The Club

MANDASUE HELLER

The Club

HODDER &
STOUGHTON

First published in Great Britain in 2006 by Hodder & Stoughton
A division of Hodder Headline

A Hodder & Stoughton Book

1

A CIP catalogue record for this title is available
from the British Library

Hardback ISBN 978 0 340 83830 3
Hardback ISBN 0 340 83830 2

Trade paperback ISBN 978 0 340 92149 4
Trade paperback ISBN 0 340 92149 8

Typeset in Plantin Light by
Palimpsest Book Production Limited, Stirlingshire

Printed and bound by
Clays Ltd, St Ives plc

Hodder Headline's policy is to use papers that are natural, renewable
and recyclable products and made from wood grown in sustainable forests.
The logging and manufacturing processes are expected to conform to the
environmental regulations of the country of origin.

Hodder & Stoughton Ltd
A division of Hodder Headline
338 Euston Road
London NW1 3BH

The Club is dedicated to my beautiful mum, Jean Heller
– for everything you have been, and still are, in my life.

Acknowledgements

I would like to thank the following – as always:

My lovely partner, Wingrove Ward; my fantastic children, Michael, Andrew, Azzura, and my gorgeous new grand-daughter, Marissa; my great sister, Ava, and her kids, Amber & Kyro, Martin, Jade, and Reece; Auntie Doreen; Pete & Ann; Lorna & Cliff, Chris and Glen; Natalie & Dan; and the rest of my family – love you all.

Many thanks to everyone at Hodder for being so supportive – again – especially, Carolyn Caughey, Isobel Akenhead, Emma Longhurst, and everybody in sales, marketing, art, etc . . . etc . . .

My agents, Cat Ledger and Faye Webber.

Norman Kaine Fairweather Brown; Betty Boo & Ronnie Schwartz; Wayne Brookes; Rosie Goodwin – thanks to you all for your help, advice, friendship, and funny e-mails – it means the world.

A big Hi! to Martina. And all best wishes to Betty's Babes – keep up the good work, guys.

Nick Austin – with thanks, as ever.

Special mention to Sarj Duggal, with thanks for the financial advice.

And lastly, eternal gratitude to the buyers, sellers, readers, reviewers and the lovely ladies at the library.

PROLOGUE

'Damn it!' Jenna cursed, peering down at the ladder zigzagging its way over her knee. Less than an hour to go, her hair was still wet, she hadn't even started on her make-up, and now she had to find another pair of tights. But it was her own fault. She should never have chanced a bath when she was so tired. Not on an important night like tonight.

She'd stressed and fretted her way through every second of the last few months, petrified that she'd bitten off more than she could chew; terrified that it would all fall apart at the last minute. Now that everything that could be done *had* been done, she should have been able to relax. But she felt worse than ever, and wished that she could run away and hide until it was all over. Still, it was too late for that. She just had to lay the fears aside and get on with it.

Taking several deep breaths to calm herself, Jenna sat down on the dressing-table stool and dried her hair. That done, she carefully applied her make-up, then changed the laddered tights for a pair of sheer black lace-top stockings and slipped her shoes on.

Looking herself over when she'd finished, she smiled. Not bad, but she could do with spending a week or two in the gym to tone her stomach after all the fast food she'd been eating lately. And a few early nights wouldn't go amiss to lighten the shadows circling her eyes. But she'd do for now.

Her mobile rang just as she reached for her jacket. Seeing the name on the screen, Jenna smiled again.

Kalli was one of the young waitresses who had worked
for her dad – and was the first to agree to come back when
Fabian contacted the staff to let them know the score. A
petite scrap-of-nothing Chinese girl, she was the prettiest
little thing, with an elfin face and warm, almond-shaped eyes.
She looked twelve, despite being almost twenty-one, but she
had the air of a much older soul because she fussed over
everyone like a mother hen. Particularly her flatmate, Austin,
who was one of the waiters. And, as soon as she met her,
Jenna.

Knowing that Kalli was probably checking up on her now
to make sure that she hadn't run away, Jenna answered the
call.

'Yes, I know I'm late, Kalli. I'm just leaving.'

'Just thought I'd best check in case you'd fallen asleep in
the bath, or something,' Kalli said concernedly.

'Who's got time for a bath?' Jenna lied, reaching for her
keys and heading for the door. 'Everything okay down there?'

'Fine – *now*,' Kalli told her. 'Maurice had a bit of a crisis
earlier, but it was nothing I couldn't have sorted out in a
nanosecond – if he'd bothered *asking*.'

'Oh?' Frowning, Jenna locked up and set off down the
stairs. 'What happened?'

'He thought someone had stolen the champagne, and
made all the boys leave what they were doing to search for
it. I didn't know what they were looking for, or I could have
told them it had been moved to the office for safe keeping.
But you know Maurice. He'd rather *die* than ask a *girl* for
help.'

Tutting softly, Jenna let herself into the residents' car park.
Maurice was the head barman. He'd been with her dad right
from the start, and still regarded him as the *proper* boss. He
had a problem with females in general, but he particularly
resented having one for a boss and had spent the last couple

of days sulking and complaining while everyone else got on with the final preparations for the party.

'Fabian gave him a bit of a roasting,' Kalli went on, chuckling softly now. 'That did *not* impress him, as you can imagine. But he wouldn't dare argue when Fabian's in that kind of mood.'

Sighing, Jenna climbed into her car. So, not only was Maurice still sulking, but Fabian was in a mood. Great! Just what she needed when teamwork was crucial to the success of the night.

Changing the subject before the nerves flared up again, she said, 'How's the queue?'

'Massive!' Kalli told her excitedly. 'And some have been waiting a good couple of hours already, so Fabian's got the security on alert in case anything kicks off when they don't all get in.'

'I'm sure we'll cope,' Jenna said, crossing her fingers. 'Anyway, I've got to get off the phone now, Kalli. See you in a bit.'

Disconnecting the call, she started the engine and eased the car out onto the road.

Turning onto Deansgate five minutes later, Jenna saw that Kalli had been right about the queue, which started at Zenith's brand new smoked-glass doors and snaked right down the block and out of sight around the corner.

It had been snowing all day, turning the roads to slush and the pavements to ice, and a fierce wind was punishing the skimpily dressed clubbers for their vanity.

The two doormen who were standing head and massive shoulders above the shivering crowd didn't seem fazed. But Jenna was sure they had to be freezing and, waving as she drove past, she made a mental note to see that they traded places with some of the other guys once everyone was inside.

Best leaving them out front for now, though, because they were easily the biggest of the security crew, and could most efficiently deal with trouble if Fabian was right and something *did* kick off.

Parking up behind the club, Jenna heard the staff talking among themselves in the main clubroom as she let herself in through the kitchen door. Taking her coat off, she hung it on a hook in the staff cloakroom, then slipped quietly in behind the bar.

Standing in the shadows, she took the opportunity to have a look around before anybody noticed her. She'd had so many wobbles since committing herself to this, convincing herself that they would never be ready on time. But not only had the building, painting, and refurbishing work been completed ahead of schedule, it looked way better than she had ever imagined it would.

The funky chrome bars that she'd had installed were gleaming; the plush new carpets were spotless; and the mega-expensive opaque-glass circular dance floor was alive with vibrant, colourful, built-in pulsar lights; while overhead, the new lighting rig rivalled that of any club Jenna had ever visited.

At Fabian's suggestion, they had turned the upper floor overlooking the dance floor into a VIP lounge, and a buffet of exotic foods had been laid out there earlier today for the invited guests, with a spectacular pyramid of sparkling glasses in the centre of it all for the champagne fountain. And little gift-packs containing expensive aftershaves and perfumes, and solid silver lighters engraved with the sword-slash 'Z' that Jenna had adopted as the new logo, had been placed on each table.

She'd been reluctant when Fabian had asked her to double the budget for the party, concerned that he was being unnecessarily extravagant on top of everything she'd already spent.

But he'd persuaded her that they needed something special to impress the A-listers – in the hope that they would spread the word to their pals and really put Zenith on the celebrity map. And, all credit to him, she had to admit that he'd really pulled it off.

One of the waitresses spotted her just then and made her jump when she called, 'Wow, Miss Lorde! You look amazing!'

Embarrassed when the rest of the staff turned her way, Jenna fought the urge to turn and run. Most of them still secretly regarded her as the boss's daughter, she knew, and if she was ever going to fill his shoes this was the time to do it.

Watching as Jenna came out from behind the bar, her thigh-length chain-mail dress shimmering like liquid silver, her hair gleaming, her eyes huge, Kalli thought that she was just the most beautiful woman she had ever seen.

And she wasn't the only one.

Up in the DJ's booth, Vibes was holding one can of his headphones to his ear as he lined up his opening tracks. Glancing out of the window when he sensed the charge in the atmosphere below, he gave a low whistle when he saw Jenna. He'd thought she was pretty special from the first time he'd laid eyes on her, but, *man*, she looked hot tonight!

Flipping a button on the console, he pushed the faders up and flooded the air with the sweet sound of: '*Sexy . . . Everything about you, so sexy . . .*'

Blushing when the staff started laughing and clapping, Jenna held up her hands, saying, 'Okay, settle down . . . he's only testing the speakers.' Stepping back then, she said, 'Right, let's have a look at you all.'

Maurice was dapper in his self-chosen outfit of white shirt, black pants, and blue velvet waistcoat; the ten young waiters and waitresses looked gorgeous in their respective silver shorts and T-shirts and minidresses that Jenna had designed for them; and the six-strong security crew exuded class and professionalism in their bow ties and muscle-enhancing black suits.

'Perfect,' she said approvingly.

'Does that go for me, too?'

Coming down from the VIP area where he'd been doing last-minute checks, Fabian strolled towards her, handsome as a devil in a dark green suit, his hair falling lazily over his smoky eyes.

Glad to see that he was in a better mood than Kalli had reported, Jenna smiled. 'Of course it does.'

'Merci,' he drawled, letting his gaze slow-dance over her. 'And may I say that *you* look sensational.'

Flipping the mike on just then, Vibes's smooth sexy voice came over the PA speakers. 'Nearly time for the countdown, folks.'

'Ready when you are,' Jenna called, turning and waving at his silhouette in the booth. Crossing her fingers then, she turned back to the staff. 'What say we get this party started?'

Gritting his teeth when the grandfather clock chimed twelve, Leonard Drake cursed under his breath. Damn Avril! They were supposed to be at the club already, and he'd been ready and waiting for a good half-hour while the driver sat in the car outside clocking up a nice bit of overtime. But *she* was still at her vanity table, plastering yet more muck onto her jowls.

Well, he wasn't bloody well having it!

Pounding up the stairs, he burst into his wife's room and jabbed angrily at his watch.

'You *do* know what time it is, don't you? We're supposed to be there by now.'

Pausing with the lipstick halfway to her mouth, Avril

flicked him a cool glance in the mirror. Then she slowly carried on with what she was doing.

'You are so infuriating sometimes,' Leonard complained. 'You know how much I've been looking forward to this. If you didn't want to come, you should have bloody well said so and I would have gone by myself!'

'No, you wouldn't,' Avril muttered, smacking her raspberry lips together. 'You never go *any*where new without me to hold your hand. I'm just a crutch, as far as you're concerned – an old pair of shoes that you slip on and walk all over.'

'Don't be ridiculous,' he retorted. 'James Lorde was a bloody good friend of mine, in case you'd forgotten, and I will *not* be late for his daughter's party!'

'You already are,' she reminded him flatly. 'And, for the record, dear, you and he were *not* good friends, you were acquaintances. There *is* a difference.'

'He was my *friend*,' Leonard asserted indignantly. 'My *father*'s friend, and then *my* friend. If he weren't, I wouldn't have received a VIP invitation, would I?'

'Temper, temper,' Avril clucked as purple blotches sprang up all over her husband's face. 'Mustn't get ourselves worked up. You know what it does to your complexion.'

Shaking his head with frustration, Leonard turned on his heel and marched out of the room.

Sighing when she heard the bathroom door slam shut down the landing a second later, Avril put the lipstick down and reached for her comb.

No doubt he'd gone to splash his face with cold water, but a blotchy complexion was the least of his worries. God only knew what he saw in the mirror these days, but he didn't seem to have realised that he was no longer the slim, handsome young man he had once been. His lovely thick hair had thinned considerably, and his once-sparkly eyes were just piggy little blobs in their puffy sockets now. But it was the belly bulging over the waistband of his suit trousers that betrayed just how far he'd let himself go. And the jacket sleeves were surely constricting the blood flow to his arms, but the vain bugger had squeezed himself into it nonetheless.

Coming back just then, Leonard tutted when he found Avril exactly where he'd left her. But knowing they would never get out of the door if he started a row, he mustered every last ounce of self-control and calmly said, 'Will you *please* hurry up?'

Without answering, Avril took a few more moments to tease her newly combed hair into shape. Then she gave it a quick spritz of lacquer before standing up.

'Thank you,' he muttered, heading for the door. 'I'll be in the car.'

Avril hissed a breath out through her teeth. She knew that she was being a bitch, but she couldn't help it. Theirs had not been the easiest of marriages, what with the demands of Leonard's political career pulling them this way and that. But she had hoped that things would mellow between them when he retired last year.

And he *had* adjusted quite well, seeming content to potter about in the garden, or shoot some holes – or whatever he called it – at the golf club. It helped that they were still invited to his ex-colleagues' dinner parties, giving him the opportunity to meet up with his cronies and keep abreast of the latest gossip while Avril and the wives swapped recipes. But just when she'd finally begun to believe that their future was settled, that damned invitation for the nightclub reopening party had arrived, and he'd started acting like a kid who'd been handed the keys to the sweetshop.

'*AVRIIILLL!*' Leonard screeched up the stairs now. 'Bloody well come *on*, will you!'

Rolling her eyes, Avril checked herself one last time in the mirror. Then she switched the lamp off and settled her mouth into an unconcerned smile before heading down the stairs.

The sooner this was over, the sooner she could get back to her book.

Across town, in his plush third-floor hotel suite, Tony Allen stopped his impatient pacing and yanked the curtain aside. In the car park below, his right-hand man, Eddie, was leaning against the white stretch limo they'd hired, chatting to the driver. When a sleek black Mercedes pulled in behind it, Tony watched the long-haired guy who was staying in the penthouse suite swagger towards it. He was dressed in tight leather pants and a girly-pink silk shirt, and was flanked by an uptight-looking older man and three blonde bimbos in micro-miniskirts. He was supposed to be some sort of megastar singer, according to Melody, but Tony couldn't say that he'd ever heard of him.

Chase Mann . . . What kind of homo name was that, anyway?

Dropping the curtain when the group had climbed into the Merc and taken off, Tony glanced at his watch. Twelve-fifteen. What the fuck was Melody playing at? She always liked to be late to be sure of making a big entrance, but this was the one night of the year when you had to be there on the fucking dot! How many times did she need to brush her hair or take her make-up off only to put it back on exactly the same, anyway?

Marching into the bedroom, he snatched the blusher brush from Melody's hand and hauled her up off the stool.

'What are you *doing*?' she squawked. 'I'm not ready.'

'Yeah, you are,' he grunted, marching her into the living room. 'Here, you can finish off on the way.' Snatching her handbag off the table he shoved it into her hands, then pushed her out the door and down the corridor to the elevator.

Melody complained all the way down to the foyer. But Tony ignored her, possessing that rare quality other men would pay to acquire: the ability to completely blank his women out.

Even those as gorgeous as Melody Fisher.

And she *was* gorgeous: angel face, devil of a sexy body, waist-length honey-blonde hair, and the most perfect tits he'd ever got his hands on – all bought and paid for by him. At thirty-two, and five-ten, she was a good deal younger than him and a little taller in her heels. But he was more than man enough to hold his own beside her, because he had that certain something about him: a menacing, brooding darkness, which, when added to his larger-than-life personality and the twinkle in his piercing eyes, created a powerful aura. *We'll have a laugh, but don't even think about fucking with me.*

'For Christ's sake, Tony!' Melody complained now, tottering helplessly on her stilettos as he pushed her out of the entrance doors. 'Do you have to act like such a fucking thug? You might get away with the He-Man shit in the fucking States, but we're in *England* now, remember?'

'Whatever,' Tony said dismissively, shoving her onto the limo's spacious back seat and climbing in beside her. Waiting until Eddie had got in up front, he tapped on the dividing window to tell the driver to get going.

Sighing loudly, Melody sat petulantly back, muttering, 'I can't be*lieve* you're stressing me out like this. Christ, I'm actually *trembling* – look . . .' Thrusting her hand out, she gave it an exaggerated shake. 'I need a cigarette,' she said then. Getting no response, she clicked her fingers sharply in front of Tony's face. 'A *smoke*, Tone, I need a smoke!'

'Not in the car,' he snapped, swatting her hand aside. 'And don't call me that. You know I can't stand it.'

'*Sorry,* I'm sure!' Pulling her skirt down over her thighs with a huff, Melody folded her arms.

Reaching across, Tony pushed the skirt back up. 'Leave it there. I don't want people thinking I'm hanging out with a fucking nun.'

'No,' she sniped. 'You'd rather they thought I was a fucking *whore.*'

'Not just any whore,' he countered, giving her a sly grin. '*My* whore. And don't you forget it.'

Melody complained all the way to the club, only stopping when they pulled up outside and she saw all the heads in the queue turn their way as people tried to see who was behind the blacked-out windows. Getting her first real buzz of the night, she fixed her top for maximum cleavage and manoeuvred her skirt to pussy level, then waited for the driver to open the door, eager to get out and bask in the admiring glances.

Tony was having none of it. He'd just spotted the paparazzi hanging about on the other side of the road, and the last thing he wanted was to wake up and find his picture splashed across the papers. Taking a firm grip on Melody's wrist when they hit the pavement, he raised an arm to shield his face from the barrage of flashing lights and yanked her to the head of the queue.

'Tony!' she griped, twisting to free herself as he paused to show the doormen their invitation. 'You're hurting me.'

'So quit wriggling.'

'These people wanted to see me. I am *famous,* you know. It kind of comes with the territory.'

Giving a scornful snort, Tony said, 'Two films does *not* a superstar make.'

'*Hollywood* films,' she reminded him tartly.

'You still ain't no Jolie,' he flipped back. 'And I'd bet my life none of these idiots have got a fucking clue who you are.'

Not yet, maybe, Melody thought resentfully, folding her arms while they waited to be admitted. *But you just wait till my agent tells me I got that part I auditioned for. Angelina flaming Jolie won't know what's hit her when I get started!*

PART ONE

I

Jenna Lorde seemed to have it all. At twenty-six she could still pass for twenty-one, even on a bad day. Slim and curvaceous, with sleek shoulder-length black hair, a flawless complexion, and exotically slanted sea-green eyes, she had a good job at a major fashion house in the West End, a nice little flat in Maida Vale – and a shattered heart, having recently discovered that Jason, her charming, funny, passionate, unbearably handsome boyfriend of six years, was married.

Dumping him as soon as she found out, Jenna spent the next few months fielding the texts and phone calls claiming that his wife meant nothing to him, that it had all been a terrible mistake, and that Jenna was the only woman he'd ever loved. When that didn't work, he tried self-righteous anger, turning up at her flat, and – more embarrassingly – her workplace, accusing her of being selfish, and telling her to stop feeling sorry for herself and think what this was doing to *him*. And, finally, he tried reasoning that, as she'd already been sharing him with his wife all along, what was the difference if they carried on now as if nothing had ever happened?

And in one particularly weak, bleak moment, when she'd been missing him like crazy, and wishing that she'd stayed in blissful ignorance, Jenna had found herself actually considering it.

Which was when she came to the conclusion that she had to get as far away from him as possible if she was ever going to get her life back on track. But just as she was about to hand in her notice at work and give up the lease on her flat, fate stepped in. She got the call telling her that her dad had died.

Going home to Manchester to arrange the funeral and sort out her dad's affairs was a shock to Jenna's system. She'd been away for eight years, and in some ways it felt like she'd never been gone. But in others, it was truly weird to be back – especially knowing that her dad wouldn't be there when she reached the house.

Having kept in touch mainly by phone over the last few years, and only paying the occasional flying visit, Jenna hardly recognised the place when she stepped off the train. Piccadilly Station had had a major revamp since she'd last been there, and so had the rest of the city. But the people were exactly the same, she soon discovered – stoically determined to retain their northern-ness as the landscape mutated around them into a pastiche of the south. She didn't know if that was a good or a bad thing, but as she wasn't planning on sticking around after the funeral she didn't really care.

The funeral was a small affair, because Jenna didn't really know any of her dad's friends to invite them. In the end it was just her, a handful of their old neighbours, and Ruth Wolff – the widow of her dad's old solicitor, who had been the one who'd let her know that he'd died.

Jenna's older sister, Claudia, didn't come – but then, Jenna hadn't expected her to, considering that she hadn't bothered coming back for their mum's funeral either. Claudia had moved to Australia fifteen years earlier, and they hadn't clapped eyes on her since. Now she claimed that she couldn't afford the air fare – despite the fact that she and her husband ran their own business and owned a sprawling ranch-style house. But she'd always been selfish, which was why Jenna wasn't surprised when Claudia demanded that her share of the inheritance should be sent over as soon as possible.

Going back to Ruth's house after the service for a small buffet, Jenna felt like an outsider as Ruth and the elderly neighbours swapped stories and reminisced about her dad. It was obvious that they had known James Lorde as a man in his own right, had chatted to him on an adult level and knew how he thought and felt about the world. Whereas Jenna had only ever known him as the dad who had been too busy running his precious nightclub, Zenith, to spend more than the occasional hour with his children every now and then. Who had nipped in and out of the house as if visiting an hotel, giving his wife perfunctory kisses on the cheek in passing and leaving the scent of Old Spice in his wake. But the man his friends talked of, who had, apparently, been the life and soul of every gathering and would give you the shirt off his back; the man who had kept the collection of porn magazines that Jenna had found hidden in his wardrobe when she was clearing the house out, who had left dirty clothes scattered around his bedroom floor, a stack of unpaid bills in the kitchen drawer, and a whole heap of empty whisky bottles beside his bed – she didn't know *that* man at all.

But, newly discovered secrets and childhood memories aside, Jenna still loved James Lorde as deeply as ever. She might not have seen him as often as her friends had seen their fathers while they were growing up, but he had always been a hero to her. A strapping man with a magical laugh, who would toss her into the air and then catch her and give her a big cuddle, who'd slip them money to buy their mum a birthday or Christmas present, who'd herd them all into the car on a Saturday afternoon and drop them off at the cinema. Even when she grew up and moved away from home, it was her dad that she still turned to for advice; him that she would phone whenever she needed a comforting voice in her ear.

Claudia had always been jealous of their relationship, calling Jenna a daddy's girl and accusing her of playing up to the fact that she was her father's favourite. But Jenna had never seen it like that – not until the will was read, and she learned that he'd left Zenith solely to her.

Wracked with guilt that Claudia might have been right all along, Jenna rang her sister, intending to tell her that she would sign half of the club over to her as soon as she could. But she immediately changed her mind when Claudia laid into her before she had a chance to say a word, calling her a gold-digging, grave-robbing tramp. Anyway, she figured that her dad must have done it this way on purpose: not because Jenna was his favourite, but because he'd known that Claudia would put the club on the market before the soil was settled on his coffin – which was exactly what she had insisted Jenna should do with the tiny semi in Rusholme where they had grown up and which he'd left to them both.

Not that Claudia would get much out of it when it went, because their dad had obviously done nothing to it after their mum had died and Jenna had left. The neglect showed in everything from the gate hanging off its hinges to the overgrown garden, from the rotting door and window frames to the stale odour of man-alone that tainted the air inside.

But, honoured as she was that her dad had trusted her enough to leave his club in her hands, there was just one major problem for Jenna: she didn't actually want it.

Taking it on would mean having to move back to Manchester, which she really didn't want to do. And she didn't even know if she was capable of running a nightclub, anyway. She'd never taken the slightest interest in the place when she'd lived here, and had resisted her dad's efforts to bring her in and show her the ropes, because she and her friends preferred the trendier student bars with their cut-price booze and cool live bands. And then she'd moved to London, which was worlds apart from Manchester when it came to club-life, so she was still none the wiser.

But then, her dad couldn't have known what *he* was doing when he started out, either, and he'd managed to keep it going for twenty years. And he'd done all the hard work, so all she'd have to do would be to walk in and pick up where he'd left off.

She just didn't *want* to.

But how could she walk away without even trying, when her dad had obviously wanted her to make a go of it?

Knowing that she owed it to him to at least consider it, Jenna decided to go down to the club and take a good look around. If her instincts told her to give it a shot, then fine, she would roll her sleeves up and throw her heart and soul into it, like her dad before her. But if they said no, she would put it up for sale. And she was sure that her dad would understand, as long as she'd given it real consideration first.

Jenna took a cab to the club and her heart sank before it had even pulled up to the kerb. Her dad had obviously missed the regeneration bandwagon when it had rolled into town after the bombings a few years back because, compared to all the bright new façades surrounding it, the club looked dated and scruffy. It had the same old scarred black doors as when he'd first bought it, and the wall was covered in messy posters, leaflets and graffiti.

It was so seedy and neglected that Jenna couldn't imagine anybody making an effort to come here for a night out. In fact, the only good thing about it was the location: smack in the middle of Deansgate, which had taken a massive upturn in recent years and was now chock-full of upmarket wine and coffee bars and swanky new apartment blocks. If she

did end up selling – which was looking very, *very* likely –
she'd get more for the postcode than for the actual building.

Using the keys that the solicitor had given her she unlocked
the door and went inside. She'd only ever been here a couple
of times, and that had been during opening hours when it
was fully lit and crammed with people, with music pumping
out at an incredible volume. Standing in the foyer now, it
just felt cold, dark, and far too quiet.

Shivering, Jenna went through to the clubroom itself,
which was pitch dark and really quite eerie. Propping the
door open with a chair, she used the sparse light from the
foyer to find her way to the lights control box which the
solicitor had told her was behind the bar. Flicking switches
at random, she had just found the one for the overhead lights
when a door opened behind her and a man walked in.

Leaping back when he saw her, he cried, 'Holy *shit*! You
scared the crap out of me!' Patting his chest then, he gave
her a sheepish grin. 'Guess you're not an armed robber,
huh?'

'Definitely not,' Jenna assured him, amused that he seemed
even more alarmed than she was – he was lean and muscular
and looked quite capable of taking care of himself. He was
also very good-looking, she noticed. Mixed-race, clean-
shaven, with ice-white teeth, unusual blue eyes and a soft
American accent.

And a broad gold wedding band on the third finger of his
left hand, which he wasn't trying to hide – unlike Jason, who
had hidden his for six long years, the bastard!

Shaking the irritating thought of Jason out of her head,
she asked the man if he worked here.

'Weekends,' he said, presuming her to be one of the waitresses who worked mid-week when DJs Fiddy or Marky Day
had their slots. 'Shame we had to shut down, isn't it?' he
murmured then, gazing around the room. 'It's a great place.

And James was pretty cool for an old guy. But nothing lasts for ever, right?'

Jenna nodded her agreement, liking him because he'd obviously liked her dad.

'It's Vibes, by the way.' He held out his hand. 'One of the DJs – or, at least, I *was*.'

'Jenna,' she told him, shaking it. 'You say the club's been closed down?' she asked then, wondering why the solicitor hadn't told her about that.

'Yeah, the day James died,' Vibes said, frowning quizzically. 'Look, sorry, I don't mean to be rude, but shouldn't you already know that if you work here?'

'I'm the old guy's daughter,' Jenna told him, smiling when she saw the information sink in and show up in his eyes.

'For real?' Drawing his head back, he peered at her face, then nodded. 'Yeah, I guess I can see it. You've got the same nose.'

But not the same anything else, he thought, because she was absolutely stunning.

Snapping himself out of it, he said, 'So I take it you're the new owner, then, huh? And you're like – what? Just checking the place out?'

'Something like that,' Jenna replied. 'I wanted to see what my instincts told me before I made any decisions.'

'And what are they telling you?'

'Not sure yet.' She shrugged. 'It'll need major renovations if I do take it on.'

'Worth it, though,' Vibes said, adding quickly, 'not that I'm trying to sway you, or anything, but – well, you know. It's a great place.'

'So you said.'

'Bad habit, repeating myself.' Vibes flashed her a sheepish grin. Then, shrugging, he said, 'Suppose I'd best let you get on with it, then. Don't mind if I just grab a bit of my gear, do you? Only Fabian's waiting out back to lock up and I don't want to keep him waiting, 'cos I don't think he was planning on sticking around.'

'No, go ahead.'

'Right, well, then.' Another smile. 'See you later, I guess.'

Watching as he strolled across the dance floor and tripped lightly up the stairs to the DJ's booth, Jenna bit her lip thoughtfully. She hadn't even considered what her decision would mean to the staff. If she sold Zenith they would all be out of a job. But even if she'd wanted to keep it open, she doubted that she'd be able to afford all the work that would be needed to bring the club into the twenty-first century. The decor was hideously old-fashioned, the seating worn and faded, the carpets so manky that she'd bet her feet would stick to them, and the bar was a huge wooden monstrosity with brass hand- and footrails that would have looked more at home in an old back-street pub – which was probably where her dad had picked it up from in the first place. It might look great in the alcohol-glazed atmosphere of night, but in this harsh overhead light it resembled a seedy old working men's club.

'Er . . . excuse me, but who are *you*, and how did you get in here?'

Jumping when she heard the accusing voice behind her, Jenna turned around and saw yet another good-looking man. This one was white, with expensively cut blond hair, slate-grey eyes, and a very good-quality suit.

Raising an eyebrow when he saw her face, Fabian King's gaze slid over the rest of her and a slow smile lifted the corner of his lip.

'You must be Fabian?' Jenna said, looking him in the eye, unamused by his leering.

His eyebrow went up another notch. 'How did you know that?'

'Vibes mentioned you.'

'I see.' Flipping into instant cold mode, Fabian frowned. Vibes had obviously tricked him into coming over, thinking he'd be stupid enough to let him in then get straight off and leave him to his little rendezvous. 'I suppose he let you in the front door, did he?' he demanded now, all set to tell her that she could damn well let herself back out the same way.

'No, I let myself in,' Jenna told him coolly, wondering what it had to do with him.

Eyes narrowing with suspicion, Fabian drew his head back and peered at her. 'How?'

'With these.' Jenna showed him the keys.

Scrutinising her face for a moment longer, Fabian clicked his fingers. 'You must be Jim's daughter?'

A flicker of a frown crossed Jenna's brow. She had never in her life heard anybody shorten her dad's name to Jim, and it didn't sound at all right. But then, maybe he'd liked it – who knew? There were plenty of things she hadn't known about him, it seemed.

'So, how are you?' Fabian asked, in a sympathetic *if you need to talk, I'm your man* tone. 'Funeral go all right?'

'I'm fine,' she told him guardedly, not liking the sudden switch from cold suspicion to warm familiarity. 'And it went as well as we could have hoped, thanks.'

'Sorry I couldn't make it,' he went on, as if he'd been invited – which he hadn't, because she didn't even know who he was. 'I would have loved to have been there, but there was too much to do over here, I'm afraid. And, knowing your dad, he'd have preferred me to get this place sorted than to waste time saying goodbye to a coffin.'

'Mmm,' Jenna murmured, thinking that his choice of words was a little insensitive, even if she did agree with what he'd said. Her dad *had* put the club first in life, so why wouldn't he in death?

Pity he hadn't thought to spend a little more money main-
taining it, though. But judging by the state of this place *and*
the house, he'd obviously let a lot of things slide lately.

'Care to join me for a drink?' Fabian was asking now.
Adding, with a cheeky grin, 'Don't worry, I won't charge
you.'

Jenna was starting to get irritated. First he'd called her dad
'Jim', which nobody had ever done – not even her mum.
And now he was offering out drinks as if *he* owned the place.

Shaking her head, she folded her arms and said, 'No
offence, but who exactly *are* you?'

'Fabian King,' he told her over his shoulder as he helped
himself to a shot of brandy. 'The manager,' he added, turning
back to her.

'*Really*?' She frowned. 'What happened to Frank?'

'Long story. Let's just say he and Jim stopped seeing eye
to eye.'

'Dad never said,' Jenna murmured, wondering what could
have possibly happened to make them fall out. Frank had
been the manager here for over ten years, and her dad had
considered him a friend as much as an employee. 'When
was this?'

'Last year,' Fabian told her, leaning back against the
counter. 'I came in to cover Frank's holiday time, originally.
But your dad asked me to stay on, so obviously I said yes.
Don't mean to blow my own trumpet,' he went on – doing
exactly that, Jenna thought – 'but this place was going steadily
downhill before I came on board. It's been a struggle, but
we're on our way back up now. Well, we *were*,' he added,
giving her a pointed look. 'Still could be, if we don't stay
shut too long.'

Taking a sip of his drink now, he carried on looking at her,
waiting for her to respond. When she didn't after a moment,
he said, 'If you don't mind me asking, what *are* your plans?'

'I haven't made up my mind yet,' Jenna told him evasively. 'But don't worry, I'll let you know as soon as I do.'

Pursing his lips thoughtfully, Fabian nodded slowly. What he really wanted to know was, if she *did* keep the club on, would he still have a job? But she hadn't been very forthcoming, so far, and he sensed that it was probably best not to push her. Yet.

Vibes came back just then, several cases of CDs in his hands and a holdall of vinyl albums over one shoulder. Avoiding making eye contact with Jenna – because Fabian was already doing such a good job of leering at her and Vibes didn't want her to think she'd landed on Planet Lech – he said, 'I'll have to leave the rest for now – if that's okay?'

'It's fine,' Jenna assured him. 'If you want to give me your number, I'll give you a ring and let you know when I'm coming in again.'

'Cool,' Vibes said, putting his stuff down. 'Never remember it off the top of my head, though, so you'll have to give me a minute to find my phone.' Searching through his pockets then, he frowned. 'Damn! Don't tell me I lost it again.'

'Don't worry about it,' Fabian jumped in quickly. 'I'll have to take Jenna up to the office to show her the books anyway, so I'll give it to her from the file. You can get off now, if you're done,' he said then, giving Vibes a pointed look. 'I'll take it from here.'

Giving him a knowing half-smile, Vibes shared a brief conspiratorial look with Jenna which conveyed his question: *Are you all right with that?* and her answer: *Don't worry, I can handle him.*

'I'll leave you to it, then,' he said, picking up his things. 'Nice meeting you, Jenna.'

'You, too. I'll give you a ring within the week.'

'Much appreciated.' Nodding goodbye, Vibes opened the door and left.

Relaxing now that the competition for Jenna's attention was gone, Fabian downed what was left of his drink and put the glass in the small sink. Then, waving her through the opening in the counter, he said, 'Shall we?'

Jenna hadn't intended to stay long, but she decided that she might as well get this over with now rather than have to arrange to come back and meet Fabian at another time. He had the air of a man who was used to women falling all over themselves to get to him, and – handsome as he undoubtedly was – she found that kind of arrogant presumption incredibly off-putting.

Unlocking a door marked *Private*, which led to the upper floor where the offices, staff bathroom and boardroom were located, Fabian led her to an office part-way along the first-floor corridor.

'This was your dad's,' he told her, unlocking the door and reaching in to switch the light on. 'Sorry about the mess, but we thought we'd best leave it alone for the time being. He was in the middle of having an en-suite bathroom built into the cupboard space, you see, but they hadn't quite finished when he died.'

Stepping in, Jenna gazed around in dismay. Fabian was right about the mess, but it wasn't the builders' debris that bothered her, it was the personal stuff. Just like at the house, there were dirty clothes, newspapers, and empty whisky bottles all over the place.

'Was he sleeping here?' she asked, frowning when she noticed the sleeping bag and pillow spread out on the small leather couch.

'He'd started to over the last couple of months,' Fabian replied, shrugging as he added, 'I guess he just got too tired to bother going home towards the end. But he figured he had everything he needed close at hand, so he was fine with it.'

Jenna felt the guilt that was already eating away at her intensify. How could she have let her dad come to this? He must have been feeling really ill, but he'd never said a word. All those times she'd phoned him, crying over Jason and ranting about her petty little troubles, he'd never once told her to shut up, or pointed out that there were worse things that could happen – like losing the will to go home to your own bed at night.

Seeing the distress in her eyes, Fabian gave her a reassuring pat on the arm, telling her gently, 'If it's any consolation, I was keeping an eye on him. And I know it looks bad, but, honestly, he was doing okay, so don't upset yourself.'

Sighing, Jenna nodded. 'Thanks.'

'No problem.' Smiling, Fabian edged past her into the room and did a quick clean-up – tossing the guilt-inducing sleeping bag and pillow out of sight down the side of the couch and sweeping the mess of coffee cartons and sandwich wrappers off the coffee table into a plastic bag.

Walking behind the desk, Jenna sat down on her dad's battered old leather chair – where, the solicitor had told her, he'd been found the morning after he died. Running her hands over the scuffed arms, she gazed around the room, trying to envisage what he'd been looking at when it happened. The builders' mess to the left, or his own mess to the right, perhaps? Or maybe the framed black and white print on the opposite wall of an old tramp on a park bench, wearing a filthy old coat and a huge toothless smile as he waved his bottle of cider in the air. Had he been thinking about work, she wondered. Or reminiscing about his life, and the family he had all but lost. Or maybe he had simply fallen asleep and slipped away with his dreams.

Jerked back to the here and now when Fabian took several folders out of the filing cabinet and dropped them onto the desk, Jenna sat up straighter and tried to focus her attention as, for the next hour, he talked her through the paper-life of the club. But the more she heard, the more concerned she became, because it seemed that her dad had died owing thousands.

'The drinks suppliers are by far the biggest creditors,' Fabian told her. 'But I've put them in the picture about the situation and they've agreed to hang fire until we know where we're at.'

'What about these?' Jenna asked, reaching for the letters that her father had obviously been ignoring because he hadn't even opened them. They were from the electricity company, the water board and BT, all threatening imminent disconnection and legal action to recover the debts.

'I have spoken to them, but you should probably think about sorting them out quickly to save having everything cut off and having to pay reconnection fees,' Fabian said. 'Everything else is in order, and the staff are paid to date,' he went on, adding, 'but we shouldn't leave them hanging too long, because some of them have already found new jobs, and it might not be so easy to tempt them to come back once they get settled.'

'Come back?' Jenna gazed at him, a deep frown creasing her brow. 'For what?'

'When we reopen,' Fabian said, jumping in at the deep end. However she responded, at least he'd know where he stood.

'I'm not sure it's even worth considering,' Jenna murmured, clasping her hands together. 'It would cost an absolute fortune to fix it up. And if most of the staff have already gone, what's the point?'

'I know it's a lot to take in, but it looks far worse than it actually is,' Fabian said. 'We went through a bit of a rough patch, but it's been getting better, and we've seen a massive upturn in customer numbers since we got the new DJs in. Particularly Vibes,' he added truthfully – much as it pained him to compliment the man. 'Fiddy and Marky Day are good, but Vibes is the best in Manchester, without a doubt. And that's half the battle won, because people don't go to clubs for the quality of the booze or the look of the place – they go to see their favourite DJs.'

'And he's that good?' Jenna asked doubtfully, sure that Fabian was just doing a hard sell because he wanted her to keep the club on.

'The best,' he affirmed. 'You'd have to see him in action to believe it. And it's not just women who love him, the other DJs pop in if they get a chance on their nights off to see what he's playing – and that doesn't happen unless they're really hot. Believe me, the guy is solid *gold*.'

Smiling at his description, Jenna said, 'Well, I'm sure you're right, but I can't see him being the answer to this mess.'

'He's a definite part of the solution,' Fabian countered bluntly. 'With a bit of effort, we could take this place to the top.'

'With respect,' Jenna said, 'I think it's going to take a damn sight more than that. *I* wouldn't go out of my way to come here – not when there are so many *decent* clubs in town to choose from. It looks disgusting from the outside, and it's absolutely horrible inside.'

'Your dad loved it,' Fabian persisted. 'And, all right, so, he let it slip a bit cosmetically, but there's a real soul to the place.'

'It's a dive,' Jenna cut in. 'My dad hasn't changed a single thing since he bought it.'

'Because he loved it exactly as it was,' Fabian pointed out. 'But it's yours now, so you can do whatever you like with it. Imagine it . . .' he went on, getting into his stride now.

'You get the builders and decorators in to revamp the interior, then you get the outside cleaned up, have a new door and sign fitted, and – *voilà*! It looks amazing, and everybody wants in.'

Sighing, because she was getting tired now, Jenna held up her hands to stop him. 'Look, I appreciate the advice, but I just can't see it, to be honest. I was considering selling up before I came here today, and now I've seen the state of it I really think that's the best bet.'

Peering at her across the desk, Fabian shrugged. 'It's your decision ultimately. But if you don't mind a bit more advice, I'd really think about it before you jump into putting it onto the market just yet, or you might end up losing out *big* time.'

'I've already thought about that,' Jenna told him. 'And I reckon I should get a fair price just for the location.'

Shaking his head slowly, Fabian said, 'I don't think you understand what I'm getting at. It's a given that the club's in dire need of modernisation, but you've got no idea what kind of shape it's in below the surface. A potential buyer would contract a surveyor to do a thorough inspection, and if they concluded that it's in as bad shape structurally as it is cosmetically, they'd have no option but to report it to the relevant authorities – and you might find yourself slapped with a condemnation order. If *that* happened, not only would you not be allowed to sell, you'd have to pay for the repairs – or, worse, demolition, which would be a *major* expense. Is that a risk you're willing to take?'

'Bloody hell!' Jenna gasped. 'Could that really happen?'

'I've seen it happen to places in better shape than this,' Fabian replied. Shrugging then, he said, 'Your choice, but I know what I'd do if it was me. I'd keep it on and bring it up to scratch, then open up and see how it went for a year or so. And if I still didn't want it at the end of that, *then* I'd think about selling, because it would be worth far more by then.'

Shaking her head, Jenna slumped despairingly down in her seat. There was an undeniable logic to what he'd said, but she just didn't want to move back to Manchester permanently. She'd only been toying with the idea because of the guilt factor, but if she did as Fabian was advising, she'd have no choice but to come back.

'Look, why don't you take some time to think it over?' Fabian suggested, seeing that she was becoming bogged down with it. 'It's still going to be here tomorrow, isn't it?'

'I suppose so,' Jenna agreed, sighing heavily.

Her dad had obviously thought he was doing a wonderful thing by her but, by *God*, she wished he hadn't bothered!

'Out of interest,' she said, reaching for her bag, 'can I ask why you closed down before you knew what I was going to do? Surely the staff would have been better off if you'd stayed open until I'd got here, and there'd have still been money coming in to pay off those debts.'

'I couldn't,' Fabian told her. 'Your dad held the licence, so it would have been illegal to sell alcohol or provide entertainment. I could have applied for a temporary change of DPS, but the solicitor was away and his secretary wouldn't give me your number so I couldn't get hold of you to get your authorisation.'

'What's a DPS?'

'Designated Premises Supervisor,' Fabian explained. '*You* could apply for it now, if you wanted to. Or, if you didn't want the hassle, you could okay it for *me* to do it. It is a bit of a ball-ache, though,' he said then – seeming, Jenna thought, to be trying to persuade her to do the latter. 'The police do a thorough background check on you, for convictions and what-have-you. And then the licensing panel demand all sorts of references and credit checks and stuff. But I don't mind putting myself through it if you can't face it.'

'I have nothing to hide from the police,' Jenna told him, smiling as she stood up. 'Anyway, thanks for your help, I really appreciate it.'

'Any time,' Fabian said. 'And if you need to talk before I see you again, feel free to give me a ring.' Reaching for a notepad, he jotted two numbers down and handed them to her. 'Home and mobile – you'll always catch me on one or the other. Day *or* night,' he added with a slow half-smile. 'I'm a very light sleeper.'

Thanking him, Jenna slipped the numbers into her bag. Then, remembering that she'd promised to ring Vibes, she located his number in the staff file and wrote it down.

'Right, then,' she said when she'd done. 'I'll get back to you as soon as I've made a decision. And in the meantime, I'll sort out those bills.'

'Good idea,' Fabian said, getting up to open the door.

Walking her down to the front door then, he let her out and waved her off, calling, 'See you soon – I hope.'

Arriving back at her dad's house a short time later, Jenna groaned when she saw the *For Sale* sign in the garden. The estate agent had been round earlier that morning to do a valuation, but she hadn't expected him to come back so soon. It felt like she was being rushed from all sides: Claudia rushing her to sell up; Fabian rushing her into making a decision on the club; and now the estate agent rushing her out of house and home.

Not that she *wanted* the house, because it held far too many painful memories for her to ever be truly comfortable there. But if she was going to be forced into staying around she'd need somewhere to sleep at night, and if the house went as quickly as the estate agent had predicted she'd find herself shelling out for hotels before she knew it – and that was an expense she definitely didn't need right now.

Making herself a coffee, she carried it through to the lounge and sat down. Kicking off her shoes, she reached for the phone and dialled the solicitor's number, hoping to sound him out about the stuff she'd discussed with Fabian. Getting no answer, she called Ruth Wolff instead.

Ruth was the only person she could think of who had known her dad for longer than she herself had. Almost seventy years old, she was still as sharp as a butcher's knife. She was also one of the most honest, no-nonsense people Jenna had ever met and, having been married to a solicitor for so long, she would have much more of an idea about the legal aspects of this situation than Jenna.

'Hate to say it,' Ruth said when Jenna had explained everything. 'But it looks like this manager chappie might be right about it being more trouble than it's worth trying to sell. A surveyor *would* be duty-bound to report a dangerous structure to the local authorities. And, let's face it, my love, your father was a one for cutting corners – bless him – so you could be opening a very large can of worms if you proceed with the idea of selling.'

'Great,' Jenna muttered. 'So I'm stuck with it.'

'Is that really such a bad thing?' Ruth asked quietly. 'Your dad wanted you to have it more than anything in the world. We were discussing it after his first heart attack, a couple of months ago, and he told me—'

'*Sorry?*' Jenna interrupted. 'Did you just say his *first* heart attack?'

'Ah . . .' Ruth murmured guiltily. 'Sorry, my love. You weren't supposed to hear that.'

Jenna felt as if she'd been punched in the stomach. 'Why didn't anybody tell me?'

'Because he didn't want to worry you,' Ruth told her gently. 'You'd had a hellish few months, but you seemed to be on the up and he didn't want to drag you back down.'

'Did he think I was so wrapped up in my own problems that I wouldn't want to know something like *that*?' Jenna gasped incredulously. 'Christ, Ruth, I wouldn't have given any of that a second thought if I'd known that my dad needed me. I'd have come straight home to look after him.'

'Which was precisely what he didn't want,' Ruth chipped in firmly. 'He couldn't bear the thought of forcing you to play nursemaid to a dying man. You've been doing so well since you left home, and he knew how happy you were – apart from the boyfriend situation, of course. He desperately didn't want you to lose all that.'

'But I've lost it anyway,' Jenna told her. 'I'd already decided to move on and start again.'

'So, why not here?' Ruth suggested smoothly. 'All he ever wanted was for you to be secure, and leaving you the club was his way of guaranteeing that. Claudia's husband runs his own business, so he didn't want *her* to have it. And, anyway, he knew that if you went for it, you'd be as passionate about it as he was.'

'Doesn't look like I've got much choice, does it?' Jenna murmured resignedly. 'But how am I supposed to pay for it?'

'Oh, that's the easy bit,' Ruth told her breezily, sounding pleased that Jenna was coming around to the idea. 'You honour the debts before anybody takes legal action. Then, once you've got a clean credit rating, you use the club as collateral and secure a bank loan to finance the work that needs doing. Simple.'

Jenna's head was spinning by the time she came off the phone. But now that she'd told Ruth she was willing to give it a go there was no turning back. She just hoped it was going to be as simple as Ruth had insisted it would be.

Phoning the bank, she made an appointment for the

following morning. Then she called Fabian and told him what she'd decided, and asked him to meet her at the club at noon tomorrow. Then, lastly, she took a deep breath and rang Vibes.

'Oh, right,' he murmured disappointedly when she told him that he should come for the rest of his things tomorrow if he liked. 'I take it you've decided to sell, then?'

Smiling, Jenna said, 'No, I've decided to *keep* it. If all goes well with the bank, I'll be getting the builders in as soon as possible. I just thought I'd better warn you, because I didn't think you'd want your stuff in there while they're ripping the place to pieces.'

'For real?' Vibes sounded delighted. 'Oh, man, that's so cool! Anything I can do to help?'

'Well, there *is* something, actually,' Jenna said, nervous now, because it was a big favour she was about to ask of him. 'Fabian reckons it could take about four months to get everything done if we started now, so I know I'll probably lose most of the staff because they won't be able to hold out for that long. But I really, really don't want to lose *you*, so I was wondering if you'd consider keeping your diary clear for when we reopen? Only thing is . . . I, er, don't think I'd be able to pay you a full wage while the work's being done.'

'Hey, don't even worry about that,' Vibes told her without hesitation. 'Money ain't an issue for any of the DJs, 'cos we all do other residencies on our free nights. You just do what you got to do, and let me know when you're ready for me. To come back, that is,' he added quickly, kicking himself for sounding like he was hitting on her. 'Anyway, four months is perfect timing for the party.'

'Sorry?' Jenna said, not understanding what he was getting at, because she hadn't mentioned a party.

'It's September now,' Vibes explained. 'So four months would take us to the beginning of January – and what better night than New Year's Eve for a reopening party? You'd have plenty of time to plan it, and you could invite all the local celebrities. It'd be fantastic publicity.'

'I don't know any celebrities,' Jenna admitted, disappointed because it really had sounded like a great idea.

'Leave that to Fabian,' Vibes told her knowingly. 'I guarantee he'll come up trumps. But do yourself a favour, and tell him it was your idea.'

'What's wrong with telling him the truth?'

'Let's just say I know enough about him to know he'd be more receptive if it came from you.'

Shrugging, Jenna said, 'Okay, whatever you think best.' Then, 'Right, well, I guess I'll see you tomorrow, then.'

'Looking forward to it,' Vibes said softly. 'Later, Princess.'

Smiling, Jenna said goodbye and hung up. What a lovely man. And what a lucky lady his wife was, because she obviously had nothing to worry about, judging by the way he'd corrected himself just now to make sure that Jenna didn't think he was flirting with her. She really respected him for that.

And resented Jason all the more.

But she wasn't going to think about him any more. From now on, she was going to put all her time and effort into the club.

Her club.

2

Jenna was standing with Fabian inside the clubroom door, greeting people as they arrived. She'd been convinced that none of the celebrities he'd invited would turn up, sure that they'd have far better things to do than try out what was in effect a brand new club, on the biggest night of the year. Amazingly, most had decided to chance it – which was a huge relief. And somebody had obviously tipped the press off, because several photographers had set up camp across the road and were busy snapping everyone who came in – which would be fantastic publicity when the papers hit the stands in the morning, just as Vibes had predicted.

All in all, everything seemed to be going really well so far. But Jenna was particularly impressed with Fabian now that she'd seen him in action. He'd been indefatigable in the gruelling months leading up to this, taking on every challenge with gusto. Jenna had done her bit, but Fabian had far surpassed her in energy and imagination. And he was totally on the ball tonight – which was a minor miracle, Jenna thought, considering he'd been at the club from early this morning, making sure that everything and everyone was ready.

His customer-service skills were exceptional. He'd known every one of the guests' names without once referring to the list and had treated them all like old friends, subtly adjusting his manner to suit their individual status: respectful to the older, more established stars, like Glenda Jackson and John

Savident; suave and sophisticated for Victoria Beckham's group; cool and flirtatious with Charlotte Church and her gal-pals, the pretty girls from *Coronation Street*, and the three blondes who arrived with Chase Mann – but not too much so with the latter, in case they came back at a later date celeb-less and expected preferential treatment; then matey with Chase himself, having met him a few times previously.

'You really enjoy this, don't you?' Jenna said when they'd wished Chase and his entourage a Happy New Year and had one of the waiters escort them to the VIP lounge.

'Usually,' he replied, adding quietly, 'but not always. Hope you've got a tissue handy.'

'Sorry?'

'The Honourable Drakes.' He nodded towards the main doors, where an older couple were just entering. 'He's got the sweatiest hands I've ever come across – and it's not pleasant, be warned.'

He wasn't wrong, as Jenna soon discovered when Leonard Drake made a beeline for her and grasped one of her hands between both of his. They were fat, wet, and very hot – it felt like being swallowed by an enormous slug.

'You must be Jenny,' he gushed. 'I can't tell you how pleased I am to meet you.' Sighing loudly then, he shook his head sadly. 'Terrible business, your father going like that. He was a good friend, and I shall miss him terribly.'

'Me too,' Jenna said, not bothering to correct his mispronunciation of her name as she slid her hand free. 'I must apologise for not inviting you to the funeral,' she said then, 'but I hadn't had a chance to go through my dad's papers at that point, and I wasn't sure who his friends were – other than those I knew personally, of course. I hope you weren't too offended?'

'Not at all,' Leonard assured her, beaming widely. *So much for Avril's snipe about James Lorde not regarding him as a friend!*

'I'm just delighted to be here now. And very honoured that you thought to invite me.'

Holding her hand away from her dress in case the sweat stained it, Jenna smiled. 'My dad wouldn't have been happy if I'd neglected his friends.'

'Especially not such an eminent one as Mr Drake,' Fabian chipped in, his eyes twinkling as he noticed what Jenna was doing with her hand. 'He was an MP for many years,' he went on – seemingly full of admiration, although Jenna was sure she caught a hint of a mocking tone as he added, 'and quite the local celebrity, too. There was a time when he was never out of the papers or off the TV.'

'That was some time ago now, I'm afraid,' Leonard murmured wistfully. 'Seems they only want young, pretty faces on screen and page these days.'

'Probably a blessing that you retired when you did, then,' Fabian said soothingly. 'Give you a chance to relax and get your privacy back. And I'm sure *you*'re happier to see more of your husband, Mrs Drake?'

'Absolutely,' Avril lied. Turning to Jenna then, she said, 'I'm Avril. Very nice to meet you, dear.'

'You, too. And I hope you have a lovely time with us tonight.'

'Oh, I'm sure we will.' Avril smiled, but the dullness in her eyes didn't escape Jenna. 'I think we've taken up enough of your time,' she said then, linking her arm through her husband's. 'Shall we, Leonard?'

Calling one of the waiters over to escort them to their table, Jenna watched as they walked away, wondering how an overweight, overly sweaty, rather unattractive man like Leonard had ever managed to net himself such a refined, lovely-looking wife.

'How well did he and my dad actually know each other?' she asked Fabian when they'd gone. 'I invited him because his name was in Dad's address book, but I don't actually remember Dad mentioning him.'

'They were friends,' Fabian said. 'But I think it was more of a business-contact kind of thing. Drake's the son of one of your dad's old college mates.'

'My dad went to college?' Jenna glanced up at him with genuine surprise in her eyes. She hadn't known that. But then, she had discovered a lot of things that she hadn't known since coming back, and this was just the latest in a long line of revelations.

'He was very intelligent,' Fabian told her. 'But he liked people to think he was a simple man, because then they wouldn't have too many expectations and he'd be free to get on with what he loved.'

'The club?' Jenna said, knowing that was what her dad had loved above everything.

'Among other things,' Fabian said, with no intention of elaborating, because he doubted that Jenna wanted to hear about her dad's extra-curricular activities at the lap-dancing clubs he frequented outside of Zenith.

'So, he met Leonard through *his* dad?' Jenna asked now.

'Yeah, Drake senior introduced them when your dad bought the place, because Leonard was working in the town hall at the time and your dad needed help getting the liquor licence pushed through.' Lowering his voice now, Fabian added, 'Don't quote me, but I got the impression it might not have been entirely above board.'

'Don't be ridiculous,' Jenna snorted, sure that her dad would never have been involved in anything less than legal. If there was one thing she *did* know about him, it was that he respected the police and the law above all else.

'Just the impression I got.' Fabian shrugged. 'Could be wrong.'

'I'm sure you are,' Jenna said with certainty. 'So, what about Mrs Drake?'

'Typical celebrity wife,' Fabian said, scathingly. 'Got used to hubby being the Tory poster boy, and wasn't too happy when his looks went and his career hit the skids and they were pushed out of the limelight. I met them last year when we hosted some old judge's retirement party in the board-room, and she was miserable as sin that night, too.'

Pursing her lips thoughtfully, Jenna said, 'I thought she seemed more sad than miserable.'

'Same thing, isn't it?' Fabian gave her a sly grin. 'Anyway, wipe your hands. You're about to meet a real live movie star.'

'Oh?' Raising an eyebrow, Jenna looked around. 'Who?'

'Melody Fisher.' Fabian nodded in the direction of the group who were just entering the foyer.

Jenna watched as the woman strolled in, pausing – seem-ingly innocently, although it just *had* to be deliberate, Jenna thought – directly beneath one of the overhead spots to light the cigarette that one of the men had just given her. Seeming not to notice that every male tongue was hanging out, she arched her lovely neck and blew her smoke elegantly into the air.

'Stunning, isn't she?' Fabian whispered, folding his arms to watch the show.

'Gorgeous,' Jenna agreed. The woman had the most incredible figure she'd ever seen: tiny waist, endless legs, and amazing breasts. 'I don't think I know her, though.'

'You will,' Fabian assured her. 'She was in a Sandra Bullock movie last year, and another with George Clooney after that. She's being tipped for the big time, by all accounts. Definitely had surgery, though,' he added conspiratorially. 'But she's been living in the States, and it's practically compulsory over there, isn't it?'

Smiling, because that was exactly the kind of thing a woman would have said, Jenna asked who the men were.

'Little one's her boyfriend, Tony Allen,' Fabian said, lowering his voice. 'Don't know too much about him except that he's American. Big one's rumoured to be a minder.'

'Rumoured?' Jenna glanced up at him amusedly. 'By who?'

'My sources.' Tapping a finger to his nose, Fabian gave her a secretive smile. 'Pays to keep your ear to the ground in this game, you know. How else do you think I found out they were here, and where they were staying so that I could send them an invitation?'

Shushing her then, he stepped forward to greet the trio as they approached.

'So glad you could make it, Ms Fisher,' he cooed, reaching for Melody's hand and lightly touching his lips to it. 'And good evening to you, too, Mr Allen. Welcome to Zenith, and may I—'

'Do I know you?' Tony cut him off rudely, sizing him up and deciding that he was a creep.

'Fabian King – manager of Zenith,' he said, holding the smile in place despite taking an instant dislike to the other man. 'And this,' he gestured towards Jenna, 'is the owner, Jenna Lorde.'

'Owner?' Drawing his head back, Tony gave Jenna a disbelieving look. 'At your age? What are you – like, nineteen, twenty?'

'I'm older than I look,' Jenna assured him, amused by his straightforward manner.

Melody had been busy ogling Fabian, who was the exact opposite of Tony. Fair, fantastic-looking, fit body. Catching the interest in Tony's eyes as he looked at Jenna, however, she snapped her attention back to them, her rival-antennae twitching. Giving Jenna the once-over, she decided there was nothing to worry about. Tony liked blondes, not brunettes, and the tits were natural – and nowhere near big enough.

Giving Jenna a wide smile, Melody stepped forward to

make her presence felt, saying, 'Yeah, me too. No one ever believes I'm not twenty-one any more.'

'I can see why,' Jenna lied, certain that Melody had to be at least thirty now that she could see her up close. And Fabian could be right about the surgery. But she was very attractive, even so. 'You have beautiful skin. You'll have to tell me your secret.'

'Do you think so?' Melody raised a hand to her cheek. 'I thought I'd gained a few lines recently.'

'Well, if you have, I can't see them. And *please* tell me you have to suffer to keep your body in that kind of shape?'

'Oh, you're a doll,' Melody purred, her face lighting up. 'You and me are going to get along fine.'

Baffled as to how a couple of words about nothing could bring Melody out of a mood so fast, Tony shook his head.

'I don't know what you just did, but thanks for doing it, 'cos I thought she was going to have a face on her all night. Pleased to meet you, Jenna.'

Surprised by the contrast of soft skin and powerful grip when she shook Tony's hand, Jenna said, 'You, too, Mr Allen.'

'Hey, it's Tony to you,' he scolded. Then, jerking his head, 'And this here's Eddie.'

Glancing up at the man, Jenna said hello, then smiled nervously when he just stared unblinkingly back down at her. She didn't know about Melody being a film star, but *he* looked like he'd just stepped off the set of *The Sopranos*. Tall, and quite muscular, he had an almost feral face, and the darkest eyes she'd ever seen.

'Best get moving before this shower of freeloaders necks all the booze,' Tony said then, casting a scathing glance around the already crowded clubroom. 'And what's the chance of getting this racket turned down, 'cos I'm going to get a fuck of a headache if I have to listen to this shit all night.'

'You're so loud, you won't even notice it once you get talking,' Melody contradicted him, rolling her eyes at Jenna. 'Nice meeting you, Jen,' she said then. 'But I'd best get him moving before he bores you to death. We'll catch up later, yeah?' Letting her gaze slide slowly over Fabian then, she said, 'Later, Babe.'

'Who you calling Babe?' Tony demanded as she took his arm and tugged him through the room.

'It's a girl thing,' she assured him breezily. 'We all do it.'

'Well, I don't like it, so quit it.'

'Okay, Babe.'

'Don't fucking push it, Mel!'

Laughing as their voices faded into the crowd, Jenna shook her head. 'They were sweet, weren't they?'

'Oh, you're good,' Fabian drawled, folding his arms and giving her a wry smile. 'I saw the way you stroked her little ego.'

'I don't know what you're talking about. Women like being complimented, that's all.'

'Yeah, I know. But other women don't normally pull it off that good. They usually make it sound sarcastic, but even *I*'d have believed that you really thought she was that young.'

'Well, if it makes her happy . . . ?' Shrugging, Jenna glanced at her watch. 'Right, I'll leave you to it, if you don't mind. I want to have a word with Jacko about replacing the doormen before it gets too late. Will you be all right by yourself?'

'I'll be fine,' Fabian assured her. 'Most of the guests are here now, anyway, so I think I'll give the go-ahead to let the motleys in.'

'*Paying customers*,' Jenna corrected him, giving him a mock-stern look before walking away.

Narrowing his eyes, Fabian gazed after her. That was the longest he'd spent with her on a one-to-one basis since she'd taken over, and she'd surprised him. In the months following her dad's funeral, she'd been so stressed that she hadn't bothered with make-up, and had practically lived in her jeans. Even in that raw state she'd been a looker, but what an absolute *babe* she was when she made the effort. And now that she'd chilled out, she was way more approachable than he'd initially thought. And if this was the real her, he reckoned that things were definitely going to pick up around here – just so long as she didn't start interfering. She might own the place, but *he* called the shots – and that was exactly how he intended to keep it.

Jacko, the head of security, was checking the fire doors on the lower floor when Jenna found him. Asking him to send some of his boys out to replace Bobby and Flex, she went to the bar and called Maurice over to ask if he'd remembered to send a drink up to Vibes.

Giving her a defiant *why-are-you-bothering-me-with-this-nonsense* look, Maurice said, 'Who?'

'The DJ,' Jenna reminded him, knowing full well that he knew exactly who she was talking about.

'Oh, *him*,' Maurice replied dismissively, already turning away. 'No. I forgot.'

Biting down on her irritation, Jenna called out firmly, 'Two glasses of champagne, please, Maurice.'

She saw the slight tensing of his shoulders, and guessed – rightly – that he was dying to tell her to piss off and get it herself. But if he thought she was going to roll over and let him disrespect her, he had another think coming.

Thanking him when he placed the drinks on the counter, Jenna nodded towards a small pile of broken glass in the corner beside the fridge.

'Clean that up before somebody slips on it, would you?'

Nostrils twitching, Maurice pursed his lips and glared at her.

Raising an eyebrow when several seconds had passed and he still hadn't moved, Jenna said, 'You *do* know where the dustpan is, don't you? Only I'd like you to do it *now*, before somebody cuts themselves and sues me for negligence.'

Giving a triumphant small smile when Maurice reached under the counter for the hand-brush, she picked up the glasses and walked away. She didn't want to add insult to injury by standing over him while he did it, but he'd needed to be put in his place – even if it *had* made her legs feel like jelly.

God, it was hard running your own business. But kind of fun once you got into the swing of it.

Carrying the champagne carefully up the narrow stairs to the DJ's booth, Jenna tapped on the door and let herself in. Vibes was leaning over the console, bobbing his head to the beat in his headphones. He smiled when he saw her, his teeth dazzling in the fluorescent lights pulsing through the window.

'Hope I'm not disturbing you,' she whispered, conscious of the microphone. 'But I thought you must need a drink by now?'

Taking the headphones off, Vibes nodded towards a case of bottled water on the ledge behind her.

'I tend to stick to that when I'm working. But I'll make an exception, seeing as it's New Year.' Taking one of the glasses, he raised it. 'Hope it's a good one, Princess.'

'Me, too.' Clinking her glass against his, Jenna took a sip. The heat in the small room enveloped her like a damp blanket. 'God, it's boiling in here,' she said, fanning a hand in front of her face. 'How do you stand it?'

'It's the equipment,' Vibes told her, wiping his brow on the fluffy white towel looped around his neck. 'There's nothing you can do about it, so you just get used to it.'

Shivering as a bead of sweat trickled down her back, Jenna said, 'Do you want me to get you a fan?'

'Nah.' Vibes shook his head. 'They just stir it up and make you feel sick. And they're noisy as all hell, which don't sound too good over the mike. But thanks for the thought.'

'Let me know if you change your mind,' Jenna said, taking another sip of her drink. Gazing out at the rapturous faces on the dance floor below, she said, 'I don't think I've ever been to a club before where everyone's dancing before they're even half drunk. I guess you *must* be as good as they say, huh?'

'Why, thank you, kind lady.' Vibes gave her a playful grin. 'Does that mean I get a raise?'

'Please say you're joking,' she groaned, gripping her glass a little tighter.

Jenna wasn't even paying *herself* yet – and probably wouldn't be able to for some time to come, because she was up to her neck with bank-loan repayments and the rent on her apartment. But she couldn't afford to lose Vibes. Fabian had told her that great DJs were stars in their own right, and that their fans followed them to whichever club they were playing at. She was lucky that Vibes had agreed to come back after she'd effectively laid him off for the four months it had taken to refurbish Zenith, but if she lost him now she'd probably lose most of her customers, too.

Seeing the fear in her eyes, Vibes quickly assured her that he *was* joking – and wondered, not for the first time, if her skin was as soft to the touch as it looked.

Shaking the thought away, he reminded himself that there was no point thinking like that. Jenna was sweet, gorgeous, and intelligent – and not in the least bit flirtatious, unlike most of the British women he'd met so far. He didn't know if it was the American accent that they got off on, or just that they had never seen a black guy with blue eyes before, but he'd been inundated with phone numbers and blatant propositions since coming over here. And while he would have lapped the attention up a few years back, now it just turned him off.

Taking the hint when he finished his drink and reached for his headphones, Jenna picked up his glass and said, 'I suppose I should get back out there and mingle. Can't hide away up here all night, can I? See you later.'

'Later, Princess,' Vibes said, pulling the headphones down over his ears and flipping the mike on to introduce the next track.

Jenna was smiling as she went back down the stairs. She liked Vibes. He was polite, gentlemanly, and really easy to be around – and to look at, of course. The perfect man, in fact. Now if only she could find one like him for herself, she'd be laughing.

But decent *single* men were as hard to find as great DJs, in her experience. And you couldn't just take their word for it when you *did* find one – as she had learned to her cost with Jason.

But there was no point raking over *those* old coals. What was done was done, and she just had to make sure that she never made the same mistake again.

3

The party was in full swing by two; everybody buzzing as they soaked up the booze and lost their inhibitions.

Great for the club, but not so good for Fabian, who had managed to get himself hijacked by a group of frisky older women. He'd tried to get away, but they seemed intent on holding him hostage on the dance floor, and every time one let go of his hand another one snatched it up.

The one he was with now was actually making him feel ill, rubbing her saggy breasts against him and winking at him seductively. Convinced that she was just waiting for the chance to go in for a full-on snog, he broke free after their third dance and lied that he'd just been summoned by his boss from across the room.

Escorting the woman back to her table, it was all Fabian could do not to scream when one of the friends grabbed him and said, 'Me next. Don't you go and forget about me, now.'

Promising to come right back as soon as he could, he rushed to the safety of his office, wondering what the hell the old witches were doing here, anyway. They weren't on the guest list, so they must have paid to get in. But surely they should be tucked up in bed with their cocoas by now, not out on the town flirting with men young enough to be their great-grandsons!

Locking the door in case anybody walked in on him, he opened his wall safe and took out a small bag of coke. Chopping a thin line on the mirror, he snorted it quickly and leaned his head back to savour the instant tension-easing buzz.

Sorted, Fabian put everything away and headed back down to the club floor with a fresh swagger in his step. Pretending that he hadn't seen the old biddies when they started waving their bingo wings at him, he headed on up to the VIP lounge to give his celebrity friends a dose of the King treatment.

Sitting at her table, surrounded by some of the brightest stars of British stage and screen, Melody should have been in her element. She wasn't happy though – as they would have known if they'd bothered to look at her. But none of them *had* bothered, which was precisely why she was so pissed off. It wasn't like she expected to be the centre of attention or anything, but there was no excuse for people being so rude as to totally ignore her.

She blamed Tony.

Ever since they'd landed two weeks ago, they couldn't go anywhere without people falling all over themselves to talk to him. And once they did, they were hooked. He'd had so many invitations to parties since they'd got here, it wasn't even funny. Everyone in Manchester seemed to think he was some kind of big shot and wanted to be his new best friend, and that really peeved Melody, because he was nothing but a big-talking hood who liked to splash the cash. Whereas *she* had two hit movies on her CV – and many more to come, if the critics who had been calling her *America's Next Big Thing* were right.

Melody had been so pleased when the invitation for tonight's party had arrived at the hotel in *her* name; thrilled that at *last* somebody had realised she was alive and kicking in Tony's shadow. But the thrill hadn't lasted long once they'd got here, because Tony only had to open that big mouth of his for the spotlight to turn firmly his way.

Brenda Thompson had been the first to invite herself to join them. She'd sailed up to their table, almost knocking Melody clean off her chair in her effort to squeeze herself in beside Tony.

'Don't mind if I join you, do you?' she'd asked, in the breathy rasp that Melody had spent hours copying as a teenager. 'But I simply *had* to meet the man behind that wonderfully evocative accent. New York – am I right?'

For a very brief moment, Melody had been thrilled to be in the presence of her long-time acting idol. But that had soon changed when she'd tried to join in the conversation and received the frosty raising of a pencil-thin eyebrow and a turned back in return. She was so offended that she nearly lamped the old cow!

And her mood hadn't improved when two bitches from a top soap came along and proceeded to air-kiss their 'good pal' Brenda and suck up to Tony, while looking down their noses at Melody. Followed by some ugly old Lovie-Dahling actor who was more plastic than Cher, and his *personal assistant*, Clive. Like Clive wasn't his boyfriend – *much*!

Chase Mann was the last straw. Despite slagging him off when they'd seen him at the hotel a couple of days back, Tony had greeted him like a long-lost mate tonight. Melody hadn't minded at first, because she'd thought that Chase would at least talk to her, given that they were closer in age and attractiveness than the rest of these idiots. But he was so stoned that he'd barely even glanced at her. And the tarty little slappers who were sticking to him like gold-digging leeches wound her up by giggling and whispering behind their hands whenever they looked at her.

Shifting irritably in her chair now, Melody glared at Tony, but he was too busy telling jokes to notice. So she gazed down at the crowded dance floor instead, toying with the idea of grabbing a good-looking man and dragging him off to the toilets for a revenge fuck. Tony would notice *that*, she was sure.

Yeah, and then he'd kill me – stone, no messing dead! These people might think he was a charming teddy bear of a man, but Melody knew *exactly* what he was capable of.

Sighing loudly, she snatched up one of the champagne bottles that were cluttering the table and poured herself a large glassful. She might as well get hammered if she had to sit here listening to Tony's boring stories all night, and watching these shitty never-really-weres laughing their facelifts off. Boring, boring, boring!

Fabian arrived at that exact moment.

'How's everyone doing?' he asked loudly, a big smile on his handsome face.

'Having a blast,' Tony grunted, giving him the cold eye. Glancing past him then, he frowned. 'Where's the boss lady?'

'She'll come and say hello as soon as she gets a chance,' Fabian assured him. 'Anything I can do in the meantime?'

'Nah, don't trouble yourself.'

Narrowing his eyes slightly, Fabian said, 'Right, well, I'll leave you to it, then.' *And I hope you choke on your free champagne, you dismissive cunt!*

'Just a minute,' Brenda Thompson called out huskily as he started to back away. Picking up her gift pack, she dangled it off the tip of her finger. 'Are you responsible for this?'

'Er, yes,' Fabian admitted. 'Is there a problem?'

'Oh, no, it's delightful,' she purred, reaching for his hand and pulling him towards her. 'I just *adore* the lighter,' she said then, gazing seductively into his eyes. 'And the perfume smells divine. But I was wondering . . .'

Peering at Fabian when he dipped his head to listen to whatever Brenda was saying, Melody felt a sickening tug in her gut when she noticed the fine white traces under his nose. Coke! Oh, God, what she wouldn't give to get her hands on some of *that* right now. But there was no chance of that with Tony keeping tabs on her. According to Mr Big Shot, '*Ladies don't touch that shit.*'

'What's up with your mush?' Tony asked out of the corner of his mouth, making her jump.

'Nothing,' Melody snapped, pushing her chair back with a dull scrape. 'I'm just fed up of all this yakking, that's all. I'm off for a dance.'

'Not on your own, you're not,' he hissed, gripping her wrist.

'Come with me, then,' she hissed back, knowing full well that he wouldn't.

Flashing her a warning glare, he said, 'You know I don't go for all that jiggy-jiggy shit. But I ain't letting you loose with all them chancers down there, so forget it.'

'What . . . so, now you don't trust me?'

'Sure I do. But you've had too much to drink, and I don't trust *them*. Eddie'll go with you.'

'Oh, come *on*,' Melody moaned, glancing at Eddie who had been leaning against the wall behind Tony all night. 'He'll scare everyone off the dance floor. Have you seen the way he's looking at people – like he wants to skin them and *eat* them.'

'Well, you ain't going alone,' Tony said flatly. 'Take it or leave it.'

'What about him?' She nodded in Fabian's direction.

'You putting me on?' Tony frowned darkly.

'Oh, for God's sake!' Melody tutted softly. 'He's *gay*, you big idiot. Can't you tell? Look at his *hair*. And the way he talks.'

Tony peered at Fabian for a moment and decided that he *did* look kind of effeminate.

'Yeah, you could be right,' he conceded. 'Okay, you can go with him – but no funny business.'

'What, like getting him to give me make-up tips?' Melody sneered.

'You know what I mean.' Giving her a hooded look, Tony turned to Fabian and clicked his fingers. 'Yo! A word.'

Extracting himself from Brenda's clutches, Fabian said, 'What can I do for you, Mr Allen?'

'She wants to dance.' Tony jerked his head at Melody. 'But she's loaded, so I want you to go with her and make sure she don't get mauled by none of them cunts down there.' Pausing, he sent a clear message with his eyes as he added, 'Wouldn't wanna spoil the night having to warn anyone off – you get me?'

'Got you.' Fabian agreed, feeling the coke buzz turn into a sharp stab of paranoia. 'I'll see she gets back in one piece.'

'You do that.' Grinning darkly, Tony reached up and patted his cheek none too gently.

'Come on, then,' Melody snapped, looking at Fabian as if she'd rather be swimming with sharks than about to dance with him.

Following her down the stairs, Fabian was conscious that his legs were shaking. He hadn't liked Tony Allen from the off, but he'd sensed something dangerous about him just now, and he was sure the threat had been aimed at him. But whether or not it had been, there was no mistaking what it had meant: if any man – Fabian included – stepped out of line with his woman, Tony Allen would take it very, very personally.

Melody's mood changed as soon as she and Fabian hit the dance floor. Smiling now, she thrust her breasts at him and yelled, 'That was fun, wasn't it?'

'What was?' Fabian yelled back, glancing around self-consciously.

'Getting you alone without raising suspicion,' Melody told him, raising her arms above her head and throwing her hair back sexily as she twirled around to a remix of Chic's 'Freak Out'. 'Course, he only let you come with me because you're gay.'

'Ex*cuse* me?' Fabian gasped, not sure he'd heard right.

'Why else would he trust me with such a good-looking guy?' she teased, bumping him with her shapely hip. 'Unless he thinks you'd be more interested in *his* bits than mine. You're not gay, though, are you, Babe?'

'Absolutely not!'

'Didn't think so.' Looking up at him through her lashes, Melody bit her lip seductively. 'You really are gorgeous, though. Bet you're hot as hell in the sack.'

Jerking back when she moved even closer and pressed herself against him, Fabian shot a nervous glance up to the VIP lounge, where, he was glad to see, Tony had his back to them.

'Jeezus!' he squawked when Melody suddenly slid her hands over his buttocks. 'Are you trying to get me shot?'

'Aw, now that's not nice,' she scolded when he pushed her away. 'I thought Tony told you to look after me.'

'I doubt he meant like *that*,' Fabian protested. 'Look, why don't I go and get you a nice cup of coffee?'

'Rather have something stronger.' Melody gave him a knowing look.

'I don't know what you mean.'

'Sure you do.' Raising a finger to her nose, she said, 'You really should check yourself in the mirror when you're finished.'

Realising what she was getting at, Fabian quickly wiped the coke traces away. Christ! If *she*'d noticed, who else had? *Jenna*? Oh, God! He'd lose his job. Then he'd lose his apartment, because he wouldn't be able to afford it. And his car. And—

Interrupting his racing thoughts, Melody said, 'Chill, Babe. I won't tell if you don't.'

Exhaling nervously, Fabian ran his hands through his hair and gave her a sheepish smile. 'Pretty careless, huh? But thanks for the warning. I would have been in real shit if anyone else had seen it.'

'No problem,' Melody drawled, a glint of something steely sparking in her eyes. 'All you have to do is give me some, and I'll never mention it again.'

'Yeah, right!' Fabian grinned, sure that she was joking.

'I'm serious,' she retorted icily. 'Give me some, or I'll tell Tony you were trying it on with me. And you *know* he'd believe me.'

'Ah, but he thinks I'm gay,' Fabian reminded her, still grinning – still sure it was a joke.

'Only because I *told* him you were so he'd let me dance with you,' Melody countered smoothly. 'But I could have made a mistake, couldn't I? It's easily done. So, how about it, Mr Manager? You going to make your new favourite customer happy. *Or . . .*'

Gazing down into her lovely face, Fabian realised that it wasn't a joke. The bitch was actually trying to blackmail him. And what the hell was he supposed to do about it? If he didn't do what she wanted, she'd drop him in it with her bad-ass boyfriend. But if he did, and got caught, he'd lose his job.

'Well?' Melody said, still managing to dance – although Fabian didn't know how, because *his* limbs felt like lead weights.

'Look, I only had a bit,' he lied, hoping that she would back off. 'If I'd known you were into it, I'd have saved you some, but I didn't.'

Narrowing her eyes, Melody pursed her lips petulantly. He was lying, she could tell, and she hated being lied to.

'Aw, now, you wouldn't be fibbing, would you?' she drawled with a mean edge to her voice. 'That's not very nice when I'm trying to be friendly.'

As friendly as a rattlesnake! Fabian thought incredulously, wondering how he'd managed to get himself caught up in this.

Softening her tone suddenly, Melody moved closer, whispering, 'I'll make it worth your while. Babe. I know you want me – I can see it in your eyes.'

Fabian glanced at the people surrounding them, terrified that someone might have heard. Under normal circumstances, if a gorgeous woman came on strong like this he'd go for it good style. But these were not normal circumstances, and he had too much to lose if anybody got hold of the wrong end of the stick. Tony Allen, for example.

'Look, I *swear* I haven't got any left,' he whispered back, praying that she believed him. 'If I did, I'd give it to you.'

'Fine,' Melody snapped, losing patience. 'I'll just have to go and tell Tony what you've been doing, then, won't I? And he hates it when anybody upsets me.' Blinking rapidly now, making her huge eyes swim with tears, she quivered her bottom lip and whimpered – loudly, 'No . . . please don't . . . I don't want to.'

Fabian's heart sank. If he hadn't seen and heard it for himself, he'd never have believed that anybody could switch it on so fast – and so convincingly. Glancing around for witnesses to verify that he hadn't touched Melody should he need to prove it, he was dismayed to see that none of the sweaty, drunken dancers were paying him the slightest attention. It would be his word against hers.

'All right,' he hissed when she started to back away with a terrified expression on her face. 'Over here.'

Motioning with his head for her to follow, he walked off the dance floor and found a quiet corner in the shade of a potted palm tree.

'I'll see what I can do,' he said when she joined him seconds later. 'There's a guy I know who might have something, but

you'll have to give me time to find him. See that door?' he
said then, nodding at the door to the offices. 'I'll leave it on
the latch. My room's on the first floor, halfway down the
corridor.'

Smiling slyly, Melody reached up and stroked his cheek.
Laughing softly when he jerked back, she waggled her fingers
at him. 'See you in ten, then. And make sure you've got it,
or I won't be a happy bunny.'

Rushing to his office when she'd gone, Fabian took out
his stash and chopped two thick lines on the mirror. Snorting
one quickly, he cursed her under his breath. He hadn't
intended to do any more tonight, but his nerves were shot
to pieces thanks to her.

Tapping on the door a few minutes later, Melody let
herself in without waiting for an answer. Seeing the line he'd
left for her on the mirror, she gave a triumphant smile.

'I see you managed to find your friend, then?'

'Yeah, but I nearly got caught,' Fabian lied, giving her a
resentful look. 'Do you know how much trouble I could get
into for this?'

Sighing remorsefully now, Melody flopped down on the
visitor's chair and crossed her legs, giving Fabian a flash of
sheer black panties.

'Sorry, Babe, I didn't mean to heavy you like that, but I
was desperate. I'm having the shittiest night *ever*. When Tony
gets on a roll, he just goes on and on, and I might as well
be invisible for all the attention he gives me. We've been
here two weeks now, and all he's done is . . .'

Listening as she poured out her woes, Fabian felt the anger
that had been holding him rigid melt away. It sounded like
she'd been having a rough time of it, and she was only kicking
out at him because she couldn't kick out at her boyfriend.
She looked so vulnerable – he felt a wave of protective indig-
nation wash over him. Tony Allen must be some kind of

idiot if he couldn't see that bagging himself a prize like Melody Fisher came at a price. Stars needed more attention than normal people – and there were thousands of men out there who would gladly give Melody Fisher the attention she was craving. If Tony Allen wasn't careful, it would be nobody's fault but his own when Melody found what she was looking for in somebody else's arms.

Fabian's, maybe.

Well, why not? What man in his right mind would refuse if she was offering it on a plate?

'Am I forgiven?' Melody peered up at him with little-girl-lost eyes.

'Yeah, sure, forget it.' Smiling, he handed her the rolled-up twenty note he'd been using as a straw.

Snorting her line, Melody leaned her head back and inhaled deeply as Fabian's gaze slid over her body. He'd had more women than the average teenage boy had had hot wanks, and most had been way up there in the looks department, but this one was something else. With the added bonus that she was almost really famous. How cool was that?

Smiling as if she could read his mind, Melody passed the note back to him and stood up. Putting a hand on his cheek, she kissed him softly on the lips.

'Thanks, Babe, I really needed that. You're a star.'

Reaching for her, Fabian's hands hit empty air when she backed towards the door, biting her lip and waving her fingers at him. He had a hard-on to die for – and another attack of paranoia coming on. Now that she'd had what she wanted, she'd have nothing to lose by dropping him in it. It might be her idea of fun.

'Hey, you're not going to do anything stupid, are you?' he asked, panic rich in his voice.

'*Would* I?' Melody teased. Then, shaking her head, she said, 'Course not, Babe. He'd kill you. And where would that leave me? I could be stuck in this stinking place for months the way he's going on, and I'm going to need you to keep me sane.' Blowing him a kiss then, she opened the door and slipped out, whispering, 'Don't worry, it'll be our little secret.'

Locking the door behind her, Fabian leaned back against it. She'd said that Tony would kill him if he found out – and he had no doubt that the man was more than capable of it.

But, no, come on. This was *England*. That kind of thing might happen every day in America, but Allen couldn't be crazy enough to think he'd get away with it over here – *could he*?

Whether or not he could, one thing was sure: Fabian would have to tread very carefully until he knew that Melody could be trusted.

Looking down when his dick gave a plaintive throb, he shook his head disbelievingly. Scary as it was to think of the trouble she could cause him, he had to admit that the hard-to-get act was a turn-on. But it was a very rare woman who could resist him for too long once he'd set his sights on her, so he wasn't worried about that. And, who knew – if their little secret *stayed* secret, Fabian might get to see a fair bit more of her than Allen had bargained for when he'd told him to keep an eye on her.

Avril Drake was bored, and becoming increasingly irritated. So much for Leonard's belief that he was as well known and popular as ever: nobody had so much as said hello to them since they'd arrived, apart from the gushing manager and the pretty young owner. And Leonard had a face like a wet weekend in Wigan. But at least it should make him think twice about dragging her back here in a hurry.

Sighing heavily, she stared wistfully down at the smiling dancers below. It wasn't that she didn't enjoy music and parties, because she did. In fact, she'd been quite the life and soul – once upon a very long time ago. But Leonard had soon stopped that, because he didn't *do* dancing and partying, claiming that it didn't suit his image. So, apart from the occasional waltz at some stuffy political do or other, she hadn't had the pleasure in a good long time.

She resented Leonard for robbing her of her best years, but there wasn't a damn thing she could do about it now because she was far too old to start again. Too settled with her life – such as it was – to face the upheaval.

Glaring at her when she released yet another heavy sigh, Leonard hissed through clenched teeth, 'Are you just going to sit there pulling that miserable bloody face all night?'

'Why?' she retorted sarcastically. 'Are you worried it'll outdo yours?'

Tutting loudly, he shook his head.

'Careful,' Avril muttered. 'You'll have people thinking that we're not quite as *together* as you'd have them believe.'

'I don't care what anybody thinks,' he grunted – blatantly lying, because that was all he'd *ever* cared about.

'If you're not enjoying yourself, why don't we just go home?' Avril suggested hopefully, feeling a sudden longing for the warm, cosy solitude of her bed.

'And make myself look a complete idiot?' Leonard snapped. 'I'm not going anywhere, so give me a break and make like you're having fun, for God's sake.'

'Fine,' she replied, a hint of hurt in her eyes. 'If you're sure that's what you want?'

'I wouldn't have said it if it wasn't,' he said, folding his arms over his belly.

'Right!' Pushing her chair back, Avril stood up. 'I'm going to dance.'

'On your *own?*' Leonard looked at her as if she'd gone mad. 'Don't be ridiculous!'

'You told me to have fun.'

'With *me*.'

'Is that possible?' Avril replied coldly.

But who was she kidding? She'd no more dance alone than Leonard would walk into a room full of strangers without her, and they both knew it.

Shoulders slumping, she pushed her chair under the table, saying resignedly, 'I'm going to the toilet – *if* that's all right with you?'

'Fine,' Leonard grunted with satisfaction. Then, looking around for a waiter, he said, 'I shall have to have words with that Jenny girl. Let her know that her staff have been neglecting her guests.'

'Don't make waves,' Avril cautioned wearily. 'And while I'm gone, could you please think about going home, because neither of us is enjoying this.'

Flicking her a dismissive glance, Leonard turned his head, his face all false smiles now as he nodded to the music and gazed around the room. He had no intention of slinking away like an unloved dog before the party was over.

Shaking her head, Avril walked calmly away. She didn't really need the toilet, she just needed a break from her husband's miserable company. Tapping a waiter on the shoulder en route to the stairs, she pointed out their table and asked him to take a very large Scotch rocks over to Leonard, in the hope that he would get drunk and cheer up.

Self-conscious by himself, Leonard agitatedly tapped his fingers on the table. He would never admit it to Avril, but she was right about him not enjoying himself. He didn't know what he'd expected when he came here tonight, but it certainly hadn't been to sit in virtual isolation. And while he knew a lot of the faces around him, having seen them on

TV or in the papers, he found it quite wounding that they obviously didn't recognise him.

But, then, maybe they did, he told himself consolingly. Maybe they knew exactly who he was, but were put off approaching him because of Avril's uninviting face.

'Your drink, sir.'

Glancing up in surprise when the young waiter placed a large Scotch on the table, Leonard said, 'Oh, right . . . thank you. Just a moment.' Pulling a ten-pound note out of his wallet, he placed it on the tray.

'You don't have to pay,' the waiter told him, holding it out. 'Everything's complimentary for invited guests tonight.'

'Yes, I know that,' Leonard blustered, having completely forgotten. 'It's a tip.'

'Oh, no, sir, I couldn't.'

'I insist.' Leonard was smiling now. 'I *want* you to have it.'

'Okay, thanks.' Returning the smile, the waiter pocketed the note. 'I'll be around if you want anything else. Just give me a wave.'

Watching as the boy walked away, Leonard shook his head, wondering how on Earth these kids managed to squeeze themselves into such tight clothing. Oh, to be young and fit again. He'd have given these boys a run for their money in his prime – before Avril got her claws into him and sucked all the joy out of his bones.

Sighing wistfully for his lost youth, he sipped at his drink and let his gaze wander. The room was packed out, but there was a particularly large gathering at a table across the room where a loud American was holding court, making every-body laugh with stories that Leonard couldn't hear.

Pursing his lips thoughtfully, he peered at the man's face. He must be very famous, judging by the way the other stars were hanging on to his every word, but Leonard couldn't quite put his finger on where he'd seen him before.

Clicking his fingers when it suddenly came to him, he thought, *Of course!* Lord Kimberley's charity auction-cum-dinner at The Lowry last week. Tony Allen – that was his name.

Feeling a small thrill of excitement when it occurred to him that it might break the ice with some of the other guests if he were to go and say hello to Allen, Leonard eased himself out of his seat and strolled over.

Edging casually in among the people who were hanging about on the edge of the circle, he manoeuvred himself in until he was close to Allen – who was too busy telling a joke to notice him. Coughing to attract his attention, the blood rushed to Leonard's cheeks when everybody turned and looked at him.

Irritated by the interruption, Tony frowned up at him. 'Yeah?'

'Oh, sorry . . . didn't mean to disturb you,' Leonard said, suddenly nervous because Allen obviously didn't recognise him. 'I, er, just saw you and thought I'd best come and say hello.' Grinning then, he added, 'Wouldn't want you thinking I was ignoring you, or anything.'

'Do I know you?' The frown deepened.

'We met last week,' Leonard reminded him. 'Lord Kimberley's do.'

'Kimberley?' Tony repeated slowly, narrowing his eyes.

'At The Lowry,' Leonard prompted, embarrassed now because people were beginning to smirk. 'Auction and dinner in aid of the dialysis unit? Lord Kimberley introduced us.'

'That the old dude with the horse-face wife?'

'Maureen,' Leonard affirmed, smiling again. 'Yes, that's them. I was sitting across from you on the long table at dinner. We discussed some of the lots.'

'Can't say I remember too much about it.' Tony shrugged. 'It must have been boring.'

'Those things often are,' Leonard agreed disloyally. 'So, I, um, guess you won't be going to his *Poloquet* party next week?'

Repulsed by the smarmy conspiratorial grin, Tony said, 'Whatever the fuck that means – *no*, I won't be going.'

Excusing herself just then, Brenda Thompson got up and squeezed her way out from behind the table.

'Do you mind?' Leonard indicated her vacated seat.

'Free country, last I heard,' Tony grunted. 'Wouldn't be here otherwise.'

Leonard laughed, but quickly stopped when Tony flicked him an irritated glance. *Okay, keep it cool*, he told himself, squeezing onto the chair. *Don't get carried away and make a fool of yourself when everything's going so well.*

Over at the bar, Kalli was casting disapproving glances in Leonard's direction as she washed a pile of glasses. She'd seen the leering way he'd followed Austin with his eyes when Austin had taken him a drink a short while ago, and she hadn't liked it one little bit.

Austin would say she'd imagined it, but she hadn't – and she knew better than most about men and their disgusting ways, having been forced to cater to all manner of filthy pigs when her father had sold her to the brothel owner in Hong Kong. Just like that fat man, *those* men had smiled like angels while making their deals with the Devil. And Austin, with his cute dimples, bleached-blond hair and baby-blue eyes, was prime meat for that kind of man.

Austin bounded over just then with a fresh order. Waving a hand in front of her face, he said, 'Oi, quit staring at the stars and get on with your job.'

Snatching the order slip from him, Kalli gave it to the other waitress and grabbed his hand.

'*Ooer*, get off!' he protested, jerking back and looking at the soapsuds in disgust. 'Now look what you've done. I'm all wet.'

'Never mind that,' Kalli said impatiently. 'What were you and that man talking about?'

'*Man*?' Austin repeated bemusedly. 'Honey, in case it's slipped your distracted attention, there's about a *zillion* men in here tonight, and I've been talking to them all, like the good little waiter I am.'

'*Him*.' Kalli jabbed a finger in Leonard's direction.

'I wasn't talking to him about anything,' Austin told her innocently. 'Oh, except to tell him that he didn't have to pay for his drinks.'

'So, what did he give you?' Kalli persisted. 'And don't lie, because I saw you put something in your pocket.'

'Check *you*, Miss Marple!' Austin teased. 'But for your nosy information, it wasn't his number, so you can drop the slapped-bum mush.' Pulling the ten-pound note from his pocket, he dangled it in front of her face for a second, then stashed it away again before the other waitress saw it and expected him to put it in the tips jar. 'Keep quiet, and I'll split it with you later.'

Sighing, Kalli shook her head. 'No, it's yours. Just be careful, yeah?'

'Okay, *Mum*.' Grinning cheekily, Austin took his newly loaded tray off the other waitress and winked at Kalli. 'See ya later, Dominator.'

Kalli pursed her pretty lips as she watched him skip away through the crowd. He was very perky tonight. *Too* perky, and she suspected that it had something to do with his boyfriend Xavier's visit to their flat earlier this afternoon. If she found out he'd been taking Es again, she'd be having very strong words with him. And Xavier would get a good telling–off next time she saw him, too.

★

It was almost four in the morning when Jenna dragged herself back up to the VIP lounge. She was exhausted, and her feet were screaming for release from her high, strappy shoes. But they would just have to wait, because nobody looked in any hurry to leave any time soon. *God*, how she wished she'd settled for a three o'clock licence instead of an all-nighter.

Making her way to a quiet corner of the bar, she smiled when Kalli came over. 'Hi, sweetheart. How's it going?'

'Fine.' Kalli peered at Jenna with concern. 'But you look tired.'

'I am. But don't tell anyone. It's not the best impression to give the customers, is it? The hostess who can't stick the pace.'

'Don't worry, nobody will notice.'

'*You* did.'

'Yes, but I see more than most.'

'I'm sure you do.' Jenna laughed softly. 'Could you get me a cranberry juice, please?' Yawning when Kalli went to get her drink, she jumped when Tony Allen suddenly appeared at her side. Throwing a hand over her mouth, she rolled her eyes apologetically. 'Sorry about that. I guess I'm not used to such late nights.'

'Not so hot on staying up all night myself, these days,' Tony drawled, giving her a lopsided grin. 'Mind if I sit down?' He patted the stool beside hers.

'Not at all.' She moved her knees to give him room. 'I'm just getting a drink. Can I get you anything?'

Settling on the stool, he said, 'Yeah, that'd be good. JD on ice. Ed?'

Sitting on the other side of him, Eddie nodded.

When Kalli had brought their drinks, Tony took a sip of his and exhaled loudly.

'Hope you don't mind me invading your space like this, but I needed to escape before I lost my mind.' He jerked his head in the direction of his table, where Leonard was sitting alone now, everyone else having drifted away. 'Kind of boring, having people agree with every word you say – especially when you know you're talking shit. But one man's idiot is another man's pain in the ass – and all that.' Reaching into his pocket, he took out a pack of cigars. 'Mind?'

'Not at all,' Jenna told him. 'Go ahead.'

Lighting up, Tony exhaled a thick plume of noxious smoke, then swivelled in his seat to gaze around.

'You know, this is quite some place you got here. I wasn't too sure at first, but it's pretty cool once you get used to it.'

'Glad you like it.' Jenna smiled, resisting the urge to waft the smoke away. She despised the smell of cigar smoke, but he *was* a guest.

'Oh, I like it.' He nodded slowly. 'A lot, as it goes.'

Jenna raised an eyebrow when he gave her a disarming smile. For a squat man who wasn't overly blessed in the looks department, he was almost handsome when he wasn't scowling.

'So, you inherited this place off of your old man?' Tony asked suddenly, catching her off guard.

Wondering how he knew, she said, 'Yes. He died a few months ago.'

'So I hear. How you coping?'

'Okay, I suppose. You just have to get on with it, don't you?'

'Guess so,' Tony agreed, leaning an elbow on the bar now and crossing his legs, as if settling in for the night. 'Mom doing all right?'

'She died a while back,' Jenna told him. 'Not long after . . .' Pausing, she flapped her hand in a subconscious *brush the pain aside* gesture. 'My younger brother was killed, you see, and I don't think she ever really got over it.'

'Jeez, that's rough.' Tony squinted at her through the smoke. 'Died of a broken heart, did she?'

'No, Alzheimer's. It was a mixed blessing, though, because it affects the memory, so she seemed to forget all about Damian once it kicked in. She didn't recognise *any* of us by the end.'

'Man, you've had it bad,' Tony commented sympathetically. 'So, now you got no one?'

'A sister,' Jenna told him. 'But I don't really see too much of her, because she married when I was quite young and moved to Australia.' Frowning now, she reached for her drink, wondering why she was revealing so much personal stuff to this stranger.

'You're doing good, considering you've had to go it alone,' Tony said admiringly. 'You can't knock yourself for that.'

'I'm managing,' she murmured.

'Better than managing,' Tony persisted. 'Like I said, this is a great place – and I should know, I've had one of my own.'

'*Really*?' Jenna was surprised. She hadn't actually considered what he might do for a living, but running a nightclub wouldn't have been her first guess.

'Yeah, but it wasn't really my bag, so I sold up and shipped out to "good old Blighty".'

Groaning at his affected English accent, Jenna shook her head. 'That was terrible.'

'Sounded better than half the clowns I've been listening to tonight,' he chuckled. 'Some of 'em sound like they're munching on their own bazoomas.'

'Ah, the *actors*.' Jenna gave him a conspiratorial smile. 'Don't let them hear you saying that. They spend good money learning how to speak like that.'

'Yeah? Well, maybe they should put their dough in the bank and save us the pain of having to listen to it.' Blowing out yet more smoke, Tony brought the subject back to her. 'So, what's your plans for this place? You got partners . . . shareholders?'

'No, it's just me,' Jenna said, irritated that she couldn't bring herself to tell him to mind his own business. None of the other guests had gone beyond congratulating her and wishing her luck for the future, but Tony Allen seemed to be probing, and she wasn't sure that she liked it.

Gazing around thoughtfully, Tony said, 'You know, anybody else messing with this much chrome would have had it looking like a slot machine, or something. But you've got it real classy. And I like the way you've got the kids dressed to match. That's a nice touch.'

Accepting the compliment with a modest smile, Jenna said, 'You've quite an eye for detail, Mr Allen.'

'Hey, come *on* . . .' Drawing his head back, he frowned at her. 'I thought I told you to call me Tony? Only ass-lickers and dick-wipes have to call me Mister – like that fat fuck back there. No offence,' he added quickly. 'I know he's your guest, an' all, but there's something not right about him. He gives me the creeps – know what I mean?'

'Mmmm.' Jenna struggled to keep from laughing out loud at the look of revulsion on his face. Leonard Drake had obviously made quite an impression, and she wondered if he and Tony had shaken hands.

'Who is he, anyway?'

'A politician,' Jenna said, jumping when Tony slapped his hand down hard on the bar.

'Ha! Shoulda known! *That*'s why he's so fucking creepy. Always on the make, those guys. Goddamn liars, too, promising shit they ain't got no intention of delivering. And *greedy* – don't even get me started. Ain't one of 'em not on *some*one's payroll!'

'It's the same for every political system the world over, isn't it?' Jenna commented bemusedly. 'Greed and deception are just part of the job description.'

'Hey, whaddya know . . .' Sitting back, Tony gazed at her

with open admiration. 'A broad with a brain – never thought I'd see the day. Most of the women I know can't talk about nothing but clothes and make-up. And those that *do* have more interesting things to say generally turn you off when they start combing their crew-cuts.'

Smiling, Jenna said, 'I'm sure I'm not the only hetero-sexual woman you've ever met who's got a mind of her own.'

'Maybe not,' he conceded. 'But you're sure as hell the prettiest.'

Jenna's smile faltered. Oh, God! She hoped he wasn't hitting on her. Apart from the fact that she wasn't attracted to him in the slightest, he was Melody Fisher's boyfriend.

Fortunately, an actress friend of Brenda Thompson decided to come and introduce herself to Tony just then, so Jenna was spared having to find out if he was trying his hand. Promising that they'd talk again soon, she made her escape.

Avril had been back from the toilet a long time when Leonard finally gave up on Tony Allen and slithered back to their table. Seeing the look of dejection on his face, she smiled tightly.

'What's the matter, dear? Did your new friend chase you away?'

'No, he did *not*,' Leonard grunted. 'For your information, it was *me* who left *him*.'

'Of course it was,' Avril murmured, fanning her face with her hand as a hot flush came over her.

'You're sweating like a pig,' Leonard muttered nastily. 'Haven't you any powder in your bag of tricks to soak it up?'

'Didn't think I'd need any.'

'Well, you do. It's very unflattering.'

'Don't take it out on *me* because *you*'ve been rejected,' Avril snarled.

'If you were watching, you know that he didn't just leave *me*, he left everybody,' Leonard informed her, feeling a little better as he said it, because he realised that it was actually true. 'He needed to discuss something with Jenny in private. But, as you're so interested,' he added, blatantly lying now, 'he asked if I'd be here again tomorrow, because he'd rather like to talk some more.'

'Oh, would he now?'

'*Yes*. And I said I'd be delighted, so there we go.'

'I see. Well, perhaps you'd better go back and tell him that you won't be able to make it because we'll be at the Buckleys' – or had you forgotten?'

'No, of course I hadn't,' Leonard blustered. 'I just thought we could come straight from there.'

'It's too far. We'd be too late to get in by the time we got here.'

'Not if we left early.'

'What, earlier than everyone else?' Avril gave her husband a disbelieving look. 'You who *always* stay till the bitter end in case they talk about you when you're gone?'

'I'm sure they'll manage without us,' Leonard muttered, wishing that she'd shut her sarcastic mouth. 'Anyway, you're always complaining that you don't get out enough, so you ought to be grateful.'

Raising an eyebrow, Avril peered at him incredulously. *Grateful?* Did he think she was a dog desperate to be walked, or something?

'It's late. Let's go,' Leonard said suddenly, snatching up his glass and downing what was left of his drink. 'I just want to have a quick word with Jenny first.'

'Why?'

'To thank her for inviting us tonight, of course.' Getting up, Leonard peered down at his wife. 'You really should lay off the drink if it makes you forget your manners.'

'Don't concern yourself with *my* manners,' Avril retorted indignantly. 'And I've only had three drinks all night, as you well know, so don't insinuate that I'm some kind of alcoholic. I might just have another, in fact,' she added defiantly.

'I've a busy day tomorrow,' Leonard informed her, as if that were the end of the matter. 'And *you*'re going to need all the beauty sleep you can get.'

Glaring after him when he walked away in search of Jenna, Avril snatched up her handbag. She didn't want to stay, but it galled her that he just assumed command as and when it suited him. She'd been asking to leave for hours and he hadn't budged, but they could go now that *he* was ready.

And she had no choice but to comply, because he'd think nothing of leaving her to make her own way home if she didn't. And he'd probably lock the gates, too, forcing her to ring through to the house to get him to open them.

Jenna was nowhere to be seen when Leonard reached the bar. Looking around, he spotted Fabian hovering in the shadows and made a beeline for him instead.

'Ah, hello there . . . I was looking for Jenny. You wouldn't happen to know where she is, would you?'

'*Jenna*'s busy at the moment,' Fabian told him, emphasising the pronunciation of her name. 'Will I do?'

'Well, I suppose you'll have to,' Leonard grumbled disappointedly. He had really wanted to talk to the girl in person – to let her know that, as a trusted friend of her late father, he was always available should she ever need any advice or guidance, or even just a fatherly chat. But it would have to wait, he supposed. Remembering his manners now, he said, 'I wanted to thank her – and yourself, of course – for inviting my wife and me tonight. We've had a lovely time.'

'Glad you enjoyed it.'

'Oh, we did. Everything was wonderful. The food, the drinks, the service – couldn't fault a thing.'

'Very pleased to hear it,' Fabian murmured distractedly, his gaze fixed firmly over Leonard's shoulder on the Allen table, where he could see Melody being touchy-feely with Tony. She'd obviously forgiven the ugly lout for neglecting her, but Fabian hoped she didn't get *too* relaxed and let anything slip.

'Are you open tomorrow?'

'Sorry?' Snapping his attention back to Leonard, Fabian frowned. 'Tomorrow? Oh, right – yes. And every night there-after. Shall we expect to see you?'

'Absolutely!' Leonard beamed, taking it as an actual invi-tation.

It was six before the club was totally cleared of guests, and by half past most of the staff had gone, too.

Bumping into Fabian on her way to the lower bar, Jenna gave him a tired smile. 'Good night, wasn't it?'

'Fantastic,' he agreed. 'Bet you're wondering what you were so worried about?'

'I wasn't worried,' she lied, her eyes twinkling because they both knew how panicked she'd been. 'You were great, by the way. I was watching you with Melody Fisher.'

Fabian blanched. *Oh, shit! What had she seen?*

'It was really nice of you to dance with her,' Jenna went on, oblivious to the wariness in his eyes. 'Not that it could have been all that hard, considering how lovely she is, but I know you only did it to help Tony out. So, well done.'

'Thanks,' Fabian muttered, more relieved than she could ever know. 'All in a day's work.'

'A very *good* one, in your case,' Jenna said. 'Staying for a drink?'

Fabian was tempted, but when he saw Vibes, Kalli and

Austin loitering by the bar he decided against it. Much as he'd have liked another one-to-one with Jenna, there was no way he was wasting his time on the hired help. Anyway, he was still on edge about the whole Melody situation and needed to get home to relax.

'Actually, I'm a bit knackered,' he said, yawning to emphasise the point. 'And I've got to come in first thing to wait for the delivery, so I'll give it a miss, if you don't mind?'

'Course not. And don't worry about that delivery. I'll come in early and help you with it.'

'No need, I've got it covered. You just stay in bed till you're good and ready.' Leaning towards her, Fabian kissed her on the cheek. 'Happy New Year.'

'You, too,' Jenna said, sitting down wearily on one of the tall bar stools.

Stepping out of the way to let Fabian past, Kalli put her hands on her non-existent hips and gazed around at the mess of glasses, plates and overflowing ashtrays littering the bar. Pushing up her sleeves, she set about clearing up.

'Leave that,' Jenna told her. 'The cleaners will do it in the morning. Come and have a drink – I think we all deserve one.' Looking around at them all now, she said, 'Thanks so much for everything you've done, guys. You've really helped make it go well tonight.'

'We *were* pretty damn good, weren't we?' Austin crowed, going behind the bar to pour the drinks.

Straddling the stool beside hers, Vibes said, 'I hope you're including yourself in that, Princess, because *you* were fantastic.'

'Hear, hear,' Kalli agreed, sitting on the other side of Vibes. 'You were brilliant, Jenna. Nobody would ever guess it was your first time.'

'*Like a virgin*,' Austin sang camply, popping the cork out of a half-full bottle of champagne that Maurice had left under the counter.

'Shut up, you idiot,' Kalli scolded. 'Jenna's trying to relax.'

'It's okay,' Jenna assured her. 'I don't mind a bit of music. Subject of,' she said then, turning to Vibes. 'You were *amazing*.'

Dipping his head, Vibes gave a modest shrug. 'I was okay, I guess.'

'Oh, come on, you were *way* hot!' Austin chipped in enthusiastically, laying four glasses out on the counter. 'When the doors opened and you hit it with the Big Ben chimes, I thought I was gonna *die*, it was that spine-tingly. And the way you came out of that gospel version of "Auld Lang Syne" and blasted straight into that Kylie remix . . . Oh, my *life*!' Closing his eyes, he hugged the champagne bottle to his chest. 'It was like getting into an ice-cold shower after a sizzling sauna!'

'I think we get the picture.' Jenna laughed. 'Now, do you think we could get the drinks?'

But it was true what he'd said. Vibes had turned the room on its head tonight, drawing people onto the dance floor and holding them there, never giving them a chance to think about sitting down as each track raised the pace of the last. But his real brilliance had shown itself in the final hour, when he'd started to mellow the mood, subtly slowing the pace down to the final laid-back bluesy smooch.

'Fantastic,' Jenna murmured, sighing happily.

'Isn't he?' Kalli agreed, resting her chin on her hand. Blushing then, she added, 'I meant as a DJ.'

'Me, too,' Jenna said quickly.

'What-*ever*!' Austin murmured amusedly.

Smiling, Vibes looped his arms around their shoulders and hugged them to him. 'You are one pair of terrific ladies – you know that?'

'What about me?' Hand on hip now, Austin tilted his head and pouted flirtatiously. 'Don't you get hugs round here if you haven't got boobs?'

'You, my friend, get a high five!' Vibes laughed, slapping

palms with him across the bar. 'I'd like to propose a toast,' he said then, picking up his glass. 'To friends . . . and to Jenna's success.'

'That's two toasts,' Kalli said, smiling slyly as she noticed that Jenna and Vibes couldn't seem to look each other in the eye for more than a few seconds at a time.

'Oh, who cares, Little Miss Perfect?' Austin tutted. 'Button up, and *bottoms* up!'

Reaching for her glass, Kalli said, 'You'd better take it easy, 'cos you're not having another one after that. And I am *not* cleaning the taxi if you throw up in the back again.'

Letting Kalli and Austin out a short time later, Jenna set the alarms and locked up, then stood with Vibes outside the front door to wait for his cab. He'd booked it from the same firm as the rest of the staff, but everyone else's had been and gone a long time ago and there was still no sign of his.

It was pitch dark outside, and absolutely freezing. Jenna was shivering, and her nose felt like an icicle, but there was no way she was leaving Vibes by himself. There had been too many reports of gangs attacking lone men in the city lately, and she'd never live with herself if that were to happen to him.

'You should go,' Vibes told her. 'It's too cold to be hanging around out here.'

'I'm fine,' she lied, smiling to disguise the fact that her teeth were chattering. 'What time did they say they'd be here?'

'Twenty minutes ago.'

'Bloody hell. I didn't realise they were that late. They've probably forgotten.'

'No worries.' Shrugging deeper into his jacket, Vibes stepped forward to look down the deserted road. 'I'll give it another five and start walking.'

'Don't be daft,' Jenna said, glancing up at him. 'My car's out back. I'll take you.'

'Nah, it's cool.' He shook his head. 'I don't want to put you out.'

'You won't be,' Jenna said firmly. 'But if you stay out here for much longer you'll be too ill to come to work tomorrow – and that's no use to me, is it?'

'If you're sure?' Vibes peered into her eyes – then glanced quickly away when it suddenly struck him where he'd seen that shade of green before.

The sea in Tahiti, when I took a honeymoon stroll on the beach with Aliya, just a few short hours after we later figured that Tashei must have been conceived . . .

Shaking the memory away before it took hold and burned, Vibes said, 'Second thoughts, I think I'd best just wait. That cab's probably gonna come racing round the corner any minute, and I wouldn't want to miss it and waste the guy's time on a day like this.'

Jenna knew better. Turning, she walked away, calling back over her shoulder: 'Come on.'

Catching up with her when he realised that she wasn't taking no for an answer, Vibes adjusted his stride to match hers. He'd never noticed quite how petite she actually was, and the glow from the street lamps gave her hair a beautiful blue sheen.

'You'll have to direct me, because I don't know my way around Withington,' Jenna said when they were in the car.

Rubbing his hands together as the heater blasted delicious hot air at him, Vibes said, 'Left at the corner and keep going straight.' Falling silent then as Jenna reversed out of the yard into the narrow alleyway, he leaned his head back against the rest and thought about how well the night had gone.

Fabian had done himself proud with the guest list, and the rest of the staff had really pulled their weight to make sure everything went smoothly. Particularly Kalli, from what he'd heard. But then, he wouldn't have expected any less of her. She might be the smallest and youngest of the wait-resses, but it was to her that they all turned when they needed help or advice.

'She's a good kid,' he said out loud. Adding, '*Kalli*,' when he realised that Jenna wouldn't know what he was talking about.

'She is, isn't she?' Jenna smiled fondly. 'I haven't known her as long as you have, but you just get the feeling you can really rely on her, don't you?'

'That's because you can,' Vibes murmured. 'And that's good, 'cos we all need someone to rely on.'

'Very true,' Jenna agreed. 'Bit of a rare luxury for me, these days, though, because I lost touch with most of my friends when I left Manchester. I've met lots of new people since I came back, but it's not the same, is it?'

'I hear that,' Vibes said softly. 'Many faces in the picture – few close to the heart.'

'Very poetic.'

'Very *safe*,' Vibes said, glancing at her out of the corner of his eye. Dawn was only just beginning to break, and the dull street lamps were casting long shadows across Jenna's tired face, but she was still one of the most beautiful women he'd ever seen. There was a proud tilt to her chin, and a dignity in the way she held herself which told him that she would be a faithful lover, or a lifelong trusted friend.

Or both, if a man were lucky enough.

Shaking the thought away, he sat up straighter and concen-trated on staying awake as they travelled out of town and into Withington.

'It's the next turning on the left, then second right,' he said when they reached the village centre. 'First house on the left.'

Pulling up at the kerb outside the corner house a minute later, Jenna smiled when she saw three grown men chasing each other around the garden with water guns. 'They look like they're having fun.'

'Oh, man, I thought the party would have been over by now,' Vibes groaned. 'Gina must be having a fit. It would have been murder getting the baby to sleep with these fools making so much noise.' Sighing now, he unclipped his seat belt. 'Best go see if I can get them to cool it.'

Reaching for the door handle now, he hesitated, unsure how to say goodbye. It was New Year's Day, but should he kiss Jenna on the cheek and wish her a good one like he would have any other female friend? Or would she think that completely inappropriate because she was his boss?

Opting for the cautious approach, he nodded at her. 'Right, well, thanks for the lift. And I'll, er, see you tomorrow, I guess.' Smiling shyly, he added, 'Don't go falling asleep at the wheel on your way home.'

'I won't,' Jenna assured him. 'See you tomorrow.'

Hopping out, Vibes stepped back to the gate to wave her off.

'Who's that?' Kenneth asked, coming up behind him with a sly grin on his face.

'My boss,' Vibes said, pushing the gate open.

'Hot *momma*.'

'Wouldn't let Gina hear you saying that.' Strolling up the path, Vibes nodded at Kenneth's friends, who were sitting on the doorstep now, skinning up. 'Happy New Year, guys.'

'Certainly is,' one of them called back in a loud whisper. 'I'm happy as fuck, me. Fancy a puff to see it in, mate?'

Shaking his head, Vibes said, 'Thanks, but I'm gonna hit the sack.' Touching fists with Kenneth then, he said, 'See you in the morning, man.'

'Sweet dreams,' Kenneth called after him as he made his way inside.

Knowing exactly what he was getting at, Vibes flipped him the finger.

4

Fabian had barely slept, but nobody would have guessed it to look at him when he was getting the club ready for opening that night. His hair was perfect, his nails buffed, and his skin glowing, thanks to a visit to Toni & Guy in between overseeing the cleaners and sorting the delivery earlier that day. It was an expensive indulgence but, in his experience, women appreciated a well-groomed man – especially a well-groomed man in a suit. And his midnight-blue Armani and silver-grey shirt couldn't have looked better if it were being strutted down a catwalk in Milan.

But he didn't just *look* good. He felt good, too.

Coming down off the coke in the restless early-morning hours had mellowed him enough to think the Melody Fisher situation through more rationally, and he'd come to the conclusion that she wouldn't dare tell her boyfriend what had happened. If everything was honest and open between her and Tony Allen she wouldn't have had to engineer getting Fabian alone like that – she'd have come right out and asked him for the coke in front of Tony. But she obviously hadn't wanted Tony to know, and that gave Fabian something to hold over her if she got out of line.

With the weight of that gone from his shoulders, he was on top form when Jenna arrived. Greeting her with a kiss on the cheek, he told her about the dozens of calls they'd received from last night's guests and customers, saying how much they'd enjoyed themselves and asking if they'd be open tonight.

'Is that good?' Jenna asked, shrugging out of her jacket and blowing on her icy fingers.

'It's *great*,' he assured her. 'Believe me, people don't usually bother giving feedback. But the machine was chocker when I got here, and the phone hasn't stopped all day.'

'Wow,' she murmured, impressed by his enthusiasm. 'Hope it lasts.'

'Oh, it will,' he told her confidently. 'I've got a feeling we're going to be right up there with the best before too long. You watch.'

'Fingers crossed.' Jenna gave him a nervous smile. Glancing at her watch then, she said, 'Best go drop my stuff in the office while I've got time.' Walking away, she turned back to call, 'You're looking good, by the way.'

Smiling, Fabian called, 'You, too.' And he meant it, because she looked sensational again, in a figure-hugging black halter-dress, and emerald necklace and earrings that perfectly matched her eyes.

The front door opened just then, letting a blast of icy air in. Turning to see who was using the out-of-bounds customer entrance, Fabian frowned when he saw that it was two of the waitresses, JoJo and Vanessa.

'It's fucking freezing!' JoJo yelped, stamping the slush off her shoes and shaking the snow out of her hair onto the polished floor.

Smile gone, Fabian marched towards them, barking, 'How many times have I told you to come round the back? Let me catch you using the front doors again and you're out! Now get that mess cleared up before someone slips on it and breaks their neck. And hurry up – or I'll dock your wages.'

The queue was even longer tonight, the crowd just as skimpily dressed despite the heavy snowfall and icy temperatures. After just half an hour, Fabian went out front and told the doormen to stop letting people in – which didn't impress those at the back of the queue who had been waiting for hours. But no amount of flirting from the girls in their best *fuck-me* outfits worked, because Fabian was determined not to reach their full quota with Joe Public punters if it meant having to turn celebrities away.

Inside, Jenna was doing the rounds: chatting to the customers who'd been lucky enough to get in, and making sure that everybody was happy. A fair few regulars from her dad's day were here, but there were many more new faces – which was a great sign, as long as they didn't drift straight back to their usual clubs as soon as the novelty wore off. James Lorde had never succeeded in luring the hard-core clubbers and A-list celebrities in, but Jenna was hoping that the funky decor would change all that. And, if last night was any indication, they were definitely on the right track.

Finished with the lower floor, she made her way up to the VIP lounge and looked around, happy to see that several of last night's celebrity guests had come back. And there were lots of soap and sports stars who hadn't made the party but had come to check the place out on the recommendation of those who had.

Spotting her just then, Tony Allen strolled over to say hello. The picture of elegance in a charcoal-grey suit, his jet hair slicked smoothly back from his brow, he said, 'Hey, look at you. You look beautiful.'

Jenna was a little surprised when he pulled her to him and kissed her on both cheeks. It was a bit familiar, given that this was only their second meeting, but she supposed it must just be the American way. Fighting the urge to fold her arms when he let her go, she said, 'Nice to see you again. How are you?'

'Cool,' Tony said, putting his hands in his pockets and gazing around. 'Had a bit of free time, so I thought I'd come and check the place out again.'

Edging in beside him just then, Melody linked an arm through his and gave Jenna the once-over. Satisfied that she looked way hotter than her, she gave her a glowing smile. 'You're looking lovely, Jen.'

Rolling his eyes ceilingward, Tony muttered, 'Christ! Why does she always have to clip the end off of everyone's goddamned name? See, if she calls me *Tone* one more time, I swear to God I'll rip her fucking tongue out.'

'Aw, shut up,' Melody scolded, playfully pinching his cheek. 'You're such a grouch sometimes.'

Shaking his head wearily, Tony said, 'Be a good girl and go amuse yourself somewhere else for a bit, will you? I wanna talk to Jenna.'

Melody would have been furious if he'd dismissed her like that a couple of seconds earlier, but she'd just seen Fabian making his way to the bar. Glad of the excuse to escape, she gave Tony a kiss and told Jenna that she'd see her later. Then she tripped away through the crowd, her hips swaying sexily.

'Cent short of a dollar,' Tony murmured, watching her go. 'But you gotta love that ass.'

Jenna smiled. They were such an odd couple: Melody a blonde bombshell; Tony short, dark and squat, and almost handsome in an ugly sort of way. If you took them at face value, you'd wonder what Melody saw in him. But there was obviously far more to Tony Allen than met the eye, and Jenna sensed that he would be deeply loyal to few – and deeply dangerous to many.

'Have you got a minute?' he asked her now.

Jenna was faintly amused when he immediately placed a hand on the small of her back and guided her to an empty table, pulling a chair out for her when they got there and waiting until she sat down before taking his own seat. Strange manners, considering she hadn't actually agreed to talk to him – arrogant presumption mixed with olde-worlde charm.

Silent as ever, Eddie sat down and folded his arms, watching the room with unreadable eyes.

'How's about a drink before we get started?' Tony said, looking around for a waiter. Spotting one, he clicked his fingers in the air. 'Yo! Three large JDs – and don't take all night about it.'

'House white for me,' Jenna chipped in quickly, a little less amused that he was presuming to order for her now.

Shrugging, Tony said, 'And a house white.' Clicking his fingers again when the boy turned to go, he pointed towards Melody, who was standing at the bar with Fabian now. 'Give her whatever she wants, and tell her not to rush back, yeah?'

Leaning towards Jenna when the waiter had gone, he nodded in Melody's direction. 'What's with that guy?'

Following his gaze, Jenna said, 'Fabian?'

'Yeah, him. D'yuh trust him?'

'Of course. He's a very good manager.'

'If you say so,' Tony muttered, not sounding too convinced. 'He's a bit of a smooth bastard, if you ask me.'

'That's just his way,' Jenna said, not wanting to sound disloyal. 'The customers seem to like it.'

'Yeah, well, I don't buy all that polite namby-pamby shit,' Tony sneered. 'He needs to get his finger out of his ass and start acting like a real fuckin' man.'

Wondering where this was coming from, Jenna frowned. Fabian hadn't done or said anything offensive, as far as she was aware, but Tony obviously disliked him for some reason.

Thrusting a twenty at the waiter when he brought their drinks over, Tony handed Jenna and Eddie theirs, then took a swig of his own, still eyeballing Fabian.

'So, what did you want to talk about?' Jenna asked, hoping to draw his attention back to her before Fabian got scorch marks on his back.

Turning to face her, Tony shrugged and took another

drink. 'You, as it happens. I've been thinking about what we was talking about last night, and I've got to admit I'm intrigued.'

Unnerved by the intensity of his gaze, Jenna said, 'There's really nothing to be intrigued about. I pretty much told you everything last night.'

Guessing what she was thinking, Tony chuckled softly. 'Relax, Angel-face, it's your mind I'm interested in, not your body – hot though it is.'

Jenna felt the blush flare across her cheeks.

'I ain't hitting on you,' Tony assured her with a chuckle. 'Melody's always saying I give off the wrong signals, and it don't usually bother me, but I wouldn't want you thinking I don't respect you, 'cos I do. That's why I want to get to know you better.' Giving her a sincere look then, he said, 'You all right with that?'

Nodding, Jenna said, 'Okay, but let's not talk about me again. I'd rather hear about you and your club. I imagine you do things very differently in the States?'

'Oh, it's different, all right,' Tony said, thinking that, for starters, a little girl like her would never get to play in a big man's game like this without a whole heap of trouble.

Blissfully unaware that he had just been the focus of Tony Allen's scorn, Fabian was enjoying making Melody grovel. She'd apologised for last night and promised that she would never try to force his hand again, but he wasn't as fooled as his easy smile would have her believe. He knew that she'd get around to asking for coke sooner or later, but he wasn't about to offer it on a plate. Far better to let her make the running so he could retain some control over the situation.

Right now, though, he was just enjoying the foreplay.

Sexy as hell in a red satin dress that clung to her hips and moulded itself to her breasts, with her hair swept up, leaving just a few long strands to frame her gorgeous face, and some serious bling sparkling at her ears, throat, wrists and fingers, Melody way out-glammed every other woman in the club – and, *boy*, didn't she know it. Fabian's dick was straining to get at her as she flirted with him, brushing up against him so that her breasts grazed his arm, fluttering her long eyelashes, and pouting her glossy red lips.

Determined to play it cool, he put a hand in his pocket to disguise the bulge and leaned casually back against the bar, gazing nonchalantly around the room.

Sensing that she was losing his attention, Melody eased her knee between his. 'Where's your head at?'

'Just wondering what your boyfriend would say if he knew what you were doing.'

'Oh, let's think . . .' Melody tapped a long red nail against her lip. 'Well, first he'd boil you in oil, then he'd hang you out to dry with a pig's head sticking out of your ass.' Looking him in the eye now, she said, 'Worried?'

'Not at all,' Fabian drawled unconcernedly. 'I'd be more worried about you, to tell the truth.'

'Tony would never hurt me.'

'You trust him that much, do you?'

'Of course.'

'Even if he found out what we're doing?'

'But he's not *going* to find out, is he? Anyway, stop depressing me. I've been dying to see you, and all you've done is talk about Tony.' Leaning closer, Melody raked her nails up his thigh, whispering huskily, 'You heard what that waiter said – he wants me to take my time. So, how about we nip to your office while no one's looking?'

'Love to,' Fabian said, glancing pointedly at his watch. 'But I can't right now. We've not been open long enough for me to pull a disappearing act.'

'Just long enough to get me wet, huh?'

'Oh, yeah?'

'Yeah,' Melody purred, gazing promisingly into his eyes. 'So don't keep me waiting *too* long, or I might have to go and find someone else to play with.' Winking sexily now, she picked up her glass and began to move away.

Lust winning out over his determination to play hard to get, Fabian reached out. 'Wait.'

Turning back, Melody looked down at his hand on her arm. 'Changed your mind, Lover?'

'Five minutes,' he told her quietly.

Tipping her head to one side, she let her gaze slide down to his groin. 'Sure you can wait that long?'

Grinning, he shook his head. 'You're going to get me into trouble, Miss Fisher.'

'We'll see,' she murmured. 'Just give me a minute to have a word with Tony, and I'll follow you down.'

Fabian exhaled slowly when Melody sashayed towards the table where Tony and Jenna were sitting chatting. He must be crazy, he reckoned, getting deeper into this after the worry of last night, but she was too sexy to resist. And where was the harm – as long as they didn't get caught?

Apologising to Jenna for interrupting, Melody cupped her hand around Tony's ear and whispered, 'Gay-Boy's offered to dance with me again. You okay with that?'

'Yeah, whatever,' he said, eager to get on with his conversation. 'But no funny business.'

Flicking her tongue into his ear, Melody giggled when he squirmed. 'That's the only funny business I'll be getting up to tonight, Tiger.' Waggling her fingers at Jenna then, she headed for the stairs, fully aware that every man in the room was following with his eyes.

Seeing Fabian going down to the lower floor, Kalli waited a couple of minutes, then poured a glass of chilled orange juice and slipped out from behind the bar. Telling Vanessa that she wouldn't be long, she nipped down the stairs and made a dash for the DJ's booth, keeping her eyes peeled for Fabian.

Smiling at Vibes who was lining up his next track, she edged in behind him and checked out the view through the three-sided window. It was the first time she'd been up there, and she was surprised how much of both the lower and upper floors you could see.

Slipping his headphones down around his neck after a moment, Vibes reached for the juice and took a long drink, then wiped his mouth on the back of his hand. 'Thanks, you're an angel.'

'You're welcome,' Kalli murmured, still looking out. 'Doesn't she look gorgeous?' she said then, sighing softly.

Following her gaze, Vibes felt something catch in his chest when he saw Jenna. She looked so beautiful, and classy with it – and *so* out of his league.

'She sure does,' he murmured resignedly. Then, 'Who are those guys?'

'One of them is Melody Fisher's boyfriend,' Kalli told him, flicking a glance at the swarthy man sitting across from Jenna. 'He's American, like you.'

'Uh huh,' Vibes said thoughtfully.

'Something wrong?' Kalli asked, gazing up at him.

'Nah, nothing,' Vibes said, shrugging off the dark sense of foreboding that had come over him when he'd looked at the man. 'So, who's Melody Fisher?'

'I'd have thought *you*'d know that, her being a big Hollywood star.'

'Can't say I've heard of her,' Vibes said, shrugging.

'She's down there dancing with Fabian somewhere,' Kalli told him, gazing out at the dance floor. 'You couldn't miss her, she's absolutely gorgeous.'

'Ah,' Vibes said, a light switching on in his head. 'Blonde?'

'Yeah. Have you seen her.'

'Oh, yeah, I've seen her,' Vibes murmured. 'So, if she's the mystery man's girlfriend, what do you reckon's going on with her and Fabian? Only they were acting real shady last night, taking off right in the middle of the party.'

'Taking off?' Kalli's eyes widened with curiosity. 'You mean they went out?'

'Got down, more like!' Vibes gave her a knowing grin. 'I saw them having a cosy chat in the corner, then he went up to the office, and she followed a few minutes later. Then *she* came out, and *he* followed *her* a few minutes later. What do you make of that?'

'Nothing good, knowing him,' Kalli snorted.

'Don't think too much of him, huh?'

'Not much,' Kalli admitted.

'Well, well,' Vibes said, chuckling softly. 'Speak of the Devil.' He nodded down to the dance floor, where Fabian and Melody were casually dancing their way towards the edge. 'If I'm not very much mistaken, they're going for a rerun.'

Glancing down at them, Kalli frowned disapprovingly. 'Dirty pig! Do you think I should tell Jenna?'

Shaking his head, Vibes said, 'Nah, you don't need to be getting involved, and neither does she. If Fabian wants to get his fingers burned, he ain't taking my two favourite ladies down with him.'

'You think so?' Kalli gazed up at him trustingly.

'I *know* so,' he said. 'Anyway, you'd best get out of here before he comes back. Wouldn't want him taking his guilt out on you.'

Nodding, Kalli said goodbye and hurried back up to her bar. Fabian was a dog, but Vibes was right to tell her to stay out of it. It would end in tears without her intervention. These things always did.

★

Locking the door when Melody came into the office behind him, Fabian pushed her up against the wall and pressed himself against her, his lips covering hers, his hands sliding over her buttocks.

'Not yet,' she gasped, holding him at bay.

'I thought you said you were wet.'

'Soaking, Babe, but I need something to *really* get me going.'

'I'll do that,' Fabian assured her breathily, reaching for her breasts and circling her erect nipples through the satin with his thumbs. 'Oh, Christ, they're incredible.'

'Yeah, I know.' Melody impatiently slapped his hands away. 'But I really, really need a line. You *have* got it, haven't you?'

'Yeah, I've got it.'

Backing off with reluctance, Fabian took the coke out of the safe and laid out two thick lines. Snorting his, he handed the straw to Melody. Moving behind her then when she leaned over, he rubbed up against her. Encouraged when she let out a tiny gasp, he eased up her skirt, groaning lustfully when he saw her diamante thongs.

'Oh, that's good,' she moaned, rocking back against him when he slipped his hand between her thighs. 'Oh, yeah . . . keep doing that.'

Unzipping his fly, Fabian freed his hard-on and slid into her. Keeping still then, afraid that he would come if he moved, he held on tight to her hips.

Melody couldn't wait. Arching her back as the coke rushed to her head, she put her hands flat on the table and bucked against him, crying, 'Oh, God, *now!*'

Pounding into her until he felt the first searing rush of ecstasy, Fabian pulled out and swept everything off the desk. Flipping her onto her back, he tore off her panties and tossed them aside, then pushed her dress up over her breasts and bit down on her nipples. Wrapping her legs around his waist, Melody sank her nails into his back, holding on tight as waves of pleasure tore through them both.

Easing herself up when her breathing had slowed, Melody shoved Fabian off and stood up. 'Oh, shit!' she moaned, looking down at the creases in her dress. 'Look at the *state* of it.'

'Don't panic,' Fabian said calmly, running his hands firmly down the material to smooth it. 'It'll be fine.'

'Best had be,' Melody grumbled. 'Tony will flip if he sees me like this. Christ, my *hair*!' she gasped then, reaching up to find the diamante clips that had been holding it in place. 'I've got to get cleaned up or we're both dead. Where's the bathroom?'

'You'll have to use the staff toilets,' Fabian told her, cursing Jenna for not getting him an en-suite when she'd had the one that her dad had started completed. 'Just let me make sure no one's out there first.'

Going to the door, he frowned when he noticed the tiny red light glowing in the corner. He was sure he'd switched the CCTV off when he came in this morning, but he must have forgotten. It would have caught the whole thing, and how damning would that be if it got into the wrong hands? But he didn't have time to erase it now, because he had to get Melody out of here before anybody caught them.

Sticking his head out, he peered both ways along the corridor, then waved her out when he saw that it was clear. Waiting for her outside the toilets, he hopped nervously from foot to foot, wondering what excuse to give if anybody came along just now.

Or, worse, what if her boyfriend had seen them coming in here?

But if Tony Allen *had* seen them, Fabian had no doubt he'd have followed them or sent his goon to see what was going on – and Fabian would be picking up his teeth right about now.

So, no, they were probably safe this time. But it had been a stupid risk to take, all the same, and he wouldn't be doing it again any time soon – even if it *had* been one of the best fucks of his life.

'How do I look?' Melody asked, coming out just then.

'Great,' he grunted, just wanting to get her out of here.

'My pants,' she squealed as he grabbed her arm and rushed her down the corridor.

'I'll get them later,' he promised, pulling her on down the stairs.

Easing the lower door open, Fabian was relieved to find a group of drunks weaving about in front of it, blocking them from view. Slipping out after Melody, he headed for the downstairs bar while she made her way across the room.

Two burly doormen were standing guard at the door to the VIP stairs, and they were refusing to let Leonard and Avril go through. When they stepped aside to let a blonde tart in a red satin dress in, Leonard almost blew a fuse. Already furious because the Buckleys' party hadn't finished as early as he'd expected, this sleight was just adding insult to injury.

It was Avril's fault for making them get here so late. If she'd bothered to tell him that the Buckleys were celebrating their silver-wedding anniversary, he'd have guessed how thoroughly tedious the party was going to be and would have invented a life-threatening illness to get out of going. At the very least, he'd have found a way of getting out of there before the toasts. But, thanks to Avril, he'd had to endure a five-course meal – very little of which he could actually stomach – followed by a two-hour session of whining neoclassical tripe from a string quartet. Then there'd been an hour of congratulatory speeches from the couple's family, friends, and associates.

Flooring his precious Jag when they had finally escaped,

Leonard reached the club in record time, only to be told that he'd have to pay twenty pounds – *each*. And, if *that* weren't insult enough, these imbecilic thugs were now refusing to let them go upstairs. It just wasn't on!

'If you don't have a VIP pass, we can't let you in, sir,' one of the doormen was telling him for the fourth time.

'But I'm a friend of the owner,' Leonard told him – again. 'And I spoke to the manager just last night, and he personally invited me back tonight.'

'Sorry, sir, but we need to see your pass.'

'No, you *don't*!' Beads of sweat burst out on Leonard's brow and upper lip now. 'I don't *need* one, because I'm a *friend* of the *owner*. Go and get her. She'll tell you.'

'Sorry, but we can't just go walkabout, sir. If you haven't got a pass, you—'

'Oh, for Christ's sake!' Leonard barked, spraying Avril with sweat as he shook his head angrily. 'This is outrageous. I will *not* be treated like this.'

'Leonard, leave it,' Avril cautioned when one of the burly doormen took a step forward. 'There's a perfectly good table over there.'

Turning on her, Leonard yelled, 'You can sit down here if you want to, but I'm not going anywhere until I get the respect I bloody well deserve.'

Hearing the commotion, Fabian made his way over to see what was going on. Reaching them just as the doormen were about to escort Leonard out, he said, 'What's the problem?'

'These *people* are refusing to allow my wife and me upstairs,' Leonard told him indignantly. 'I've told them that *you* invited me, but they're being deliberately obstructive. And they wouldn't go and get Jenny to verify that I'm a personal friend. They just keep going on about bloody VIP passes.'

'I'm sure they didn't mean any offence,' Fabian told him,

his tone placatory. 'It's my mistake. I must have overlooked you when I was allocating passes. Why don't you let me get you a drink by way of apology?'

'Very kind,' Leonard grunted, casting a last glance of displeasure at the doormen as Fabian waved him up the stairs. 'You really ought to have strong words with these chaps about their treatment of your personal guests, you know.'

'Oh, I will,' Fabian assured him, sharing a conspiratorial glance with the grinning doormen – who resumed their places as if nothing had happened.

Following Leonard and Avril up, he escorted them to the bar and told Vanessa to give them whatever they wanted. Then, apologising again, he promised to sort out the VIP pass as soon as he had a minute.

'That was so humiliating,' Avril hissed when he'd gone. 'Why do you always have to throw your weight around?'

'I wouldn't need to if people knew their places,' Leonard retorted self-righteously. 'And if it wasn't a problem for the manager, I don't see why *you*'ve got to make an issue of it.'

'Because I'm the one you made a bloody fool of.'

Bored now, Leonard flapped his hand dismissively. 'There's an empty table. Go and sit down. I'll be over in a minute.'

'Why, what are you doing?' Avril asked, unwilling to sit by herself when she didn't even want to be here in the first place.

'Getting another drink,' Leonard informed her frostily.

'We've only just got these.'

'Yes, and at the rate you were putting them back last night you'll need another before your backside hits the seat.'

'Oh, don't start that again,' she moaned.

But Leonard wasn't listening. He'd just spotted Tony Allen and Jenna sitting together across the room.

Turning to see who he was staring at, Avril's lips puckered with irritation. 'Go on, then. Go and see your new friend, why don't you?'

'I'll go when I'm good and ready,' he muttered, sticking his hand into his pocket in an attempt to look casual.

'You're so full of crap!' Avril spat, turning on her heel and marching away. She knew full well that he wouldn't go over to the man while she was watching, because he didn't want her to see him being shooed away again. He must think that she was a complete fool.

Stepping aside to let Brenda Thompson and her obscenely young male escort pass, Leonard downed his drink and turned back to the bar. 'Scotch rocks,' he said, keeping half an eye on Tony. 'And a G-and-T, please.'

'Anything else?'

Shaking his head, Leonard said, 'No, thanks.' Then, on impulse: 'Actually, yes . . . I was here last night, and, um, a young man served me. Blond, about so tall.' He held a hand up to his nose. 'He was wearing a gold stud in his ear, and I think he might have had a pierced eyebrow.'

'That'll be Austin,' Vanessa said, dipping her voice to ask, 'he didn't do anything to upset you, did he?'

'Course not.' Smiling, Leonard reached into his pocket for his cigarettes. 'He was very helpful, as it happens.' Lighting up, he rested an elbow on the bar. 'Is he, um, working tonight?'

'Yeah, he should be around somewhere.' Gazing out over his shoulder, Vanessa scanned the room, then shrugged. 'Can't see him. Would you like me to tell him you're looking for him?'

'Erm, no, it's okay,' Leonard said quickly. 'I'm sure I'll bump into him before the night's out.'

'Yeah, probably.' Smiling, Vanessa placed his drinks on the counter and held out her hand. 'Nine-eighty, please.'

Leonard blanched. Almost ten pounds for two drinks? Outrageous! He'd have to make sure that Avril didn't go overboard tonight, or he'd be bankrupt come the morning. Tugging his wallet from his pocket, he peeled off a ten-pound note and thrust it at her, telling her to keep the change as he snatched up his drinks and walked away.

'How generous,' Vanessa muttered.

Spotting Austin a few minutes later, she waved him over. 'That fat guy over there's looking for you. But don't expect a tip, 'cos I only got twenty pee.'

'You should learn to be nicer to the customers,' Austin told her, with a cheeky grin.

Making his way over to Leonard's table, he gave Avril a polite nod. Then he turned to Leonard, saying, 'I was told you were looking for me, sir?'

Eyes narrowed to slits, Avril gave a scornful snort. 'Oh, I'm sure he was, dear, but I doubt you'd be so eager to—'

'Shut up!' Leonard hissed, giving her a warning glare. Blushing now, he said, 'Please excuse my wife. We came straight from a dinner party, and I'm afraid she may have had one too many.'

'Nonsense!' Avril snarled. 'I'm just telling the boy that he might expect to be run off his feet catering to you.'

'Shall I come back later?' Austin suggested, taking a step back.

'Preferably when I'm not here,' Avril snapped. Then, tutting, she shook her head, reminding herself that it wasn't the boy's fault her husband was such a shit. Downing the drink that Leonard had just brought her, she held the glass out. 'A large G-and-T, please.'

Doing the same, Leonard said, 'And I'll have a—'

'Scotch rocks,' Austin finished for him. Then, feeling Avril's glare boring into him, he said to her, 'That *was* what you told me to get for him last night, wasn't it?'

Smiling tightly, she said, 'Excellent memory, dear. Shows you have the makings of a good barman.'

'Thanks,' Austin said, sure that she'd meant it as an insult. 'And yours is a large G-and-T. I won't forget. Can I get you anything else?'

Oh, I'm sure Leonard could think of something, Avril thought bitterly.

'No, thanks,' she said. 'That will do for now.'

Turning on her when Austin made his escape, Leonard said, 'What the hell was *that* all about? You bloody well embarrassed me.'

'Not half as much as you *constantly* embarrass me,' Avril shot back, looking at him with disgust. 'Or yourself, for that matter.'

'I don't know what you're talking about,' he retorted indignantly. 'You're only being like this because the boy remembered me.'

'No, I'm being like this because *you* went out of your way to look for him.'

'I did not!' Leonard lied. 'The girl on the bar must have got the wrong end of the stick. She asked if we'd been happy with the service so far, and I mentioned that the boy had been very helpful last night, that's all.'

'And she just happened to know *which* boy you were talking about? How very convenient.' Shaking her head disbelievingly, Avril folded her arms.

'You're just miffed because nobody's paying *you* any attention.'

'Oh, bugger off!'

'Where are you going?' Leonard demanded when she pushed her chair back and stood up.

Leaning towards him, Avril patted his hand. 'Don't worry, dear, the little boy will be back soon to keep you company. Anyway, I thought you were supposed to be meeting that awful man again?' Casting a glance in Tony Allen's direction, she sneered. 'Doesn't look much like he's waiting for you, though.'

On his way back with the drinks just then, Austin waited until Avril had gone, then approached Leonard with a smile. 'There you go, sir. One G-and-T, and one *very* large Scotch rocks.'

'Thanks.' Sighing wearily, Leonard reached for his wallet and handed him a twenty. 'Keep the change,' he said, running a hand through his hair. Wiping it on his trousers when it came back wet, he slumped down in his seat, looking thoroughly dejected.

Gazing down at him, Austin shook his head sympathetically. The poor sod's wife was a grade-A bitch to talk to him like that in public. Christ, *gays* were supposed to be bitchy, but they weren't a *patch* on so-called loving wives when it came to verbal emasculation. Thank God *he*'d never have to put up with some razor-tongued harridan ripping *his* balls to shreds.

'Look, I hope you don't think I'm being nosy,' he said when Leonard glanced up at him questioningly. 'But is everything all right? Only your wife seemed a bit upset.'

'My wife is perpetually upset about something or other,' Leonard muttered, his belly rising and falling as he gave another deep sigh.

'My mum's the same,' Austin confided quietly. 'Her mate reckons it's the menopause, but nobody dares mention it, 'cos she, like, *totally* flips.'

Looking into the boy's bluer-than-blue eyes, Leonard felt a mirthless chuckle bubble up in his throat. Oh, if only it were as simple as the menopause. At least there was medication for that.

'Anyway.' Austin flapped his hands. 'I just wanted you to know that I understand. And if you ever need to talk . . . well, – you know.'

Leonard's eyes misted a little as it struck him that the boy was being sincere. It was so unexpected that he didn't know quite how to react. It had been so very long since anybody had shown him any compassion or understanding.

'You're very kind,' he murmured gratefully.

'No problem.' Austin gave him a pitying smile. He couldn't bear to see people upset – unless he'd caused it, in which case they deserved it, so it didn't count.

'Do you, um, have a girlfriend?' Leonard asked suddenly.

'God, no!' Austin yelped. Then, glancing quickly around, he whispered, 'I'm not that way inclined.'

'Ah, I see.' Nodding thoughtfully, Leonard drummed his fingers on the table for a moment, then said, 'Are there many – you know – *places* for you young people to meet?'

'Oh, yeah!' Austin subconsciously adopted a girlish hand-on-hip stance. 'The Village is *fabulous*.'

'Really.' Leonard nodded again. 'Well, that's good, isn't it? I mean, it would be terrible if you had to hide away.'

'There's none of that, these days,' Austin told him breezily. 'We're out and about all over the place. In fact, you'd be surprised how many of us there are.' Pausing then, when it occurred to him that this man was of an age that he might not actually approve, he shrugged. 'We tend to stick to our own places, though, so it's not like we're shoving it in anyone's face.'

'Probably just as well.' Leonard sighed again. 'There are a lot of ignorant people in this world.'

'Tell me about it,' Austin muttered, thinking of some of the scrapes he'd found himself in before now. It was his own fault, because he got a perverse kick out of flirting with straight men, but you never knew which way they would take it. Nine times out of ten they laughed it off – and some even played along. But the odd one would turn nasty and batter you senseless. Much as he liked to pooh-pooh Kalli's concerns, he *did* know that he should be more careful.

Like now, for example, chatting away to this man like they were mates when the man was probably only being friendly because his wife was such a bitch and he was grateful to have somebody on his side – *not* because he was interested.

Not that *Austin* would be interested even if *he* was, because he preferred the classic tall, dark and handsome type – like Vibes. Now *there* was a man he'd be only too happy to . . .

Stopping the thought dead before it showed up in his shorts, Austin said, 'Right, well, I'd best go back to work. Shout if you need me.'

'I will,' Leonard said quietly. 'Thanks again.'

'I was watching that,' Kalli hissed when Austin came back to the bar. 'What's going on with you two?'

Raising a prim eyebrow, Austin said, 'Er, he's *married.*'

'That doesn't usually stop you.'

'No, but I'm behaving myself – Guide's honour. I *do* listen to you sometimes, you know.'

'Glad to hear it,' Kalli murmured, not sure that she totally believed him.

'I don't half feel sorry for him, though.' Austin glanced back at Leonard, who looked thoroughly miserable again. 'His wife treats him like a *dog.* You should have heard her tearing strips off him just now. It was brutal. And she didn't even care that *I* was standing there.'

'Keep out of it,' Kalli told him firmly, sure that the fat man probably deserved whatever his wife threw at him. 'And promise you'll stay away from him.'

'Okay, I promise,' Austin agreed wearily, crossing his fingers behind his back.

'Without the crossed fingers.' Folding her arms, Kalli raised an eyebrow and gave him a stern look.

Grinning, Austin brought his hands up and waggled his fingers. 'Is that better?'

'Much,' she said, giving him a satisfied smile and walking away.

'Yeah, but I didn't promise that time,' Austin whispered to her retreating back. If she thought he was letting one of the other waiters nab his big tipper, she had another think coming.

Still buzzing more than an hour after her visit to Fabian's office, Melody was amusing herself by winding up Tony's celebrity friends.

Calling, 'Cheers' to nobody in particular, she slurped her drink and smacked her lips loudly – to the obvious disgust of those close enough to hear. Then, slamming the glass down, she lit one cigarette after another, blowing her smoke into other people's faces, and rudely jumping in and out of their conversations.

Tony was watching Melody with suspicion. She couldn't seem to sit still, and she was being way louder than usual, pushing herself into conversations that didn't concern her and tossing out insults disguised as compliments. If he didn't know better, he'd swear she was on something. He was sure she wasn't, though, because she didn't know anyone to score off. But, high or not, she was definitely acting up – and he wasn't impressed.

Excusing himself after a while, he got up and jerked his head at her. 'Yo. Over here a minute.'

'What's up?' Melody asked, jiggling to the music as she followed him to the bar, her eyes darting every which way.

'That's what I want to know.' Tony gave her a piercing look. 'You're acting weird. Are you on something?'

'Oh, give me a break,' she snorted, putting her hands on her hips. 'I decide to get into the swing of things, and you have to go and ruin it by accusing me of all sorts. I don't *have* to talk to your boring friends, you know. I was only making an effort for *you*. But if that's all the thanks I'm gonna get . . .'

'That'd better be all it is,' Tony said in a low voice. 'If I find out you've been doing something—'

'You'll what?' Melody interrupted cockily. 'You can't tell me what to do, Tony. I'm your girlfriend, not your daughter. Though, Christ knows, you're *old* enough to be my fucking dad.'

'That's right,' Tony warned her quietly. 'You just keep flapping that mouth and see what it gets you.'

Catching the glint in his blacker-than-black eyes, Melody struggled to bring herself under control. It was mega-difficult with the coke still coursing through her veins, but her deeper instincts screamed at her to behave before he flipped out and she managed to latch on to a sliver of common sense and quieten down.

Pouting now, she looped her arms around his thick neck and dipped her head to drop little kisses on his face.

'Sorry, Sugar-Wugar. I'm trying to be nice, but the nasty people don't like me – and that upsets me, 'cos I haven't done nothing wrong.'

Gazing down into her cleavage, Tony felt his anger evaporate. Man, she was one horny bitch.

'Nah, they're just jealous 'cos you're such a doll,' he told her, giving her nipples a tweak. 'But if that's your idea of being *nice*, quit it, for fuck's sake. It sounds more like insults to me.' Chuckling now, he said, 'And don't think I didn't hear you telling that broad she's lucky she's going bald.'

'Yeah, well she is,' Melody said playfully. 'All she has to do is open the window and her little nest's dry. Me, I gotta spend two hours drying this little lot.' Reaching up, she ran her hands through her own lusciously thick hair.

'Smart-mouthed bitch.' Tony laughed, copping a handful of ass. 'Just pack it in, yeah?'

'If you say so,' Melody agreed, slipping her arm through his. 'But you'd best start paying me some attention, or I might get bored and start amusing myself again.'

Catching Fabian's eye when they passed him on their way back to the table, Melody gave him a little wink and let her gaze slide to his groin. Smiling when he blanched, she cupped her hand around Tony's ear and whispered, 'How's about we cut out early and go fuck our brains out?'

Sure that Melody had been whispering about him, Fabian beat a hasty retreat to the safety of the lower floor. Yet again, the buzz was well and truly shattered, and the stabbing paranoia was back with a vengeance. He needed a hit of vitamin C to bring him down.

Going to the bar, he snapped his fingers at JoJo and demanded a fresh orange juice.

'Yes, *sir*!' she muttered, her slim nostrils flaring with irritation as she flipped her platinum hair back over her shoulder and marched to the fridge. Pouring his drink, she slammed the glass down on the counter in front of him. 'Anything else?'

Fabian narrowed his eyes meanly. 'Who am I?'

A confused frown flickered across JoJo's brow. What kind of whacked-out question was *that*?

'Who *am* I?' he repeated slowly.

'Fabian,' she replied. Adding, 'Mr King,' when he carried on staring at her. Then, 'The manager.'

'At last she gets it,' Fabian snarled. 'Me manager – *you* waitress. And if you ever dare speak to me like that again, you'll find yourself out on the street where you belong. Got me?'

'Got you.' Lifting her chin proudly, JoJo bit her tongue to prevent herself from telling him to go fuck himself. She needed this job too much to give him an excuse to sack her.

'Good!' Fabian snatched up his glass. 'And don't forget it.'

Sticking two fingers up at his back when he walked away, JoJo snarled, 'Yes, Mr King . . . no, Mr King . . . and would you like me to suck your tiny little dick while I'm at it, Mr King?'

'Ex*cuse* me?' Austin gasped, coming up behind her in time to catch this last bit. 'Don't tell me you've got the hots for Fabulous Fabian? Oh, my fucking *life*, girl. Just wait till I tell the others.'

'Fuck off,' JoJo snapped. 'He's a jumped-up little twat.'

'That's more like it,' Austin chuckled. 'Anyway, forget him. Have you got my thingy?'

'Shut *up*!' Glancing quickly around, JoJo grabbed his arm and dragged him into a corner. 'Fucking hell, man, you're going to get me shot with that big mouth of yours.'

'Sorry. I wasn't thinking.'

'You never do.' Scowling, JoJo reached down her top and pulled out a small plastic bag of tablets. Taking one out, she shoved it into his hand. 'There. And don't ask me for any more tonight, 'cos you're acting too hyper.'

'Can't help it.' Austin grinned. 'I'm buzzing off this place. Don't you think it's *fab* since old man Lordey kicked it?'

'Would be if we had a different manager,' JoJo agreed, smiling now because Austin's glee was infectious. 'Glad *you*'re here, though.'

'And Kalli.'

'Yeah, *right*,' JoJo muttered, wondering what everyone saw in the miserable little Chinky. Always telling people what to do, and giving it with the inscrutable-eyes business. JoJo couldn't stand her.

'See you later, Terminator,' Austin said, already dancing away.

'Oi, money,' JoJo called after him. 'You still owe me for the last one as well, and I've got to buy a leccy card on my way home or I won't be able to have a bath.'

'Stop whinging,' Austin said, whipping a tenner out of his shorts and shoving it in her hand.

'Oh, that's gross,' she complained, holding it away from herself. 'It's still warm. And I bet it *stinks* of bummy cock.'

'Oi, you cheeky whore. I'll have you know I spray my willy with Lynx every ten minutes.'

'Yeah, and I have to cut *mine* off every night 'cos it keeps growing back.'

'I always knew you were a man,' Austin snorted.

'With tits like these?' JoJo retorted sarcastically. 'Yeah, right.'

'Call *them* tits?' Austin shot back. 'I've seen better on the trannies down the Brittania.'

'Fuck off!'

'Love you too.' Blowing her a kiss, Austin danced away with his E clutched in his hand. Waving as he passed Leonard and Avril on their way out, he called, 'See you later, Mr and Mrs D.'

'Did you *hear* that?' Avril snapped, glaring after him. 'Mr and Mrs D, indeed! Who the bloody hell does he think he's talking to?'

Ignoring her, Leonard struggled to hide his smile as he continued on out of the door. The boy had not only shown him a kindness tonight, for which he would be eternally grateful, but he'd obviously gone to the trouble of finding out their names, too – which quite took the sting out of what had otherwise been another thoroughly miserable night.

He still hadn't managed to speak to Jenny alone yet. And he'd missed the opportunity to chat with Tony Allen, too, because the man had left early – with the same sluttish blonde whose easy passage into the VIP lounge had so enraged Leonard earlier.

Still, it was nobody's business but Allen's if he chose to

pick up prostitutes. It wouldn't make Leonard think any less of him. All Leonard had ever wanted was to be a part of the celebrity circles he'd spent so many years on the edges of; to have people acknowledge that he was still a force to be reckoned with. And what better way of gaining the recognition he craved, than by being associated with Tony Allen, who obviously had the power to draw influential people to him.

At closing time, Jenna eased herself onto a stool at the lower bar while Fabian saw everybody out. Apart from the twenty minutes or so that she'd spent chatting to Tony Allen earlier, she hadn't sat down all night and, once again, she was exhausted.

Smiling when Vibes joined her, she said, 'You look as wiped as I feel.'

'I am,' he admitted, covering a yawn with his hand.

Popping her head out of the kitchen door just then, Kalli said, 'I'm making coffee if anybody wants one?'

'Oh, yes, please,' Jenna said.

Telling her that he'd love one, Vibes picked up a beer mat and turned it over and over on the bar, wondering how to ask Jenna the questions that had been on his mind all night. Deciding that the direct approach was best, he said, 'You know that man you were talking to earlier – Melody Fisher's boyfriend. He's American, right?'

'Yeah.' Jenna nodded. 'Not that you'd ever guess that you two came from the same place,' she added, smiling as she thought how different Tony's loud, aggressive accent was compared to Vibes's altogether softer, more laid-back drawl.

'What's his name?'

'Tony Allen. Why? Do you know him?'

Narrowing his eyes, Vibes pursed his lips as he rolled the name over in his mind. 'Don't think so,' he said after a moment. 'I just thought he looked kind of familiar. What do you know about him?'

'Not a lot,' Jenna admitted, thanking Kalli when she put their coffees and a small sugar bowl on the counter. 'I met him for the first time last night. He's only been in England for two weeks, apparently – brought his girlfriend over for a break, because she's been working so hard. Isn't that sweet?'

'Mmmm,' Vibes murmured, stirring sugar into his cup.

'Something wrong?' Jenna asked, curious about his response.

'Not sure,' he replied quietly. Then, shrugging, he said, 'Nah. I'm probably way off track. Don't worry about it.'

'Worry?' Jenna repeated, frowning now. 'Well, if there's one thing guaranteed to *make* me worry, it's being told not to.'

Sighing, Vibes ran a hand over his face. He should have kept his mouth shut, but it was too late now. Jenna was waiting for an explanation.

'Look, don't quote me, because I could be totally off the mark,' he said. 'But he's got a look about him, that's kind of like . . .' Pausing, he shrugged. 'Let's just say he looks connected.'

Gazing blankly back at him, Jenna shook her head.

'To the mob,' Vibes said quietly.

Laughing incredulously when she realised what he meant, Jenna said, '*Tony*? Don't be daft! He's far too charming to be involved in something like that.'

'Hey, don't be fooled by the friendly face,' Vibes warned her. 'Some of the most charming guys in the States are connected. Sophistication and charisma are tools of the trade for those guys.'

Smiling now, sure that he was wrong, Jenna said, 'Oh, come on. I'm sure you'd be able to tell if someone was into something like that.'

'You're too trusting,' Vibes told her quietly. 'Look, tell me to mind my own business by all means, but can I ask what you were talking about?'

'Nothing really.' Jenna shrugged. 'We were just comparing notes, because he had a club of his own. I think it amuses him that a woman can run an empire without a man to guide her. Apparently, it wouldn't be so easy for me in the States.'

'True,' Vibes admitted, peering shamefacedly down into his coffee. 'It's still a bit of a man's world over there, I'm afraid.'

'I suppose I should be grateful that *you* don't think like that, then?' Jenna teased. 'Or you'd never have stayed on to work for me after my dad died.'

'Sure I would,' Vibes murmured, smiling shyly as he added, 'women are *way* more appreciative.' Forcing himself to look at her then, he said, 'But, seriously . . . about that guy. Like I said, I could be wrong, but just in case I'm not, do yourself a favour and don't get too involved with him.'

Seeing the concern in his lovely blue eyes, Jenna nodded her agreement. She knew that he wouldn't make something like that up for the sake of it, but even if he *was* right, Tony was just a friendly customer as far as she was concerned – nothing more, nothing less. And whatever he did or didn't do when he was at home was none of her business.

Finishing her coffee now, she changed the subject, asking Vibes if he had anything planned for tomorrow.

'Nah, I'm just gonna laze around,' he told her. 'Gina's taking the baby to her mom's, so I'm planning on catching up on my sleep while it's nice and quiet. She's a cute little thing, but, *man*, does she make noise now she's teething.'

'Painful.' Jenna gave him a sympathetic smile. 'So, Gina's English, is she?' she asked then, not wanting to seem like she was being nosy, but curious to know about Vibes's wife.

'Yeah, she's from Yorkshire,' he said. 'Took a bit of getting used to the accent, but she's a great girl. And lord only knows how she copes, what with the baby crying all night, and Kenneth making an unholy mess wherever he goes. The guy can't put *nothing* back where he found it.'

'That drives me crazy,' Jenna said, laughing softly. 'I like everything to be in its place, but Jason just thinks I'm a neat freak.' Clamping her mouth shut as soon as the words slipped out, she gritted her teeth angrily. Why the hell was she still talking about that bastard in the present tense? Would she *never* be free of him?

Vibes sighed softly. So, there was a Jason, was there? Well, at least he knew for sure now, so he could stop wondering. Shame, though, because he had a feeling that he and Jenna could have had something. But, hey, who was he kidding? She was his boss – end of.

5

Before Jenna knew it, Zenith had been open for a full month and was doing better than she'd ever dreamed possible. The publicity that they'd received after the opening party had certainly helped, especially the picture of Chase Mann on the front of the *Evening News*, with the club's smoked-glass doors with the etched gold 'Z' clearly visible behind him. That had proved to be a huge draw for young girls from all over the country, who turned up in their droves, desperate to get near the sexy rock star – and, hopefully, be the one he chose to take back to his hotel at the end of the night. But he was usually so out of it by the time he left that his manager would literally have to carry him out.

Shots of various stars coming and going had begun to feature regularly in some of the nationals' gossip pages since then and Jenna kept a close eye on them, making sure that the publicity stayed positive. So far, it had all been good, and she couldn't have been happier as her profits climbed steadily. She was actually contemplating paying herself a wage instead of just covering her living expenses if things carried on as they were, and she might even think about taking a day off, too. A whole day to just lounge around in her nightclothes and watch TV, read, or listen to music. Or maybe she'd take a drive out to the country and lie on a nice secluded river bank somewhere, watching the swans float serenely by. Or she could visit the cemetery and put flowers on her parents' and Damian's graves. *Any*thing that didn't involve the club, because she'd been living and breathing it for five solid months now.

As had Fabian.

In her office with him at the end of the month, counting the takings ready for banking in the morning, Jenna noticed the dark hollows under his eyes, and the yawns that he kept covering with his hand, and realised that, like her, he hadn't had a single day off since this had started. But while it was one thing for *her* to give up her life for the sake of the club, it was quite another to expect him to sacrifice his.

Pouring two glasses of wine when they had finished, she joined him on the couch and told him it was time that he took a break.

'I don't need one,' Fabian replied without hesitation. 'I'm fine.'

'No, you're not,' Jenna laughed. 'You're shattered.'

'I am *fine*,' he repeated firmly.

It was a lie, but he wasn't about to admit that Melody Fisher was the real cause of his exhaustion. He'd never met a woman who could out-fuck him before – and that was saying something. But it was no longer the thrill that it had been at the start. Quick dash to the office whenever she clicked her fingers. Quick snort. Quick shag. No talking. No affection. No satisfaction. Fabian was beginning to understand what his past conquests had meant when they'd complained that he only wanted them for their bodies. Not that he wanted a relationship, or anything, but it was *so* cold that he was finding it increasingly difficult to get aroused. Although it didn't seem to have affected Melody's ability to orgasm. The woman was insatiable.

But it wasn't just the sex that was wearing him out. The coke situation was doing his head in, too.

Melody had been in every single night since the reopening party, and she expected Fabian to have her supplies ready and waiting. But it didn't seem to have occurred to her that he actually had to *pay* for it. And it was more expensive than ever right now, because there was a shortage and the dealers were milking it. And there was all the other stuff to take into consideration, too – like all the running around he was having to do to get hold of it, and his increasing paranoia at the thought of being caught in possession of it and losing everything he'd worked so hard for.

If Fabian could've turned back the clock he'd have wiped his damn nose before setting foot out of his office that first night, because if Melody hadn't caught him she'd have had nothing to hold over him. He would probably still have shagged her, but it would have been on *his* terms. Now she had him over a barrel and it could only get worse, because the more frustrated she got about Tony's seeming reluctance to take her home, the more coke she demanded. And the more she took, the more she craved it. It was a vicious circle, and Fabian was terrified that she would get careless one of these days and drop a bomb that would explode in his face.

He was so worried, in fact, that he had kept the CCTV tape that he'd accidentally recorded of them that first time. Initially, he had intended to destroy it in case it got into the wrong hands. But then he'd decided that it would be better to keep it as insurance – proof that she'd been a willing participant, should she ever cry rape or anything stupid like that. It would be an absolute last resort, though, not something he would bring out unless she gave him no choice. And then he would have to run, because Tony Allen would probably try to kill him.

Right now, though, Fabian was stuck between the rock of meeting Melody's demands and the very high ledge of not doing so. And there wasn't a thing he could do about it, except sit it out and pray that Tony would agree to take her home soon.

Watching Fabian as he wallowed in his thoughts, Jenna
shook her head. If he was as fine as he made out, how come
he was struggling to keep his eyes open? And why was his
chin getting closer and closer to his chest? Tapping his leg,
she smiled amusedly when his head jerked up.

'Not tired, huh?'

'I'm fit as a fiddle,' he grunted, sitting up straighter and
widening his eyes. 'There. Do I *look* tired?'

'You were practically asleep,' Jenna pointed out. 'Anyway,
I'm not asking you, I'm *telling* you to take a break. I'm sure
we'll manage without you for a week or two.'

'I don't *want* you to manage without me,' Fabian countered, frowning now. 'You might decide that you don't want
me back.'

Before Jenna had a chance to deny this, there was a knock
at the door.

'Guess what I've just heard . . . ?' Kalli burst in without
waiting for an answer, her pretty face glowing with excitement. Stopping in her tracks when she saw Fabian, she said,
'Oh, sorry. I thought you were alone.'

Assuring her that she wasn't interrupting anything, Jenna
said, 'What have you heard?'

Flicking a nervous glance at Fabian, who was giving her
the cold eye, Kalli said, 'Austin's friend works at Morgan's,
and he reckons their door takings are right down. And The
Nest is supposed to be even worse. They've started a happy
hour to try and bring the customers back, but it isn't
working.'

'Wow!' Smiling, Jenna turned to Fabian. 'That's great,
isn't it?'

'Yeah, great,' he murmured. 'Is that it, Kalli?'

'Er, yes.' Kalli backed towards the door. 'I just thought
Jenna would want to know. Anyway, I'd best get going.
Austin's waiting for me.'

Turning to Jenna when they were alone again, Fabian said, 'I don't want to burst your bubble, but that might not be as good as you think. It's one thing losing a few customers, but nobody can afford to lose too many. If the other clubs realise we're the cause, they're going to get pissed off.'

'But that's just part and parcel of business, isn't it? Nobody's got the monopoly on customers.'

'No, but businessmen aren't the most magnanimous of people when their profits are under threat.'

'Well, that's not very fair,' Jenna said, frowning now. 'It's not my fault if my club's more popular than theirs. They should make more of an effort to keep people interested.'

'True, but that won't stop them blaming you. Just don't be surprised if they start playing dirty, that's all I'm saying.'

'Dirty? How?'

Shrugging, Fabian said, 'Slashing their door prices. Going all out on drinks promotions so that we can't compete. There's all kinds of ways they could get at us. And if it costs them more in the short term, they might figure it's worth it to put you in the red.'

'That's outrageous,' Jenna gasped. 'We're only charging the going rate on the door, and the drinks aren't cheap, so it's not like we're undercutting anyone. What am I supposed to do? Sack all the DJs so nobody wants to come?'

Peering into her angry eyes, Fabian smiled to himself. She was clueless about the cut-throat nature of this highly competitive business, but she looked so damn raunchy when she was pissed off, if she wasn't his boss he'd be tempted to . . .

Whoa, there! He pulled himself up short. He might go there one day – when Melody had gone and his dick had recovered. But not now. He was too knackered to even *think* about getting it up.

Sighing resignedly beside him, Jenna finished her drink

and shrugged. 'Oh, well. If anything happens, I'll just have to deal with it, won't I? But I'm proud of what we've achieved, and I've got no intention of lowering my standards to satisfy whoever can't match them.'

'Fair enough,' Fabian said approvingly. She had balls, you had to give her that. Finishing his own drink then, he put his glass down and got up. 'Think I'll make a move,' he said, stretching languidly. 'Anything you want me to do before I go?'

Smiling up at him, Jenna said, 'Yeah, book yourself a holiday. Just let me know when you're going and I'll have the agency send a temp in to cover for you.'

Sensing that she wouldn't stop going on about it if he didn't seem to make an effort, Fabian agreed to think about it, but he had no intention of doing it. This was *his* club, and there was no way he was leaving the way clear for some chancer to come in and take over – like he had with his predecessor.

Anyway, there was no way he was risking going off the scene while Melody was still in town. If she started suffering coke withdrawal symptoms and he wasn't there to make her feel better, there was no telling what she'd do. And he didn't fancy coming back to find Tony Allen and the goon waiting for him.

Across town just then, dropping Fabian in it was the last thing on Melody's mind. Not long back from the club, she'd been banished to the bedroom of the hotel suite that was fast becoming home – to Tony, at least – while he and Eddie got on with some 'private' business in the lounge.

Melody was sick to death of Tony and his secrets. Every night for weeks he'd been dropping her off here after the club and pissing off out to God only knew where with Eddie. And on the rare occasions that he actually stayed in, he spent all his time with Eddie, having conversations that she wasn't allowed to join in with. She'd given up trying to listen through a glass, because the walls were too damn thick and she could never make anything out, so she invariably went to bed to catch up on her beauty sleep. But she was way too wired to sleep tonight, so she decided to call her agent, Scotty Nash, on the off chance that she might actually reach him this time.

Melody had been here for six weeks now, and to start with Scotty had called daily to tell her what was happening back home, and to ask when she was coming back, because he had big things planned for his 'favourite girl'. But two weeks ago he'd suddenly stopped calling, and she had found it impossible to get through to him since. If she called his office, his secretary said he was in a meeting; and whenever she tried his mobile it was either switched off or he just wasn't answering – and she suspected the latter to be the case.

Realising that her mistake was to always call him from her mobile, the number of which he obviously knew and could therefore ignore, she decided to trick him by using the hotel line. Asking the operator for an international line, she tapped Scotty's number into the bedside phone and settled back against the pillows.

'Ah ha!' she crowed when he answered on the second ring. 'So glad I caught you when you weren't busy – *for once!*'

'Melody,' Scotty said, his voice betraying that she had been dead right about him avoiding her. 'Hi, Sweets. How are you? I've been meaning to call, but you know how it is this end. Work, work, work!'

'Yeah, and I'm supposed to be your most important client,' Melody reminded him icily. 'So, what's happening, Scotty? What have you got lined up for me?'

'It's been a bit hectic lately,' Scotty said evasively. 'What with the Oscars coming up, and the preparations for Cannes, and everything.'

'What about my audition?' Melody cut in impatiently. 'Have you been in touch with the producers?'

'Sure, I've been in touch. But you know how it is with those guys – too many dinners to eat, too much booze to drink.'

'Never mind that, what are they saying about *me*?'

'Ah, well, that's the thing, see . . .' Scotty sounded like he was sweating now. 'They, um, kinda passed.'

'Passed?' Melody repeated croakily, feeling like a bucket of ice water had just been tipped over her head. 'What do you mean, *passed*? They didn't want me?'

'Something like that, I guess. But, hey, you know . . . there'll be other parts.'

'I don't want *other* parts,' Melody whined. 'I want *that* part. Why didn't you get it for me, Scotty? You're supposed to have stayed on it. That's what I pay you for, you dumb shit!'

'Hey, don't be ragging on me,' Scotty shot back at her. 'It ain't my fault you took yourself out of the picture for so fucking long and let them producers forget you exist. I did warn you. You know how competitive this market is.'

'It's only a *holiday*,' she gasped. 'It's not like I'm never coming back.'

'Try telling them that,' Scotty countered. 'These guys got better things to do than sit around waiting on someone who ain't even in the news no more.'

'I'm not?' Melody murmured, feeling sick now because she'd been a regular column-filler before leaving – if not quite the headliner she'd planned on becoming once the Julia Roberts film was in the bag.

'Nope. Not a thing in weeks,' Scotty told her – sounding remarkably unconcerned, she thought, considering that he should have been tearing his hair out thinking up ways of keeping her name in print while she was away: feeding gossip to the press, leaking rumours – *any*thing to keep her out there.

'So, have they cast the part yet?' she forced herself to ask – not wanting to hear an affirmative, but needing to know if there was still time to get home and rectify things. If they hadn't chosen anyone else yet, she might still be able to persuade the producers that she was their girl. Or maybe she could go directly to Julia. She'd read through the scene with Melody at the audition and had said she was fantastic. If Melody could get to her—

'Remember that girl, Deanna Shelby?' Scotty cut into her thoughts.

'*No*,' Melody muttered, feeling sicker than ever. 'Please don't tell me *she* got it?'

'Yup. *Wowed* 'em, by all accounts – really blew them away.'

'How?' Melody gasped. 'She might as well *be* me – but without the talent. She's a fucking freak! Copying my style, and turning up at all the same auditions.'

'Well, it's obviously working for her,' Scotty commented snidely. 'Word is, it was actually a toss-up between you and her for a while. But she's been getting herself out and about since the audition, and you've disappeared off the face of the earth, so it wasn't that tough a decision in the end.'

'But that's not fair!' Melody whined. 'I'm the real deal, she's just a fucking clone! And the critics—'

'Are raving about Deanna now,' Scotty jumped in. '*She*'s their *Next Big Thing* now. And you should see the headlines she's been getting. *Boy*, that girl knows how to get herself column inches!'

Hearing him chuckle at his end, a light switched on in Melody's head.

'You're representing her, aren't you?' she demanded icily.

'Well, *hell*, yeah,' Scotty admitted. 'I'd have been a fool *not* to when she was practically begging me, don't you think?

I mean, now she's in there with Julia, it's gonna be mucho buckolas all the way.'

Melody slammed the phone down.

Scotty had told her everything she needed to know. She was on her way out; the door was already closing behind her. The fickle producers who had so recently wined and dined her had already forgotten her; and Scotty scumbag Nash was effectively dumping her, because he'd be too busy pouring all of his time and energy into his new money-cow from here on in.

And Deanna Shelby was the biggest cow going!

The ugly witch had crawled out of the woodwork last year and come trailing after Melody like the annoying slug that she was, copying Melody's clothes, getting the same hair colour and extensions, and the same porcelain veneers. She'd even gone to the trouble of finding out which tuck-and-suck man Melody had used, and got herself the same boobs, nose and lips. She'd been so desperate to *be* Melody, and it looked like she'd finally achieved her aim. In six short weeks she had stepped neatly and completely into Melody's shoes – and there wasn't a goddamned thing Melody could do about it, because she was wasting away over here, in the no man's land they called Manchester, England; while Deanna was stealing her thunder back home.

And it was all Tony's fault for bringing her here in the first place, on this holiday that he'd booked behind her back as a 'reward' for all the hard work she'd been doing lately. The holiday she'd never even wanted, and hadn't enjoyed one fucking bit!

Screaming with frustration now, Melody snatched her glass of brandy off the bedside table and hurled it at the wall.

In the lounge, Tony heard the sound of shattering glass and, fearing that Melody had had an accident, rushed in to see if she was all right.

Stepping back when a piece of glass crunched under his shoe, he looked down at the shards embedded in the thick carpet, then up at the wet patch staining the expensive flock wallpaper as the brandy dripped slowly down.

'What the fuck are you doing?' he demanded, glaring at Melody, who looked like a madwoman, sitting in the middle of the bed with her face a mess of tears and her hair all over the place. 'Have you lost your fucking mind? I'll have to *pay* for this.'

'*Good!*' she screamed, balling her hands into fists and slamming them down on her thighs. 'You *should* pay for what you've done to me, you bastard!'

'Keep it down,' he barked, closing the door. 'You want the whole fucking place to hear you?'

'I don't *care!*' Melody wailed, snatching up a book and throwing it at him. 'You've ruined my *life!*'

Narrowing his eyes, Tony frowned deeply. She was acting crazy, and he didn't have the first clue what was eating her.

'I just spoke to Scotty,' she yelled at him accusingly. 'And guess fucking *what*, Tony? I didn't get that part I was after!'

'Is that it?' he sneered. 'You just cost me thousands, all because you didn't get one fucking part?'

'Is that *it*?' she screeched, really blazing now. 'Don't you get it, Tony? I'm *finished*! They picked some big-titted long-legged *freak* who thinks she's *me* – and it's all *your* fault, because *you* kept me *here* when I should have been *there!*'

'Aw, quit freaking out,' Tony grunted, laughing at her now. 'I told you you was no good from the start, but would you listen? No. So now you're gonna have to feel what it's like to hear it from the rest of the world.'

'No good?' Melody repeated incredulously. 'What kind of crap is *that*? I'm great – everyone's been saying it. I knocked them dead in that Clooney film!'

'Aw, get over yourself,' Tony shot back at her. 'You're an

average actress, and it was an average film. Yeah, they was hyping you for a while, but only 'cos they had nothing better to do. Do you think they'd have forgot you so fast if you was great? Jolie could take *ten* years off, and they'd be lining up with their tongues hanging out if she said she wanted to come back. You're away six weeks and they can't even remember your name. Think about it.'

'You got the hots for her, or something?' Melody demanded jealously. ''Cos you sure sound like it – always comparing me to her. If she'd kept her fucking clothes on she wouldn't be *half* as famous as she is, but I don't suppose you care about that, do you?'

'Clothes on, clothes off – who gives a shit?' Tony replied scathingly. 'Fact is, *she*'s got it, and *you* ain't – not for the kind of acting you want to do, anyway. I always said you should stick to doing what you do best.'

'Oh, yeah, you'd like that, wouldn't you?' Melody hissed. 'And there was me thinking you actually *loved* me. Well, I guess I know the truth now, don't I? You don't love no one but *you*. Well, that's it, Tony. I've had it with you and your shit. First thing tomorrow, I'm going home – without *you*!'

'No, you ain't.'

'Oh, right, so you're allowed to do whatever *you* want but *I*'ve got to do what *you* tell me?' Melody demanded. 'That the way it works in your thick head?'

Tony didn't answer. He just stared at her with rapidly darkening eyes. A sure-fire warning that Melody was too fired-up to heed.

'Well?' she continued, thrusting her chin out at him, her eyes sparking with pure hatred. 'That how you think it is with us, Tone? You do whatever the fuck you want, and I just go along with it – like all them fucking *whores* you used to be hooked up with?'

'You remember what you was doing when I picked you up?' Tony cut in quietly.

'What's *that* got to do with it?' she spluttered. 'Christ, Tony, have you any idea how *sick* I am of listening to your macho crap? I've been *begging* you to go home, but you've been so busy making friends with these up-your-ass morons round here, you don't give a toss what you're doing to my career. Well, you can go screw yourself if you think I'm staying now, 'cos I'm going home, and I'm gonna get my life back on track without *you* hanging round my neck like a flaming millstone.'

'That right?' Tony snarled, losing patience now. 'Let's see how far you get without *this*, then, eh?'

Marching to the dresser, he wrenched open the drawer and took out her passport. Slipping it into his back pocket, he looked around for her handbag.

Guessing what he was thinking, Melody lunged across the bed, but Tony beat her to it. Shoving her roughly aside, he snatched the bag up off the floor and rifled through it until he found her credit-card wallet.

'Give that back!' Melody screamed, throwing herself at him and beating him with her fists. 'That's mine! You've got no right!'

The punch sent her sprawling across the bed. Winded, she lay on her back, blood from her cut lip trickling down her cheek. Staring up at him with huge, terror-filled eyes when Tony came and stood over her, she held her breath.

'Look what you done now,' he said, his voice deceptively soft as he unzipped his fly. 'Gone and got me all worked up.'

'You can't be serious?' she gasped when he flopped his dick out and started rubbing it. 'You can't expect me to *sleep* with you after what you just did?'

'What makes you think I'm asking?'

'You can't *force* me. Eddie's out there.'

'And what's *he* gonna do?' Tony gave a nasty laugh. 'He don't give a flying fuck about you. Anyway, you think he's never heard me putting a smart-mouthed bitch back in her place before?'

'But I'm not like the others,' Melody cried. 'You said I was special.'

'You was till a minute ago,' Tony said, shoving her legs apart.

'No!' Melody yelled, struggling with him as he climbed on top of her. 'Pack it in, you twisted bastard! I don't want you to touch me. I hate you! You make me *sick*!'

Grabbing her hair with one hand, Tony forced her head down into the mattress and gave her a couple of hard slaps. Bringing his face down then, until their noses were touching, he hissed through clenched teeth, 'Make you sick, do I? Well, what do you think your moaning and whining does to me? You think you're so fucking special, but you're a demanding, talentless, money-grabbing, pig-thick *whore*, who's only ever been good for one thing – and you ain't even so good at *that* no more!'

Realising that she'd pushed him way too far, Melody stopped struggling and gazed tearfully up into his eyes. 'I'm sorry, Tony,' she murmured in a tiny remorseful voice. 'I didn't mean it. It just slipped out because I was mad at you about that film. It's my fault.'

'Yeah, I know,' he snarled. 'And so's *this*, 'cos you should learn to zip it when you're told to. You was nothing but a whore when I found you – a filthy little tramp who spread her legs for any cunt who had the price of a wrap of smack. I took you away from all that and turned you into something decent, and you repay me by telling me I make you *sick*?'

Crying for real now, Melody held on to Tony's wrists to ease the pressure of his grip on her hair.

'Please, Babe, I don't want to fight. I swear I didn't mean it. You've been good to me, and I don't deserve you, but you know I love you, don't you? You're the only one I've *ever* loved. And I haven't looked at anyone else in the whole time I've been with you, so that's got to tell you something.'

'You couldn't be stupid enough to look at no one else while you're with me.'

'And I haven't.' Reaching out, Melody stroked his cheek. 'You're everything I've ever needed or wanted. Please, hon . . . let's just forget this ever happened and get back to how we were before.'

Breathing hard, Tony peered dark and deep into her eyes. 'Yeah, all right, I'll forget it, but I'd best not hear any more shit about going home, 'cos it ain't happening – not till *I* say so. And before you get any smart ideas about running away,' he said then, his voice so low that she could barely hear him, 'just remember that I bought and paid for every inch of this body. *And* this . . .' He gripped her face and squeezed it hard. 'All mine. And nothing that's mine gets away from me till I'm good and ready for it to be gone. You got that?'

Wincing with pain, Melody nodded.

'Good girl.' Smiling nastily, Tony let go of her face and patted her cheek hard. Pushing himself up then, he got off her and zipped himself up.

Sitting up gingerly, Melody watched as he walked to the dressing table and straightened his clothes. Then, opening a tub of wet-look gel, he slicked his hair back.

'Are you going out?' she asked, sure that this would all be over if she could just get him to come to bed.

'Yep.' Splashing on aftershave now.

'Do you have to?'

'Don't know how long I'll be gone,' Tony said, as if she hadn't even spoken. 'Don't wait up.'

Lying down when she'd heard him and Eddie leave,

Melody let the tears of self-pity slide down her cheeks. She'd always prided herself on succeeding in taming him where his other women had failed, but she'd been stupid to confront him like that – and really, *really* stupid to tell him that she was leaving, because that was a red rag to a bull with a control freak like Tony. If only she'd kept her mouth shut, she could have waited for the right opportunity and sneaked away. But he would never let her have her cards and passport back now that the battle lines had been drawn.

And there was nothing she could do about it, because nobody could help her. Not Eddie. Definitely not Fabian. And it was more than her life was worth to even *think* about involving the police. All she could do was carry on acting the loving, doting girlfriend until Tony trusted her again – however long that took. And she might as well forget getting her career back on track, because if it wasn't already over it sure as hell would be by the time she escaped – if she ever did.

'She all right?' Eddie asked as he and Tony headed down to the car park where the taxi they had ordered was waiting.

'She's fucking lucky, is what she is,' Tony grunted. 'But I got more important things to think about right now. That call I got just before she kicked off? That was Ronson saying the Feds have just pulled Zorba in, and they got the Johnson brothers as prosecution witnesses.'

'Might be a good time to make the money disappear,' Eddie muttered, holding the door open for him. 'While the heat's on and no one's looking too hard.'

'Could be right,' Tony agreed, pursing his lips thoughtfully as they climbed into the cab.

He was quiet on the ride to the casino, thinking everything over. He'd given Melody a hard time just now, but better that than have her run back to the States to a certain

death. If she did but know it, he'd saved her life by dragging her over here when he had, because she'd be in a
concrete box at the bottom of the Hudson by now – and,
to teach Tony a lesson, Zorba would have taken great delight
in fucking her front, back, and inside out, before personally
pouring the liquid cement over her screaming head.

But she didn't know that – and she wasn't *going* to, because
Tony didn't trust her. He didn't trust *any*body all the way,
except maybe Eddie. But he definitely didn't trust *her*, not
while she was so mad at him for fucking up her career.

It couldn't have come at a better time, as far as he was
concerned, because, brilliant as *she* thought she was, she
hadn't reached the point of being unforgettable to the public
yet, so it wouldn't be too long before she was plain old Fiona
Dawn again. And when she was, Tony would marry her,
ensuring himself a permanent ticket to stay in England.
Nobody would give a toss *who* she married by then, so there
would be no publicity. No publicity – no way of Zorba
reading about it and knowing where to look for him.

In the meantime, he had to find a way of investing the
money he'd stolen while Zorba's men were concentrating
their efforts on getting to the Johnson brothers. And they
would get to them, because in all the attempts the Feds had
ever made there had never been a witness *yet* who'd made
it into court to testify against Zorba. Tony had until then to
get something sorted, but the way things were going it wasn't
looking too good.

Ripping the money off had been too good an opportunity
to miss, and Tony had whacked it into his bank back home
before anyone realised, withdrawing the bulk in a draft and
the rest in cash a couple of days later. Then he'd grabbed
Melody and Eddie and jumped on the first plane to England,
thinking it would be a doddle to set himself up in business
and make himself untraceable once he got here. But it was

proving to be much harder than he'd anticipated because the British banks were tougher than Fort Knox to get into. With no paper proof as to how he'd come by such a large amount of money, they wouldn't touch him.

Stuck with almost one hundred gees in US bills that needed changing over, he'd been going into the local bureau de change every few days, changing a couple of hundred at a time. And, by night, he'd been rotating around the few casinos that Manchester boasted, playing the tables like a butt-lucky novice. But you could only win so many times without raising eyebrows, so he was having to lose as well – which was time-consuming, and more than a little frustrating, because he could have wiped them all out in a single night if he'd been free to play his usual game.

But while that might be tedious, it was at least doable. But the million-dollar bank draft wasn't. With no account to deposit it in, he was stuck with it. And, in his pocket, as it had been the whole six weeks he'd been here, it wasn't worth the paper it was printed on.

But something would come up, Tony was sure, because he was nothing if not determined. Sooner or later, he would find a way around the mess. But until then he would have to carry on doing what he was doing – and keep a very close eye on Melody to make sure she didn't do anything stupid and blow him sky-high.

Still awake when Tony came back a few hours later, Melody kept her eyes firmly closed and pretended to be sleeping when he came into the bedroom and stood over her. Wincing when he traced a finger over her bruised lip, she held her breath, praying that he didn't try and wake her.

Leaving her be, Tony slipped his jacket off and hung it over the back of the bedside chair. Then he went into the bathroom, closing the door behind him.

Peeping out through half-closed eyes to be sure he'd really gone, Melody eased the quilt back and tiptoed across to his jacket. Stare riveted on the door in case he came back and caught her, she slipped her hand into his pockets, hoping to find her passport and cards. They weren't there, but there was a thick wad of cash in the inside pocket. Taking it out, her eyes widened when she saw that they were all twenties and fifties.

There must be thousands of pounds there – but what could Tony possibly have been doing to make this kind of money in just a few hours? And, more to the point, *who* had he done it with, because he didn't know the city well enough to have made the kind of contacts he'd need for this.

Or did he?

Tony *had* been putting himself about quite a bit since they'd got here, and who knew what he'd been organising? He could have recruited himself a gang and had them out robbing banks, for all she knew. She wouldn't put it past him. And it wouldn't matter that he'd had more than enough to start with, because men like Tony could never get enough.

But wherever this money had come from, it might be Melody's only opportunity to get her hands on any cash for months, and she'd need it if she was ever going to escape. It was a huge risk, because Tony might have counted it, but he wouldn't necessarily think that *she*'d taken it. He might think he'd lost it, or that whoever he'd done his 'business' with had ripped him off.

Deciding it was worth the risk, Melody slid a small bundle of the notes out and put the rest back where she'd found it. Looking around then for somewhere to hide it, she remembered the jumbo pack of sanitary towels in her toiletry bag. Tony would never think of looking there – he hated anything to do with *that* side of women.

Taking one of the individual packets out, she carefully

unwrapped it and took the towel out. Putting the folded notes in its place, she rewrapped it and slotted it back in between the others. Perfect.

So perfect, in fact, that she could probably get away with replacing every towel like that over time. If she took just a little whenever she found money in Tony's pockets, she'd soon have enough for a plane ticket. All she'd have to do then would be find her passport and she'd be free.

Hearing the toilet flush, Melody rushed back to the bed and pulled the quilt over herself, just as Tony came back.

Glancing at her, he quietly picked up his jacket and went into the lounge. Taking the money out, he stashed it right down inside the couch with the rest – US currency to the left, British banknotes to the right. Hardly the ideal hiding place – but it would have to do for now because he certainly couldn't be carrying it around in his pocket.

And Tony couldn't afford to make too many more mistakes like the one he'd just made, either. Fortunately, Melody had been asleep, but he might not be so lucky next time, and if she got her hands on that kind of money and did a runner, he was fucked.

He had to get this moving. Now.

6

Jenna had just had her morning shower and was sitting on the bed brushing her hair when her mobile rang. Reaching for it, she smiled when she saw Vibes's name on the screen.

'Good morning. How are you?'

'Not too good, actually,' he said, sounding uncharacteristically glum. 'There's something I need to talk to you about. Have you got a minute?'

'Course I have,' she assured him. 'Fire away.'

'I suppose I could have waited till I saw you tonight,' he said. 'But I thought you'd appreciate having as much warning as possible.'

'Warning?' she repeated questioningly. 'Is something wrong?'

'Nothing for you to worry about,' he told her quickly. 'It's just that I had a call a couple of hours ago – from back home. And, well . . .' Pausing, he inhaled deeply. 'Thing is, I've got to go back.'

'Oh, right,' Jenna said, her heart sinking. 'When?'

'Flight's booked for Monday.'

'*This* Monday?'

'Uh huh.'

'Wow. That soon?'

Sounding as sick as he felt, Vibes said, 'I'm real sorry, Jenna. If there was anything I could do to change it, I would. But something's come up and I've got no choice. It's, um, family stuff, you see.'

'You don't have to explain,' Jenna told him quickly, sensing from his tone that he didn't really want to discuss it. 'Just tell me how long you'll be gone so that I can arrange someone to cover for you.'

'That's the thing,' Vibes said quietly. 'I don't know how long this thing is gonna take, or even if I'll be *able* to come back when it's over. It all depends what happens when I get there. Not that I don't want to,' he added quickly. 'But there's no point making promises I can't be sure of keeping, is there?'

'I suppose not,' Jenna murmured. Then, pulling herself together because Vibes was obviously feeling bad enough about this without her making him feel worse, she said, 'Well, I can't say I won't miss you, because I will – we *all* will. But there will always be a place for you at the club if you do make it back.'

'That's real nice of you.'

'Rubbish!' Jenna laughed to ease the tension. 'I'm not being nice, I'm being selfish. You're the best DJ in town. I'd be a fool to close the door on you. Subject of,' she said then, crossing her fingers tightly, 'are you going to be able to make it in tonight, or were you planning to finish as of now?'

'God, no!' Vibes said quickly. 'I wouldn't dream of dropping you in it like that. Anyway, I've got to do my last weekend. It wouldn't feel right to go without saying goodbye to everyone.'

Sighing with relief, Jenna said, 'Okay, great. Well, I guess I'll see you tonight, then.'

Hanging up, Vibes dropped his head into his hands. That had been one of the hardest calls he'd ever had to make, and he felt terrible for leaving Jenna in the lurch like this. But he'd meant what he'd said: there was no way he could have contemplated leaving without saying goodbye to everyone at the club – customers included.

It was Friday now, which left just three short days to get the most out of everything he was about to lose, because he would probably never see the place again once he had gone. Or Jenna, or any of the others at the club. He'd stay in touch with them all, of course, but it wouldn't be the same as seeing their faces every day, hearing their voices, sharing their laughter and tears.

But, while he would miss them, it was Kenneth he would miss the most. Kenneth, his homeboy, who had moved to England and had invited Vibes to come and stay for a few weeks – never once so much as hinting that he'd outstayed his welcome as those weeks rolled into almost two years. He owed Kenneth big for that. He owed him his *sanity*. And Gina, too, because between them they had dragged Vibes out of the pits of hell and helped him back on his feet. And for that, he would be eternally grateful to them both.

Tapping on the door just then, Kenneth popped his head around. 'Everything all right?'

'Cool,' Vibes lied, forcing himself to smile. They didn't need to be worrying about him any more than they already were. 'I've just told my boss I'm leaving.'

'How'd she take it?'

'Fine, I guess.' Shrugging, Vibes stood up. 'I said I'd work out the weekend – give her time to get a replacement.'

'You sure that's wise?' Kenneth asked, concerned that it would all be too much for him. 'You're leaving Monday, and you're not gonna have much time to settle in when you get there before everything gets rolling. Don't you think you'd be better taking this time out to really get your head around it?'

'I hear what you're saying,' Vibes replied softly. 'But I think it's better if I keep myself occupied right up till I get on the plane, 'cos then I'll have nothing to do *but* get my head around it.'

'Still planning on staying at Tyler's?'

'Couldn't say no after Delores was so good to me, could I?' Sighing deeply, Vibes shook his head. 'Gonna be tough, though, 'cos you can see my house from his front yard.'

'Don't go if it's gonna be too much for you,' Kenneth said quietly. 'I'm sure Ty's mom will understand.'

'Nah. I've got to face it some time. Can't keep running for ever.'

'True, but you don't have to torture yourself by staying that close. You could find a motel near the courthouse. And if money's an issue, I can always—'

'Thanks, bro, I appreciate the offer, but I'm fine for cash,' Vibes assured him. 'And I've made up my mind to do it this way for my own sake. The deeper the wound, the faster it heals. Right?'

Chuckling softly, Kenneth said, 'I don't know where you heard that, but if you come down to A and E when I'm working a Saturday shift, you'd know what a crock it is. The deeper the wound, the louder the screams and the more blood to mop up, in my experience.' Shrugging then, he said, 'But you know your own mind, so I ain't gonna preach. And you know I'm at the end of the phone if you need me – any time.'

'I know.' Vibes nodded. Then, glancing down at his watch to hide the tears in his eyes, he said, 'Man! Is that the time? I can't be chatting to you all day. I got things to do.'

'Well, don't let me keep you,' Kenneth said, stepping aside. 'Just don't go *over*doing it, yeah?'

Jenna's mood sank like a stone after the call. She'd always known that Vibes would have to leave one day, but now that it was imminent she was absolutely dreading it. Not only because she might never see *him* again, but because she was bound to lose customers, too – and that would be a massive blow when everything had been going so well. But she wouldn't try to persuade him to stay. He had his own life to live, and she just had to get over it – and hope to God that she found a decent replacement.

But she would deal with that later. Right now, she had a leaving gift to buy.

Heading into town, Jenna spent hours searching for the perfect 'something' to thank Vibes for all his hard work. She wanted it to be personal, but not *too* personal; expensive, but not over the top. But that proved much harder than she'd anticipated, because nothing seemed quite right.

Forced to make a snap decision when the shops began to close around her, she rushed back to the first jeweller's she'd visited on King Street and bought the chunky matt-silver watch that had caught her eye in the window. It cost way more than was probably decent for a boss to spend on an employee, but she was beyond caring by then. And she didn't have to justify herself to anybody, so what was the harm?

Jenna had to pause for thought when the jeweller asked if she'd like to have it engraved, though. 'To . . . with love from Jenna' would have been perfectly acceptable for anybody else but, given the illicit feelings she'd been harbouring towards Vibes lately, she was paranoid about giving the wrong impression – to him *or* to his wife.

Sticking to safe ground, she plumped for the sword-slash Z logo – to remind him of his time at the club, but not necessarily of her.

Dropping into the club now on her way home, she'd just popped the watch into the wall safe when her desk-phone rang. Reaching for it, she said, 'Hello?'

'That you, Jenna?' It was Tony Allen. 'Sorry for disturbing you outside of work hours, but I needed a favour.'

Frowning, Jenna glanced at her watch, hoping this wasn't going to take too long. She'd been in town much longer than she'd intended already, and she needed to go home and eat, then get ready for tonight.

'Actually, it's more advice than a favour,' Tony went on. 'You got time to talk?'

'Well, I *am* in a bit of a rush,' Jenna said, trying not to sound like she was fobbing him off. 'But if you want to give me the gist of what it's about, we could discuss it in more detail tonight.'

'I was thinking more along the lines of calling in on you now, so we could have a proper chat without distractions,' Tony said. 'But I guess if you're busy, you're busy.'

'Sorry.'

'No problem. I could probably do with a shower, anyway, so I guess I'll catch up with you tonight. It's only a bit of business advice, so it shouldn't take too long. Just need some facts about British business – laws and regulations, that kind of stuff.'

'Ah, well, I might not actually be the best person to talk to,' Jenna admitted. 'I'm a bit of a novice, as you know, and I haven't had to deal with too much of that side of things yet.'

'Oh, right,' Tony murmured. 'Oh, well, not to worry. I'll just have to think of someone else.'

'You could always try Leonard Drake,' Jenna suggested, remembering what Fabian had said about Drake having helped her dad.

'Who?'

'The politician.'

'That fat creepy guy?'

'Mmm.' Jenna bit her lip to stop herself from laughing. 'I believe he used to have something to do with the liquor licensing board, so he ought to know something about business law.'

'Worth a try,' Tony said thoughtfully. Then, 'Yeah, why not? Go on, then, give me his number. I'll give him a ring.'

'I don't actually have it on me,' Jenna lied. 'Maybe it would be better if you waited to see him at the club.'

'He might not come in tonight, and I don't really have time to waste,' Tony said. 'Just see what you can do for me, will you? I'll leave you my room number so you can call me back when you get it.'

Jotting the number down, Jenna promised to get back to him. Putting the phone down then, she chewed on her thumbnail, wondering how best to deal with this. It wouldn't be right to give the Drakes' number out without their consent, but would it really hurt if *she* rang and passed the message on? Tony would only keep ringing if she didn't, and she would feel awkward if she had to keep lying.

Opening the desk drawer, she reached to the back for her dad's old address book and looked up Leonard's number.

'Oh, hello, Mrs Drake?' she said when Avril answered. 'Sorry to disturb you, but this is Jenna Lorde.'

'Sorry, *who?*'

'Jenna Lorde – from Zenith, on Deansgate. I was wondering if I could have a quick word with your husband?'

'Oh?' Avril's voice was filled with suspicion. 'Leonard's not here at the moment. May I take a message?'

'It's just about somebody who's trying to contact him,' Jenna explained. 'They asked me for his number, but I didn't think it my place to give it out, so I thought I'd best pass the message on and let Mr Drake deal with it himself.'

'And who would this person be?'

'One of my customers – Tony Allen.'

'I see. And I don't suppose you'd have any idea *why* he'd like to speak with Leonard?'

'None whatsoever,' Jenna admitted. Then, 'Look, I'm really sorry. I probably shouldn't have bothered you, but he did say it was important. So, if you'd like his number . . . ?'

'I suppose so.' Avril sighed audibly. 'Just give me a moment to find a pen.'

Apologising again when she'd passed the number on,

Jenna put the phone down and shook her head. Avril Drake had sounded so unfriendly, but Jenna could hardly blame her. Your home was the one place where you should be able to relax without people you barely knew disturbing you.

Groaning when the phone began to ring again, she closed her eyes, praying that it wasn't Tony Allen calling back already. What was she supposed to say? That she didn't want to give him the Drakes' number, but had passed *his* number on to them? It seemed quite insulting put like that.

Reaching for the receiver, she was about to say hello when a deep male voice hissed, 'I've been watching you, and I hope you're ready to die, cunt, 'cos I'm gonna slice your fucking throa—'

Slamming the phone down as if it had burned her, Jenna stared at it when it immediately began to ring again, at exactly the same time as somebody knocked on the door.

Vibes was smiling when he popped his head in, but soon stopped when he saw the expression on her face. Coming in, he closed the door.

'Hey, what's up?'

Jenna shook her head. 'Nothing. It's all right.'

Frowning, Vibes looked at the still-ringing phone. 'Aren't you going to answer it?'

'No.' She shook her head again, and folded her hands together in her lap.

'Want me to get it?' he offered, wondering even as he said it if he ought to be interfering. What if it was her boyfriend, and they'd had an argument?

'Would you mind?' Jenna gazed up at him, her cheeks flushed now, sure that he must think she was acting like a silly little girl.

'Course not.' Still frowning, Vibes snatched up the receiver and barked, '*YEAH?*' There was a moment of silence at the other end, then the dial tone. Shrugging, he hung up. 'No one there.'

'Good.' Releasing a jagged breath, Jenna stood up and came around the desk.

Reaching out when she tripped on the waste-paper basket, Vibes peered down at her. 'Hey, you're shaking. What's going on, Princess?'

Conscious of the musky scent of his aftershave and the warm strength of his solid arms as he held her, Jenna gave a nervous laugh. 'Nothing. I'm just being stupid. It's not the first time I've had a malicious call, and I doubt it'll be the last.'

'Malicious?' A spark of anger flared in Vibes's eyes. 'Who was it? What did they say?'

'No idea who, but he didn't say anything I haven't heard before.' Embarrassed for making so much out of nothing, Jenna sighed. 'It took me by surprise, that's all. But I'm fine now. Honestly.'

'Sit down,' Vibes said, pushing her gently but firmly towards the couch. Perching beside her then, he nodded towards the now-silent phone. 'Looks like my voice did the trick, anyway.'

'Thanks. Saves me having to waste the police's time – like they haven't got enough to do without chasing round after silly women who get freaked by stupid phone calls. Anyway, forget about it.' Flapping her hand now, Jenna sat back. 'What brings you in at this time of day?'

'I came in to pick something up and saw your car out back,' Vibes said. 'And I had a favour to ask, so I thought I'd best see you now before we get too busy.' Giving her a sheepish smile, he said, 'I know it's a liberty, but is there any way I could leave some of my gear here when I go? Only, there's no room back at the house, and I don't want to leave it in storage 'cos it'll get wrecked. I'll find some-where else if you haven't got the space, but—'

'It's fine,' Jenna assured him. 'You can leave it in here.'

'You sure?' Vibes asked. 'There's a couple of decks, and a whole heap of CDs. And you don't even want to *know* how many albums.'

'Will it fit back there?' Jenna indicated the space between the back of the couch and the wall.

Glancing over, Vibes shrugged. 'I guess so. But it shouldn't be in your way too long. I'll send over for it as soon as I know what's happening.'

'It won't be in my way. Take as long as you need.'

'Thanks. You're an angel'

Their gazes met, and Jenna was conscious of her heart thudding noisily in her chest. She knew it was so very, very wrong, but she just couldn't help herself wondering what if . . .

The phone began to ring again.

Spell broken, Vibes jumped up and rushed to it. Snatching it up, he yelled, '*WHO IS THAT?*' Then: 'Oh, sorry, sweetheart, didn't mean to shout. Just a minute.' Turning to Jenna, he grimaced guiltily. 'It's Kalli.'

Passing the phone to her when she came over, he glanced at the clock on the wall behind her. It was almost six-thirty, and he still had tons to do back at the house. Mouthing for her to call him if she needed him, he backed out of the door.

Waving, Jenna sat down, aware that she was shaking again.

'Is everything all right?' Kalli asked, concerned because it was so unusual for anybody else to answer Jenna's phone – and even more unusual for Vibes to shout.

Exhaling slowly to calm herself, Jenna said, 'Everything's fine. What can I do for you?'

Not sure whether she believed her, but aware that it was none of her business, Kalli decided to let it go. If Jenna wanted her to know, she'd have told her.

'Can Vibes hear me?' she asked now.

'No, he's just gone,' Jenna said. 'Why? What's up?'

'Nothing, really. Well, apart from him *leaving* – which is just the worst thing ever.'

'He told you?'

'Yeah, he rang this afternoon.'

'I see,' Jenna murmured, biting down on a sudden twinge of jealousy. Why *wouldn't* he call Kalli? she asked herself sharply. They got on really well, and Vibes had actually known her for longer than he'd known Jenna, so of course he'd want to tell her something like that.

'I wanted to get him a going-away present,' Kalli was saying now. 'But I've been looking for ages, and I still haven't found anything. I wondered if you might have some ideas?'

'I'm sure he'd love anything you chose to give him,' Jenna assured her. 'But don't spend too much, because I've already got him something – from all of us,' she added, deciding that it was probably best to keep it impersonal. Especially so, after that little fit of green-eye. 'But please don't tell anyone, because I want it to be a surprise.'

'I won't tell a soul,' Kalli promised. 'But can I ask what it is, only I'll be dying of curiosity if I have to wait to see it.'

'It's a watch,' Jenna told her. 'And I've had the club logo engraved on the back.'

'Oh, he'll absolutely love that,' Kalli said approvingly. 'It'll remind him of us every time he looks at it.'

'That's what I thought. Anyway, I was thinking we should present it at closing time on Sunday.'

'I can't wait to see his face,' Kalli said softly. 'He'll be so p-*pleased*.' Giving a tiny sob then, she said, 'Oh, I'm sorry, but I'm going to miss him so much.'

'We all will,' Jenna murmured, biting her lip as tears flooded her own eyes. Blinking them back, she pinched herself hard to snap herself out of it, then said, 'Right, well, I'd best get on.'

'Me, too.' Kalli sniffed softly. 'Any idea what I can get him?'

Thinking about it for a moment, Jenna said, 'The other DJs have been putting together CDs of their nights, and I know Vibes likes Marky Day, so why don't you see if you can get something of his?'

'He won't be in till Wednesday,' Kalli pointed out disappointedly. 'That's too late.'

'You should be able to pick one up at that white-label place at the back of the Corn Exchange,' Jenna told her. 'I'm sure someone said they'd been selling them from there.'

'That would be brilliant,' Kalli said, sounding a lot happier now. 'I'm still in town, so I'll nip over there now. See you later.'

Hanging up, Jenna dropped her face into her hands and rubbed at her eyes. She would hold it together if it killed her, but it was going to be harder than she thought to say goodbye to Vibes. And she'd have to deal with it alone, because she couldn't let *anyone* know that she'd allowed herself to like him as much as she did.

Snatching her jacket off the back of the chair, Jenna slipped it on and picked up her bag – just as the phone started to ring. Sure that it was the malicious caller again, she rushed out, slamming the door much harder than she'd meant to behind her.

In his own office along the corridor, Fabian had just laid out a thin line of coke on the mirror. Thinking that someone was kicking one of the doors in when he heard the bang, he swept the incriminating evidence into his drawer and grabbed the little rubber cosh he kept under the desk.

Easing the door open, he peeped out into the corridor, dreading coming face to face with Tony Allen and the goon; terrified that they had found out about him and Melody and were hunting him down. Shaking with relief when he saw Jenna outside her door, struggling with her handbag, the strap of which seemed to be caught, he hurried towards her.

'Need a hand there?'

'*Shit!*' she squawked, spinning around with a hand on her heart. 'Do you *have* to sneak about like that?'

'Sorry.' Frowning, Fabian ran a trembling hand through his hair. 'You looked like you were having problems, and I thought you might need—'

'I'm fine,' she cut him off testily, wrenching the strap free. 'I just need to get out of here.'

'Your phone's ringing,' he called after her as she abruptly turned and walked away.

'Thank you, Fabian,' she snapped without looking back. 'But I *have* got ears!'

Staring after her, a glint of anger sparked in Fabian's eyes. What the hell was *that* all about? He'd only been trying to help, but the moody bitch had practically bitten his head off. And if there was one thing he hated, it was women treating him like a prick!

Going back to his office, Fabian kicked the door shut and took his stuff out of the drawer to finish what he'd started.

Hissing, 'Fuck!' when his own phone started to ring, making him spill the powder onto the desktop, he snatched up the receiver. Hearing Melody's voice, he narrowed his eyes nastily.

'I can't hear a word you're saying,' he told her, dabbing at the coke with a wet fingertip. 'You'll have to speak up.'

'I *can't*,' she whispered urgently. 'Tony's in the shower, and he could come out any minute. I just wanted to see if you can get me something extra for tonight – only I want some to bring back here with me, because I'm stressed to the max.'

'My guy's out of town,' Fabian replied coolly, taking it out on Melody because Jenna had pissed him off.

'Can't you get it off anyone else?'

'Depends.'

'Oh, come on, Fabian, don't mess me about. Can you get it or not?'

Saying nothing, Fabian retrieved what he could of the coke and rubbed it over his gums. Sliding down in his seat then, he swung his feet casually up onto the desk.

'All right, how much?' Melody hissed. 'If that's what this is about, name your price.'

'Did I mention money?' he drawled, beginning to enjoy himself. She'd never offered to pay before; she *must* be desperate. 'I just don't know if I can get hold of anything right now, that's all.'

'*Please*,' she begged, a note of hysteria creeping into her voice. 'I *need* it, Fabian . . . Are you still there?'

Sighing wearily, he said, 'Yeah, I'm here. All right, I'll try and sort something out. But I'm not making any promises. And, seeing as you brought it up, I *will* need you to pay for it.'

'Fine.' She gave a relieved sigh. 'How much?'

'We'll talk about it later.'

'It had better be good,' Melody said, hanging up.

'Who was that?' Tony asked, coming out of the bathroom with a towel slung loosely around his spreading gut.

'Room service,' Melody lied, the colour draining from her face.

'Did you tell them the bar needs restocking?' he asked, whipping the towel off and rubbing his hair with it.

Averting her eyes from his hairy nakedness, Melody shook her head. 'No, I forgot.'

'So what *did* you tell them?'

'That I wanted a sandwich,' Melody said, her eyebrows puckering together as she turned to look at him now – exactly as she would have done if she'd been innocent. 'Christ, Tony, what's with all the questions? Don't you trust me, or something?'

Grunting, 'I don't trust no one,' he strolled into the bedroom, dropping the towel en route. 'I need a rub-down,' he called back to her, the mattress springs complaining loudly as he threw himself down on the bed.

'I'm busy,' Melody muttered, reaching for a bottle of bright red nail-polish to paint her toenails. It was obvious what he wanted, and she *so* wasn't in the mood.

She'd accepted that she would never escape alive unless Tony chose to let her go, or – God willing – died. And she was willing to play the game as usual, but no *way* could she bear the thought of him touching her right now. Her stomach was so tight, she might just throw up in his face.

'Yo!' Tony barked from the doorway just then, making her jump because she hadn't heard him get up off the bed. 'Am I talking to myself here, or what? I said, what's taking so long?'

Biting down on her anger and resentment, Melody took a deep breath and said, 'Sorry. I'm just getting ready for tonight.'

'You got plenty of time for that. But this can't wait. Look.'

Turning her head, Melody gave a silent groan when she saw that Tony was waggling his hard-on at her.

'Aw, not now, hon,' she murmured. 'My nails are all wet.'

Tony's eyes narrowed. *Not now, hon* . . . ? What kind of shit was that?

'You forgetting that little chat we had last night?' he snapped, marching over to her.

Shaking her head, Melody shrank back, pressing her head deeper into the cushion to escape the bitter stench emanating from his groin.

'I just don't feel so good, that's all.'

Peering at her face, Tony noticed the lack of colour in her

cheeks and the dark rings under her eyes. And the deep purple bruise around her lip.

'Yeah, maybe you don't look so hot,' he relented. 'Maybe *I* should be giving *you* a rub-down, huh?'

Tensing when he reached for her, Melody shook her head. 'It's all right, Babe. A shower should do it.'

'Aw, come on,' he insisted, his tone cajoling now as he went behind the couch and started roughly kneading her shoulders. 'It won't take a minute, and you know I'm good.'

The damp heat of Tony's palms on her bare shoulders made Melody's stomach churn. But she steeled herself and let him carry on, scared of him sensing her revulsion and kicking off again.

'How's that?' he asked after a while.

'Great,' she lied, her knuckles white from clenching her fists so hard. 'You're the best, Babe.'

'You'd better believe it.' Tony slipped his hands down to her breasts and tweaked the rigid nipples – the result of tension, not desire. 'Methinks the lady's looking for a fucking,' he said, chuckling huskily.

'Please, Tony . . . I can't. I—'

'Sure you can.' Coming back around the couch, Tony aimed his resurrected erection at her mouth.

Knowing there was nothing for it but to get it over with, Melody closed her eyes and opened her mouth. The right flick of her tongue would bring him off in two seconds flat – as long as she didn't puke first.

Just as she'd predicted, it was no time at all before Tony was done. Leaving a slimy trail on her chin, he swaggered towards the bedroom, whistling to himself as he scooped up the towel he'd discarded earlier to wipe himself.

Melody waited a couple of seconds, then strolled calmly into the bathroom. Locking the door, she made a dash for the toilet and puked all the frothy semen down it.

Trembling when the retching finally stopped, she stepped under the shower and leaned back against the cold tiles as the steaming water lashed down on her. She felt like shit. And, yes, she knew it was her own fault for starting on the coke again, but she needed *some*thing to get her through. And at least it wasn't smack. Coke she could handle, but smack was a complete bastard to get off once you were hooked.

It was nice when you were doing it, though, wasn't it? The voice she hadn't heard in a long time whispered into her ear. *Made you feel wonderful, didn't it – warm, and safe, and insulated.*

Snarling 'Fuck off!' under her breath, she turned the shower to cold to blast the monkey off her back.

She hadn't touched smack in five years, and had thought that she was well and truly clear of it. But it was true what they said: once a junkie, always a junkie. There was something about it that you just couldn't forget. Like your first true love: fantastic when you were in each other's arms, but so murderously bad when you were apart that all you wanted to do was get back together again.

It was an endless cycle of pleasure and pain. And a damn sight cheaper than coke, which just made it all the more attractive. But the real price came later – as Melody knew only too well. And there was no way she was going down that route again.

Fabian had better come through for her tonight, or she didn't know what she would do. But what a fucking little weasel, asking her to *pay* for it! She'd like to see what he'd do if she made him pay for all the good sex he'd had off her. He wouldn't be able to afford to *look* at her tits, never mind touch them.

Tony was still undressed when she went into the bedroom, standing in front of the mirror in all his glory, spraying Lynx all over his furry body. Almost choking on the toxic fumes, Melody sat down on the bed to dry her hair.

'Room service never showed,' Tony said, glancing at her in the mirror.

Smiling nervously at his reflection, she shrugged. 'Oh, well.'

'Oh, well, nothing,' he snorted, turning suddenly and sauntering into the lounge. 'I'm gonna bell the lazy bastards – see what's taking 'em so long.'

Squeezing her eyes shut when she heard him yelling down the phone, Melody prayed he wouldn't mention the sandwich she'd never ordered.

Coming back a few seconds later with the phone still clutched in his hand, Tony jerked his head towards the door.

'They're sending someone up to restock the booze. Get something on and let them in, will you? And don't come back till I give you the all-clear,' he said then, sitting down heavily on the bed. 'I got a couple of calls to make.'

Pulling her dressing gown on, Melody did as she was told, pulling the door firmly shut behind her.

When the room-service boy had been and gone, she poured herself a neat vodka and switched the TV on. Sitting down on the couch then, she leaned her head back against the cushions and gazed unseeingly at the screen.

All day she'd been trying to hold it together and act like everything was normal. But Tony was getting on her nerves big time, and Fabian had really pissed her off. She didn't know how much more she could take before she snapped and did something stupid.

Like drug Tony, take her credit cards and passport and book herself onto the first flight home.

And, as a parting shot, she might just let Tony in on her and Fabian's little secret while she was at it. From the plane, of course. She wasn't stupid enough to imagine she'd be able to tell him *that* little snippet face to face and survive.

But it was never going to happen, because she'd have to incapacitate Eddie as well – and there weren't enough drugs in the *world* to knock out that big idiot.

'You've had a call,' Avril said when Leonard came in from the golf club that evening.

Folding her arms, she watched from the living-room doorway as he heaved his clubs into the cupboard beneath the stairs. Straightening up, he rubbed at the small of his back.

'From?'

'That girl, Jenna, from that nightclub you keep dragging me to,' Avril told him, her tone conveying her disapproval. 'Apparently, your *friend* Tony Allen is trying to contact you.'

'Oh?' Leonard's eyebrows shot up.

'Mmm. He called her for your number. Which I found a little surprising, actually, because I'd have thought he'd already have it if you're the good friends you claim to be.'

'Would you please stop saying *friends* as if it's an insult,' Leonard snapped. 'And tell me exactly what she said.'

'*Exactly* what I've told you. Tony Allen called her for your number, but she felt it inappropriate to give it to him without okaying it with you first, so she left *his* number instead.'

'You've got Tony Allen's number?'

'Isn't that what I just said?' Sighing irritably, Avril shook her head. 'Really, Leonard, these golfing sessions seem to be affecting your memory.'

'Don't be ridiculous,' Leonard muttered, walking past her into the lounge and looking around. 'I trust you wrote it down?'

'Of course.'

'Well, do you think you could tell me *where*?'

Avril's nostrils flared as she inhaled deeply and pursed her lips. She had been in two minds about telling her husband about that call, and had only done so in the end because he'd have been sure to find out as soon as they next went to the club. It was annoying, though, for this to happen now, when she'd been so sure that Leonard was on the verge of giving up his new-found zest for the nightlife.

They had gone to that club every single night without fail for the first two weeks. But that had tapered off to just a couple of nights a week recently, and Avril had sensed that Leonard was becoming disheartened with the whole experience. And like any canny mother having to deal with a wilful child, she had therefore decided to stop complaining about it, knowing that if she allowed it to run its course Leonard would quit going of his own accord. Whereas if she were to try to *make* him stop, it was guaranteed to have the opposite effect. And it seemed to have been working. Until now.

'Do you think I should call him?' Leonard murmured, peering nervously at the number on the pad.

'Well, that's the only way you're going to find out what he wants, isn't it?'

'I suppose so. Yes, you're right.' Nodding decisively, Leonard flopped down onto the couch and reached for the phone. 'I'll do it now.'

Going back to her chair, Avril picked up her knitting and feigned a lack of interest as he made his call.

'Oh, hello, is that Mr Allen?' Leonard said, sitting up straighter all of a sudden – as if, Avril thought, he were talking to a superior. 'This is Leonard Drake. We, um, met at the *club*?'

Avril shook her head ever so slightly, wondering why on earth he was introducing himself as if it were *he* who had precipitated the contact.

'Oh, no, it's not a problem at all,' Leonard said now, making Avril's eyebrows pucker with irritation because he sounded so toadying. 'Yes, I could be there. Absolutely.

What time? Ten? Yes, that's perfectly acceptable. Right, well, ten it is, then. I shall look forward to it.'

'What did he want?' Avril asked when he'd hung up.

'To meet at the club tonight,' Leonard told her, getting up and heading for the drinks cabinet.

Watching him out of the corner of her eye, Avril noticed that his hands were shaking.

'I thought it was supposed to be urgent?' she said quietly. 'That was the impression the girl gave when she rang.'

'Yes, well, he's too busy to talk right now,' Leonard said, pouring himself a Scotch. 'Apparently, he would have liked to have spoken to me earlier, but nobody thought to let me know at the time.'

'And how was anybody supposed to do that?' Avril asked, knowing full well that he meant that *she* should have done it. 'You left your mobile here.'

'You could have reached me at the clubhouse. They would have called me in.'

'Yes, well, I didn't.' Sighing, Avril laid the knitting aside again. 'Still, I'm sure you're quite satisfied with the outcome. I'll just go and see what I've got in the wardrobe, shall I? Wouldn't want to embarrass you by wearing something I've been seen in a thousand times already.'

'Don't put yourself to any trouble,' Leonard said, smiling suddenly – which immediately roused Avril's suspicions. 'I know you don't really like the place, so there's no need for you to tag along if you'd rather stay at home tonight.' Another smile. And a bead of sweat on the brow. 'We'll only be talking business, and it's hardly fair to make you sit alone.'

Avril returned his smile, her teeth firmly clenched beneath her tight lips.

'Not at all, dear. I shall be there for you, as always.'

★

Relaxed after a shower and a rest, Jenna went back to the club with her tail between her legs. Finding Fabian doing a stock check in the storeroom, she gave him a sheepish smile.

'I just wanted to apologise for talking to you like that earlier. I was completely out of order, and it should never have happened.'

Getting a waft of Chanel No. 5, which evoked immediate memories of a particularly horny several-night stand with a foxy pole-dancer in Ibiza a few years back, Fabian's handsome lips arced in a secret smile.

'Don't worry about it,' he said, flicking his gaze over her body. She looked great, as usual, and the sincerity in her gorgeous eyes made them an even richer shade of green. 'Feeling better now?'

'Much, thanks.' Jenna smiled, reluctant to explain what had made her so jumpy earlier. He'd only think she was stupid for letting an idiot on the other end of the phone get to her like that – and he'd be right. 'I just had a bit of a headache, but it's gone now. Anyway, I wanted to set things straight with you before we open. And I promise it'll never happen again.'

Knowing the power of magnanimity, Fabian gave her a reassuring smile. 'It's cool, Jenna. You've been working too hard, that's the problem. Any time you want a break, just say the word. I'm more than happy to look after things.'

'Isn't that what *I*'ve been trying to tell *you*?' Jenna raised an eyebrow. 'I seem to remember that you were supposed to be booking yourself a holiday.'

'Is that the time?' Fabian said, grinning as he pantomimed looking at his watch. 'Best get out of here before we get locked in. And who's going to look after the place without us?'

'Okay, I get the point. You don't want time off. Well, fine. You just keep working till you can't stand up for exhaustion.'

'You and me both,' Fabian quipped, waving her out and

locking the door. Strolling up the stairs beside her then, he said, 'So, it's Vibes's last night on Sunday?'

'Mmmm,' Jenna murmured, wishing that he hadn't reminded her.

'Thought of anyone to take his place yet?'

'Don't ask,' she groaned. 'I've been ringing everyone, and no one can step in at short notice. Marky Day's going to call me later to let me know if his friend can do it, but I don't know what we're going to do if he says no.'

'Glad you said that,' Fabian said, grinning. ''Cos I know the perfect guy. Fresh in this morning from a winter season in Tenerife and looking for a residency, at least until summer.'

'Can't be too well known if he's been out of the country,' Jenna commented worriedly. 'Won't that be a bit of a risk for the weekend slot?'

'Do you know how many Brits spend their summers partying in places like that?' Fabian said. 'And then they have to come back to this damp, dark dump, with nothing but memories to carry them through to the next year. Imagine how chuffed they'd be if they found out we'd got one of the guys who was spinning the tunes when they were having the best time of their lives. They'll *kill* to get in. You watch. He'll wipe Vibes off the map in no time.'

Still smiling, Jenna kept her mouth firmly shut. Fabian could think what he liked, but in her opinion Vibes was going to be a hard act to follow.

Still, she didn't have an awful lot of options right now and something was better than nothing. And if this guy didn't work out she didn't have to keep him.

'I'll leave it with you,' she said. 'But I hope you're right about him being good, or we're in trouble.'

'Oh, he's good, don't worry about that,' Fabian assured her. 'I'll go and give him a ring – and hope I catch him before someone else snaps him up.'

7

Tony was dressed and ready to go when he came out of the bedroom. Frowning when he saw Melody dozing on the couch with the TV blaring, still in her dressing gown, her unstyled hair as dry as a scarecrow's, he reached down and gave her a rough shake.

'Yo! It's time you was getting ready. Eddie'll be here in a minute.'

'Uh . . . ?' Waking in confusion, Melody struggled to open her eyes. 'What time is it?'

'Eleven.' Lighting two cigarettes, he passed one to her.

Dragging deeply on it, she shivered. 'Christ, it's cold in here. Have you got the air-con on?'

'Jeez, you *must* be ill. It's hotter than a goddamn furnace.'

'I'm freezing,' she moaned, wrapping the gown tighter around herself.

'Go to bed if you're not feeling right. Sleep it off.'

'No! I'll be fine. Just give me a minute.' Jumping up, Melody stumbled into the bedroom.

Coming out of his own small room two floors up a short while later, Eddie trotted down the stairs and tapped on the door.

'Ready?' he asked when Tony let him in.

'Near as dammit,' Tony affirmed, pouring them both a drink and handing Eddie's to him. 'Just waiting on Mel.'

'You get through to that guy yet?' Eddie asked, going to the window to check if the taxi had arrived.

'Yeah, he rang earlier. I said we'd meet him at the club.'

'Reckon he'll know anything useful?'

'He's got to know more than us,' Tony said. Then, with a shrug, he added, 'Whether or not it's useful is anyone's guess.'

Walking in just then, Melody peered at them suspiciously. 'What you talking about, Tone?'

'Nothing for you to worry about,' he told her dismissively.

Casting a resentful glance at Eddie who was standing by the window, his face as impassive as ever, Melody folded her arms. These two were so far up each other's backsides, it wasn't even funny.

'What you stewing about now?' Tony demanded, giving her a dark look.

'I suppose *he* knows?' she muttered accusingly.

'Pack it in!' Tony barked, downing his drink and slamming the glass down on the table. 'He's family, so don't fucking push it.' Stalking to the door then, he jerked his head for them to follow.

Leonard and Avril arrived at the club at five to ten. Slapping his money down on the pay-desk, Leonard propelled Avril into the clubroom with a hand on her elbow.

Jerking her arm out of his grip, she said, 'Don't push, Leonard.'

'"*Don't push*",' he mimicked under his breath as she strode on ahead with her nose in the air. He'd push her, all right – right out of the bloody door with her suitcases if she carried on like this.

Following Avril up to the VIP lounge, Leonard headed for the bar while she went and found them a table. Glancing around while he waited for the waitress to fill his order, he spotted Tony Allen in a corner booth. The blonde hooker was with him again, and the weird tall man.

But, thankfully, none of the sycophantic fan club was around for a change.

Scolding himself for feeling so nervous about this meeting, he reminded himself that once upon a time – many years ago, admittedly – he had prided himself on being able to tackle any situation head-on. He'd stood tall in his years as party news-spokesman, and had given confident, informative after-dinner speeches since retiring. So why on earth he was so nervous about approaching one man for a civilised chat, he didn't know. Especially when the man had requested the meeting in the first place.

Telling himself to get a grip, Leonard downed both his *and* Avril's drinks when they came, then tossed a ten-pound note to the waitress and marched across to Tony.

'Hello, there. I hope I'm not late?'

'Bang on time,' Tony said, peering up at him with a hint of amusement in his penetrating eyes.

Christ, the guy was ugly. And fat. And where the fuck all that *sweat* came from was anybody's guess, but it sure wasn't normal.

'Take a seat,' he said after a moment. 'Drink?'

Squeezing himself onto the bench seat, Leonard said, 'Yes, thank you, that's very kind. Scotch rocks, please.'

Ordering their drinks, Tony sat back and peered at him. Intimidated by the scrutiny, Leonard slipped a finger into his collar to loosen it as a trail of perspiration snaked down the side of his face.

The sight of it, coupled with the pungent stench of fear and excitement coming from his sodden armpits, made Melody's already sensitive stomach flip.

''Scuse me,' she muttered, lurching to her feet and scrambling to get out from behind the table without touching Leonard.

'Where you going?' Tony asked her sharply.

'To the toilet,' she said. Then, to Leonard, who still hadn't moved: 'Will you *please* let me out!'

'Yo!' Tony barked. 'Don't be rude to our guest.'

Melody opened her mouth to retort that Leonard was no guest of hers. But the look on Tony's face stopped her.

'Sorry,' she mumbled instead, giving Leonard a tiny sick smile. 'Could you please let me out? I really don't feel too good.'

'Thought you said you was better?' Tony frowned.

'I thought I was,' she lied. 'Must be a bug.'

'Best go back to the hotel, then.' Turning to Eddie, he clicked his fingers. 'Take her back, will you?'

'No!' Melody yelped. 'I'll be all right in a minute, hon – honest. I just need to go to the ladies' and splash some cold water on my face. Really, I'll be fine.'

Watching as she made a dash for the toilets, Tony jerked his head at Eddie. 'Go see if they got any antacids in the first-aid kit, or something.'

'Actually, I've always found that peppermint cordial works rather well,' Leonard volunteered. 'That's what my, um, wife usually takes when she feels under the weather.'

Nodding at Eddie, Tony waited until he'd gone, then took out a pack of cigars and lit one. 'So, you're married?' he said, offering one to Leonard.

'Oh, yes.' Leaning towards him for a light, Leonard sat back and pointed Avril out. 'That's my good lady wife over there.'

Glancing at her, Tony saw the crossed arms and furious scowl. 'She don't look too happy.'

'She's fine,' Leonard assured him breezily. 'She's just got a few things on her mind, that's all.'

'What, like wondering where her drink is?' Tony chuckled, noticing the lack of glasses on her table. 'Think we ought to send her one over?'

'Well, I, um, *yes*, I suppose we should,' Leonard splut-tered guiltily. 'I was actually in the process of ordering when I spotted you.'

'What'll she have?' Tony clicked his fingers at yet another waiter.

'G-and-T.'

Ordering a double and asking for it to be taken to her, Tony sat back and gave Leonard an amused smile. 'Well, well . . . who'd have thought you was married? Tell the truth, I had you down as a queer.'

The blush covered Leonard's face like wildfire. 'God, no! We've been married for twenty-eight years.'

Nodding slowly, Tony surmised that his first impression was spot on. The man could have been married for ever, but he was definitely gay. And that he was so keen to hide it could prove very useful in the future.

Letting the squirming worm off the hook – for now – he said, 'So, you're a politician?'

'Er, yes,' Leonard said, recovering his composure with difficulty. 'How did you know?'

'I make it my business to know these things. So, tell me Lenny – don't mind if I call you Lenny, do you?'

Thrilled by the familiarity, Leonard shook his head. 'Not at all.'

'Lenny it is, then.' Tony smiled. 'So, tell me, Lenny – what exactly is it that you do?'

'Well, to be absolutely truthful, I'm retired,' Leonard told him. 'But I still have quite a lot of clout.'

'How so?' Tony squinted at him through the smoke.

'Oh, you know . . .' Leonard gave a modest shrug. 'I still have irons in various fires. Most decisions that are made in local government fall to a panel of my closest friends, you see, so it's inevitable that my advice should be sought from time to time. I'm *very* well respected.'

'I imagine so,' Tony lied, paying the waiter when he brought the drinks over and ordering the same again.

'Oh, yes,' Leonard went on, gaining in confidence as the drinks he'd already had began to loosen his tongue. 'I was quite the high-flyer in my time, so people tend to take my opinions seriously.'

Reaching for his drink, Tony took a long sip and peered at him over the rim of the glass. Was this guy for fucking real? One minute, sweaty little mouse; the next, raving egomaniac.

'So, that other shit you mentioned,' he said. 'The local-government stuff. What kind of influence would you say you've got with that?'

'Oh, plenty,' Leonard told him conceitedly. 'I've been at it for a long time, you see – know all the ins and outs.'

'That's good to know,' Tony murmured. ''Cos that's kind of what I wanted to talk to you about. See, I've been thinking about investing in something over here, but I don't know too much about your laws, and I don't want to get started on something only to hit a brick wall.'

'Confidentially,' Leonard said, leaning toward him and lowering his voice, 'every law can be, if not broken, then certainly *manipulated*. If you know the right people, of course.'

'That right?'

'Oh, yes. Because everything comes down to a human decision in the end, and every man can be swayed.'

'You mean bought?'

'In some cases,' Leonard conceded. 'But it's not always necessary for actual cash to change hands. Quite often it's a simple case of favour for favour. You rub my back, I'll rub yours – so to speak.'

'So, say someone was thinking about setting up a casino over here,' Tony said smoothly. 'Who would he have to know to get a smooth ride?'

'Oh, it would be terribly difficult,' Leonard said knowledgeably. 'They'd have to have a considerable amount in
the bank to begin with.'

'Say that wasn't a problem?'

'Well, then an application would have to be made to the
Gaming Commission – which is top-level security stuff.'

'Not like the "old friends" stuff *you*'ve got going, then?'

'Oh, no, I'm afraid casinos are way out of my league,'
Leonard admitted. 'It involves all sorts of legal bodies, you
see. Police, Customs and Excise, Inland Revenue.'

'I see,' Tony murmured. 'So, they'd want to know all sorts
of stuff about you.'

'*Every*thing,' Leonard affirmed. 'And, believe me, there is
nothing they can't uncover once they start delving. The
gambling industry is notorious for its connections to organised crime, and this government has to be seen to be taking
a stand. If the individual concerned were foreign,' he went
on, guessing that Tony wasn't asking hypothetically, 'they
would have to provide records from the police in whichever
country they had come from, too.'

Taking all this in, Tony nodded slowly. The casino idea
was an obvious non-starter: there was no way he could allow
anyone to delve so deeply into his affairs, because there were
far too many things in his past that needed to stay buried.
But just because *that* was out of the question, it didn't mean
that he couldn't get involved in something else.

'What about a gig like this?' he asked, flicking his cigar
ash casually onto the floor. 'How easy would it be for a
foreigner to set up a nightclub?'

'Somewhat easier than a casino,' Leonard told him. 'But
you'd still have to undergo the security checks, I'm afraid,
because you're still talking alcohol and entertainment
licences. If that were going to prove *problematic*,' he said
then, 'my advice would be to consider investing in a going

concern, which would allow you to build a credit history on the back of somebody who had already been passed by the relevant boards.'

Nodding thoughtfully, Tony mulled this over. There was no way he could put himself under any kind of scrutiny, and he knew enough about Melody's background to know that she had several convictions on her record from when she'd lived here before, so it might not be so easy to open something in *her* name, either. What he needed, it seemed, was to find somebody squeaky-clean to hook up with. Somebody who would be the public face of respectability while Tony sat back and watched his dirty money get clean.

Reaching for his glass, he raised it. 'Cheers, Lenny. You've given me food for thought there.'

'Well, I really haven't done much of anything,' Leonard said. 'But anything I can do in the future, you need only ask.'

'Much obliged.' Taking another puff on his cigar, Tony said, 'So, tell me about yourself. Got kids?'

Flattered that Tony seemed so interested in him, Leonard said, 'Yes, two. Boy and girl. They're both grown now, of course, with families of their own. But they're doing well for themselves. Son in banking, daughter married to a stock-broker.'

'That right?' Tony remarked, clocking up more potentially useful future contacts. 'You must be very proud.'

'Oh, I am.' Smiling, Leonard laced his fingers together over his gut. 'We Drakes have a prestigious financial history, as it happens. My grandfather was a name in the Bank of England, and amassed himself a fortune from share-trading, which my father inherited and quadrupled before he was thirty. Made quite a name for himself in politics, too.'

'That why you went into it?'

'For my sins.' Leonard grinned. 'We're a very traditional

family, so the sons tend to follow the fathers. Not that my son followed *me*,' he added – with a hint of bitterness, Tony thought. 'You'll have to meet him sometime,' he said then, imagining the look on Rupert's face when he saw the connections his stuffy old father had been making since he and his wife Barbara had last deigned to visit. 'Perhaps we could arrange a dinner party? I'm sure Avril would be delighted to have you. She's a wonderful hostess.'

Flicking a surreptitious glance at Eddie who had just come back with a glass of peppermint cordial in his hand, Tony said, 'That'd be great. And I'm sure Melody would enjoy getting to know her. Give me a call sometime – we'll work something out.'

'Oh, I will,' Leonard said eagerly. 'I'll have Avril get on to it as soon as we get home.'

'You do that,' Tony said. Then, nodding in Avril's direction, he said, 'She's looking kinda lonely.'

Glancing at his wife, Leonard was about to say that she was fine but quickly decided against it. He didn't want to give the impression that he didn't care about her – not when he'd just been gushing about his marvellous family. And not when Tony had admitted that he'd thought Leonard was gay, because that was absolutely the last label a man in his position needed. The general public might be heading in a more accepting direction, but politicians were lagging sadly behind, and Leonard had seen for himself how cruelly and absolutely some of his former peers had been excommunicated when news of that nature leaked out.

'I guess I should go and pay her some attention,' he agreed, casting a fond smile in her direction. 'She's such a trooper. And my pals adore her.' Grinning conspiratorially now, he added, 'Quite jealous, most of them. Wishing they could have a little bit of what *I* get at night – if you know what I mean?'

'Mmm,' Tony murmured, wishing the guy would quit the blokey guff and piss off.

'Lovely-looking woman,' Leonard went on, still gazing in Avril's direction as he struggled to get his gut out from behind the table.

'Sure is,' Tony agreed, easing his cuff back and glancing pointedly at his watch. 'Man, look how late it is. Wonder where Melody's got to.'

'Right, well, it was good to talk to you,' Leonard said, loudly enough for the nearby celebrities to hear – making sure they knew that he and Tony were friends. 'Call you soon about dinner.'

After a quick visit to the toilets to throw up, Melody had gone looking for Fabian. Finding him chatting up two tarty-looking women on the edge of the dance floor, she waved to catch his eye, then slipped back into the shadows to wait for him.

'Did you get it?' she demanded when he reached her.

Drawing his head back, Fabian frowned. 'Is that it? No, "Hello, nice to see you"?'

'Please don't play games,' she hissed. 'I can't deal with it right now. I feel like shit.'

'Yeah, you don't look so good,' he agreed, the frown deepening when he noticed her bruised lip. 'What's happened to your mouth?'

'I walked into a door,' Melody told him evasively.

'You sure Tony didn't do it?' Fabian persisted, worried about her now. And about himself.

'Course not,' she snapped. 'I told you he'd never hurt me. Now, have you got it or not?'

'Yeah, I've got it.' Glancing nervously around, Fabian pulled the wrap out of his pocket.

Snatching it from his hand, she said, 'How much?'

'Later. Go and sort yourself out, then come and find me when you get a minute.'

'Fabian . . .' Reaching out as he began to move away, Melody gave an apologetic shrug. 'Sorry, Babe. I know I'm being a complete shit, but I'm just—'

'Don't worry about it,' Fabian cut her off, giving her an understanding smile. 'We'll talk later, yeah?'

Squeezing the wrap tightly in her hand when he walked away, Melody slipped back into the ladies' and locked herself in a cubicle. Laying out a line on the toilet cistern, she leaned down and snorted it straight. To hell with hygiene – she needed this.

'Are we celebrating something?' Avril asked, glancing up at Leonard suspiciously when he returned to their table with a bottle of champagne and two glasses.

'We most certainly are,' he beamed, seeming to have totally forgotten that they had barely been speaking when they'd arrived. 'I've just had a most interesting chat with Tony Allen.'

'Oh yes?'

'Yes, indeed. And I've invited him and his lady friend to dinner, so we'll have to get our heads together and come up with something wonderful. Oh, and I was thinking, maybe we should invite the children. It's been a while since we all got together, and it would be nice to see the little ones.'

Drawing her head back, Avril peered at him incredulously. He detested having the grandchildren in the house, almost as much as they detested coming.

'To my beautiful wife,' Leonard said suddenly, handing a glass to her and raising his own. 'And good times ahead.'

If Avril hadn't already had the large gin-and-tonic that Tony had sent over, and the two she had ordered for herself in Leonard's absence, she'd have been highly suspicious of this sudden lift in his mood. But she was feeling quite mellow at the moment – enough to be grateful that her usually dour husband seemed happy for a change. So, touching her glass to his, she smiled.

'To good times.'

And she damn well hoped he meant it, because she'd had more than her share of bad times recently, enough to last her a lifetime.

Melody felt and looked much better when she came back from the toilets. She'd regained some of her colour, and her eyes were sparkling again.

'I was just about to come looking for you,' Tony told her. 'I had some broad check out the bathroom, but you weren't there.'

'The upstairs ones were full, so I had to use the down-stairs ones,' Melody told him, sitting down.

'Feeling better now?'

'Yeah, loads. Must have been that chicken I had for lunch. I thought it tasted a bit funky.'

'Better tell the Drakes not to put chicken on the menu when we go for dinner, then, eh?' Tony said, handing the peppermint cordial to her. 'Wouldn't want you hurling all over their table, would we?'

'Dinner?' Melody repeated with a grimace. 'Aw, not tonight, Tone? There's no way I can eat tonight.'

'Nothing's been arranged yet,' he assured her. 'I'll let you know when, and Eddie can take you shopping for some new clothes.'

'What do I need new clothes for?' she asked, not relishing the thought of being babysat by Eddie. Shopping was supposed to be fun, not torture. And how was she supposed to ask him if something suited her when he'd barely said two words to her in three years?

'These people have got money,' Tony said, relighting his cigar. 'We don't wanna turn up looking like trash, do we?'

'Tony, honey,' Melody purred, leaning towards him and flicking her tongue into his ear. 'I *never* look like trash.'

Tony's eyes narrowed as the saliva from her tongue left a ghost of a tingle in his ear. If he wasn't very much mistaken . . .

But, no, she couldn't have. She didn't have a single cent in her purse – he'd made sure of that. And nobody was idiot enough to give coke away for free. Anyway, she'd only been to the bathroom, so unless some broad had set up shop in there – which he very much doubted – she couldn't have got her hands on anything.

Taking a sip of the cordial just then, Melody grimaced. 'Ugh! What the hell's *that*?'

'Peppermint, to stop you feeling sick.'

'Guaranteed to *make* me sick, more like,' she complained. 'I can't drink that, hon. Get me a proper drink, will you?'

'You feeling all right?' Tony asked, his eyes giving nothing away as he watched her wriggle about in her seat.

'Yeah, I feel great,' Melody said. 'Always do after a good vomit. And I love this song. *I don't see nothing wrong . . .*' she sang, squeezing his thigh under the table, '*with a little bump and gri-ind.*' Pouting prettily now, she slipped a finger in through the button of his shirt and played with the hair on his chest. 'Mind if I go dance while I'm in the mood?'

'Yeah, why not?' Tony agreed, moving her hand. 'Find Gay Boy and have a couple of spins with him while I finish my drink.'

'Thanks, Babe,' Melody chirped, jumping up without hesitation. 'See you in a bit.'

Turning to Eddie when she'd gone, Tony said, 'Go keep an eye on her. She goes near anyone other than the queer, come get me.'

★

Fabian was having a drink at the downstairs bar when he saw Melody come down the VIP stairs and make her way to the dance floor, where she stood on her tiptoes and looked around. Putting his glass down, he set off towards her, to see if she was okay. He was a bit worried about that bruise on her mouth. There was no way she'd done it walking into a door – but if Tony had done it, what else was he doing to her? She definitely wasn't her usual self at the moment.

Halfway there, Fabian spotted Eddie in the crowd behind her and stopped in his tracks, half expecting to see Tony as well. Frowning when he realised that Eddie was alone, and that he seemed to be trying to mingle casually while keeping a close eye on Melody, his heart thudded painfully in his chest. Eddie was following her. And it had to be on Tony's orders. But why? What did he suspect? The drugs – or that she'd been shagging Fabian's brains out for a solid month?

Shaking wildly now, fearing for his life, Fabian edged back towards the bar, planning to slip quietly away before anybody noticed he'd gone. He would give Jenna a ring on her mobile as soon as he was out, tell her he'd had to rush off to visit his sick mother, or something.

'Oi, watch it, you wanker!'

Spinning around, Fabian found himself faced by three unfriendly-looking men. The one in the middle was glaring at him, his hand dripping with drink that had spilled out of his glass.

'Sorry,' he apologised. 'I didn't see you there.'

'No fucking kidding.'

Sensing that the man was spoiling for a fight, Fabian glanced around for the security guys, but there were none in sight. Needing to stub this out before it escalated and led Eddie straight to him, he switched on his smooth manager smile and offered the man a fresh drink – on the house.

'On the house?' The man looked him up and down. 'You the boss, then, are you?'

'Manager,' Fabian told him, waving him towards the bar. 'Just tell the barman what you want, and I'll sort it out.'

'What about me mates?' The man jerked his head at the others who were smirking over his shoulder. 'You ain't just ruined my night, you've ruined theirs an' all.'

Fabian's nostrils twitched with irritation. The cheeky bastard was pushing it now, but there were still no security guys around so there wasn't a lot he could do about it. And – worse – Melody had just spotted him and was heading his way, with Eddie in slow pursuit.

Trapped, Fabian smiled his best matey smile at the man who was posing the more immediate threat and said, 'All right, just this once. But don't tell anyone, or they'll all be banging into me for free drinks, eh?' Going behind the bar then, he clicked his fingers at Maurice en route to the kitchen door. 'Give them whatever they want, but don't charge them.'

'As long as you don't blame *me* when the receipts don't tally,' Maurice muttered to his back. Then, smiling tightly at the three louts, he said, 'What'll it be, gents?'

'Three cognacs' the man told him, finishing what was left of his original drink and sliding his glass across the bar. '*Triples.*'

Reaching the bar just then, Melody eased her way in between the men to ask Maurice where Fabian had gone.

'Who knows, who cares,' he muttered, shrugging unconcernedly as he went to get the men their drinks.

Leaning an elbow on the bar, the man Fabian had bumped into gave Melody a lingering once-over. 'All right, darlin'? Haven't I seen you somewhere before?'

'Very likely,' Melody said, flicking him a mildly dismissive glance. She usually enjoyed being recognised, but she wasn't in the mood right now.

'Yeah, I know who you are. You're that bird out of *Baywatch*.'

Gritting her teeth, she said, 'No, I'm not.'

'Yeah, you are,' the man persisted. 'I never forget a good pair of tits, me.' Laughing he held his hands to his own chest. 'Red swimsuit, running down the beach. Phwoar!' Clicking his fingers now, he said, 'Pamela Anderson!'

'You need glasses,' Melody told him sharply. Why did people always think it was a compliment to mistake her for that vacuous tart? She was Melody Fisher. Her name spoke for itself. At least, it had started to in the States, but these ignorant thugs obviously hadn't caught up yet.

'Gonna let me buy you a drink, then, Pammy?'

'For Christ's sake, I am *not* Pamela fucking Anderson. Just back off and go find someone else to wank over, will you!'

'She likes me,' the man said, grinning at his mates.

'In your dreams,' she muttered, tapping her long fingernails on the bar. God only knew why he thought he stood a chance. He was nowhere near good-looking enough, and he had the worst case of cheap-gold-overload she'd seen since that awful gangsta-rap crew's album launch in LA last summer.

'In *my* dreams,' the man drawled, still grinning. 'I'll give you the best fucking dreams you've ever had, darlin'.'

'Will you just piss off!' she hissed, giving him a dirty look. 'I'm not interested – all right?'

Coming up behind her now, sandwiching her in between his mates and the bar, one of the men ran a hand over her backside, whispering, 'Nice arse, love. Be even nicer with my dick in it.'

'Get your fucking hands off me!' Melody yelped, jerking her arm back to elbow him in the stomach.

Laughing, the first man grabbed her wrist and held on to it. 'Now, now, no need for violence, Pammy. We'll play fair, won't we, lads?'

'Yeah, we'll pay,' the second one said. 'I've got a tenner to spare. What'll you do for a tenner, love?'

'All three of us, by the look of her,' the third one quipped, sliding a hand up her thigh. 'Get that bruised gob sucking cock, did you?'

'Back the fuck *off*!' Melody shouted, twisting angrily around so that her back was against the bar. 'If my boyfriend sees what you're doing, he'll *kill* you!'

'Oh yeah?' the first man laughed. 'And who's your boyfriend, then? David fucking Has-a-toss?'

Feeling a tap on the shoulder, he was still laughing when he turned around. The head-butt came from nowhere, splitting the bridge of his nose and knocking him spark out.

'Fuck are you playing at, y' cunt!' one of his mates snarled, launching himself at Eddie as the other one snatched a bottle out of a girl's hand and smashed it on the bar.

'*FABIAN!*' Maurice yelled at the top of his voice, pushing the kitchen door open. 'Get in here quick! Those blokes are attacking that big ugly American!'

Halfway out of the back door, Fabian groaned. He didn't want to get involved, but he could hardly justify running out in the middle of a situation now that he'd been told about it.

'Get security,' he told Maurice, coming back in.

Back out in the bar, bar stools were going down and people were leaping out of the way as feet and fists started flying. The man with the bottle was dancing around his mate and Eddie, trying to get a clear shot with the jagged edge.

Hand over her mouth, Melody pressed herself back against the bar as Eddie sidestepped one of the men and brought his elbow down hard on the back of his neck, sending him sprawling on the floor. Then, grabbing the other one's arm, he twisted it around and pulled it high up his back, making him drop the bottle and fall to his knees in agony. But just as he was about to snap the arm, three of the doormen waded in and pulled them apart.

'Right, you, *out!*' Jacko barked, gripping the lapel of Eddie's jacket. 'You're barred.'

'*Don't!*' Melody yelled fearfully, seeing the smile on Eddie's lips.

Thinking she was talking to him, Jacko said, 'Sorry, love, but he's out. Can't have shit like that going on in here.'

'It wasn't him,' Fabian said, coming around the bar just then. 'It was them.' He nodded at the other three who were being held by Bobby and Flex now. 'They were harassing the lady, and he was just helping her out.'

Nodding, Jacko let go of Eddie. 'Sorry, sir.' Then, jerking his head at his guys, he said, 'Get 'em out.'

Holding on to his bleeding nose, the first man gave Eddie the evil eye as Bobby dragged him past. 'Big mistake, pal. We'll be seeing you again.'

Staring intensely back at him, Eddie's smile deepened.

Shuddering, Melody folded her arms. It wasn't the first time she'd seen Eddie fight, but it never ceased to shock her when he did because he was like a robot: no noise, no emotion, just vicious, economical action. And that smile was seriously creepy.

'What's going on?' Tony asked, reaching them just then. 'You all right, Melody?'

Nodding, she said, 'Those blokes were harassing me. But Eddie sorted them out.'

'I thought *you* were supposed to be looking after her?' Tony turned on Fabian angrily.

'He wasn't here.' Melody jumped in quickly. 'He was out back, and I was waiting for him when those guys started feeling me up.'

'Feeling you up?' Eyes murderously dark, Tony glared at Fabian. 'What the fuck are you running here? Some kind of whorehouse, that the men think they can come in and have any woman they lay fucking eyes on?'

'I really had no idea what was happening,' Fabian replied honestly. 'If I had, I'd have dealt with it.'

'Oh yeah? *How?*' Tony sneered. 'Hit 'em with your fucking *purse?*'

'Leave it, Tone,' Melody said, looping an arm around his waist and resting her head on his shoulder. 'It wasn't his fault. Anyway, I told them to get the fuck away from me or you'd kill them.' Giggling now, she added, 'Then Eddie came and nearly did it for you. Should have seen him, hon – he was a *monster.*'

'Yeah, well, they'd better not come back,' Tony growled, still eyeballing Fabian. 'I see them in here again, your guys best stay clear, 'cos they're mine. Got that?'

Fabian was relieved that Eddie obviously hadn't been watching Melody because of him, but this was something he couldn't afford to agree to. There were procedures, and they had to be followed to the letter.

'Much as I'd love to okay that, Mr Allen, I'm afraid I can't,' he said, flapping his hands in a nothing-I-can-do-about-it gesture. 'My guys are highly trained, fully licensed doormen, but our insurance doesn't provide for unauthorised persons interfering with troublemakers. I'm sure you understand?'

'All I understand is that you ain't got a fucking clue about *real* security,' Tony retorted sharply. 'Eddie had it in hand way before your lot got involved – but what would have happened to Melody if he hadn't got to her in time?'

'I can only apologise for that.'

'Yeah, well, apologies don't mean *shit* when you got blood on your hands.'

Melody's beautifully lifted brow puckered into a ghost of a frown as it suddenly occurred to her to wonder how come Eddie *had* managed to get to her so quickly. Her confrontation with those men couldn't have lasted more than a minute, but even if he'd seen it start he'd never have made it down the stairs and through the crowd in that time. He'd have had to have jumped over the balcony and run like mad, in which case there would have been a pile of bodies in the wake of his enormous frame. But there weren't, so he must have already been down here – close enough to reach her in time to rescue her, but not so close that she had noticed him.

He'd been following her!

Shocked by the realisation, Melody cast a nervous glance at Tony, thinking exactly what Fabian had thought: that it had to have been on Tony's orders. But why? What did he suspect?

Turning up just then, having been told about a disturbance at the lower bar, Jenna caught the antagonism in Tony's eyes as he glared at Fabian.

'Everything all right?' she asked.

'Fine – *now*,' Tony spat, shooting a poisonous look at Fabian as he added, 'No thanks to *him*. He was nowhere to be fucking seen while she was out here being molested by some dirty bastards.'

'Molested?' Jenna gasped, turning to Melody. 'Are you okay? What happened?' Spotting the bruise on her lip, she said, 'Oh, please don't tell me they did that to you? Let me go and call the police. They need to be caught and punished.'

'No!' Self-consciously raising a hand to her mouth, Melody shook her head. 'I did this on a door. Those guys were just trying it on, but Eddie sorted it out, so there's nothing to worry about.'

'Well, as long as you're sure?' Jenna said. Then, turning to Fabian, she said, 'Where are those men now?'

'Jacko and some of the boys are throwing them out,' he told her, folding his arms.

'Good. And make sure they don't get back in again, because I don't want that kind of customer.'

'Now, *that*'s the response I expected,' Tony said, sneering at Fabian. 'That's all you'd have had to do to show me you was taking this seriously. None of this shit about insurance and "unauthorised interfering".'

Coming to Fabian's defence, Jenna said, 'To be fair, Tony, there *are* strict guidelines when it comes to security.'

Looking at her for a moment, Tony sighed and ran a hand through his hair. 'Sure there are. Sorry. I just get kinda heated when anyone disrespects Melody like that.'

Fabian raised an eyebrow but kept his mouth shut. The bastard could apologise to Jenna, but not to the person he'd been yelling at. But that was fine. Fabian didn't need an insincere apology, anyway. And at least he didn't have to leave the country just yet. But if this had taught him anything it was that this thing with Melody had to stop – now. And he would tell her so the first chance he got. Once she realised that it was for her own good as well as his, he was sure that she'd back off.

'Can I get you a drink?' Jenna was asking Tony now.

Glancing at Melody, pale and shaking beside him, Tony shook his head. 'I think I'd best just get her back to the hotel.'

'Of course,' Jenna said, peering at Melody with concern. 'I'm so sorry your night ended like this. But I hope it won't put you off coming back?'

'The hell it will!' Tony snorted. 'Take more than a couple of idiots to run *us* out of town. See you tomorrow.' Putting an arm around Melody's shoulder, he walked her out, with Eddie following on behind.

'That man is so bloody ignorant,' Fabian complained under his breath.

'Don't take it personally,' Jenna said, smiling at his outraged expression. 'He was only angry because somebody disrespected Melody. I'm sure you'd be the same if it was your girlfriend.'

'Mmmm,' Fabian murmured, thinking that she couldn't be more wrong. There were too many maniacs in this world to risk getting beaten, stabbed – or worse – over a woman. And in a city like this, where everybody seemed to think that fear represented respect, 'worse' was the more likely outcome of any confrontation these days.

Which reminded him . . .

'I'd better have a word with Jacko and make sure they keep the front doors locked.' Fabian glanced at his watch. 'There's still a couple of hours to go, and those guys might come back mob-handed.'

'Just because they got kicked out?' Jenna asked. 'Surely not.'

'No, because they got a good *kicking*,' Fabian said, pointing to the floor behind her. 'One of them left that – and I don't think he's going to just crawl away and forget about it.'

Glancing to where he was pointing, Jenna grimaced when she saw the pool of blood. 'My God. What happened?'

'Eddie knocked seven shades out of them.'

'*All* of them?'

'Yep.' Fabian nodded slowly.

Exhaling loudly, Jenna said, 'Bloody hell. I guess your sources were right about him being a minder. And a bloody good one, too, by the look of it.'

Fabian stared at her, amazed that she was treating it as a joke. Tony Allen and his goon were serious trouble waiting to happen, but she didn't seem to have a bad word to say about them.

'You're probably right about locking the doors,' Jenna said now. 'But if anything happens, we'll call the police and let them deal with it.'

'Yeah, whatever,' Fabian said distractedly. 'See you in a bit.'

Watching as he walked away, Jenna frowned. Had she just

imagined it, or had he been a bit off with her just now? She couldn't see why, though, so maybe he was just upset about Melody and those guys.

Shrugging it off, she turned back to the bar and called, 'Maurice – could you get someone to come and mop this mess up, please?'

8

The men didn't come back that night, or the next, and Jenna forgot all about them as, all too soon, Sunday came around.

Determined not to disgrace herself and reveal her true feelings about Vibes leaving, Jenna forced herself to smile and chat to the customers as usual as the night wore on. She noticed that the rest of the staff were a little subdued, but that was only to be expected, she supposed, because none of them were looking forward to saying goodbye to him.

At the end of the night, when the music stopped, the house lights came up, and the last of the customers had finally left, she locked the doors. Then she called the staff together on the dance floor.

Going up to the DJ's booth, where Vibes was quietly gathering his stuff together, Jenna asked him for his radio mike. Then she went out onto the top step and jerked her head for him to follow.

Frowning questioningly, he came out and looked down at everyone standing below. 'What's going on?'

'You'll see,' Jenna told him quietly. Switching the mike on then, she said, 'Thanks for staying behind, everyone. Now, as you know, Vibes is leaving us tonight . . .'

Down below, Kalli shushed Austin when he let out a loud sob.

Smiling sadly because she knew exactly how he was feeling, Jenna took a deep breath.

'Anyway,' she continued, 'I'm sure you'd all like to join

me in wishing him the best for the future – wherever and whatever that may be.' Pausing as a cheer went up, she took the gift-wrapped box out of her pocket. Waiting until she had quiet again, she said, 'As a mark of our appreciation, I'd like to present this to Vibes.'

'What's she doing?' Fabian muttered, folding his arms. 'She didn't tell me about this.'

'I think she wanted it to be a surprise,' Kalli said, glancing innocently up at him. Smiling then, she went back to watching the presentation, aware that Fabian was fuming beside her because she had obviously been in on the secret and he hadn't.

'So, Vibes . . .' Jenna turned to him now. 'This is for you – from all of us.'

Taking the box, Vibes shook his head. 'I don't know what to say.'

'Don't say anything – just open it!' one of the waitresses yelled.

'Okay, okay!' Laughing, Vibes tore the paper off and opened the box. Seeing the watch, his mouth dropped open and, wide-eyed, he turned to Jenna. 'You shouldn't have done this,' he whispered. 'It's *way* too much.'

'You deserve it,' she whispered back.

Taking the watch out of the box, Vibes turned it over in his hand. Seeing the engraved logo, he shook his head and traced his finger over it.

'To remind you of us,' Jenna said, getting a little choked as she saw the tears in his eyes.

'I could never forget you,' he murmured, looking into her eyes and then glancing quickly away. Then, pulling himself together with an effort, he looked down at the people below and smiled. 'Thanks, y'all. This means the world.'

'For he's a jolly good fellow . . .' Austin start singing in a choked voice, urging the others to join in. 'For he's a jolly good fellow . . .'

A short time later, when he'd said his goodbyes and most of the staff had gone, Vibes brought the last box of albums up to Jenna's office and put it behind the couch with the others.

'All done,' he said, rubbing the dust off his hands. 'Sure it won't be in your way?'

'It's fine,' Jenna assured him. 'Join me for a last drink?' she asked then, holding up a bottle of brandy.

'Love to.' Sitting down on the couch, Vibes leaned his head back and exhaled wearily. 'Man, I'm gonna miss this place.'

'Aw, you'll forget all about us once you're back home with your friends, seeing all the old sights,' Jenna said over her shoulder.

'No, I won't,' Vibes murmured truthfully. 'How could I, with *this* to remind me?' Flipping the box open for the umpteenth time, he gazed at the watch and shook his head. 'You really, really shouldn't have done this. These things cost the earth.'

'Everybody chipped in,' Jenna lied, bringing their drinks back and sitting down. 'And if it's any consolation, I think it's a fake.'

'Hope so,' Vibes chuckled, knowing full well that she was joking. 'I can just see them letting a black guy through Customs with a genuine Rolex without tossing his ass in jail.'

'You're not serious?'

'Nah, just fooling,' Vibes said, grinning as he added, 'You *do* have the receipt, though, right?' Laughing at the look of horror on her face, he said, 'Relax, Princess. It was a joke.'

'Thank God for that,' Jenna said, laughing softly. 'If I'd had to give you the receipt, you'd have known that it only cost two quid.'

'You're crazy, you know that?' Shaking his head, Vibes sipped at his drink. Leaning forward then, he put the glass down on the table and took something out of his pocket. 'Since we're giving gifts,' he said, suddenly nervous, 'I, er, got *you* something, too. It's sort of like a thank-you, 'cos you've been real good to me since you took over.' Handing her a small black velvet box, he said, 'Hope you like it.'

'You didn't have to,' Jenna murmured, gazing down at it with genuine surprise.

'Yeah, well, I wanted to.' Vibes shrugged, hardly daring to look at her.

Opening it, she gasped when she saw the delicate gold necklace with its semiquaver charm made up of tiny diamonds.

'For the lady who always strikes the right note,' Vibes said, his voice low and husky.

'Thank you *so* much,' Jenna murmured tearfully. 'It's beautiful.'

'Let me fasten it for you,' he offered, taking the chain from her trembling hands and looping it around her neck.

Just inches away from each other, their gazes met and, before either of them could stop themselves their lips were locked in a kiss so sweet and tender that Jenna felt as though she were drifting away.

Coming to her senses suddenly, she pulled back and covered her burning cheeks with her hands.

'Oh, God, I'm so sorry. I shouldn't have done that. It was completely out of order.'

'No, it was my fault,' Vibes said, disgusted with himself for taking advantage when he knew that she had a boyfriend. She must think he was a complete slime-ball. 'I'm really sorry.' Then, getting up he said, 'I guess I should go.' Shrugging, he added, 'It's late, and I've got that early start tomorrow.'

Mad at herself, and convinced that Vibes must be, too, Jenna nodded. 'Yeah. You're going to need all the sleep you can get. I know what it's like flying long-haul when you're strung out. It's not good.'

'Tell me about it,' Vibes said, trying desperately to lighten the atmosphere – he couldn't bear to leave her like this.

Taking a deep breath to bring herself under control, Jenna stood up and linked her hands together. 'Right, well . . . I guess this is it, then.'

'Guess so,' Vibes murmured. 'I'll, er, be in touch – about the gear, yeah?'

'Don't worry about it,' Jenna told him, smiling now. 'It's not a problem. Anyway, I hope you'll let us know how you're getting on from time to time? Everybody's going to be asking after you.'

'Course.' Vibes nodded, admiring the way that she'd put them back onto a professional footing. Reaching out on impulse then, he gave her a quick hug and turned abruptly away. 'See you, Princess.'

Sitting down when he'd gone, Jenna closed her eyes and traced a finger over her lips, where she could still feel the softness of his; still taste the sweetness. But, she kept on telling herself, she should never have done it. He belonged to another woman, and this time she didn't even have the excuse that she didn't know: he had never once tried to hide his wedding ring.

Jumping when somebody tapped on the door, she sat up, hoping wildly that it was Vibes, even though she knew how very, very wrong that would be.

It was Kalli.

Her pretty eyes red and swollen, the girl came in and sat down next to Jenna. She gave her a tentative smile. 'Are you all right?'

Exhaling slowly, Jenna nodded. 'Yeah, I'm fine. You?'

'Oh, you know.' Kalli shrugged.

'Drink?'

'Best not,' Kalli murmured. 'Austin's already drunk enough for both of us. I just wanted to make sure you were okay before I took him home.'

Reaching out, Jenna squeezed Kalli's hand. 'Thanks, sweetheart. But really, I'm fine.'

Nodding, Kalli took a tissue out of her pocket and dabbed at her eyes. 'I know we'll all miss him – but you'll miss him the most, won't you?' Looking up then, her gaze was filled with such understanding and compassion that it pierced the wall that Jenna had been building ever since she'd heard that Vibes was leaving.

Jenna lowered her head. 'I won't deny that I like him. But it's wrong, and I've just got to get over it.'

'Why, if he feels the same about you?' Kalli asked softly.

'Oh, don't!' Jenna groaned, swiping at the tears she'd been holding at bay for so long. 'I know you mean well, but I shouldn't be thinking things like this about a married man. It's just not right. And if you knew what I'd . . .' Stopping herself, she shook her head. 'I should know better, that's all.'

Looking at her, Kalli nodded. 'You've got to do what's right for you.'

'Thanks,' Jenna said, taking a deep breath. 'Phew,' she said then, giving a sheepish little laugh. 'It's been quite a night, hasn't it?'

'And then some,' Kalli agreed. 'It was nice, though, wasn't it? I'll never forget the look on his face.'

Touching the necklace, Jenna smiled wistfully. 'Me neither. Anyway, you'd better go,' she said then. 'Austin will be waiting.'

Tutting softly, Kalli rolled her eyes. 'I suppose I'd better get him out before he drinks his way through all the left-overs. You sure you're okay?'

'Absolutely fine. See you tomorrow.'

Glancing at her watch when Kalli had gone, Jenna groaned when she saw that it was almost four a.m. She was so tired, she felt that she could just lie down right here and go to sleep.

Leaping to her feet as soon as she'd thought that, she snatched up her jacket and bag and headed for the door. Her dad had spent every last minute of his life at this place – eating, drinking, sleeping and, eventually, *dying* here. No way was she going down that same road.

Letting herself out, Jenna drove home and went to bed – then lay staring sleeplessly up at the ceiling as the dawn crept slowly in.

Another time, another universe, things might have been different. But, here and now, it was never going to happen, so she had to let go of the longing and concentrate on the real things in her life. And, right now, the club was the only real thing she had.

9

Melody was still in bed when Tony and Eddie went out the next morning. Pretending to be asleep when Tony popped his head round the door to check on her, she waited until she'd heard them leave, then went to the window and eased the edge of the curtain back to make sure that they really were going and not just tricking her. Seeing them climb into a cab down below a couple of minutes later, she watched until it had driven out of the parking lot. Then, taking the last of the coke Fabian had given her, she got dressed and set about searching for her passport and cards.

They hadn't been in his pockets when she'd searched them after he finally fell asleep last night, so Melody figured he must have hidden them somewhere in the suite. Turning the place upside down now, she spent the next few hours searching every drawer, cupboard, corner and shelf. She had even been prepared to risk her expensive acrylic nails by sticking her hand down the back of the couch. But she had been so disgusted when she took the cushions off and saw the caked-in dust and bits of disgusting shrivelled-up foodstuffs edging the gap that she couldn't bring herself to do it. There was no way Tony would have put his hands down there if she couldn't. He hated dirt even more than she did.

Gazing around the room when she'd searched every nook and cranny, she groaned with despair. She had to put it right before Tony got back or he'd know what she'd been doing, but she loathed cleaning almost as much as she loathed him right now. But it had to be done.

Standing by the door, Melody waited until she heard the maid's trolley rattling along the corridor. Nipping out when she heard the maid going into the room next door, she nicked an armful of cleaning sprays and cloths, and a pair of rubber gloves.

Putting the TV on, she flipped it onto Sky's MTV Base channel, and danced her way around the room, singing along to the American R&B songs she'd been missing so badly. Tony liked Sinatra and all that boring old shit, so that was all she ever got to hear these days.

Quite enjoying herself once she got started, she'd worked up a fair sweat by the time Tony and Eddie came back later that evening.

'Fuck's got into you?' Tony asked, gazing around the spotless lounge in amazement.

'I was bored off my skull,' Melody lied, gathering the cleaning equipment together.

'Where did you get that?' Tony asked, suspicious about how she'd managed to buy anything with no money.

'The maid left the trolley outside the door, so I helped myself,' Melody told him, putting it all out of sight in the bathroom. Coming back, she peeled her rubber gloves off and pushed her damp hair away from her flushed face with the back of her hand.

'Shoulda gone down to the gym and built up a sweat down there while you had the chance,' Tony grunted, taking his jacket off and slinging it over the back of the chair. 'You've put on a bit around the middle lately.'

'Thanks a fucking bunch!' she snapped. 'I can't help it if I'm bleeding.'

'Aw, for Christ's sake, do you *have* to?' he groaned, snatching up a bottle of vodka and two glasses and flopping

down on the couch. 'It's bad enough I have to know about
it at all without you shoving it down my throat.'

'Sorry for being a *woman*, I'm sure,' Melody sniped. Then
folding her arms, she raised an accusing eyebrow when he
poured two shots and handed one to Eddie. 'Don't I get
one?'

'No,' Tony said, grinning at her look of outrage. 'You're
taking a shower and getting dressed, 'cos we're taking you
for a spin in the new car.'

'You've got a car?' Melody frowned. 'Why?'

''Cos I'm sick of paying fucking cab fares.'

'But you're not legal to drive it,' she reminded him. 'You
haven't got a licence.'

'You'd be surprised what you can get your hands on if
you know the right people to ask,' Tony told her, smiling
mysteriously. 'Anyway, never mind that. Go get cleaned up,
and be quick about it, 'cos we're going out to eat. Then
we're going to the club.'

'It's a bit old, isn't it?' Melody complained when they set
off in the ancient bronze BMW a short time later. 'Couldn't
you have got something a bit sportier?'

'We ain't in the States now,' Tony reminded her. 'Anyway,
sporty's out, executive's in. And this baby is a classic.'

'Classic what?' she muttered, folding her arms and glaring
out of the window. 'Banger?'

'Quit griping, or I'll kick you out and you can make your
own way back,' Tony warned her.

Snorting softly, Melody thought, *Chance would be a fine
thing.* But there was no point saying anything, because he
didn't mean it. Anyway, it *was* pretty comfortable, she
supposed. And it beat the constant cabs, because at least
now he might take her somewhere other than the club without
moaning about the expense.

London, maybe, so she could see something she recognised. Some*body* she recognised, even. Somebody who might be able to bung her a bit of cash and help her to get out of this hell-hole.

But she'd still need her passport – damn him!

'By the way,' Tony said, twisting around in his seat to look back at her. 'Me and Eddie might take off for a couple of days.'

'Oh?' Melody sat up a little straighter. 'Where?'

'Not sure yet,' he told her evasively. 'But don't worry,' he added, giving her a pointed look. 'I'll be close enough to keep an eye on you – make sure nothing bad happens.'

Sinking back down, Melody sighed. So, he'd be spying on her. Great!

'What am I supposed to do with myself?' she asked sulkily. 'It won't be much fun stuck in the room all day, and you know I don't like going into clubs on my own.'

'You ain't going to the club without me,' he told her, setting her straight from the off. 'Not after them guys hassled you like that.'

'Aw, Tone, that's not fair,' she complained. 'They wouldn't dare go back there – not after what Eddie did to them. Anyway, Gay-Boy will look after me.'

'He didn't do such a great job of it the other night, did he?' Tony reminded her flatly. 'You ain't going – period. Anyway, you'll have to stay put to make sure no one gets at our stuff. And there's plenty to occupy you at the hotel till we get back.'

'What, like, facials and flaming massages?' Melody muttered. 'Yippee!'

Still sulking when they reached the club that night, Melody ignored Tony's friends when they swarmed around him as usual. She hated them all. Especially those who were doing well in the soaps, because every last one of them was shit, and she didn't see why they should be allowed to get on with their stupid little careers when her much bigger, brighter one was in tatters.

Grunting a reluctant hello when Leonard Drake brought his wife over to introduce her, Melody folded her arms and glared at the floor when Avril took the chair beside hers. All she wanted was to get to Fabian, but there was a fat chance of that with Tony watching her. And now she was stuck with Granny Grump.

Greeting Leonard warmly, because he'd decided he could potentially be of use to him, Tony said, 'Hey, everyone, meet my friend, Lenny. Some of y'all probably know him already. He's one of your big-shot politicians.'

Leonard felt like a king when everyone turned to look at him. And no humiliating smirks this time, just interested smiles.

'I know you,' Brenda Thompson said, peering up at him. 'Where from . . . where from . . . ?' She clicked her fingers suddenly. 'That time in Brighton with Tony and Cherie. We all went on to the hotel afterwards and got blitzed on champagne, and everybody ended up in the swimming pool.'

Leonard was about to tell her that she'd attached him to the wrong party, but decided against it. Why burst the first little bubble of recognition he'd had in years?

'Wonderful night,' he lied, taking her hand and kissing it. 'And you're looking just as lovely now as you did then.'

'Oh, you old flatterer.' Brenda laughed huskily.

'And so it begins,' Avril muttered, rolling her eyes and sighing heavily.

'*What?*' Melody said irritably.

'Oh, nothing, dear. Just talking to myself.'

'What's everyone drinking?' Tony asked, looking around for a waiter.

'Champagne,' Brenda said, putting her arms in the air and swaying to the beat of the music. 'More champagne for everybody!'

'I think she's had more than enough already,' Avril murmured under her breath.

Ordering several bottles of champagne, Tony said, 'So, how's it going Lenny?'

'Pretty good,' Leonard said, squeezing past Brenda to sit beside him. 'I'm glad you're here, actually,' he said then, lowering his voice to add, 'I've been thinking about our little discussion last night, and I've got a couple of suggestions.'

'That right?'

Back on their side of the table, Avril said, 'Leonard tells me you're coming for dinner?'

'Mmmm,' Melody murmured, not wanting to get into a conversation.

'I'm looking forward to having you,' Avril went on. 'It'll be such a relief to have some good female company while they *man* talk.' Sighing now, she shook her head. 'You know, I spent *years* listening to Leonard prattle on about politics and high finance, and when he retired I actually thought I'd heard the last of it. Then he met *your* chap, and now he's back on the business buzz like he's never been off it.'

'I know what you mean,' Melody muttered. 'Tony's always yapping on about it.'

Leaning a little closer, Avril whispered, 'You wouldn't mind, but they're so *boring*, don't you think?'

Casting a resentful glance at Tony, Melody thought, *Too right he's boring.*

But Tony hadn't always been like that. In fact, he'd been a lot of fun to start with, always dragging her out to the casinos and nightclubs, and showering her with flowers and gifts. And he'd been proud to show her off to his high-rolling friends back then, too, relishing the look of envy in their eyes as he paraded her around with the fantastic new face and body he'd paid for. But there had been none of that over here. And after that fight, she doubted she'd ever see the fun times again, because he'd made it quite clear that he had no intention of going home any time soon. And there was nothing she could do about it, unless she fancied more of what he'd given her the other night. And she knew enough about him to know that he could do far, far worse than give her a cut lip.

'Is everything all right, dear?' Avril asked her quietly.

Sighing heavily, Melody shrugged. 'Yeah, I'm fine. Time of the month, that's all.'

'Oh, I don't envy you,' Avril murmured. 'Mine have finished now, thank the Lord. Not that *Leonard*'s noticed. But that's okay, because I can still use the old PMT as an excuse for biting his head off if he annoys me. If only more of us knew how to use it to its best advantage, we'd have these buggers whipped in no time, eh?'

Smiling now, Melody actually looked at Avril for the first time. Whether it was the fickleness of Hollywood rubbing off on her, or just her own innate vanity, but women who fell on either side of the sixteen-to-thirty-five threat range were usually invisible to her. But Avril was quite nice-looking for her age – which Melody guessed to be around fifty. Her skin was reasonably smooth, except for a few crow's-feet around the eyes, and a slight sagging of the jawline; her eyes were a lovely purply-grey shade; and her hair was a nice rich auburn, which looked almost natural, Melody thought.

And she was actually talking *to* Melody, not at her or about her, like the rest of the snotty bitches around the table. Jenna was all right, but apart from her, and now Avril, not one woman had actually given Melody the time of day since she'd got here.

Sensing that the girl was scrutinising her, Avril smiled.

They were of a different generation – although maybe not as far removed as their appearances might have anybody believe, because Melody was obviously older than she looked once you saw her up close. But Avril recognised the look of frustration and boredom in the younger woman's eyes, and guessed that she, like Avril, had secret depths of which few were probably aware – least of all the men they had chosen to saddle themselves with.

Leonard was a blustering, self-important man, with not the least understanding of the female psyche. To his mind, women should be exact replicas of his late mother, Ethel, who had been the epitome of the good Conservative wife: never less than perfect in appearance; her food never less than Michelin standard; her home never less than immaculate; her husband never less than the most important man in the world to her. How she had managed to maintain those standards into her eighties and still manage to walk, talk, and breathe fire, Avril did not know, but she was the reason that Avril would be forever lacking as a wife in Leonard's eyes.

And this poor girl's partner was no better, Avril thought, looking at Tony Allen now. He might have a different approach than Leonard, in that he was obviously a lot livelier and far more self-confident, but the controlling edge was undoubtedly there. She could see it in his eyes when he looked at Melody: a dark, watchful sharpness that betrayed his need to know that she was doing only that of which he approved. And Melody's obvious depression, combined with the tarty clothes and make-up, told Avril that she had probably succumbed to his demands. She was the classic fantasy whore: there to satisfy her man's sexual desires, but not expected – or allowed – to have an opinion of her own.

'You girls ready for another drink?' Tony called over just then, breaking into their thoughts.

Smiling politely, Avril said, 'That would be lovely.'

Turning back to Melody then, she muttered, '*Girls*, indeed! My dear, if that man's penis is even *half* the size of his ego, you must surely be the luckiest woman alive.'

Laughing, because it had been so unexpected, Melody said, 'I can't believe you just said that!'

'I haven't always been an old trout,' Avril told her amusedly.

Nudging Leonard as he watched their women chatting, Tony said, 'They seem to have hit it off, huh?'

'They certainly do,' Leonard said quietly, his eyebrows raised with amazement. Avril usually took time to warm to new people, but he would never in his wildest *dreams* have imagined her giving Tony's sluttish girlfriend the time of day. But then, she knew how important his friendship with Tony was to him, so she was probably pushing her distaste aside for his sake.

To be fair, he had to admit that she'd been quite pleasant today. She'd discussed his plans for the dinner party with more enthusiasm that he'd anticipated, and had even suggested that he buy himself a new suit for the occasion, pointing out that his wardrobe needs might have *changed* a little over recent months. Which was rather diplomatic of her, he thought, given that she *could* have just said that he'd let himself get fat, as he knew to his shame that he had. But he was pleased that *she* had suggested it, because he'd been wanting to update his wardrobe since they'd started coming to the club but had resisted for fear of raising her suspicions about his motives.

All in all, Leonard was quite pleased with *every*thing just now. He was beginning to feel like his old self again and, with Tony Allen as a friend, he had no doubt that he would soon be right up at the top of the social tree.

Avril was having a hot flush. 'Phew!' she said, fanning a hand in front of her face. 'That wine is rather strong. I think I'd better go and powder my nose.'

Seeing a chance to escape from Tony's watchful gaze, Melody reached for her handbag. 'I'll come with you.'

'Just going to the little *girls'* room,' Avril told the men as they passed. 'Won't be long.'

Strolling off to the VIP toilets together, Melody's mind went into overdrive, wondering how she could get away from Avril for long enough to find Fabian.

As luck would have it, there was only one free cubicle. Telling Avril to go ahead and take it, Melody waited a second, then tapped on the door.

'The sanitary-towel machine isn't working,' she called through. 'I'm just nipping down to the other toilets. Won't be a minute.'

'I'll wait here for you,' Avril called back. 'I need to touch up my make-up, anyway.'

Hissing a jubilant 'Yes!' under her breath, Melody cracked the main door open and peeped out to make sure that Tony wasn't watching. Slipping out then, she darted down the stairs.

Fabian jumped when Melody ran up behind him and grabbed his arm.

'What are you doing?' he hissed, glancing nervously around for Eddie.

'I haven't got time to chat,' she hissed back, tugging him towards the office door. 'I just need you to give me something.'

'*I* haven't got time, full stop,' he retorted, prising her hand off his arm. 'We're busy, and I need to be on the floor.'

'It'll only take a minute,' Melody persisted. '*Please*, Fabian. I'm desperate.'

'I'm not in the mood for sex,' he told her bluntly. 'Anyway, I've been meaning to talk to you about that, because I think we should quit while we're ahead. It's been great, but it's getting too dangerous. You *do* know you were being followed, don't you?'

'Yes, I know,' she said, frowning now. 'But Tony's busy right now, so stop messing about. Anyway, I don't want sex, I just need some coke.'

'Keep your voice down!' Fabian muttered, taking his keys out. 'Okay, I'll give you some, but this is the last time, Melody – and I mean it. I thought I was going to get my legs broken the other night.'

Peering up at him, Melody's frown deepened. 'Hang on . . . how did *you* know I was being followed?'

'I saw Eddie watching you.'

'Is that why you took off?'

'What did you expect me to do? Wait for you to start mauling me, so Tony would know for sure there was some-thing going on?'

'I do *not* maul you!' Melody retorted indignantly.

'Yeah, whatever.' Unlocking the door, Fabian ushered her quickly through.

Taking his stash out of the safe when they reached his office, he ripped a square of paper off a letter-headed sheet and tipped a little of the coke onto it.

'I need more than that,' Melody told him, taking one of the fifty notes she'd stolen from Tony out of her bra and thrusting it into his hand. 'Just give me the bag.'

Looking from the money to the bag, Fabian frowned. If he gave all the coke he had to her he'd have to go out and score again when they'd closed – which was a ball-ache, *and* dangerous at that time of night. But fifty quid was fifty quid.

'All right,' he agreed, tipping the wrap back into the bag and handing it to her. Taking the money, he slipped it into his pocket and waved her to the door. 'Let's go.'

'Do you have to be so cold?' she asked, giving him a

reproachful look. 'I thought we were friends. And I won't see you for a couple of days, so the least you can do is be civil.'

Sighing, wondering why she was determined to make this difficult, Fabian said, 'Look, I'm not being funny, Melody, but I can't take this. It won't be long before your boyfriend puts two and two together – if he hasn't already.'

'He doesn't know about us,' Melody assured him. 'But, yeah, you're right, he *is* watching me. I think he thinks I'm doing drugs, or something.'

'Oh, great!'

'Don't worry, he doesn't know it's coming from *you*,' she said, slipping the bag into her bra before he got any ideas about taking it back.

'Oh, come on, Melody, you're not exactly discreet, are you?' Fabian retorted. 'You'll probably neck most of that before you go back up to him and make it really bloody obvious that you're off your head. How long before he links it back to me?'

'Will you quit freaking out,' she snapped, annoyed that he was more concerned about saving his own skin than the shit *she* was going through. 'He doesn't suspect you of anything. And, for your information, *no*, I *won't* neck half of this now, because it's got to last until Tony comes back.'

'From where?'

'How the hell should *I* know? You don't seriously think he tells *me* anything, do you? He's the most secretive bastard I've ever met. All I know is, him and Eddie are pissing off for a couple of days and I've got to stay at the hotel like a good little girl. And this –' Melody patted her breast '– is the only thing that's going to keep me sane. So, *sorry* for being such a pain, Fabian, but it's not exactly a barrel of laughs for *me* right now, either.'

'Yeah, I know,' he murmured, running a hand over his

face. 'Sorry, but I'm just really wound up about your boyfriend's goon following you. I was about to leave the country.'

'Leaving me to get mauled by those losers,' Melody reminded him sourly. 'Yeah, well, thanks for that, Fabian, 'cos I was this close to getting raped.' Raising her hand, she pinched her fingertips together. 'They wouldn't have stopped if Eddie hadn't made them. They'd have probably dragged me into the toilets, or waited for me outside, or something.'

'You can't blame me for that,' Fabian said indignantly. 'I had no idea what was going on.'

'Oh, forget it.' She sighed. 'But next time you see me getting followed, do me a favour and tell me, yeah?'

'Sure,' he agreed. Then, '*Now* can we go?'

Nodding, her eyes clouded with disappointment that he could be so dismissive, Melody walked out with her head held high.

Strolling to the downstairs bar as she dashed back up to the VIP toilets, Fabian told Maurice to get him a large brandy. He felt guilty now. The look on Melody's face had got to him. She'd looked so defeated and let down, and he supposed he *had* let her down, because this wasn't all her fault. Under different circumstances, he'd have been delighted to be involved with her, because she was gorgeous, and sexy, and really quite nice once you scraped the Hollywood gloss off. But she was just too dangerous to be around. And *he* was too damn handsome to risk having his face scarred for life over her.

Tony looked at Leonard with a wry smile on his face. Maybe the guy wasn't quite as stupid as he looked, after all. He'd just made a suggestion that was so obvious, Tony didn't know why he hadn't thought of it himself.

'You know what?' he said approvingly. 'That's not such a bad idea.'

'Well, I did a lot of thinking after we spoke last night,' Leonard said, feeling more than a little pleased with himself. 'I was trying to think of anybody I know who might be looking for investors, and Jenna came to my mind. I'm not sure what her status is regarding finances, but it occurred to me that she must have spent rather a lot to overhaul this place, because her father certainly didn't leave it like this. It was a bit of a mess when he had it, actually. But that's by the by. I just thought it might be worth asking her.'

'Well, there's only one way to find out,' Tony said, pushing his chair back when he spotted Jenna making her way to the bar just then. 'Let's go ask her.'

'You want me to come with you?' Leonard said, a little surprised because he'd thought that Tony would want to keep this between himself and Jenna.

'It was your suggestion, so why not?' Tony shrugged. 'Anyway, she doesn't really know me, so she might get a bit nervous about me launching something like this on her. But you're an old friend of her dad, so she's bound to feel safer with you there. Don't mind, do you?'

'I'd be delighted,' Leonard agreed proudly.

Jenna was in no mood for talking. She'd spent the whole day moping about, first at her apartment, where she'd wandered restlessly from room to room, and now here at the club, where she just couldn't seem to escape Vibes's presence.

She'd been thinking about him all day, wondering if he'd got any sleep; if he'd made his flight on time; if he'd got through Customs without being hassled about the watch.

If he felt as guilty as she did about that kiss.

Desperate for the night to finish so that she could go home and escape in her dreams, she'd come up to the bar now to have a quiet drink to see her through the next two torturous hours. But no sooner had she got her glass of wine in her hand than Tony, Leonard, and Eddie came over.

Going with them to an empty booth when they said they had something to discuss with her, Jenna frowned when Tony sat on one side of her and Leonard on the other. And Eddie dragging a chair up to the table so that he was facing her just completed the claustrophobic circle.

Forcing herself to smile politely, she looked from one to the other of them, saying, 'What can I do for you?'

'Remember when I called you?' Tony said, taking the lead. 'Said I needed advice about some business ideas I had going?'

'Friday,' Jenna murmured, remembering it clearly, because that was the same day that Vibes had told her he was leaving.

'Yeah, Friday,' Tony said, frowning because her eyes had clouded over. 'You all right, Jen?'

'Uh?' Snapping her gaze back to him, she nodded. 'Sorry . . . yes, I'm fine. What were you saying?'

'Well, you suggested I talk to Lenny,' Tony continued, watching her carefully. 'And we did have a chat that night, which kind of put me right about a couple of things.'

Cutting in here, oblivious to Jenna's distracted state, Leonard said, 'You see, Tony was having a little difficulty knowing what to do with his money.'

'I want to set something up over here,' Tony jumped back in. 'And I was thinking along the lines of a casino, to start with, but Lenny pointed out that I'd be wasting my time pursuing that, because—'

'Oh, it's an incredibly tough procedure,' Leonard chipped in. 'Terribly difficult.'

'So, *any*way . . .' Tony said, frowning at Leonard to shut him up. 'Then I was thinking along the lines of opening up something like *this* place. As you know, I've had one of my own already back home, so it seems kinda logical to stick to what I know best.'

'Yes, I remember you saying,' Jenna muttered, feeling a little sick from having to twist her head from side to side to look at each of them as they spoke.

'Well, Lenny kind of scotched that for me, as well,' Tony said.

'Because that's equally hard for a man in his position,' Leonard interrupted. '*Sorry*,' he said then, holding up an apologetic hand.

'Anyway, like he said, it seems *that* might be a bit of a problem, too,' Tony went on. 'Me being foreign, and all. But then he suggested I should think about investing in a going concern, instead of trying to set something up from scratch. And I've been mulling it over all night, but I couldn't think where to start, 'cos I don't really know anyone well enough yet to approach them. But then he suggested I talk to you.'

'I don't think there's anything I can tell you that Leonard probably hasn't already,' Jenna said. 'I've already told you that I don't really know very much about the business side of things yet.'

'No, you don't get me,' Tony said, smiling now. 'He meant talk to you *about* you. Well, not *you* personally,' he added quickly, 'but this place.'

'Oh, you mean as in talk to me about investing in the club?'

'Exactly.'

'Well, I'm flattered that you thought of me,' Jenna said, smiling apologetically. 'but I'm not really looking for a partner right now.'

'I'm not suggesting leaping headlong into a fifty-fifty deal, or anything like that,' Tony assured her, sensing that she needed convincing. 'It's just that *I* need something to put my money into, and I'm pretty sure *you* could do with an injection of ready cash. I know you inherited the place, and

Lenny's told me how much work you've done to get it like this, so I figure you must be up to your neck in it with the bank.'

Choosing her words carefully, because she didn't want to offend him, Jenna said, 'That's not something I feel entirely comfortable discussing, actually, Tony. With respect, I like to keep my business private.'

Looking at her, Tony said, 'I understand that, and I wouldn't want you to think I was trying to pressurise you. But will you at least think about it?'

Sighing, Jenna shrugged. 'There doesn't seem much point when I already know the answer.'

Looking at her for a moment, Tony nodded respectfully. 'I appreciate the honesty, but don't rule it out altogether, yeah? If you ever think about taking a partner in the future, you know where I am.'

'Of course,' Jenna said, relieved that he wasn't going to push it. 'I doubt it'll happen, though,' she added, just to be sure that he wouldn't go away thinking it was a done deal. 'And you might not even be here by then, anyway. But if you are, you'll be the first to know.'

'That's good enough for me,' Tony said, smiling again. 'Me and Lenny will put our heads together and come up with something else in the meantime. Right, Len?'

'Absolutely,' Leonard agreed, feeling as if he'd let Tony down somehow. 'Anything I can do – you know that.'

'Well, good luck with that,' Jenna said, standing up. 'And I'm always willing to talk if you ever want to discuss anything – not that I'll be much use to you. But, if you'll excuse me, I think I'd better get back to work.'

'Take it easy,' Tony said.

Having got up to let Jenna out, Leonard sat back down and sighed heavily. 'Sorry about that. It probably wasn't one of my better suggestions.'

'Hey, don't knock yourself,' Tony told him. 'It was a good idea. Anyway, who knows . . . she might still go for it at some point.'

'Yes, but what are you going to do now?'

Winking at him, Tony said, 'Don't you worry about me, Lenny. Something will come up. And you've been a great help already.'

'I tried,' Leonard murmured dejectedly, wishing there was something more that he could do.

Sitting back, Tony sipped at his drink, narrow-eyed as his mind ticked over new possibilities. He liked the idea of hooking up with Jenna, but that wasn't going to happen for a while, if at all. But Leonard was a different matter. Tony had a feeling he'd be a pushover if he was handled right, and he sure had the necessary qualities to make him useful: came from a moneyed background; owned a mansion; had been something of a name in politics. But, best of all, Leonard was so desperate to *be* somebody that he'd probably agree to just about anything Tony asked now if it meant being allowed to bask in his limelight.

'You know, you've surprised me,' he said, switching the charm on and looking at Leonard with respect. 'First time I met you, I thought you were a bit flaky.'

'Flaky?' Leonard repeated, wondering if that were good or bad.

'Yeah, you know, sort of out there,' Tony elaborated, leaving Leonard none the wiser. 'But you're a pretty astute guy when you get right down to it, aren't you? Real keen business sense.'

Flattered, Leonard gave a modest shrug. 'Well, I do all right, I suppose.'

'Better than all right from what I've heard,' Tony said. 'I mean, politics is a tough business, what with all the corruption you hear about. But to come out the other end as straight as you, that takes something extra. I really admire you for that.'

'Well, it's not easy,' Leonard admitted. 'I've already told you how much – shall we say – *underhanded* stuff goes on in government. So, yes, it is rare to come out untarnished.'

'Takes special smarts, if you ask me,' Tony said, tapping a finger on his temple. Taking his cigars out then, he offered one to Leonard. 'Which kinda makes me wonder,' he went on, lighting his own and holding the flame out to Leonard, 'why you retired so young. I mean, look at all that experience, all that nous, *wasted*. And you're only, what – forty-four, forty-five?'

'Well, actually, I'm a little closer to fifty,' Leonard admitted, puffing the cigar to life.

'Sure don't look it,' Tony told him. 'But, whatever, I'd still say you was too young to be putting yourself out to graze like that. Don't you reckon, Ed?'

Nodding, Eddie smiled. 'I reckon.'

Taken aback as much by the smile as by the fact that it was the first time he'd ever heard Eddie speak, Leonard blinked rapidly.

'Know what I think your problem is?' Tony gazed at him thoughtfully. 'I don't think you've ever let yourself be who you really are. Am I right?'

Dropping his gaze, Leonard reached for his glass as the heat rose to his cheeks. 'I, um, don't really know what you mean.'

'Sure you do,' Tony said, his voice soft and low. 'See, I knew what you was from the off.'

Leonard's hand was trembling now. *Please, God, no . . .*

'But I think other people misunderstand you,' Tony went on, in full schmooze mode now. 'They see the politician, and assume you're the same as all the rest. But you're not the same, are you, Lenny? You're decent, and honest, and generous enough to spare a stranger like me the benefit of your knowledge.'

Still shaking, Leonard glanced up. He'd been so sure that Tony was going to mention the 'Q' word again, and he didn't think he could have coped with an outright confrontation.

'Hey, see what a good guy this is?' Tony said, turning to Eddie and shaking his head incredulously. 'Give him a fucking compliment, and he gets all choked. Now, that's a *real* man.'

'Sure is,' Eddie agreed, playing along. He didn't know quite where this was headed yet, but if he knew Tony – and he did, better than anyone – he was setting the guy up for some kind of sting.

'Yep,' Tony murmured, sighing now. 'Just a shame you're retired, 'cos I reckon we could kick some serious ass if we put our heads together. But you've still done something good for me tonight, Lenny.'

'I have?'

'Oh, yeah.' Reaching for his drink, Tony nodded. 'See, I've been walking around with this million-dollar bank draft in my pocket, thinking I was never gonna find a genuinely honest person to entrust it to. But you've shown me that the good guys do exist, so now I just gotta relax and wait for the right one to come along.'

Peering at him, Leonard frowned. 'You've got a *million-dollar* banker's draft?'

'That what you guys call it, huh?' Reaching into his pocket, Tony showed it to him. Shrugging, he put it back. 'Not that it's any use at the moment, mind.'

'With respect,' Leonard said worriedly, 'I really don't think you should be carrying it around like that.'

'Sure as hell can't leave it at the hotel.'

'Wouldn't it be safer in the bank?'

'How?' Tony looked him in the eye. 'Do you know how

much shit someone like me has to go through to open an account over here? I tried, but they want all kinds of paperwork that I haven't got. And I can't even use my old US one no more, 'cos I emptied it out to get this draft, thinking I'd easy find something to invest it in over here.'

'There must be something you can do,' Leonard murmured. 'I had no idea you were talking about that kind of money. Why don't I speak to my son?'

'No point,' Tony said, finishing his drink. 'Without the paperwork to prove that these are legitimate funds from selling my club, no one will touch it.'

'Can't you contact whoever bought your club and get duplicates of the contracts?' Leonard suggested helpfully.

Laughing softly, Tony shook his head. 'That ain't the way things work in my neck of the woods, Lenny. See, it turns out the guy I sold it to wasn't quite as honest as you and me, and he only wanted it to pull some kind of insurance scam. Couple of weeks after he takes it off my hands, *poof*! Biggest fire *I* ever seen.' Sighing now, he flapped his hands in a what-can-you-do gesture. 'No contracts, no records, no nothing left to prove it was ever even there – or that *I* ever had anything to do with it when it was.'

'My God,' Leonard muttered. 'How awful.'

'So you can see my predicament,' Tony said. 'Not one of your fine banks will touch me – and I can't say I blame 'em.'

'There's got to be a way around this.' Leonard frowned. 'A banker's draft isn't like a cheque. It's as good as having the physical money in your hand.'

'Yeah, well, soon as I find someone to invest it with who's willing to put it in their account till I'm sorted, I'll be rolling,' Tony said. 'Till then, it's just gonna have to stay right where it is.'

'That might not be so easy,' Leonard pointed out. 'You see, whoever takes it off your hands is going to have to prove where *they* got it from to be able to deposit it, and if no physical asset to that value had changed hands, or service been done to justify it, the bank would likely query it, which would lead them straight back to you.'

Looking at him, Tony's eyebrows knitted together. 'You got to be kidding me?'

'I'm afraid not,' Leonard said sympathetically. 'You see, there would still be the burden of proof, and I can't imagine any legitimate businessman being willing to risk his own finances being investigated. A corrupt one might, but you don't want to be involved with that kind of person, do you?'

'No, I don't,' Tony muttered running a hand through his hair. 'Oh, man, that's a downer. What the hell am I supposed to do now?'

'I really don't know,' Leonard said, feeling guilty for having burst Tony's bubble. 'But let me have a think about it, because I've plenty of colleagues with experience of this kind of thing. *Some*body ought to have a suggestion.'

'Hey, no offence, but I don't want no one knowing my business,' Tony said quickly, his voice ringing with disappointment. '*You* I trust, but I wouldn't trust no one else with that kind of information.'

'Oh, God, no, I wouldn't dream of telling anybody,' Leonard assured him. 'But leave it with me. I'll do whatever I can.'

Glancing at Eddie, Tony gave him a sly half-smile. The big fat worm was wriggling nicely onto the hook. Now all they had to do was wait for him to bite himself in the ass, and they would be part-way to a solution.

In his lounge later that night, when they had got home from the club and Avril had gone to her bed, Leonard sat on the couch with a glass of Scotch in his hand, his mind working overtime. He really wanted to help Tony out; not only because they were friends, but because Tony had done something for him tonight that money couldn't buy: he'd given him back his self-respect.

Leonard had never admitted his real reasons for taking early retirement. But it hadn't been for the sake of enjoying his last years without the pressures of politics, nor to spend more time with the family, to potter about in the garden, nor play golf, nor any of the other recreational excuses that many of the older guard had used upon standing down. It had been to escape the indignity of being shuffled further back into the political wastelands and the humiliation of knowing that the youngsters who were infiltrating the party had no clue who he was. He had not wanted to suffer the injustice of having to kowtow to the snot-nosed bastards as they rose through the ranks, nor had he looked forward to the indignity of having to ignore the condescending smirks and disrespectful remarks they made behind his back.

He hadn't *wanted* to retire: he'd been forced to. And, in taking that step, he thought that he had killed off every last shred of hope of ever regaining his place in the public eye. But then he'd met Tony Allen, a man who had everything that Leonard craved: power, presence, and a firm foothold with the rich and famous.

With Tony's help, Leonard had tonight found himself welcomed into the celebrity circle that he'd spent years trying to break into. His early moments in the press and on TV as a political poster boy and spokesman had given him a taste for it, but he'd only ever managed to achieve local renown – and that hadn't been nearly enough. He'd wanted the general public to recognise him, and for the stars to think of his name when they organised their parties. And now that he'd finally got a foot in the door he was determined to stay there. But, for now, he was just visiting that world as Tony's guest, and if Tony tired of him before he'd made his own mark there he had no doubt that he'd find himself cast out again in a heartbeat. So he needed to do something to guarantee that Tony would continue to want him around, and helping him out with his problem seemed the best bet. But how?

A light switched on in his head when his gaze came to rest on the Matisse hanging over the fireplace: the huge ugly old oil painting that his father had bought as an investment, and which his mother had liked so much that she'd made Leonard promise to let it hang there for all time – despite knowing how much he hated it.

My God, that's it! he thought, sitting bolt upright in his seat.

Getting up far more quickly than a man of his size should have been able to, Leonard went to the door and checked that Avril wasn't moving about. Closing it quietly when he heard nothing, he rushed back to the couch and reached for the phone. He knew it was late but he was sure Tony wouldn't mind.

'I think I've got the answer,' he said when Tony answered. 'Remember we were talking about you finding somebody to deposit your money for you? Well, how about me?'

'You?' Tony replied cautiously. 'I don't know, Lenny. I thought you said it'd be too difficult – that the bank would still come back to me.'

'Not necessarily,' Leonard went on excitedly. 'You see, it occurred to me that *I* could *earn* that money – if, for example, I decided to sell one of my assets.'

'What, so you want me to buy something off of you?'

'No, no. I wouldn't actually have to sell anything, I could just *say* I had. You see, I have a number of rather valuable paintings in my possession, which the bank knows about because of the insurance. Now, if I were to produce a sales receipt for some of these, the bank would have no reason to

doubt its legitimacy, because it's an entirely feasible trans-
action. Then I could deposit your banker's draft as
"payment", and when you've managed to open your own
account I can simply transfer it.'

'But wouldn't they want to know why you were giving me
the money back if I'd bought the paintings?'

'Yes, but I would claim that I had received the payment
in advance, and that the overseas buyer – *yourself* – had asked
me to hold on to them until they were able to collect, which
would explain my need to retain the insurance cover. Then
I would simply claim to have changed my mind before the
handover, and transfer the money as a refund.'

'But I'm not really buying them?' Tony asked.

'No, but the bank would *think* you were,' Leonard said
patiently. 'So when I transfer the money all they'll need to
know is that I'm repaying the person who paid me in the
first place. Which would work out perfectly for you,' he
added, 'because *you* would have the original receipt to show
to *your* bank, proving that you had legitimately owned the
asset that you were now, in effect, selling. Do you see?'

'I think I do,' Tony said, chuckling softly. 'Man, I gotta
say that's some kind of genius. You got it all covered, don't
you?'

'It just seemed so logical,' Leonard replied modestly. 'My
father was always buying and selling, so there's a family
history of major financial transactions such as this. And no
earthly reason, therefore, why it should raise any eyebrows
if *I* were to take up the tradition.'

'Well, I'm choked that you'd offer to do that for me,' Tony
said sincerely. 'And it *would* solve my problem.' Pausing
then, as if something were troubling him, he said, 'But, you
know what, Lenny? I'm gonna suggest we sit on it for now,
'cos it's a huge risk.'

'It's no risk to me,' Leonard assured him, touched that

Tony was being so considerate in light of how difficult his own situation was. 'I'd still have my paintings, so I've nothing to lose. You're the one who'd be taking a leap of faith by handing your money over.'

'Hey, if there's one thing that ain't in question, it's your honesty,' Tony said without hesitation. 'But I still want you to have a good think about it, 'cos I don't want you committing yourself and then regretting it. If you want to go ahead after that, great. But if not, I'd totally understand.'

Leonard knew that he *would* go ahead, because there was simply no reason not to. But Tony was right to insist on him making an informed decision. Who in their right mind would want to hand over a million dollars to a foolhardy idiot who jumped headlong into things without thought?

'Okay,' Leonard said. 'I'll talk to you again when I've thought it through some more. But could I ask you to keep this quiet?' he asked then, almost whispering now. 'You see, I don't want Avril to get wind of it. I, um, have a separate account, you see, which she knows nothing about.'

Smiling slyly at his end, Tony said, 'She'll never hear a thing from me, Lenny, you got my word on that. And if it makes you feel any better, I won't even tell Melody. It'll be just you, me, and Eddie. Agreed?'

'Agreed,' Leonard said, sighing with relief. The last thing he wanted was for Avril to find out. Not that it should, but if, God forbid, anything *were* to happen between depositing the money and repaying it, she would not only strip the flesh from his body as far as his house and assets were concerned, she would suck the marrow right out of his bones, too. And Tony's money would be bound to get caught in the crossfire.

Back at the hotel, Tony put the phone down and relayed the conversation to Eddie with a grin on his face.

'Sure we can trust him?' Eddie asked, reaching for the vodka bottle to refill their glasses. 'It's a lot of dough to risk on a stranger.'

'Yeah, well, we can't do nothing with it if we don't,' Tony pointed out. 'Anyway, he ain't gonna fuck us about. He's got too much to lose. He messes up, we take him and his lovely wife to pieces. Then we'll go and take what's ours, 'cos there's gonna be a set of million-pound paintings sitting there with my name on 'em.'

'Yeah, but he wants to transfer the money to your account after it's sorted, and you can't get one,' Eddie reminded him.

'Not yet,' Tony conceded. 'But I'm sure the fat boy will be happy to hold on to it until we can.'

'You reckon?' Eddie asked doubtfully. 'Sounds to me like he's only willing to do it because he thinks it's a short-term deal. Can't see him wanting to drag it out too long, or he's gonna start getting jumpy about his paintings.'

'Leave him to me,' Tony said, chuckling softly. 'I'm gonna have him licking the shit off of my shoes before too long – you watch.' Raising his glass now, he said, 'Nearly there, Ed.'

Raising his own glass, Eddie sipped at his drink, frowning thoughtfully. Leonard Drake might well be sincere, but there were too many potential holes in the plan for it to run as smoothly as he and Tony seemed to think it would.

Leonard's wife, for starters.

Eddie was a people-watcher, and Avril Drake had something about her that told him she wasn't the dumb little wife she made herself out to be. There was a keenness in her eyes that a lot of broads didn't have and, like Eddie himself, she listened – hard – and was smart enough to keep her own mouth shut while she was taking everything in. And that was a rare and dangerous quality in a woman, because ladies like that were so unobtrusive it was easy to forget they were there, and before you knew it they had a shit-load of information on you that you didn't even realise you'd given away – and they had sussed out exactly how to use it against you.

Tony would be wise to keep Melody well away from her, in Eddie's opinion. Melody wasn't stupid by any means, but she was a damn sight more stupid than Avril Drake, and if Avril wanted to get something out of her, Eddie had no doubt that she'd soon know everything that Melody knew. And, unlike Melody, who had swallowed Tony's story without question, Avril would probably rip it to pieces and then spend as long as it took putting it all back together until she had the complete picture.

Still, Leonard must know what she was like or he wouldn't have asked Tony to keep her in the dark about their plan to deposit the money in his account. So as long as Melody never got to know the real facts about their situation, they shouldn't be in too much danger. But Eddie would be watching them both closely, nonetheless.

10

Tony was still sleeping when Melody woke up the next morning. Easing the quilt back, she got up and pulled her dressing gown on, then tiptoed into the bathroom to take a shower. She felt quite light-hearted for a change. She'd accepted that she couldn't escape – yet – but she was looking forward to having a bit of time to herself while Tony was away. Two whole nights of not having to wait in dread anticipation of him returning from wherever he and Eddie kept disappearing to, a brief respite from the nightmare prospect of him coming back into the room and climbing on top of her. Bliss!

She'd taken to pretending to be asleep when he came in. Sometimes she actually *was,* but that didn't stop him. Asleep, awake, unconscious – he didn't care. She could be *dead,* and he'd probably still go for it if he was horny enough.

Coming back to the bedroom with a towel wrapped around her hair a short time later, Melody quietly opened the dresser drawers and lifted her clothes out onto the floor.

'What you doing?' Tony asked, waking up just then and eyeing her with suspicion as she rooted through the pile. 'I thought I said you wasn't coming with us.'

'Don't panic, I'm only looking for this,' Melody said, finding the Lycra exercise suit she wanted and pulling it out. 'Think it'll still fit?' she asked, holding it up against herself.

'Not with the weight you've been putting on,' he grunted, reaching for a cigarette.

'Which is exactly why I'm going down to the gym,' she retorted, wishing he'd drop dead. Snatching up the other clothes, she stuffed them back into the drawer. 'Got to do *some*thing to amuse myself while I'm under house arrest.'

'Don't get smart,' Tony warned her, pushing the quilt back.

Pulling a face at his hairy back when he strolled naked into the bathroom, Melody stuck two fingers up when he kicked the door shut. He said *she*'d put on weight, but he should take a look in the mirror sometime, because those bulges were more like industrial cargo carriers than love handles. No wonder her bones were aching, having to bear *that* pounding her into the mattress night after night.

Three long years she'd been tolerating it, telling herself that it was worth it for the money, the presents, and the surgery he'd paid for to help her achieve her acting aims. But it was getting harder and harder to stomach now that she'd tasted Fabian's forbidden fruits. Not that she *loved* Fabian, or anything ridiculous like that, but he was a hell of a good-looking man, with such a different approach to fucking than Tony's rodeo saddle-up-and-ride-'em-hard style. Tony seemed to think that orgasms were a man's right, and women should be grateful if they chanced upon one along the way. But Fabian was the exact opposite, priding himself on his abilities to bring pleasure.

And boy, *had* he!

Melody had fucked a lot of men in her time, but none had ever come close to hitting the spot as often as Fabian did. They'd only had snatched moments together since their fling had started, but he had never failed to satisfy her, and she would miss that now that he'd called it off.

Not quite as much as she would miss the coke, though. But that was just tough, because she was in no position to start heavying him about it. Not now that Tony was on her case – and definitely not now she knew that Eddie had been following her. If Tony suspected her of something, it really wouldn't be wise to stir him up about another man. Better to say and do nothing, and let whatever was going on in his head die down – and use the time between to think up ways to escape.

Coming out of the bathroom in his dressing gown just then, Tony picked up the phone and called room service to order breakfast for three. Then he called Eddie's room and told him to come down.

'Your mobile's ringing,' Melody told him, reaching for it. Looking at the screen she frowned. 'How come you never have no names come up like normal people?'

Snatching it off her, Tony said, 'And how come you never mind your own business, like normal people?'

Walking into the lounge, he pulled the door firmly shut behind him and answered the call.

'Yo?'

'I was about to give up on you,' Ronson said.

'Yeah. Well, I'm here now,' Tony grunted. 'What's up?'

'I'm just watching the news. One of the brothers is out.'

'Out?' Tony repeated, lighting another cigarette and sucking on it hard.

'Of the picture,' Ronson elaborated darkly. 'Seems they got to him in the armoured truck on the way to some military base where they were going to hold him till the trial. Guard's a straight-A medal plate for thirty-odd years, then he goes and switches sides. Takes out Johnson and the other guards, then gets himself snipered getting out of the truck, so he don't even get to pick up his dough. Go figure, huh?'

'But they still got the others?' Tony asked. 'They could still make it to court?'

'What's the chance of that?' Ronson snorted. 'Word is, they've changed the plan and decided to chopper the others to some other high-tech nuclear bunker now. But for Zorba's guys that just narrows down where to start looking, don't it? Anyway, I'm keeping the news on 24-7, so I'll keep you updated.'

'Thanks,' Tony muttered.

'No problem,' Ronson said. Then, 'So, how's it going in sunny Rio? Carnival started yet?'

'Nah, not yet, but I'll send you a ticket as soon as, so you can come over and join in.'

'They still got the bare-ass parades?'

'Sure have,' Tony lied. 'I can see the main street from the hotel, so I'm getting a bird's-eye of the *un*dress rehearsals when the floats go past.'

'Lucky bastard,' Ronson chuckled. 'I've all but forgot what a pussy looks like since that bitch dropped the fucking syph bomb on me.'

'Didn't think a little thing like that would stop you fucking your way round the world?'

'It wouldn't have. But I only went and passed it on to a freaking *cop*, didn't I? Bitch threatened to bust my ass for attempted fucking murder if I "knowingly" gave it to anyone else before I got myself clean. Only reason she didn't report me straight out is 'cos she'd have had to admit she spends her free time trawling the bars picking up lowlifes.'

'Like you, huh?' Tony chuckled.

'Hey, I'm no lowlife, I'm just smart enough to choose the bars where easy pickings like her hang out,' Ronson countered. 'I mean, come on, man, what's the point in going upmarket when them bitches expect you to take 'em out to a fucking fancy restaurant before they'll open their legs. I ain't paying for no bitch to get fat.'

'Better than paying for syph shots,' Tony pointed out.

'True,' Ronson said, sighing. Then, 'Anyway, subject of whores, any sign of Melody yet?'

'No, there ain't,' Tony snarled. 'But don't worry. I ever get to Australia, I'm gonna track the bitch down and take her out.'

'You do that,' Ronson said nastily. 'And make sure you give it to the pilot she took off with, an' all.'

'Don't worry,' Tony grunted. 'I ever see him again, he's a dead man.'

'Too right,' Ronson agreed. 'And you want to get yourself checked out for the clap while you're at it. You never know what the cunt was up to before she shafted you like that. Don't be leaving it too late like me.'

'I hear you,' Tony said, glancing at his watch now. He needed to cut the call. If Zorba had already got to a top-notch guard, he could certainly find out where Tony's phone signal was coming from. 'Anyway, look, man, I gotta hit it. Let me know as and when anything happens, yeah?'

'Will do. Keep it cool, Tee.'

'You, too.'

Disconnecting, Tony smoked the rest of his cigarette and mulled over this new information.

Zorba's people were obviously pulling out all the stops to get his case dusted. Tony had to get his shit sorted, because they would come after him with everything they had soon as Zorba was free. He was all right for now, because Ronson was the only person he had any contact with back home – and *he* thought they were in Brazil, so that was all he'd ever be able to tell anyone, even if they tortured him. And he thought Melody had left him and taken off with a pilot to Australia, so nobody would put him together with her now.

Still, now that Leonard was hooked the bank draft wouldn't be a problem; and he and Eddie had the car, so it wouldn't take long to change the rest of the money over. It would just be a matter of utilising it after that without Tony's name being attached to it. And he knew exactly how to do that.

Stubbing the cigarette butt out, Tony got up and went to get dressed.

Kissing Tony goodbye when he and Eddie left a short time after breakfast, Melody made her way down to the hotel's state-of-the-art gym with a spring in her step. Despite his snipes about her weight, she knew how hot she looked in her Lycra get-up, and was quite looking forward to the envious glances of the women who congregated there in the mornings to gossip as they wobbled their bingo wings and created earthquakes with their thighs on the treadmills and exercise bikes.

Strolling in with her shoulders back and her chest out now, she smiled to herself when the pudding club's chatter turned to an immediate low hum as they turned their surreptitious attentions to her. Putting her bag down beside a free tread-mill, she tied her hair up, aware that the bitches were eyeing her every move. Doing some sexy warm-up stretches then, as if she hadn't noticed them, she got onto the treadmill and programmed herself a two-mile jog. She'd just set off when the door opened and Chase Mann walked in.

The low hum turned to an excited buzz as the women recognised him. Walking past them as if they weren't even there, Chase came to a stop at the weights machine next to Melody. Noticing her, he gave her one of his famously sexy smiles and put his bag down. Then, taking off his jogging pants and leaving just a pair of shorts to showcase his great thighs, he put a foot up on a chair to tie his trainer laces. Frowning questioningly, he glanced back up at Melody.

'Hi,' she said coolly, breathing easy as she got into her stride. She still hadn't forgiven him for ignoring her at the club.

'Hi,' he said, still frowning. 'Sorry, but don't I know you?'

'I don't know,' she replied, not bothering to look at him. 'Do you?'

Unused to women being anything less than on the point of fainting if he spoke to them these days, Chase was intrigued. Either she was using the old I'm-not-interested trick to try and hook him and drag him in, or she genuinely didn't recognise him – and how likely was *that*? Every bird in the UK, Europe, the States and Japan recognised him by now.

Putting him out of his misery – because he was obviously having a hard time coming to terms with not being instantly adored – Melody said, 'We met at Zenith.'

'Zenith?' Chase frowned again.

'Nightclub, New Year's Eve,' Melody helped him out. 'I was with my boyfriend, you had three tarts hanging off your wallet.'

'Ah,' Chase murmured sheepishly. 'The blonde bomb-shells.'

'More like bomb*sites*,' Melody muttered scathingly.

'Probably right,' Chase agreed, with another sheepish smile. 'I think I was a bit the worse for wear that night.'

'And the next,' Melody reminded him. '*And* the next, come to that.'

'Yeah, well, I was getting myself geared up for the German tour,' he said, quite enjoying the novelty of not being fawned over for a change.

'Is that where you've been?' she said, starting to glow now with the running. 'Thought I hadn't seen you around for a while.'

'Oh, so you noticed, did you?' Chase asked, grinning now.

'Yeah, but only 'cos me and my boyfriend used to put bets on how many women we'd see getting out of the penthouse lift in the mornings. I think your record was five.'

'Not all mine,' Chase told her quickly. 'That was a party.'

'Weren't they all?'

'So, this fella of yours,' Chase said, sitting down on the weights bench now and reaching for the bars. 'Have I met him?'

'Everyone in Manchester has probably met him by now,' Melody replied, with just a hint of sarcasm in her voice. 'His name's Tony Allen.'

'Ah.' Chase remembered. 'American. Big minder.'

'That's the one.'

'Right, yeah.' Glancing around now, mock-scared, he said, 'Hey, he's not watching us now, is he? Only I don't want him thinking I'm chatting you up or anything.'

'If he was here, you'd be talking to him, not to me,' Melody said, coming to the end of her jog and punching an extra mile onto the clock at speed-walking pace. 'You were certainly more interested in him last time we met.'

'Can't remember, I'm afraid,' Chase admitted. 'But if I was rude, I'm sorry. I was a bit wasted. That's why I'm here now, actually. Under orders to get my shit together.'

'Orders from who?'

'Record company.' Chase rolled his eyes. 'They're on my case. Reckon I single-handedly fucked up the tour.'

'And did you?' Melody asked, watching his muscles tighten with his exertions.

'Nah, I just got bored,' he said. 'Sick of doing the same old songs over and over, hearing the same old shit guitar riffs, and them drums pounding in my head. So I left the band to it a couple of times and got off for a spliff. But they reckoned I should have waited till the set was finished and not walked off stage halfway through a song.'

'Yeah, but that's your job,' she pointed out logically. 'If you stop putting your heart into it, your fans will find someone else to spend their money on, won't they?'

'Oasis have been getting away with it for years,' he countered. 'And I sell as many records as them, easy.'

'If you say so,' Melody said, switching the machine off and reaching for her towel.

'Don't you believe me?' Chase asked, letting the weights

go and standing up, reluctant to end the conversation. 'I've got platinum discs all over the place. My last album went triple, here *and* in the States.'

'Oh, I know you're big,' Melody said, her eyes sliding surreptitiously to his shorts as she patted the sweat from her neck. 'But you know what they say: the higher you are, the further you fall. Why risk everything you've worked for for a spliff? If I was you, I'd be working my backside off to stay up there.'

'I suppose,' he murmured glumly. 'It's just really hard to keep at it when you've got no choice.'

'Take it from me, it's a damn sight better than not being able to do it at all.'

'That the voice of experience?'

'Mmm,' Melody murmured, not really wanting to talk about it, because it was still too raw and she just might end up screaming.

'So, you're a singer, too, are you?' Chase persisted.

'Actress,' she told him, putting her towel back into the bag. 'Hollywood stuff. You probably won't have seen them if you've been working.'

'I watch shed-loads of DVDs on the tour bus,' Chase said, realising that she was about to leave and wanting to delay her. 'Tell me what you've been in – I might have seen it.'

'Okay,' Melody said, smiling now, because she always got a buzz talking about her films. 'I did *Help Wanted* with Sandra Bullock last year, and *Gentle Rain* with George Clooney a few months ago.'

'Seen the first one,' Chase told her. Then, smiling sheepishly, 'Don't remember seeing you in it, though. Which part did you play?'

'Sandra's room-mate.'

'No way!' Drawing his head back, Chase looked at her hard. 'She was really plain.'

'Er, that's why they call it *acting*,' Melody said, delighted that he'd obviously been telling the truth and had seen it.

'Christ, you were good,' he said admiringly. 'I mean, *I* thought you were, anyway, the way you and Sandra bounced off each other. And when you had to team up and go undercover as hookers to get in with the bad guys, you were so kind of . . .' Pausing, he shrugged. 'Realistic, I suppose. But now I'm seeing you in the flesh, I'm realising how good you *really* were. To make anyone believe you're that plain and frumpy when you're actually . . . well, pretty hot, I guess.'

'Yeah, well, I thought I was pretty good,' Melody said, sighing now because it was bringing up memories that she didn't want to be thinking about right now.

'So, what's next?'

Shaking her head, Melody said, 'Nothing. I'm taking a break at the moment.' Shrugging then, she added, 'Knowing my luck, nobody will want me by the time I get back, anyway.'

'You've got to be kidding,' Chase said sincerely. 'I mean, I know I didn't recognise you, and probably still wouldn't if you hadn't told me who you were in the film. But you've got talent. Why wouldn't they want to use you again?'

Oh, let's see, Melody thought bitterly. *Maybe because they've got a clone going by the name of Deanna Shelby to keep them occupied. And she hasn't got a control-freak man forcing her out of the limelight.*

Anyway, nobody ever *did* recognise her, so she might as well stop kidding herself. The Sandra Bullock film had come up before her biggest bout of surgery, so it hadn't been as hard as Chase imagined for her to act the part of a plain girl. And she'd been in a black wig for the whole of the Clooney film, so even though she'd had the tits and lips by then, still nobody would know it was her unless she darkened her hair. In taking on character roles, she'd missed her chance to be known as herself. The Julia Roberts film would have given her that, and she'd have been right up there with the best after it hit the screens. But that was gone now, so she might as well give up dreaming about it.

'I, um, don't suppose you'd fancy having lunch with me, would you?' Chase asked her suddenly. 'Only I haven't had a decent chat in weeks. Not one that doesn't include the words "fuck-up" and "or else", anyway.'

Looking at him, Melody thought, *Why not?* Tony wasn't here to stop her, and nobody at the hotel could think enough of it to go running to him with stories when he got back. They'd be just two guests having a chat over lunch. And it would be nice to talk to someone who appreciated her for her abilities, instead of putting her down or mocking her.

'Yeah, okay,' she said, picking up her things. 'Just let me go take a shower and get dressed.'

'Meet you in the lobby. Half an hour all right?'

'That's fine.' Smiling, Melody left, blatantly ignoring the envious gazes of the fat women.

Lunch gave Chase and Melody a chance to air their grievances against the people who they saw as screwing up their lives. Melody stopped short of telling him the whole truth of her situation, just in case it ever got back to Tony, but she felt better for having a good old general moan. And Chase felt better that somebody had actually listened to his gripes about touring without telling him to pull himself together. Although Melody did manage to persuade him that he must still have a love for his music buried inside him somewhere, and that he should stop seeing it as something he was doing for everyone else and start doing it for himself again.

Taking their conversation up to the penthouse suite, they wasted the afternoon lying on the huge circular bed, getting stoned and giggling at their reflections in the overhead mirror as Chase's albums played on a loop over the built-in speakers.

'I think I'm a convert,' Melody told him when the first album came around again. 'I'm an R'n'B girl usually, but I could really go for some of this stuff. Not the really rocky ones, 'cos they're just noise, but definitely the ballads. You've got a lovely voice.'

Thanking her, Chase leaned up on his elbow and peered down into her eyes, which were sexily half-closed. 'You've got a lovely voice, too,' he said. 'And a lovely face.' He stroked a finger down her cheek. 'And a lovely body.' He let the finger continue on down to her breasts.

'And you've got a lovely dick,' Melody giggled, not trying to stop him.

'How do you know?' he asked.

'I was looking at it when you were doing the weights. You really should wear underpants if you're going to sit with your legs apart, you know.'

'Yeah, and you should wear a bra when you're running on the treadmill,' Chase said, smiling seductively. 'Those nipples send out "come and get me" signals.'

'So what are you waiting for?' Melody murmured, peering up at him with a challenge in her eyes.

'The right time,' Chase said softly. 'I've had too many meaningless fucks in this bed. I want this time to be different.' Pausing now, he bit his lip. 'How do you feel about coke?'

'With my brandy?' Melody asked, knowing exactly what he was getting at. 'Yeah, great.'

'No, with a *straw*,' he said, rolling across to the bedside table and reaching into the drawer for his stash.

Looking at the glistening white heap he tipped onto the mirror, and at the gold purpose-made snorting straw, Melody licked her lips. 'My, my, you *do* know how to keep a lady happy, don't you, Mr Mann?'

I I

Jenna was not in a good mood when Friday came around. Ever since she'd taken over the club, this had been the start of Vibes's weekend slot, and she'd looked forward to it more than any other night because, even without the attraction, she'd liked him more than the other DJs, and preferred his style of music. But he wouldn't be here tonight – or ever again.

Spending the day in the office, doing the books and getting all of the mundane paperwork out of the way to keep herself occupied, she locked up when she'd finished in the afternoon. She intended to go into town and do some shopping, then head home and get ready for tonight. Her dark mood deepened when she got down to the club floor and saw Fabian showing his friend up the stairs to the DJ's booth. Watching from the doorway as the man strutted into the small room and stood silhouetted in the window, his head bobbing to an imaginary beat as he got a feel for the place, Jenna decided there and then that she didn't like him.

In her – admittedly limited – experience, DJs fell into one of three categories: the gift-of-the-gab tossers who thought themselves *hilarious* and super-cool, and who interrupted every track to make supposedly witty comments; the flashy, smooth-talking lover-boys who dressed better than the punters and spent the whole night focusing on one "special lady" on the dance floor, with the aim of taking her home at the end of the night – and her mate the next; and, lastly, the genuine talents – like Vibes – who weren't looking for the sex, and who didn't have to impress with gimmicks or catchphrases or fancy clothes, because their pure love of music shone through without effort.

And *this* one, Jenna surmised when Fabian led him back down the stairs to the dance floor, and she took in the sunglasses perched on top of the scruffy bleached-blond head and the junkie-surfer-boy clothes complete with patterned knee-length shorts and flip-flops, was a definite gift-of-the-gab merchant. She didn't care *how* good Fabian reckoned he was, she just *knew* he was going to be terrible.

Bringing him over to meet her, Fabian said, 'This is the guy I was telling you about, Jenna. Bubba Zee – Jenna Lorde.'

'Enchanted,' Bubba drawled, giving her a cheeky grin as he added, 'Don't worry, Fabes has filled us in on what a slave-driver you are, so I'll stay out of your way as much as. Just chuck a wet bone in the cage every so-so, and I'll be sorted.'

'Ex*cuse* me?'

'He means he'd like a drink taken up to the booth for him now and then,' Fabian explained.

'I see,' Jenna replied coolly. 'Well, I'm sure *you* can arrange that, Fabian.'

'Hey, Babes, don't stress,' Bubba said. 'I was only joking.'

'I'm not stressing,' she snapped. 'And don't call me *Babes*.' Turning to Fabian, she said, 'I've got some things to do in town, then I'm going home. I'll be back by ten. Call me if you need me before that.'

'Do I get the job?' Bubba called after her as she walked away.

'Depends if you're any good,' she called back without looking at him.

Watching her, Bubba whistled softly. 'Man, she is *fit*. Just like Liz Taylor at her wank-inducing best.'

'Told you.' Fabian gave him a sly grin. 'Don't think she likes *you* much, though.'

'She will.' Bubba gave an unconcerned shrug. 'I just take a bit of getting used to.' Looking slowly around then, he pursed his lips. 'Kinda *Hit Man & Her* meets *Come Dancing* on the Starship Enterprise, innit?'

'Wouldn't let Jenna hear you describing it like that,' Fabian chuckled. 'It's her pride and joy, this place. She spent an absolute fortune getting it like this.'

'Nowt wrong with it that can't be fixed,' Bubba said. 'Just needs something – I dunno – a bit *sexier*, maybe.' Giving Fabian a nudge then, he said, 'Remember that gig I had in Crete, where they wouldn't let the girls in till they took their tops off and rode the pole? *That*'s what this gaff needs. Bit of sleaze and grit, and we'd have 'em piling in from all over.'

Snorting softly, Fabian shook his head. 'Don't really think that's the kind of place Jenna's looking to run here.'

'And there was me thinking *you* was the decisions man,' Bubba teased.

'Cat – skin – plenty of ways,' Fabian replied enigmatically. 'Right – so have you got everything you need?'

'Just about,' Bubba said. 'But I wouldn't mind a shufti through that stuff you said the last guy left. Sounds like he had some good imports.'

'I don't know,' Fabian said uncertainly. 'I really don't think Jenna would like it.'

'Aw, man, you've lost your balls but *good*!' Bubba laughed. 'And if that's what working for a woman does to you, I don't think I'll be sticking around too long.'

'I didn't say no,' Fabian retorted, annoyed that Bubba was taking the piss. 'It's just that it's all locked in her office.'

'Haven't you got a key?'

Pursing his lips, Fabian thought about it. He *did* still have the key, although Jenna didn't know that. And would it really

hurt if he let Bubba take a couple of bits? Vibes would probably never come back for it, anyway, so nobody would be
any the wiser. And the customers had loved his music, so it
would benefit the club.

'Okay,' he said. 'But don't mess anything up in there, and
don't take too much. And don't tell a soul, or it'll be my
arse on the line.'

'My lips are sealed,' Bubba assured him, grinning slyly.

Jenna was even more irritated by the time she'd finished her
shopping and gone home. There must have been an idiot
convention in town, because people were running around
like fools. She couldn't count how many times she'd been
barged into on Market Street, and she'd come very close to
punching the woman who had deliberately run over her foot
with that shopping-laden pram in the Arndale. Her toes were
still hurting.

Tutting when her mobile began to ring just as she was
struggling to get her bags through the door, she dropped
everything in the hall and kicked the door shut. Then she
dragged the phone out of her pocket, answering it without
even looking at the screen because she was too busy kicking
her shoes off.

There was a moment of static, then, 'Hello, Jenna . . . you
there?'

Her heart lurched at the sound of his voice. 'Vibes? Is that
you?'

'Yeah, it's me. How you doing, Princess?'

'Fine,' she told him, hopping through to the lounge and
sitting down on the couch, her bad mood evaporating in an
instant. 'It's really good to hear from you. Everybody's been
asking about you all week.'

'How are they all?' Vibes asked, thinking that nothing had
ever sounded sweeter than Jenna's voice.

'They're good,' Jenna said, laughing softly as she added, 'Austin's been moping about all over the place, but we knew that was going to happen, didn't we?'

'He's a good kid,' Vibes said. 'Never met anyone quite like him before, but he's cool. And how's Kalli?' he asked then.

'Being an absolute sweetheart, as usual,' Jenna told him. 'Missing you like crazy – but then, who isn't?'

There was a slight pause as Vibes wondered if he ought to ask after Jason. He hadn't met the guy, but he *was* Jenna's boyfriend, so it would be only polite. Deciding against it, he asked about the club instead.

'Pretty normal, so far,' Jenna told him. 'But tonight's going to be the tester. Fabian's hired a guy who's just come in from Tenerife, and he reckons he's really good. But *I* think he's going to be terrible.'

'Oh?' Vibes murmured, feeling a little envious because he wished he was still there, getting ready for *his* show tonight.

'He just *looks* wrong,' Jenna explained, not wanting to say what she really meant: that nobody would suit her, because they weren't him. 'Anyway, I don't want to talk about that. Tell me what you've been doing? Have you seen lots of your old friends?'

'Yeah, a few,' Vibes said quietly.

'You must be having a great time?' Jenna said, her voice a little wistful now as she stroked the necklace around her throat.

'I guess,' Vibes said evasively. 'Anyway, I'd best let you get back to what you were doing. I just thought I'd let you know I got here okay, and make sure everything was cool back there.'

'Everything's fine,' Jenna said, wishing she could keep him talking but knowing she had to let him go because his wife was probably waiting for him to go off and do something more exciting. 'Well, thanks for calling. I'll let everyone know you're all right.'

'Take it easy, Princess.'

'You too. Bye.'

Disappointed that it had been such a short call, Jenna hung up and thought about the little that they had actually said to each other. It was so obvious that he had only called out of courtesy and hadn't wanted to get into anything deep. But she supposed that he was still feeling bad about that kiss and had decided it was best not to give her the wrong idea – in case she misinterpreted it again and got false hopes that he would ever feel the same about her as she did about him.

Still, at least she knew he was all right.

Sighing, Jenna got up and went to retrieve her shopping. Vibes wasn't coming back, so she might as well let go of the past and start looking to the future.

Lying back on the bed when he'd disconnected, Vibes gazed around the room. It was his best friend Tyler's kid brother's room, and even though Nate was eighteen and in college now, rooming with a bunch of his music-class buddies over in Harlem, all his stuff was still here. Every shelf was crammed with books, CDs, and Little League trophies, every corner stacked with magazines, while the closet was packed with clothes and sneakers. But Vibes didn't mind the lack of space; it just felt good to be surrounded by reminders of his old life.

The life he'd lived and loved before it was all snatched away from him.

Almost three years had passed since that awful night, and now he was having to face the bastards who had stolen his family from him. Sitting across from them in the courthouse, watching them smirk and pass secret hand-signal messages to each other as if they were in school detention while the prosecution outlined its case against them.

His beautiful wife Aliya, their gorgeous three-year-old daughter Tashei, his precious mom, and his own kid brother Dylan – all gone. Shot to pieces in their beds by the gang who had broken into their home in the middle of the night, mistaking it for the crack-house next door.

And, like the prosecutor had said yesterday, they must have known as soon as they got in there that it wasn't no crack-house. Apart from the fact that there was actual furniture in there, rugs on the polished floors, and pictures on the clean walls, no crack-house had ever smelled that good. They *must* have known. And, knowing, they could have walked straight back out and gone after the piece of shit they were really looking for. But they had chosen to take a look around instead, to see what they could steal before they went on their way. But Dylan must have woken up and, being the brave kid that he was, gone into the hall to confront them and protect his mom. And they'd shot him dead, just like that, then gone from room to room taking out the rest of them as they slept in their beds, just so they could still go after the bastard next door without fear of being identified.

And Vibes hadn't known a thing about it until he got home and saw the police crawling all over the place, because he'd been too busy at his gig downtown – the gig he'd taken on at the last minute, despite Aliya asking him not to.

She'd been getting on his case a lot back then, worrying that she was losing him because he was spending more time behind his decks than he did in her bed and concerned that Tashei would grow up hardly knowing what her daddy looked like. But he'd carried on regardless, taking every gig that came his way and justifying it by telling Aliya that he was doing it for them, to get the money to move them to a nicer place – away from the drugs that had been slowly creeping into their neighbourhood, and the gangs that had started to form on the street corners.

Vibes had been so wrapped up in his future plans that he'd been blind to the present dangers. And by the time he'd opened his eyes, it was too late, because all he could see then was his family lying side by side on the slabs in the morgue.

The gang had escaped, but Vibes hadn't. The pain had torn him to pieces, and the guilt that he hadn't been there to protect them had eaten him up so bad that he'd started acting crazy, sleeping in the yard all day, and sitting up all night with a gun in his hand.

Tyler's mom had made Ty go drag him back to her house in the end, where she'd watched over him like a baby for the next few months, forcing him to eat and drink and remember that he hadn't died with his family.

Vibes had been slowly recovering when Kenneth got in touch and invited him to go stay with him and his new wife, Gina, over in England. And getting on that plane had completed the process, making him strong enough to come back here now and do what had to be done. At least now he could look out at his house across the road without thinking that he was going to die from the pain. And one day he might even be able to face going over there to sort through the things he'd left behind. But not yet, because he needed all his strength to get him through the next few months.

When this case was done, and those boys were behind bars where they belonged, *then* he would tackle the rest. And then he would sit down and make plans to start his life over.

Maybe back in England.

And, maybe, depending what happened between now and then, he might tell Jenna how he felt about her when he got there – if her damn fool of a boyfriend still hadn't gotten around to putting a ring on that bare third finger of hers.

Until then, he wouldn't call her again, because it was just

too hard to hear her voice and then have to say goodbye. And he didn't need to be going into that courtroom and facing those bastards with that kind of pain in his eyes. When they looked at him, Vibes wanted them to see nothing but contempt.

12

Some of the regulars did drift away after Vibes left, but more decided to stay and check out his replacement. And Fabian's posters advertising Bubba's arrival in town drew a fresh crowd of *his* fans, so the club was as busy as ever, which pleased Jenna. Despite her initial determination to find fault with him, she had to admit, once she'd seen him in action, that Bubba was good. Not as good as Vibes, of course, but better than a lot of the other DJs she'd heard. And his music wasn't too far removed from Vibes's style, so at least it wasn't a major change for the regulars.

While having a drink at the VIP bar one Friday night a few weeks on, Jenna frowned when the music suddenly stopped and she heard screaming and shouting from the public area. Rushing to the balcony, where a lot of the celebrities were already gathered, she gasped when she saw a mass brawl going on all over the lower floor. Rushing down the stairs, she'd just reached the bottom when Fabian came through the door.

'What the hell's going on?' she asked.

'Nothing to worry about,' he said, relieved to see her. 'Just go back upstairs and stay there. I'm going to lock this to make sure nobody gets at the celebs. I've already called the police.'

'I'm coming with you,' Jenna said when he started backing out of the door.

'I'd rather you didn't,' he said. 'Someone's supposed to have seen a knife.'

'Oh, my God,' she gasped. 'Nobody's been—'

'Not as far as I know, but I don't want to take any chances. Please, Jenna. Just go back upstairs and let me deal with this.'

Just then, Tony and Eddie came thundering down behind her.

'Need a hand?' Tony asked, cracking his knuckles.

'No!' Fabian told him quickly, sensing that things would get far worse if these two got involved. 'I've got it in hand. The police are on their way.'

Shrugging, Tony said, 'Okay, well, I guess they can handle it, huh?' Looking at Jenna then, he frowned. 'You ain't going out there, are you?'

'No, she's going back up where it's safe,' Fabian said before she could answer.

'Good.' Tony gave him a nod of approval. Looking at Jenna then, he said, 'Come on, I'll get you a drink – we can watch what's going on from the balcony.'

Feeling a little railroaded, Jenna reluctantly agreed.

The fight had turned into a full-scale battle now; feet and fists flying every which way, and chairs and tables being used as both weapons and shields. Thankfully, it was reasonably short-lived, because as soon as the police sirens cut through the screams and grunts the perpetrators booted the emergency doors open and took off into the night.

It took a while for the rest to realise that they were fighting fellow victims and quit, and then they stood around in panting, confused groups, trying to figure out how it had started in the first place. But nobody had seen it coming, so it was impossible to make any sense of it.

Several of the customers were taken by ambulance to the local hospital to be checked over, but, fortunately, there were no serious casualties. And with all the guilty parties gone already, the police couldn't make any arrests. So, after advising Jenna to put her doormen on alert to stop it happening again, they left her to clear up the mess.

And what a mess it was. Furniture overturned, the floor littered with shattered glass, blood everywhere. But at least it was all cosmetic, so Jenna supposed it wasn't too bad. At least she wasn't facing a huge bill to replace fixtures and fittings.

Piecing it together from what had reportedly been seen and heard, they knew that at least four fights had broken out simultaneously around the room, each started by groups of at least four men who had, their victims claimed, been drinking and chatting quietly together before it kicked off. But at exactly midnight, each of these groups had suddenly jumped up and started laying into anyone and everyone. And because nobody was sure who they were defending themselves against, they inevitably ended up fighting whoever was closest to them.

Sitting with Fabian at the bar when the last of the customers had gone, Jenna shook her head. 'I've never seen anything like that.'

'Me neither,' he admitted. 'I didn't have a clue what was happening. One minute everyone was dancing, the next they were screaming and fists were flying. I was waiting to see if Jacko and the guys could handle it, but when I heard someone say they'd seen a knife, I was straight on the phone.'

'Good job you did call the police,' Jenna said. 'I dread to think what might have happened if it had gone on any longer.' Taking a sip of the coffee that Kalli had just made her, she sighed. 'Remind me to call the hospital tomorrow to make sure that pregnant girl was all right.'

'She should be,' Fabian said, covering a yawn with his hand. 'Probably more shocked than anything. I don't think anybody actually touched her.'

'I hope not,' Jenna murmured. 'Do you think this had anything to do with those guys who were hassling Melody that time?' she asked then. 'You did say you thought they'd come back after Eddie beat them all up like that.'

'Could be, I suppose.' Fabian shrugged. 'No way of knowing for sure, though.'

'Hi, guys,' Bubba said, coming over just then. 'Good night, huh?'

'I hope that was a joke?' Jenna frowned up at him. Not that she thought he meant it nastily. He was actually quite nice when you looked beyond the garish clothes and in-your-face banter.

'Would I joke about a thing like that?' he teased, flipping her a wink. 'You look tired, Babes.'

'I am. And I thought I told you not to call me that.' Giving him a mock-stern look, she finished her coffee and stood up.

'Not going, are you?' Bubba asked, squeezing onto her stool before she'd even moved away from it.

'Want me to reserve you a place in my grave?' she quipped, stepping back so that he could get his legs straight.

'Only if we both drink the elixir of everlasting life, so we get to make love for all eternity,' Bubba said, grinning.

'What, and have nothing to look at for all eternity but your disgusting hair?' Jenna shot back playfully. 'I don't think so.'

Frowning, Fabian pursed his lips. Jenna had hated Bubba to start with, and it really bugged him that they had such an easy relationship now. Bubba talked to her as if they were flirty mates, and she didn't seem to mind – which really pissed Fabian off, because he could never imagine himself talking to her like that and getting away with it.

'Right, I'm going,' she said, sighing now as she looked around the room. 'It's going to be a hell of a morning clearing this lot up.'

'Leave it to the cleaners,' Fabian told her, reasserting his own place in her life as the caring, take control, relieve-her-of-her-burdens manager that she could trust above all others.

'I'll be here early, so I'll make sure it gets done properly. You just have a lie-in.' Kissing her on the cheek then, he said, 'Don't worry about tonight. Fights are inevitable when you've got so many people drinking in one place. But we don't tend to get more than the odd scuffle, so this was probably a one-off.'

'Thanks,' Jenna said, smiling gratefully for the reassurance. 'Night, Bubba,' she said then.

Saluting her, Bubba said, 'Night, boss.' Turning to Fabian when she walked away to get her coat and bag from her office, he grinned. 'When's the wedding?'

'What are you talking about?' Fabian asked, going behind the bar and tipping his coffee down the sink.

'You *lurve* her,' Bubba teased. 'I know you, my friend, and them hots have turned into a burning flame of red-hot lust.'

'Don't talk shit,' Fabian snorted, pouring two doubles and handing one to Bubba. 'I like her, but there's no way I fancy her. She's way too cold. I prefer them hot and heavy.'

'Not if you're talking about that tart with the huge tits I saw you sloping off with the other night,' Bubba said, chuckling softly. 'A pure case of *who let the dogs out*. Where did you take her for the big bang, anyway. Up to your office?'

'I wasn't talking about *her*,' Fabian said dismissively. 'But how did you know about that, anyway?'

'You'd be surprised how much I can see from the pod,' Bubba told him, smirking now. 'I've counted seven different tarts in the last two weeks getting your dubious pleasures. You must have a kennel club up there by now. What do you do, lure them up with your big meaty chews?'

'Fuck off. They're not all ugly.'

'Most of 'em are. Man, you've got to start looking at their faces instead of their tits, 'cos you're in serious danger of losing your babe-magnet rep if you keep going for any old barker.'

'Yeah, well, you wouldn't say that if you knew who else I've shagged,' Fabian said, adding smugly, 'and dumped.'

'Go on,' Bubba said, sighing exaggeratedly. 'I know you're dying to spill.'

'Melody Fisher,' Fabian told him, watching his face carefully.

Shrugging, Bubba said, 'Am I supposed to know her?'

'You know her,' Fabian insisted. 'Blonde, absolute stunner, best tits in England. Sits in the corner of the VIP lounge, surrounded by the stars.'

'The Mafia moll?' Bubba laughed. 'Fuck off! There's no way you've had that.'

'She's not a Mafia moll,' Fabian said, frowning again. 'She's an actress.'

'She might well be, but them blokes she hangs with are *pure* Mafia,' Bubba declared. 'Haven't you seen *The Sopranos*, man? He's Tony Wotsisname through and through.'

'His name *is* Tony, as it happens,' Fabian said. 'But he's not Mafia. He's just a thug.'

'You think what you like,' Bubba snorted. 'But I knows what I sees.' Shaking his head now, he grinned at Fabian. 'So, you reckon you've shagged her, do you? And when was that, then? In your wildest wet dreams?'

Before Fabian could answer, Jenna came back. Calling, 'See you tomorrow, guys,' she waved and made her way behind the bar to leave. Popping her head back in after going into the kitchen, she said, 'Everybody's gone from back here, Fabian, so can you just check the toilets again before you lock up? I don't want to come in tomorrow and find some injured person got locked in and died.'

Assuring her that he would check, Fabian waited until he'd heard the back door close, then went and got himself and Bubba another drink. 'Want to see something?' he asked, handing Bubba's glass across the bar.

'Only if it comes with something white and buzzing,' Bubba said, pulling three twenty-notes out of his pocket and slapping them down on the bar.

Picking them up, Fabian slipped them into his pocket and, grinning, gave a mock bow. 'Care to accompany me to my office, sir?'

'Not if you think you're gonna shag me when we get there,' Bubba laughed. 'I'm not one of those easy girls, you know,' he said then in a feminine voice, getting off the stool and putting a hand to his breast. 'I am a laydee. And it takes more than a couple of drinks to get *my* bloomers orf.'

Up in the office a few minutes later, Fabian took his stash out of the safe. Then he reached for the DVD of him and Melody that he kept there for safe keeping.

He hadn't needed to play the insurance card yet – and probably never would, because Melody seemed to have lost all interest in him lately. But he still couldn't bring himself to destroy it, and he sometimes took a look at it just to remind himself of those fantastic tits and that beautiful pussy. Maybe one day he'd get rid of it. But not just yet.

'What's it about?' Bubba asked, picking it up and turning it over in his hand as Fabian sorted him a wrap from the stash bag. 'It's got no title.'

'Let's just call it *Bubba eats shit*,' Fabian said smugly, handing the wrap to him. Laying out two lines from his own stash then, he snorted one and pushed the mirror across the desk.

'Better be good,' Bubba said, watching as Fabian went and unlocked the cupboard housing his DVD player and small monitor screen. 'I'm not getting all hyped up on this to watch Mary fucking Poppins. I want action, man.'

'Thought you'd have given the dolls up a long time ago,' Fabian quipped, slotting the disc into the machine.

'Eh?' Holding his breath, Bubba squinted at him.

'Action Man,' Fabian repeated. Shaking his head when Bubba just shrugged, he said, 'Never mind.' Going to his chair then, he sat down and pressed play on the remote.

The screen lit up and Bubba frowned when a shot of the office came up. 'What's this, dude?'

'Watch,' Fabian said, licking his lips, his eyes taking on a beady coke glow.

Exhaling impatiently, Bubba licked his fingertip and dabbed at the traces on the mirror. He'd got it halfway to his mouth when Fabian walked into shot on the screen, quickly followed by Melody Fisher, looking hot as hell in a red satin dress, cut up to here and down to there, her long legs amazing in glossy flesh-coloured stockings.

'Oh, man,' he said huskily, leaning forward for a closer look. 'I've only seen her from the distance before, but she is *fit*.'

On screen, Fabian laid out two lines of coke and snorted one. Handing the straw to Melody then, he came up behind her as she leaned down to snort hers and ran his hands over her body.

'Jeezus!' Bubba drooled. 'Look at the arse on that.'

Back on screen, Fabian was rubbing up against her.

'Oh, that's good,' screen-Melody moaned, rocking back against him when he slipped his hand between her thighs. 'Oh, yeah . . . keep doing that.'

'You dirty fucking dog!' Bubba chuckled as he watched screen-Fabian free his hard-on and slide into her, holding on tight to her hips, his face a mask of restraint. 'Yeah, that musta took some doing, guy. I'd've been ramming it home by now. I'm hard enough just fucking *watching* it.'

On the screen, Melody arched her back and put her hands flat on the table, bucking against Fabian, crying, 'Oh, God, *now!*'

And Fabian obliged, pounding into her for a while, then pulling out and sweeping everything off the desk with the back of his hand. Flipping Melody onto her back, he tore off her panties and tossed them aside, then pushed her dress up over her breasts and bit down on her nipples as Melody wrapped her legs around his waist and sank her nails into his back.

Looking at Fabian with admiration in his coke-glazed eyes when the screen went blank, Bubba grinned. 'You're hung like a fucking *elephant*, man! How come you never let on about *that* when we was doing the summer gigs? I could've earned a sweet little backhander selling your services to the ladies.' Laughing now, he added, 'And I bet a good few of the lads would've paid for a bit of you, an' all. We could have been minted.'

'All right,' Fabian said, smiling. 'You were supposed to be watching her, not me. So, now do you believe me?'

'Oh, yeah, I believe you,' Bubba said, reaching out across the desk to stroke Fabian's thigh. 'But I think I love *you*. Oh, take me now, hot boy! I need you. Oh . . . Oh!'

'Pack it in,' Fabian laughed. 'Or I might just sell this tape to the Sunday papers.'

'You what?' Bubba squawked. 'Don't tell me you're taping us now?'

'You'll find out if you keep messing about,' Fabian warned, getting up and taking the DVD out of the machine. Locking it back in the safe, he said, 'Fancy going on to somewhere else? I'm too wired to go home, and there's a new all-night pussy club just opened in Salford.'

'Bring your dick and I'll think about it,' Bubba said, grinning for the camera in the corner as he added, 'We always had such good sex when we were a couple, didn't we? Shouldn't be so different now we're just friends.'

'We were never a couple,' Fabian said to the camera, playing along.

'Oh, how could you deny me like that?' Bubba wailed, pretending to cry now. 'I thought I was the one.'

'Get out,' Fabian laughed, shoving him towards the door.

★

The rest of the week passed without incident after the fight, and everybody had forgotten about it by the time Friday came around again. But in an almost exact replica of the previous week, midnight hit and suddenly there was mayhem on the lower floor.

'I don't believe this!' Jenna gasped as, yet again, Fabian told her to stay in the VIP lounge with the stars, and locked the door to keep them safe.

And yet again, Tony and Eddie offered to help, only to be told that the police were on their way.

'You think you've got a problem?' Tony asked Jenna, sipping his drink beside her as they watched the fight from the balcony.

'Well, *obviously*,' she snapped. Throwing a hand over her mouth then, when she saw three men kicking another in the head as he lay on the floor, she said, 'Oh, my God! They're going to kill him!' Spotting her head of security wading through the crowd below, she waved her arms and pointed the victim out, yelling, '*JACKO* . . . Help him!'

Shaking all over when Jacko and Flex yanked the men off the victim, Jenna backed away from the balcony and sat down heavily on a chair.

Coming and squatting down beside her, Tony took her hand in his. 'You okay?'

'I think I'm going to be sick,' she muttered.

'It's gonna be all right,' he assured her, his voice quietly confident. 'Soon as the police come, the bastards who started it will take off like last time.'

'Do you think it's the same people?' Jenna asked.

'Could be.' He shrugged. 'Anyone been putting the screws on you lately?'

'What do you mean?' Frowning, Jenna gazed at him.

'Seems a pretty typical trick to me,' Tony said. 'Had it

happen once in my place back home. Some guys came in and started a ruck. Did it again the next week. Then the next, some dude comes in and tells me he can sort it all out for me – for a price.'

'You mean like a protection racket?' Jenna asked.

Chuckling softly, Tony said, 'Yeah, I guess that was the intention. But they didn't figure on *me* being the owner.'

'What happened?'

'Enough that they never bothered me again,' Tony said, his eyes dark as he peered into hers. 'But I'm a man.'

Frown deepening, Jenna said, 'What difference does that make.'

'Unfortunately for you, quite a lot,' Tony told her quietly. 'I mean, face facts, Jen. What are you gonna do if some guy comes threatening to break your legs unless you pay up?'

'Call the police,' she replied indignantly.

'Oh, yeah, sure,' Tony laughed. 'Is that after the nasty man's *gone*, or when he comes back, pissed off 'cos you didn't do as you were told?'

'Christ, do you have to make it sound so awful?' Jenna muttered sickly. 'I'm sure people probably get away with that stuff in the States, but it can't happen here.'

Shrugging again, Tony gestured dismissively with his hands. 'Hope for your sake you're right.'

Interrupting them just then, Fabian said, 'Sorry, Jenna, but the officer wants a word.'

Looking over at the police sergeant who had come upstairs with Fabian and was standing by the toilet door now, conspicuous in his yellow coat, his flat hat in his hand, she nodded.

'All right, bring him over.' Turning back to Tony then, she said, 'You'll have to excuse me for a minute.'

'No worries,' he said, patting her hand again and standing up. 'I want to get Melody back to the hotel, anyway. You got my number if you want to talk.'

Thanking him, Jenna said goodnight, then stood up to greet the police officer when Fabian brought him over. Taking him to a quiet corner table, she waved for him to sit down.

Sergeant Dave Poole was a little overawed, not only because he was surrounded by so many famous faces but because Jenna was one of the most beautiful women he'd ever seen – and being around the same age, he might well have chatted her up if they'd met here when he was in his civvies.

Sitting awkwardly on the edge of his seat now, he said, 'I thought we'd best have a chat, because I'm a bit concerned about what's going on here.'

'You and me both,' Jenna murmured.

'It's just that there seems to be a bit of a pattern developing.' Pausing, Poole shifted self-consciously in his seat when two girls from *Hollyoaks* stopped by to say goodnight to Jenna on their way out. Clearing his throat when they'd gone, he said, 'I'm concerned that you weren't better prepared after last week.'

'How?' Jenna peered at him incredulously. 'My doormen have been really vigilant all week, but everything's been as quiet as usual. There were no signs that anything was going to start again tonight.'

'So, they didn't see any of the same men from last week coming in tonight?'

'Nobody knows who they were,' Jenna reminded him. 'Hundreds of men come in every night. It could have been any of them.'

'What about gangs?'

'We don't let *gangs* in,' Jenna told him, a frosty edge creeping into her voice. 'In fact, we've got a strict policy not to allow groups of more than four men *or* women in at a time. And since last week, the doormen have been watching the queue like hawks, making sure that there were no groups that seemed even to know each other.'

Jotting something in his notepad, Poole said, 'What about stag parties?'

'They have to book in advance, and they're shown in independently of the queue,' Jenna told him. 'But we haven't had any parties in during the last two weeks, so that's not an issue.' Sighing heavily then, she said, 'Look, I know it must be a pain for you to have to come out again for nothing, but we've done everything we could to prevent this, and I don't know what else we *can* do, short of banning men altogether. And I don't think *that* would be very good for business, somehow.'

'No, of course not,' Poole agreed, closing his pad and putting it back in his pocket. 'All I'm saying is, you're going to need to tighten your security, because . . .' Pausing, he shrugged. 'Well, you're probably aware that there's been a lot of unrest about the levels of drink-related violence in the city recently, and certain bodies are demanding action.'

'So they should,' Jenna said, fully agreeing. 'I think it's disgusting.'

'They're going for a zero-tolerance approach,' Poole went on, not sure that she was getting the picture. 'The aim being to make club owners more responsible. If they push it through, you might find that you get billed for the police time.'

'You mean I'd have to *pay* for calling you out?' Jenna gasped.

'Obviously, we'll always respond to any emergency,' Poole assured her. 'But there could well be financial consequences in the future, depending on what we find when we get there.'

'I see,' Jenna murmured, pursing her lips angrily. 'So, if something like this happens again, I won't only have to pay to clean it up and replace anything that's broken, I'll have

to pay your wages as well – even though I pay my taxes and
do my damnedest to run a respectable club?'

Shrugging, Poole stood up. 'I'm not saying it's going to
happen, just warning you that it might. All I can suggest for
now is that you make sure your security are on the ball, 'cos
my super might get a bit touchy if we're called out for the
same thing again next week. And, between you and me, he's
been known to petition to have licences revoked.'

'That's outrageous,' Jenna said, standing up herself now.
'There are fights going on all over the place, all the time,
but just because I call for help when it happens to me, I'm
in danger of getting my licence revoked?'

'I wouldn't *not* call us,' Poole warned her. 'Not if there's
a chance somebody could get seriously hurt as a conse-
quence.'

'This is the second time anything like this has happened,'
Jenna reminded him indignantly. 'It's not exactly a notorious
trouble hot spot, is it?'

'None of the bad ones start off bad,' Poole pointed out
quietly. Nodding then, he gave her an apologetic smile.
'Hope we don't meet under these circumstances again, miss.'

'Me, too,' she retorted icily.

Fabian caught up with Jenna at the foot of the VIP stairs
after he'd shown the police out and locked the doors.

'Everything all right?'

'Not really. Christ, look at the state of it again. The cleaners
will have a fit.'

'Never mind them. If they don't like it, there's plenty more
who'll gladly take their places. What did the sergeant want?'

Relaying the conversation that she'd had with Poole, Jenna
shook her head angrily. 'I just don't see what else we can do.'

'Well, you can stop worrying about the licence, for
starters,' Fabian told her firmly. 'They would never revoke
it over a couple of little incidents like this. There would have

to be serious problems on a regular basis, and you'd have to be seen to be doing nothing about it.'

'Yeah, well, I don't want to risk it,' Jenna muttered, folding her arms. 'Can you get Jacko to arrange for the guys to come in tomorrow? I think we need a meeting to review security.'

'They're doing everything by the book,' Fabian reminded her, not wanting her to blame them. 'But I'll see what I can do.'

'Thanks. And I think we should take a look at the CCTV tapes from this week and last week – see if we can spot any of the same people in the thick of it when it kicked off.'

'I've already checked last week's, and you can't see anything specific,' Fabian told her. 'They're not very good angles on the interior cameras, unfortunately. They mainly cover the doors, and the fights have started well out of range. All you can see is a lot of men running out of the fire door – from behind, so you can't see their faces.'

'Great.' Jenna tutted. 'So, we need some of those cameras that scan the room?'

'Have you any idea how much it would cost to install enough of them to cover the whole place?' Fabian asked her.

'More than my licence is worth?' Jenna asked, raising an eyebrow.

'Well, no, obviously that's worth more,' Fabian conceded. 'But I think we need to calm down and think this through before we go jumping in at the deep end. I genuinely don't think we've got as much of a problem as you think. This looks bad, but it could be a lot worse.'

'That's what I told myself last week,' Jenna said. 'But I'm starting to wonder.'

'Let's just hang fire and see what happens,' Fabian urged. 'We'll have a talk with the lads, if that makes you feel better. But I really think this is a one – well, a *two*-off.'

'I hope so,' Jenna murmured.

★

Just as Fabian had predicted, the fights *were* a two-off. But the next week brought a completely different problem.

An anonymous caller had apparently tipped the police off about somebody selling drugs in the men's toilets, and Jenna could do nothing but stand by and watch as the police swarmed all over the club, stopping people from leaving, searching them, and taking their details. She felt terrible when the dogs were brought in and sniffed out several of her customers, who were immediately arrested for possession of cannabis and cocaine – a couple of possessors of the latter substance being celebrities.

The VIPs were not amused to be made to come down to the lower floor to give their details in earshot of the 'everyday people'. Some even threatened to sue if anything untoward happened as a result of their addresses being overheard, and Jenna wasn't sure if the threats were aimed at her or the police. What she *did* know was that she would probably never see some of her star guests again, because they wouldn't want to risk their reputations being tainted by being associated with a club that was getting a bad reputation. And that they would most probably spread the word among their friends, too.

It was all so dispiriting after everything had been going so well. But if Jenna had thought the drug bust was bad, worse soon followed. This time it happened on the Saturday, taking them all by surprise, because they had expected it to be the Friday again, as per the developing pattern that Poole had spotted.

Armed police burst in this time, weapons drawn as they ordered the terrified clubbers to hit the floor. They were responding to reports of a gang of men seen entering the club with a sub-machine gun. But eventually they left when they had searched the entire place and everybody in it, and had found no guns of any description.

No arrests were made, but it was enough to put a huge black mark against the club. Jenna just knew that things were going to start going to hell on a bobsleigh if she didn't put a stop to the nonsense soon.

She'd already figured out that it was personal before Fabian reminded her about the conversation they'd had that time, when he'd warned her that the other club owners might start playing dirty if she became too successful and stole too many customers. Fearing that he could be right, she took the Sunday off and spent the whole day calling into every other club in town to speak to the owners, managers or whoever was available to beg them – if they were behind it – to stop.

Jenna was worn out by the time she'd finished, and her instincts told her that the other club people had all been telling the truth when they'd said that they weren't involved. But she didn't know if her instincts could be trusted any more, so she was still none the wiser.

Tony Allen had been lucky enough to be out of town on the two occasions when the club was raided, sparing him the indignity of being searched and questioned. Coming in on the Sunday night, he came straight over to where Jenna was sitting at the VIP bar, having a miserable, solitary drink.

'Hey, beautiful,' he said softly, giving her a hug. 'I hear you've been having some more trouble while I've been away?'

'You could say that,' she murmured, her eyes telling a clear story of her inner despair.

'Bad, huh?' Tony said, peering at her with sympathy.

Snorting softly, Jenna waved her hand. 'Take a look around and tell me what you see.'

Glancing around the lounge, Tony shrugged. 'All right, so it's not as busy as usual. But it ain't the end of the world. It'll get back to normal once you find out what's going on and who's behind it.'

'And how am I supposed to do that?' Jenna asked hopelessly. 'I've tried everything. The security crew have been on full alert, but they haven't seen any of this coming. And some of the staff have already walked because they're so freaked out. And you don't even want to *know* how many customers I've lost.' Sighing now, she took another sip of her drink and shrugged. 'But it's not your problem, so I guess I shouldn't be moaning to you about it.'

'Hey, that's what friends are for,' Tony said quietly, his voice so kind and sincere that Jenna felt like crying.

Biting down on it, Jenna said, 'Thanks, that means a lot right now. But forget about me. You've got your own worries, haven't you? Any luck finding something to invest in yet?'

Shrugging, he slipped a hand into his pocket, reaching for his cigars. 'Not yet, but me and Lenny have teamed up now, so it shouldn't be too long.' Lighting up, he squinted at her through the smoke. 'He's a pretty savvy guy when you get to know him. And straight as a die, so it can't hurt, can it?'

'I suppose not,' Jenna agreed.

'We've had meetings with a few companies,' Tony went on. 'But it's got to be exactly right before we commit to anything, 'cos we're talking a lot of money, the two of us combined.' Chuckling softly now, he said, 'Mind you, he makes *my* contribution seem like diddly-squat, what with his millions and his mansion in Alderley Edge. You ever been there?'

'No.' Jenna shook her head. 'I don't really know him all that well. He was my dad's friend.'

'So he tells me,' Tony said, taking another drag on his cigar. 'Had a lot of time for him, by all accounts.'

'I would hope so.' Jenna smiled fondly, ignoring the smoke swirling around her face. 'My dad was a lovely man. Bit unorthodox in some respects, but his heart was always in the right place.'

'He'd be real proud of you, I imagine. The way you've handled all this shit that's been happening.'

'I don't know about that.' Sighing deeply, Jenna blinked back the tears and gazed around. 'He really loved this place, you know. He bought it for next to nothing and kept it going for twenty years. Me, I come in and strip it bare, because I think I can do it better. But I've not even been open six months, and I've almost lost it.'

'Hey, quit being so hard on yourself,' Tony told her firmly. 'This is a glitch, that's all. Someone's fucking with you, but you'll ride it out and come back stronger than ever.'

'We'll see,' Jenna said, her tone clearly conveying how much she doubted it.

'Yeah, well, you know where I am if you need me,' Tony said, patting her hand reassuringly.

'How's she doing?' Eddie asked when Tony came back to their table a short time later.

'Pretty much as you'd expect,' Tony told him quietly. 'Cracking under the pressure.'

'Offer any solutions?'

'Not yet,' Tony said, a flicker of a smile lifting his lip. 'But it won't be long.'

13

The next month was agonising for Jenna, who could only watch helplessly as things went from bad to worse. Nothing spectacularly bad happened, just lots of little things that added up to a grand nuisance. Like every cab company in town receiving crank calls and sending cabs out only to be told that they hadn't been ordered, which resulted in the club being blacklisted so that none of her customers could get a cab unless they walked to the cab offices.

In an attempt to rectify the falling customer numbers, Jenna tried everything. Drinks promotions that lost her even more money – and attracted drunken youths who inevitably disturbed the other customers, which resulted in even more walking out never to return. Door promotions, where girls didn't have to pay to get in one week, men the next, which didn't work at all. She even arranged a themed night, which bombed so badly that Fabian warned her she was turning the place into a joke.

Nothing Jenna did made any difference, and nobody seemed to be able to offer a solution. Fabian had never experienced anything quite like it, so he didn't know what to suggest other than to wait it out and hope it died down when whoever was behind it got bored. And the police were no help either, because they had made it quite clear that they thought she had allowed the situation to develop by attempting to run a club when she didn't have the first clue about the business.

And they were right, because Jenna had come into this believing that she could just pick up where her dad had left off, with nothing to qualify her other than her belief that if James Lorde could do it from scratch so could she. But she'd been so wrong, and she knew that now. There was obviously some sort of secret formula, and you either had the recipe or you didn't. And she quite patently didn't.

But if she'd thought that what had happened so far was bad, worse was yet to come.

Leaving her office late one Saturday afternoon, having spent the day fretting over the appalling accounts books, Jenna waved goodbye to Fabian and Bubba who were doing something with the speaker system down on the club floor. Letting herself out of the back door, she locked it and walked across the yard to open the gate.

It was already fairly dark out, but not quite enough for the security lights to come on when she stepped into their path. Unlocking the gate, she pushed it open, then went to get into her car to reverse it out. But just as she reached for the car door's handle, four figures darted in from the dark alleyway and surrounded her.

It happened so fast that Jenna was too shocked to scream – which was probably a good thing, she quickly realised when she saw the men, because they would no doubt have silenced her in an instant. Anyway, there was nobody in the club to hear her, except Fabian and Bubba, and there was no way they could handle these guys on their own, so they were better off not knowing. She just hoped the infra-red CCTV cameras were picking it up, so at least she'd have something for the police to work on when it was over.

Trying her damnedest to stay calm and collected now, she said, 'I don't have a lot of money on me, but my purse is in my bag. Take it.'

Laughing, one of the men brought his face down close to hers. His breath warm on her cheek, he said, 'I don't want your money, sexy.'

Terrified that she was going to be raped, Jenna held his gaze, determined to remember his face. 'What *do* you want, then?' she asked shakily.

'To make your acquaintance,' he replied, his voice lightly mocking now. 'This is just a friendly *pre*-visit, so to speak – to let you know that we can get to you, any *time*, any*where*. You've been having a lot of trouble lately, and I think it's time we stopped fucking about and got us a little system going. Understand?' Smiling when she nodded, his eyes glittered like jet in the scant light. 'Good girl, Jenna. Because it winds me up like fuck having to say the same thing twice, so things should be nice and easy next time we meet, eh?'

Jenna's heart felt like a shard of ice had fallen through it. He knew her name!

'For the record,' he went on, stroking a finger down her cheek now. 'If I hear that you've been talking to the police, we'll be paying you another little visit – at that nice little apartment of yours. Ten Clifton Quay House, yeah?' Smiling again as he watched the information sink in, he added, 'Nice plants you got for the balcony last week, by the way. And the new kettle's pretty funky, too.'

Jenna was barely breathing now. They knew her name, where she lived, *and* that she'd bought new plants and a kettle. They must have been watching her. Or, *worse* – been inside her apartment. But how? It was alarmed, and the doors were manned by security, and there were CCTV cameras in all the corridors.

'Bye for now, sexy,' the man said now. 'And don't forget – no police, or you and me are gonna have *real* problems.'

Turning from her abruptly then, he and his friends walked out the way they'd come.

Holding her breath until she was sure they'd gone, Jenna rushed to the gate and relocked it, then ran to the back door, her heart beating furiously in her chest as she scrabbled to get the key into the lock.

'That you, Jenna?' Fabian asked, coming through from the bar with a glass of brandy in his hand when he heard the back door slam shut. Seeing the panicked look on her face, he put the glass down on the table and rushed to her.

'What's happened? Are you all right?'

'Some m-men,' she stuttered. 'They came in when I opened the gate and p-pushed me into the corner.'

'What did they do to you?' Fabian asked, his eyes full of concern as he took her arm and led her to a chair. 'Did they touch you?'

Shaking her head, Jenna sat down. 'Not really.'

Frowning, Fabian went to the back door.

'Don't!' she yelped, thinking that he was going to open it and go looking for the men. 'There were four of them.'

Tugging the bolts across, he said, 'Don't worry – I wasn't being a hero. I just wanted to make sure they couldn't get in if they came back.' Reaching for his glass now, he handed it to her. 'Take it,' he insisted when she shook her head. 'You need it. You're shaking like a leaf.'

Thanking him, Jenna sipped the drink and exhaled nervously when the liquid burned a soothing path down her throat.

'Tell me what happened,' Fabian said, pulling a chair up beside hers and reaching for her hand. 'What did they look like?'

'Quite big,' she said, squinting as she tried to recall the details. 'They were wearing dark clothes, but three of them had their hoods up so I couldn't really see them. They were white, though, I think. And the main one had short black hair, and brown eyes.'

'Are you sure? It is dark outside.'

'I'm sure. He had a gold hoop earring in his right ear, with a little thing hanging off it – like a boxing glove, or something. And a thick gold neck-chain with a dog on it.'

'Well, that's good. The police should be able to do some-thing with—'

'No!' Jenna glanced up, her eyes filled with fear. 'No police.'

Patting her hand to calm her down, Fabian said, 'I know you've had a shock, Jenna, but we can't just leave this or they'll think they've got away with it and come back.'

'They *are* coming back,' she murmured, sliding her hand free. 'They said they'd be seeing me soon.'

'Why? Are they after money?'

'No, I offered them my purse, but they didn't want it.'

'I don't get it,' Fabian muttered. 'If it wasn't a mugging, and they didn't touch you, what *did* they want?'

'I don't know,' Jenna admitted quietly. 'But they said they'd be coming back to get a system going, or something. I'm not quite sure. Then they said they'd come to my apart-ment if I talked to the police.'

Bubba had come in while they were talking. Hearing this, he came over and straddled a chair. 'Sorry, but I couldn't help overhearing, and if you want my advice you'll keep zipped about this until you know what they're after, 'cos the Babs won't be able to do nothing but have a word, and that's just gonna piss them off.'

'*Babs*?' Jenna repeated confusedly.

'Babylon,' Bubba said. Then, seeing that she was still none the wiser: '*Five-O*?'

'Police,' Fabian explained.

'Yeah, them,' Bubba said. 'They could really fuck it up if you send them after these blokes when they haven't really done anything. And you can't be doing with that – not if they know where your pad is.'

'Are you sure they know where you live?' Fabian chipped in. 'They might just have been saying that to frighten you.'

Taking another sip of the brandy, Jenna said, 'They knew I'd got a new kettle. How would they have known about it unless they'd seen it?'

'Did they actually describe it?' Fabian asked, raising an eyebrow. When she shook her head, he smiled reassuringly. 'There you go, then. We had a fair bit of publicity after we opened, don't forget, so most of Manchester probably knows you moved back to take over your dad's club. It wouldn't be too hard to figure out that you'd have bought yourself a new *kettle*, would it?'

Looking up at him, annoyed by his patronising tone, Jenna said, 'So how did they know about the new plants I bought for my balcony last week, then? That's pretty specific, don't you think?'

'They must be watching you,' Bubba said immediately, echoing the conclusion that Jenna had already reached. 'And if they are, it ain't worth trying to second-guess them.'

'So what's she supposed to do?' Fabian argued, irritated that Bubba was contradicting him when he was trying to get Jenna to calm down. 'They're obviously trying it on, seeing if she's scared enough to do what they say. They're prob-ably watching from somewhere right now, waiting to see if she's called the police. If they see a squad car pull up, we'll probably never see them again. But when they don't, they'll know they've got to her, and they'll keep coming back.'

'They'll come back either way,' Bubba said, shrugging as he added, 'that's how these guys work.' Looking at Jenna now, he said, 'What was that you said about getting a system going?'

'I don't know,' Jenna murmured, trying to remember. 'I think he said he'd heard I'd been having trouble, and it was time to stop fucking about and get us a system going.'

'Protection,' Bubba declared. 'They've obviously been behind all the shit that's been happening, and now they're going to charge you to make it stop.'

'If that's true, there's not enough to pay them,' Jenna said wearily. 'The takings are so low that I was just considering closing down to cut my losses.'

'You're not serious?' Fabian gasped. 'You can't do that. This place has been going for years. It's an institution in Manchester.'

'Do you think I don't know that?' Jenna snapped, guilt making her defensive. 'I don't *want* to close, I just can't see a lot of choice. We've lost so many customers recently it isn't even funny. And you can play spot-the-celebrity these days.'

'Look, let's just calm down and talk this over,' Fabian said, desperate to find a solution. This was his club as much as it was hers. He'd been running it when her father was around, and he'd carried on when Jenna got here. It had been a little more of a challenge to manipulate her as easily as he had James Lorde, but he'd managed, and he liked Zenith just how it was. If she were to close down now, he'd have to find a job somewhere else, and he didn't want to have to go through the hassle.

Sighing, Jenna shook her head. 'I don't want to talk right now, Fabian. I appreciate the concern, but I'm just too tired. I just want to go home and get my head down for a couple of hours, or I'll never make it through tonight.'

'Why not take tonight off?' Bubba suggested. 'I'm sure everyone will pull together and keep it running smooth. You need a break.'

'I can't,' Jenna said, her eyes dark with worry. 'I'd only be wondering what was happening here while I was away. What if those men come back and threaten anyone else? Or hurt someone, even.'

'We'll deal with it,' Fabian said, agreeing with Bubba that Jenna was better off at home.

'I can't,' she said again, more firmly this time. 'It'd probably be even worse at home. I need to be here.'

'Well, you know we've got your back,' Bubba said. 'Anything happens, we're right in there.'

'Let's hope it doesn't get to that,' Jenna said standing up. Anyway I'd better go, or I'll have no time to get ready.'

'Want us to walk you through the yard?' Fabian offered.

Shaking her head, Jenna said, 'No. I'll get a taxi out front.'

'What about when you get home? Are you going to be all right going in?'

'Yeah, I'll get the security guard to come in with me. Stop worrying, I'll be fine.'

'Ballsy lady,' Bubba commented when she walked out.

'Mmm,' Fabian murmured. 'Let's just hope she doesn't try to handle this on her own, or it could get a whole lot worse.'

Going home, Jenna did exactly what she'd said she would and got the guard to come into the apartment with her. She had him check every room, window and door – under the pretext of being concerned about an ex-boyfriend breaking in – thanked him and gave him a ten-pound tip, asking him to let her know if he saw any suspicious men hanging around.

Then, closing all the curtains and blinds, she turned on every light and took a shower. Feeling a little less tense after that, she poured herself a glass of juice and carried it into the bedroom, locking the door behind her. All she wanted to do was throw her hand in and run away. But she was shackled to the club now, up to her eyes in loan and mortgage repayments, and she couldn't afford to even *contemplate* giving it up with all that hanging over her.

Sighing, Jenna sat down heavily on the bed.

Is this it? she thought, looking around. *Am I going to spend the rest of my life locking myself into rooms, too scared to drive my own car home, having to ask a stranger to check out my apartment before I dare to go in?*

'No, I am *not*,' she said out loud, slamming the glass down on the bedside table and reaching for her handbag.

She might not be able to deal with this alone, but she knew one person who might be able to help.

Taking the number out of her bag, Jenna reached for the phone.

'Hello, Tony? Sorry to disturb you, but I think I need to see you . . .'

14

'Right, first things first,' Tony said, sitting forward with his elbows on his knees. 'You go back to work tonight as if nothing's happened.'

Frowning, Jenna plucked at the corner of a cushion. It was an hour since she'd called Tony, and he had arrived a short time ago with Eddie, and – for some strange reason – Leonard. Sitting with them in her apartment now, Jenna felt awkward, because it was the first time she'd had visitors since moving in, and they were all so big that they made her usually spacious lounge seem small and claustrophobic.

'I don't think I can do that,' she said now. 'What if they come back?'

'Believe me, they won't,' Tony told her with absolute certainty.

'How can you be so sure?' she asked, sincerely doubting it.

'Because I know how these guys work,' Tony said, his voice calm, his eyes reassuring. 'I will personally guarantee that you won't be bothered again.'

'I wish I could believe that,' Jenna murmured wearily. 'These last few weeks have been horrible. I just want to get things back to normal.'

'I hate to say it,' Tony said. 'But I did warn you. Men like that prey on women like you, trying to run a business on your own. There's too much money for them to resist.'

'But that's just it – there isn't,' Jenna said, glancing up

with desperation in her eyes. 'If there was, I'd probably pay
them to keep them off my back. But there's barely enough
coming in now to pay the wages, never mind anything else.'

'That bad?' Tony asked.

'Worse.' Shaking her head, Jenna ran her hands through
her hair. 'God, I don't know what I did to deserve this, but
I'm in such a mess. I'll be okay for another few weeks, but
only because we did so well at the beginning. After that . . .'
She shrugged. 'I'm seriously thinking of closing down.'

'Oh, no, you mustn't,' Leonard chipped in. 'Your dad
wouldn't want you to.'

'I know.' She sighed despondently. 'But he wouldn't want
me to go through this, either.'

'You don't have to,' Tony said. 'Not now, because we're
going to help you.'

Glancing up at him, Jenna gave him a defeated smile. 'I
hope you can.'

'You *know* I can, or you wouldn't have called me,' Tony
reminded her. 'So, now I'm here, you've got to trust me
enough to do what I say. And that means going back to work
as if everything's hunky-dory, yeah?'

'All right,' Jenna agreed. 'But can I call you if anything
happens? Only I really don't want to involve the police.'

'Smart decision,' Tony said, slipping one of his cigars out
of the pack. 'D'yuh mind?'

Jenna would have preferred that he didn't smoke in her
lounge because the smell would linger for days. But if the
alternative was the smell of her own blood when those men
came round to 'visit', so be it.

'I'll get you an ashtray,' she said, getting up. 'Can I get
anybody a drink?'

'Scotch all round, if you've got it,' Tony said, following
her into the kitchen.

Closing the door when they got there, he said, 'You do

know I'm going to sort this, don't you?' Holding on to her hand now when she passed him a saucer for his cigar ash, he added, 'And there won't be no comeback, 'cos when I deal with something it stays dealt with.'

Looking into his eyes, Jenna saw the same dark intensity that she had seen when she'd first met him. She had sensed then that he would be deeply loyal to his chosen few, and deeply dangerous to many others. She was getting a taste of what that actually meant now, because he must consider her a friend or he wouldn't be there.

'Hey, what's the matter?' Tony asked when her eyes suddenly filled with tears. 'Is there something you haven't told me?' Anger in his voice now, he said, 'They didn't touch you, did they? 'Cos if they did, they won't just be dealt with, they'll be—'

'No.' Shaking her head, Jenna bit her lip to bring herself under control. 'I'm just glad you're here,' she said, aware that her chin was quivering. 'I didn't know who else to turn to.'

Pulling her to him, Tony held her, saying quietly. 'Well, I'm glad you chose me, 'cos I got a lot of time for you. You know that, right?'

Feeling safe for the first time in weeks, Jenna rested her head against his broad chest and nodded.

'I told you a while back that you and me would make a good team,' he told her then. 'And I offered to be your partner. Do you remember that?'

Sniffing softly, Jenna gave another nod.

'Well, I'm offering the same thing now,' Tony went on. 'Only I want you to really think about it this time, 'cos I can stop *these* men coming near you again, but what's gonna happen when the next lot decide to try it on and I'm not here to protect you?' Feeling Jenna tense in his arms, he rubbed her back soothingly. 'Hey, I'm not trying to scare

you, but you gotta be realistic. You got more than just these
guys to worry about, by the sound of it, and I can help you
all round. We can help each other, in fact, 'cos I got the
money you need, and you got what I need to be able to stay
over here.'

Jenna's mind was whirling. She hadn't wanted a partner.
Her dad had done without help for twenty-odd years, and
she'd wanted to do the same. But the thought of going through
more of what she'd been through recently just sapped all the
fight out of her. And Tony was right – what would she do if
this happened again and he wasn't here to help her? And, as
he'd said, he needed her just as much as she needed him.
Could she really deny him the chance to make a go of it over
here when he was putting himself out for her like this?

'Okay,' she murmured, feeling a rush of relief as soon as
the word was out.

'Okay?' Easing her away from him, Tony gazed down at
her. 'You said that, right?'

Looking up at him, Jenna smiled. 'Yeah, I said it. I'll let
you buy into the club. On one condition.'

'Name it.'

'I keep fifty-one per cent. It might seem petty, but the
extra one is for my dad.'

Mulling it over for a second, Tony nodded. 'You got a
deal. But I've got a condition of my own.'

'What's that?' Jenna reached behind her for the kitchen
roll. Ripping a piece off, she blew her nose.

'That you draw the contracts up in Lenny's name,' Tony
said, perching on the back of one of the kitchen chairs now.
'It's my money, and I'll be your actual partner, but that's
the way I want it.'

'It's not illegal, is it?' Jenna asked worriedly.

'Hey, come on, now.' Tony drew his head back. 'Do I
look like a dodgy guy to you?'

'No, but . . .' Pausing, Jenna shrugged. 'It just seems weird.'

'Granted it ain't the most conventional way to do business,' Tony said. 'But if you knew what I've been through since I got here, you'd understand. I was walking around with a million dollars in my pocket and nowhere to put it before Lenny offered me a helping hand. That's why I want to do this for him now. We both know how bad he wants to be part of the whole club scene, and this is my way of thanking him for everything he's done. With the added benefit of me getting my feet through the door, without the hassle of having to produce papers I ain't got and can't get.'

'Are you sure Leonard *wants* to be involved?' Jenna asked. 'And are you really sure *you* want to do it like this? It's a massive risk handing over that much money and letting him put *his* name to *your* business. What if he decides to cut you out? You'd have no proof that it's got anything to do with you.'

'You kidding me?' Tony chuckled. 'Lenny's a diamond. I'd trust him with my life. You must know how decent he is, what with him and your dad being friends and all.'

'I suppose so,' Jenna murmured. Then, 'Well, I guess if you're both okay with it, there's no reason for me to object, is there?'

'Partners, then?' Tony held out his hand.

'Partners.' Jenna shook it.

'And no one knows about our arrangement, but me, you, Ed and Len. Agreed?'

'Agreed.' Laughing softly now, Jenna shook her head, wondering what on earth she'd let herself in for.

PART TWO

15

Unlocking the door, Tony walked into the larger of the club's two storerooms. It was a vast space, with rough brick walls and a dirty cement floor, situated behind the wall housing the DJ's booth. It spanned the entire width of the club, and had several sub-rooms and alcoved sections. It was also freezing, stank of damp, and was too far away from the back yard and the bars to make it practical for storing alcohol, so all it was used for was storing the cleaning supplies and equipment.

Switching on the light now, Tony held the door open for Jenna to precede him in.

'I was thinking that if we moved all this out,' he said, waving at the boxes of toilet rolls, kitchen towels, soaps and disinfectants that were stacked floor to ceiling along one wall, 'we'd have room for a small bar. And if we take these down –' he indicated the ancient built-in shelves that lined the opposite wall '– we could put in seating. Then we could lay down a small dance floor over here,' he went on, walking across to the back wall. 'Toilets in that section, and a small kitchen in that, where we can get us a chef to do special-occasion dinner parties, and what have you. The rest is just cosmetics – change the overheads to wall lights, give it a good paint job, and it'll be perfect. What do you think?'

'I think we don't need another VIP area,' Jenna told him, repeating what she'd already said before he'd insisted on dragging her in here to take a look. 'The celebrities like to be separated from the general public, but that doesn't mean they don't get a kick out of flaunting themselves in front of them. They *want* to be seen up there in the lounge. It's like a "you can look at me in my castle, but you ain't getting in" kind of thing.'

'Yeah, maybe some of them *do* like being visible,' Tony conceded. 'But there's plenty more who'd rather keep their leisure activities hidden.'

'If we're talking *illegal* activities,' Jenna said, folding her arms now. 'I don't want any of that in my club.'

'*Our* club,' Tony reminded her softly. 'And, no, I'm not talking illegal, I'm talking *private*. Take it from someone who knows, Jenna, there's stars out there who don't want to risk having pictures of them falling over drunk, or taking their mistresses out for dinner and a dance sold to the papers. They're the real stars – the real money. And there's no one in town accommodating them at the moment, so if we got this off the ground we'd have us some real kudos.'

'I don't know,' Jenna murmured. 'I just think it's a waste of money for something we don't really need – because it would cost a fortune to get it up to scratch. And we'd need permission to open it up as a public area, and that means being inspected by the Planning Department – which I'd really rather not have to get into,' she added, remembering why she hadn't sold the club in the first place.

'Believe me, it won't be wasted money,' Tony assured her. 'And the planning aspect won't be a problem, because Lenny's still got friends in high places.'

'I'm sure he has,' Jenna muttered. 'But I doubt even they could pass this without raising eyebrows.'

'Aw, quit worrying,' Tony said, flapping his hand as if he weren't concerned in the slightest. 'Lenny's already worded up a couple of his guys, and it's practically a done deal, so that ain't a problem. And there's a shit-load of politicians chomping at the bit to get at it. We won't even have to advertise, 'cos these people got an inbuilt radar for safe places to play. All I need is for you to say yes.'

'I'll think about it,' Jenna lied, hoping that he would be satisfied with that for now. And, knowing him, by the time she got around to telling him no, he'd have already moved on to something else. Glancing at her watch now, she said, 'Right, I'd better get home or I'll never be ready in time. You staying here?'

'For a while,' Tony said, still gazing around, envisaging the private members' club that he *would* set up – with or without Jenna's approval. He liked her, so he'd let her believe that her thinking about it meant something, but he would go ahead regardless.

Jenna was frowning as she made her way across the club floor. She'd been desperate when she'd phoned Tony that day, but he had taken immediate control, telling her that he would sort it all out. And he had done exactly that. She didn't know *how*, and she didn't *want* to know: she was just grateful that it had been so effective. The men who had threatened her hadn't shown their faces again, and there hadn't been a single worrying incident at the club since, apart from the odd little scuffle – which was totally normal and which the security guys were more than able to handle. Now, almost two months into the partnership, the club was well and truly back on its feet, with a full customer turnout and a full VIP lounge every night.

Jenna couldn't have been happier about that, but she was finding the transition from sole owner to partner a little harder than she'd anticipated. She felt dwarfed by Tony's larger-than-life personality, and she had to admit that it peeved her that certain members of staff had jumped so fast onto his side of the new ship. Maurice, in particular, was thrilled to have a male boss again, and Jenna had to battle not to jump down his throat when she saw him sucking up to Tony after he, Maurice, had treated her with barely concealed contempt for so long.

The major problem that she had with the new situation was the way Tony walked around as if it was *his* club. *His* club, *his* rules, *his* way or the highway. Some of his ideas had worked really well, like throwing a party for all of the original New Year's Eve guests, to bring them back into the fold. And the advertising campaign he'd organised, comprising posters being put up all around town, adverts in the press, radio plugs, and even back-of-bus ads, to let the public know they were back on track. But others were just plain annoying. Putting Eddie in charge of security a week after coming on board without even consulting her, for example. That had *really* pissed her off, but by the time she'd heard about it Jacko had already walked out in protest, taking three of the doormen with him. Fortunately, Bobby and Flex stayed and brought in a few of their friends to fill the spaces, so everything was pretty much back to normal on the security front. But it still annoyed her when she thought about it.

Still, Tony was here now and there was nothing she could do about it, so she tried not to let it get to her too much. Jenna reminded herself – frequently – that Tony could think he was in control, but that didn't make it true. She still had the extra one per cent, and everybody knew it was her club really. And, generally speaking, things *were* going pretty well, so she supposed she shouldn't complain.

Letting herself out into the yard now, she forced herself to smile when she saw Leonard manoeuvring his Jag in beside her car. He was here all the time these days, but he wasn't too bad when you cut through the pretentiousness. The only problem Jenna actually had with him was that he was so far up Tony's backside it was difficult to know where the one ended and the other began. And with Eddie completing the triangle of power, she felt a little overwhelmed at times.

'Hello, there,' Leonard called to her now, jumping out when he'd parked and greeting her with a kiss on the cheek. 'And how are we tonight?'

'I'm fine,' she lied, opening her car door. 'You?'

'Grand,' he told her, his smile a mile wide. 'Tony around?'

'Inside,' she said curtly, climbing into the car.

Rushing to the gate to close it after her, Leonard leaned down with his hands on his knees when she pulled up alongside and wound her window down.

'Could you make sure it's properly locked, please,' Jenna said. 'The delivery guys have left the beer crates outside again, and I don't want anybody getting at them. In fact, you'll probably see him before I do, so could you tell Maurice to bring them inside as soon as he gets here?'

'My pleasure,' Leonard said, waving as she reversed out.

Going in through the back door when he'd locked the gate, Leonard made his way through the kitchen into the clubroom just as Tony came out of the storeroom.

'You took your time,' Tony called, dusting his hands off. 'I thought you said you'd be here this afternoon. I was waiting for you to give me a hand.'

'Avril wanted me to take her into Didsbury to pick up some material, then she wanted me to wait for her to get ready so I could drop her at her women's-forum thingummyjig,' Leonard said, going to him.

'And what the good lady wants, the good lady gets, eh?' Tony shook his head scornfully. 'Well, now you're here, you can help me move these boxes. I don't know where Eddie's got to, but he's getting a bit fucking good at disappearing when I want him nowadays.'

'He's out front having a smoke with a couple of the security chaps,' Leonard told him, slipping his jacket off and looping it over the back of a chair. 'I passed them on my way in.'

'Figures,' Tony grunted, propping the door open with a box and waving Leonard into the room. 'Right, I want all this shit out. We'll put it in the boardroom for now.'

'I take it Jenna's agreed, then?' Leonard asked, rolling up his shirtsleeves.

'Sure she has,' Tony lied, passing one of the boxes to him. 'Did you speak to your guys?'

'Yes, I rang round before Avril dragged me out. They're all thrilled with the idea.'

'And you told them about the membership fee?'

'Yes, and it's quite acceptable. Lord Kimberly had a bit of a grumble, but he'll stump up once he realises that he'll have a place to hide away from Maureen and hang out with the chaps.'

'I don't imagine he'll be too averse when he realises what he's gonna get for his money,' Tony said, grinning.

'Jenna doesn't know about any of that, does she?' Leonard asked. 'Only I don't think she'd be too happy if—'

'She don't know nothing, and she ain't gonna,' Tony cut him off. 'She might stick her nose round the door when we get up and running, but she won't be interfering, don't you worry about that.'

'And you're sure those girls won't say anything?'

'No one's gonna say a word,' Tony said, getting irritated now. ''Cos they know what'll happen if they do. So quit freaking out.'

'Okay,' Leonard murmured, aware that he was getting on Tony's nerves.

Working on in silence until all the boxes were stacked on the dance floor, Tony glanced at his watch.

'Right, I gotta get back to the hotel. I need to get washed and changed, and check Melody's all right.'

'Oh, dear, is she still sick?'

'Something like that,' Tony grunted, shrugging into his jacket. 'See you later.'

'Bye for now.' Watching as he walked out – the front way, obviously planning to pick Eddie up at the door – Leonard looked at the boxes and sighed. The club would be opening in a couple of hours, so they obviously couldn't stay where they were. Big job for one man, but, oh, well . . . If it shifted another couple of pounds off his waist he wouldn't complain.

Lifting the first box, he'd just reached the office door and was struggling to unlock it when Fabian came in.

'What's going on?' he demanded, looking from Leonard to the rest of the boxes.

'I'm taking them to the boardroom,' Leonard told him. 'Tony wants them out of the storeroom.'

'Oh, does he now? And why's that?'

'Because we're going to be converting it.'

'Into?'

'A, um, private members' club,' Leonard muttered, not sure whether he should be telling Fabian anything but unable to bring himself to tell him to mind his own business. He was the manager, after all.

Peering at Leonard narrow-eyed, Fabian put his hands on his hips. 'Does Jenna know about this?'

'Yes, and she's quite happy about it,' Leonard replied, wondering why the man was giving him such a hard time. He had never been as unfriendly when Leonard had been just a customer, but he'd been decidedly frosty lately and it was beginning to grate.

Giving a grunt of disapproval now, Fabian shook his head and unlocked the door. Propping it open, he said, 'Make sure you stack them neatly, because I don't want them getting in the way. And be quick about it, because we need them off the dance floor before the customers arrive.'

'Well, maybe if you gave me a hand it'd be a lot quicker?' Leonard suggested, but Fabian was heading up the stairs already as if he hadn't heard him. Exhaling loudly, Leonard shook his head. There really was no excuse for such rudeness.

Going into his office, Fabian slammed the door, muttering 'Fucking idiot!' under his breath. He couldn't stand Leonard. Couldn't stand him hanging around all the time. But there was nothing he could do about it, because he was Tony's *friend*. And Tony was *God* – everyone knew that!

Jenna had obviously lost her mind when she took them on, and Fabian was getting seriously pissed off with the lot of them. In fact, he'd have been tempted to walk out like Jacko, but he didn't see why he should have to. This had been his club before any of them came along. He'd run it when James Lorde had been alive, and he'd carried on doing exactly that when Jenna took over – even if she hadn't realised it. But it was getting to be a bit of a joke now that there were three chiefs stoking the fire.

Still, it couldn't last for ever. Sooner or later, Jenna would come to her senses and realise that she didn't want to be involved with a thug like Tony. All Fabian could do was cross his fingers and wait.

Melody was still in bed when Tony reached the hotel. Walking into the bedroom, he shook his head at her, a glint of disgust in his eyes.

Pulling a sulky face, she said, 'You don't have to look at me like that. I can't help it if I don't feel well.'

'You're a fucking hypochondriac,' he snapped. 'There's nothing wrong with you. You just need to get your ass up out of that bed and quit moaning.'

'I didn't expect you to understand,' she muttered, pulling the quilt up higher around her chin.

Sucking his teeth, Tony went to the wardrobe and took

out a suit. Laying it over the back of the chair, he opened the drawer and took out some clean underwear, then went into the bathroom, slamming the door on her miserable face. He didn't know what the hell was wrong with her, but she was doing his head in with all this moping about.

Back in the bedroom, Melody rolled over in the bed as another bout of shivering kicked in. Chase had gone off on his tour of the States a day and a half ago – and she had been counting every single second of every hour in slow motion since, because he had forgotten to leave his stash with her like he'd promised. Or, more likely, he'd accidentally-on-purpose taken it with him – the selfish bastard. He knew that she didn't know anyone else to get it off, and now he was going to be away for months, so not only did she have to put up with Tony again with no relief, she had to face going cold turkey as well. And it was already killing her, so God only knew how she was going to get through the worst of it without Tony finding out.

Chase was such a bastard for slipping that smack into the coke that time.

Thought you'd like it, he'd said. *Thought you'd get off on the different textures of the stone.*

Yeah, right! He hadn't done it for *her*, he'd done it because *he* was a junkie, and like all junkies he'd wanted her to be a junkie with him. Such generous people, these smack-heads, always looking for someone to share the experience with.

Coming back from the bathroom just then, Tony grabbed Melody's dressing gown and threw it at her, saying, 'Get up. I've had enough of this shit. You're coming to the club.'

'Aw, no, Tone,' she moaned. 'I can't.'

'Get the fuck up,' he growled, glaring at her.

Peering up at him over the edge of the quilt, Melody knew she had two choices: get up – or stay put and get battered, and then be *made* to get up.

'Okay,' she muttered, an expression of pure martyrdom on her face as she eased the quilt back and sat up. 'But I'm only doing this for you, so don't expect me to put on a show when we get there.'

'I expect you to get your face on, get dressed up, and get your ass on the dance floor and make like you're having fucking fun, is what I expect,' Tony said, spraying himself with deodorant and reaching for his shirt. 'I own the place now, and you ain't even shown your face there in weeks. Always too busy in the fucking gym, or getting your freaking nails and hair done. Well, enough's enough, 'cos the gym obviously ain't doing you no good, and your hair looks like shit.'

'I take it you approve of my nails, then?' Melody sniped under her breath as she stomped into the bathroom.

Sticking two fingers up at the door as he ranted on behind her, she reached in to turn the shower on. Stepping beneath the hot spray, she winced as it poured over her head and face. It felt like thousands of tiny pins digging into her flesh, and her stomach was tied in a sickening knot of tension. But she couldn't refuse to go to the club again, because Tony would get really mad. Still, it might not be so bad, as long as she didn't have to sit with Tony and his sycophantic fan club. And she hadn't seen Fabian in a while, so that would be nice.

Fabian! Of *course*! Why hadn't she thought of that before, instead of lying in bed thinking that the world was falling down around her. Fabian could get her something to take the edge off. He wouldn't want to see her suffer like this.

Filled with anticipation now, Melody hurried her shower and rushed back into the bedroom to get ready.

Tony took off as soon as they got to the club. He no longer entertained his star friends at his table now that he was the owner, he spread himself about instead, visiting them at *their* tables, making his presence felt in every corner.

Alone at her table, Melody was so busy looking around for Fabian that she didn't notice Leonard approaching. She jumped when he stood right in front of her.

'Shit! You scared the fucking life out of me.'

'Sorry.' Frowning, because he wasn't used to hearing women swear like that, Leonard leaned down to kiss her on the cheek – a habit he'd picked up from Tony, but one which Melody, for one, didn't appreciate, because, while Leonard had undoubtedly lost weight, gained in confidence and regained a little of the once-famous sparkle in his eyes, his weight loss wasn't enough yet to have rectified the excessive sweating. 'Are you feeling any better?' he asked now. 'Tony told me you'd been sick. Nothing too bad, I hope?'

'No, I'm fine,' Melody murmured, glancing pointedly past him, wishing he'd get lost.

'Shame I didn't know you were coming,' Leonard went on, not taking the hint. 'Avril would have loved to have seen you, I'm sure. She was only saying the other day that we should arrange another dinner party. And, you never know, my children might actually be free this time.'

'That would be nice,' Melody lied, getting to her feet. 'Sorry, Leonard, you'll have to excuse me. I'm starting to feel a bit sick again.'

'Oh, dear. Well, off you go.' Stepping back to let her pass, Leonard called, 'Shall I tell Tony you're still not feeling well?'

'No, leave him,' Melody called back over her shoulder. 'I'll be fine in a minute.'

Seeing Tony chatting with Robbie Williams at the bar, Melody made a dash for the stairs. He'd liked Robbie ever since he'd done the Rat Pack tribute album, so he would spend hours with him, given half a chance. And Eddie would be busy doing what he did best – finding people to intimidate in his new role of security chief. Which left Melody plenty of time to find Fabian and get sorted out.

Dashing around the lower floor looking for him now, she spotted him at the foot of the stairs to the DJ's booth and crept up on him.

'Hello, stranger . . . remember me?'

Turning round, Fabian raised an eyebrow when he saw her. Melody hadn't been in much since Tony had bought into the club, and he was a little shocked by how much weight she'd lost. Looking her over surreptitiously, he saw that her voluptuous body was in danger of becoming thin – and that wasn't good, because she'd been perfect as she was. And her face was beginning to suffer, too, he noticed: her cheeks were gaunt, her eyes dull.

'How are you?' he asked, half expecting her to say that she'd been ill.

'I'm all right,' she said, smiling up at him flirtatiously. 'Have you missed me?'

Folding his arms, determined to keep this impersonal, Fabian said, 'I've been too busy. Your boyfriend likes to keep us on our toes.'

'Don't talk to me about him,' Melody grunted. 'I get enough of him at the hotel.'

'Still there, are you? I'd have thought you'd have found yourselves somewhere more permanent now that you've decided to stay.'

'Hey, Tony might have decided, but I haven't.'

'Oh, right.' Fabian shuffled his feet uncomfortably. 'So, what have you been doing with yourself?'

Smiling secretively, Melody said, 'You don't want to know.'

Guessing that she must have found another supplier, Fabian said, 'Ah, well. I'm sure you've been having fun.' Glancing at his watch then, he said, 'Right, well, lovely to see you, but I'd better get moving before your boyfriend complains that I'm not pulling my weight.'

'Is he giving you a hard time?' Melody asked, delaying him because she hadn't hit him for what she really wanted yet.

'Not really. He just makes you feel like he's watching you all the time.'

'Tell me about it,' Melody snorted. Then, smiling again, she said, 'But he's not watching us now. So, how's about we nip up to your office – for old times' sake?'

'I don't really think that's a very good idea,' Fabian said, glancing around nervously.

'Aw, go on,' Melody persisted, fluttering her lashes at him. 'We always had fun, didn't we?'

'Yeah, and look how it ended up.'

'We don't have to do *that*. But I could use a little line, if you've got one. And you know I've never said a word to anyone, so you can't say you don't trust me.'

Inhaling deeply, Fabian thought about it, then nodded. 'All right, but we'll have to be quick. And if anyone comes up, I'm just going to say I'm showing the new boss's girlfriend around. Okay?'

'Fine by me,' Melody said, already licking her lips in anticipation.

Up in his office, Fabian laid out two lines. Letting Melody go first, he did his, then locked everything away again.

Rubbing his hands together, he said, 'Ready, then?'

'Just give me a minute,' Melody said, pinching her nostrils together because her eyes were smarting. 'Wow, what's in that? It's really tingling.'

'I think it's been cut with something,' Fabian said, shrugging. 'Don't worry. You get used to it after a while.'

'So, you've got quite a bit, then, have you?' Melody asked snidely. 'Enough to spare an old friend some to take away and see her through the night?'

Peering down at her, Fabian frowned. She was acting weird; her tone was wheedling, and a bit pathetic. And she looked awful, he thought again.

'Have you been doing smack?' he asked, the words coming out of his mouth as soon as the thought entered his head.

'No,' she lied, dipping her gaze.

'Oh, Christ, you *have*,' he said quietly. 'What the hell are you playing at, Melody? That's the worst thing you could possibly do.'

'Don't you think I know that?' she snapped, annoyed that he was preaching and trying to ruin what little buzz she'd got off the line. 'It wasn't *my* fault. Chase spiked my coke with it.'

'Chase?' Fabian repeated. 'Chase Mann? You've been seeing *him*?'

'Well, what was I supposed to do?' Melody retorted accusingly. '*You* didn't want me – you made that perfectly clear.'

'I was *scared*,' Fabian shot back. 'Bloody hell, Melody, did you think it was fun having to look over my shoulder all the time in case your boyfriend was sneaking up on me with a baseball bat?'

'I told you I wouldn't say anything,' she reminded him. 'Didn't you believe me?'

'Not at the time, no,' he replied bluntly. 'You're too unpredictable.'

'I am *not*,' she gasped, looking up at him with pain in her eyes. 'You're making me out to be some kind of idiot, and I'm so sick of being treated like that. Tony talks to me like I'm a piece of shit. Eddie doesn't talk to me at all. *You* turned your back on me. The only one I had left was Chase. And at least he listens to me, and doesn't talk down to me all the time.'

Watching as Melody's eyes filled with tears, Fabian felt the old stab of sympathy in his gut. She was a beautiful woman, who had, just a few short months ago, had the whole world at her feet. He knew she'd been frustrated about Tony's reluctance to go home, but there was more to this story, he was sure, otherwise she'd have given up on Tony and gone back to Hollywood where she belonged. But she was still here: obviously still frustrated, twice as unhappy as last time he'd seen her, and desperate enough to be taking smack.

'Want to talk?' he asked.

Shocked when she burst into tears, he reached out and patted her on the shoulder, almost falling over when she immediately jumped up and threw herself into his arms. Hesitant at first, because this was what he'd wanted to avoid, he relented after a moment and held her to him.

'I'm sorry,' Melody sobbed, her tears soaking his jacket. 'But it's been so awful. Tony's got my passport, and he won't let me go home. And now my agent's dumped me because he's got a new bitch to push. And Chase went and slipped smack into my coke!'

'All right,' Fabian said softly, patting her back as she wailed. 'Come on, stop crying. You're making a lot of noise, someone's gonna hear you.'

'Sorry,' Melody said again, making little wet choking noises as she tried to quieten down. 'I've just been feeling so bad. I might as well tell Tony everything and let him get on with killing me. At least I'd be out of this misery.'

'Don't talk rubbish,' Fabian said firmly, still holding her as her shoulders heaved. 'You can't tell him anything, because he'll kill you, me, *and* Chase.'

'I don't want to get you in trouble,' Melody cried. 'But I'm so fed up of this. He won't even let me have any money.'

'You've got your own, haven't you?' Fabian said, wondering why she was letting Tony control her like this. 'You must have earned a fair bit from the films.'

'Yeah, but Tony's got my credit cards,' Melody told him. She seemed to be slowing down with the crying at last. 'He took everything off me months ago, because I said I was going home without him.'

'If things are that bad between you, why wouldn't he just let you go to be rid of you?' Fabian asked, rubbing her back soothingly.

'Because he reckons he owns me.' Reaching up, Melody dabbed at her nose with the back of her hand. 'Sorry, I've made a bit of a mess of your jacket.'

'Don't worry about it,' Fabian said, easing her away from him. 'Sit down – I'll get you a drink.'

Pouring two straight brandies, he handed one to her and perched on the edge of the desk.

'So, what makes him think he owns you?' he asked, wondering if he really ought to be getting this involved again.

Shrugging, reluctant to reveal the surgery she'd had at Tony's expense, Melody said, 'He kept me when I was struggling to make it in Hollywood, so now he reckons it's payback time.'

'Why don't you run away?' Fabian suggested. 'You must have friends you could stay with? And once you're safely out of the way, you could send the police to get your things. He couldn't threaten *them*.'

'No!' Melody looked up at him with genuine fear in her eyes. 'You don't know him. He'd kill me if I ever sent the police after him. That's the one thing I wouldn't get away with.'

'Why? What's he scared of?'

'God knows. I don't know *half* of what he gets up to. But whatever it is, Eddie's in on it. *And* Leonard – but they're just using him.'

'How so?'

'Oh, I don't know. But they've got to be getting *some*thing out of him. Why else would they be letting him hang around with them? It certainly isn't because they like him – not if you heard the way they talk about him behind his back.'

'Yeah, I wondered about that,' Fabian said, frowning thoughtfully.

'Yeah, well, don't go saying anything,' Melody warned him, worried that she might have said too much. 'If Tony finds out I've been talking about him, I'm dead.'

'I won't say anything,' Fabian assured her. Glancing at his watch then, he said, 'Subject of, we'd best get moving before he comes looking for you.'

'Before we go,' Melody said, reaching out to stop him when he went to stand up. 'I'm sorry for asking, but is there any chance you could spare a bit more coke? Only that line didn't really do anything. Guess I've built up a bit of a tolerance, huh?'

'Bloody hell, Melody, how much have you been doing?'

'Unlimited supplies.' She gave him a sheepish grin. 'Chase always has loads.'

'And Tony's never noticed?'

'He was too busy working his way in here,' Melody sneered. 'Anyway, he thought I was at the gym, or the hairdresser's, and there's no way he'd ever set foot in a place like that. He hates anything to do with women's things, and exercise is a dirty word to him.'

'Okay,' Fabian said, getting up and going back to the safe. 'I'll give you some more for now, if it helps. But you need to quit the other shit, or you're gonna be in a real mess.'

'I never wanted it in the first place,' Melody said, her voice glum. 'But I can't just quit without something else to see me through.'

'And coke's going to do that, is it?'

'It's totally different, but better than nothing. Have you never tried smack?'

'Never,' Fabian said, splitting his stash in half and looking in his drawer for a spare bag. 'It wrecks your looks.'

'Not always,' she muttered defensively.

'Don't kid yourself,' he murmured, glancing up at her. 'Come on, Melody, you must *know* you look like shit. And don't tell me it's worth it, 'cos you've just been in floods of tears telling me your life's in pieces.'

'Because of *Tony*,' Melody countered. 'I was coping when I had the smack. And I'm only like this now because Chase pissed off with it and I don't know anyone else to get it off.'

'So as soon as he comes back, you're just going to start all over again, are you?'

'*No.*'

Fabian shook his head. One minute she was saying she didn't want to do it, then she was defending it. But there was no point trying to talk her out of it, because she would do whatever she was going to do, whatever anybody said.

Slipping the bag into her bra when he handed it to her, Melody said, 'Thanks. I'll try and make it last for a couple of days, but do you think you'll be able to get me some more? I've still got a bit of money stashed away, so I'll pay.'

Folding his arms, Fabian sighed. Another lie? She'd just been crying that Tony wouldn't let her have any money, now she reckoned she had some stashed away.

'I'll see what I can do,' he said.

'Great,' Melody said, her voice filled with relief as she stood up. 'And thanks again for this.' She patted her breast. 'You've been a real friend.'

'Don't worry about it,' Fabian said, going to the door and checking the corridor. 'All clear. But if anyone sees us going out, just tell them I've been showing you the offices and the boardroom, okay?'

'Whatever you say.'

They were halfway down the stairs when Tony walked in through the lower door with Brenda Thompson.

'What are you doing here?' he asked Melody, his narrowed eyes flicking from her to Fabian.

'Being shown around, seeing as *you* couldn't be bothered doing it,' Melody said accusingly, giving Brenda the cold eye. 'What are *you* doing?'

'Same,' Tony grunted. 'Brenda's never been backstage before. Thought I'd give her the guided tour.'

'Hardly compares to a *real* backstage,' Melody muttered, folding her arms, wondering if this old bitch . . .

But no. There was no way Tony would touch it. She was about thirty years too old, for starters. And ugly.

Turning to Brenda now, Melody gave her an icy smile. 'You're in for a real treat. I've never been so bored in my life.'

'Yeah, well, you won't want to stick around for a second viewing, then, will you?' Tony said, waving Brenda on ahead. Turning back as they passed on the stairs, he said, 'Yo, Fabian. Make sure she gets back up to the VIP lounge all right, 'cos I don't want no repeats of the last time you was supposed to be looking after her.'

'Absolutely,' Fabian replied evenly, refusing to let show in his eyes the anger that Tony was *still* blaming him for that incident with the men who had hassled Melody, even though he hadn't even been there.

Seeing Jenna at the bar when he had escorted Melody back to her table, Fabian went over to have a word.

Smiling up at him when he reached her, she said, 'I'm just taking a five-minute break. Care to join me?'

'Yeah, thanks.' Sitting down beside her, Fabian waved Kalli over and ordered himself a brandy. Then, turning back to Jenna, he said, 'Can I ask you something? About Tony.'

'Oh, yes?' Jenna said, a flicker of something that Fabian couldn't quite read passing through her eyes.

'Yeah, I was just wondering what's going on,' he said. 'Only, I found Leonard moving stuff out of the storeroom earlier, and he said Tony had told him to because they were converting it.'

'Did he now?' Jenna said coolly. She hadn't known about that, and it pissed her off that Tony was obviously planning on going ahead without waiting for her answer. 'I don't suppose you'd know where he put it?'

'In the boardroom,' Fabian told her, sensing that she might not be as happy about this as Leonard had suggested – if she knew at all. 'He reckons they're going to turn the store-room into some kind of private members' club.'

'Yes, well, we did discuss it,' Jenna said, not wanting to admit that Tony was walking all over her.

'I see,' Fabian said quietly. 'Well, I guess you know what you're doing. But I'd appreciate being told when these kind of decisions are made, because it's pretty hard to do what I'm supposed to do if things keep changing. I mean, what am I supposed to say if the staff hear something and ask me about it and I don't know anything?'

Sighing, Jenna gave him a weary smile. 'I understand what you're saying, and I'll try to keep you informed in future. But you might have to bear with me, because Tony's a bit . . .'

She paused to find the right word, and Fabian went through a whole list in his mind that would have fitted the gap perfectly: presumptuous; arrogant; rude; dismissive; crooked; bent; *bastard*.

'Impulsive,' Jenna said. 'He's got all these ideas floating round in his head, and he likes to get stuck in while they're fresh.'

'But the final decisions are still *yours*?' Fabian asked, concerned that she might be losing control.

'Of course,' she said, meeting his gaze. 'My dad left the club to me. I might have screwed up and had to take a partner to keep us afloat, but that doesn't mean I'm going to let Tony take over.'

'Glad to hear it,' Fabian murmured. 'And who knows?' he said then. 'One day, when everything's going great again, you might be able to buy him out and get it back to how it used to be.'

'You never know,' Jenna replied quietly, doubting that Tony would ever relinquish his share now that he'd finally got it.

'So, this private thingy,' Fabian said now, his expression clearly showing what he thought of the idea. 'Is it actually necessary on top of the VIP lounge?'

Smiling, because he was echoing exactly what she had already said, Jenna shrugged. 'Tony seems to think so.' Leaning towards him now, she added conspiratorially, 'Anyway, I'd have thought you'd be pleased, if it means you seeing less of him and Leonard?' Finishing her drink, she put her glass down and got up.

'See you,' Fabian said, smiling now because she obviously saw more than she let on.

As she walked away, Jenna's smile quickly turned into a tight-lipped frown. She wasn't amused about Tony presuming that she would okay his plans, and she would have words with him when she saw him. Yet again, he'd made her feel as if her opinion counted for nothing in her own club, and she was getting pretty bloody sick of it.

Jenna didn't get a chance to confront Tony until the end of the night. Every time she'd seen him before that, he'd been talking to somebody or other and she hadn't wanted to disturb them. Catching him as he was about to leave, she called him to one side and said, 'So, what's this I hear about you moving those boxes out of the storeroom?'

'Just thought I'd make a start,' he told her, giving her a cheeky grin. 'No point hanging about if you were only going to say yes anyway, was there? And the faster I get the builders in, the faster it's done, eh?'

Looking at him, Jenna sighed. She wanted to reprimand him for going over her head; wanted to say that she still had the extra one per cent, and that he should respect that and wait until she had given him the go-ahead before he put his plans into effect. But she knew that they would be wasted words, because he was obviously hell-bent on going his own sweet way.

'As it happens, I *was* going to give you the go-ahead,' she said instead, refusing to let him think that he'd got one over on her. 'But I expect your builders to keep the noise and mess to a minimum,' she went on, asserting what little authority she had left. 'And they absolutely must not get in the way of the club, so no late nights rushing to get finished. Okay?'

'Oh, absolutely,' Tony drawled, giving her a wry smile. 'They'll be here at eight-thirty tomorrow morning, so they won't be disturbing no one. And the first thing they'll be doing is opening up that back door that's bricked up, so they won't even need to set foot in this side once that's out of the way.' Winking now, he said, 'Chill, partner. I've got it all in hand.'

'Oh, I'm sure you bloody have,' Jenna muttered under her breath as he walked away. There were times when she really regretted taking him on, and this was one of them.

16

As Tony had promised, the building work caused minimal upheaval to the rest of the club. They had unbricked and replaced the old door with a heavy-duty security one, and had used that as their entry point since, so Jenna had barely even seen anyone coming and going. In fact, she'd all but forgotten they were in there when Tony called her down from her office three weeks later to take a look.

'What do you think?' he asked, throwing the adjoining door open and stepping back to let her go in ahead of him. Hanging back in the doorway, he folded his arms. 'Pretty cool, huh?'

Looking around, Jenna's eyebrows crept up. It looked exactly as he'd described it to her that time: small dance floor complete with its own tiny DJ box, gleaming buffed-oak bar, plush seating area, signposted kitchen and toilets. It was classily decorated, too, in subtle shades of scarlet, green, and muted gold, the wall lights adding a warm glow to the whole.

'It looks great,' she said, truthfully. 'But how on earth did you manage it? You only mentioned it for the first time a few weeks ago.'

'Hey, you know I don't like hanging around when I get an idea,' Tony said, shrugging casually. 'I just told the builders what I wanted, and left them to it.'

'Yes, but how did you get them to finish so fast?' Jenna turned to look at him now. 'It took my builders almost two months to finish my office bathroom, and that was already half done.'

'It's a man thing.' Tony grinned. 'You just gotta know the right thing to say.'

'What, like, do it fast or I'll break your legs?' she teased.

'*Now* you're getting it.' Tony chuckled. 'But, hey, don't knock it if it works. And as you can see, it does.' He waved a hand around the room.

Taking another look, Jenna nodded. 'Credit where it's due, you've done an amazing job. So, what's the plan?'

'We open tonight,' Tony told her, relighting the cigar he'd been chewing throughout. 'Lenny's got a load of his old buddies coming in, and I've got some folks lined up, too. It'll be a blast.'

'Do I get an invite?' Jenna smiled up at him.

'Hey, you don't need no invite,' Tony told her, throwing an arm around her shoulder. 'But I don't think you'll like it much, 'cos it's gonna be a lot quieter in here than out there. Just a load of old guys smoking and drinking, and chatting about the good old days, when the jitterbug ruled and women knew their place at the kitchen sink.'

'Oh, so you've aimed this firmly at the ancient MCP crowd, have you?'

'The stinking-*rich* MCP crowd,' Tony said, giving her shoulder a squeeze. 'A grand a year in membership fees,' he lied, knocking a full thousand off the price he had set and already received from quite a lot of his new members. 'And for that, they get their own entrance and exit out of the public glare; a free glass of champagne every visit; and we got us a top-notch chef to dish up the grits. Can't be bad, huh?'

'Hate to admit it, but you could be onto a winner,' Jenna said, gazing around again. 'I didn't think we needed another VIP area, but this is nothing like the lounge.'

'That *was* the intention. No offence, but the decor up there ain't what these folks are used to. They want this posh old shit. And Lenny helped me out on that, so I'm figuring it must be spot on.'

Nodding, Jenna said, 'It reminds me of one of those gentlemen's clubs you see in the old Sherlock Holmes films.'

'Perfect. Just what we wanted.'

'Well, you got it,' Jenna said, walking back out into the main clubroom. 'So, I guess I won't be seeing much of you if you're going to be spending all your time locked away in there?'

'You'll see me,' Tony assured her. 'But locked away is kind of what I wanted to talk to you about, 'cos there's gonna be no access from this side of the club. Once the door's shut, it stays shut till the club's closed.'

'That's a bit impractical, isn't it?' Jenna said. 'What if I need to see you?'

Shrugging, Tony said, 'You'll have to give me a ring and let me know you're coming, so I can get Eddie to let you in round back.'

'Outside?'

''Fraid so.' Tony shrugged again. 'If we open the adjoining door, the Zenith punters will see straight into The Diamond, and that'd negate the absolute privacy guarantee, wouldn't it?'

'The diamond?' Jenna gazed at him blankly.

'Oh, yeah, that's what I'm calling it,' Tony told her. 'Got a nice ring to it, don't it? The Diamond Den.'

'Very original.'

'Yeah, I thought so. Anyway, Eddie'll be doing the security to make sure that no jokers try getting in from this side. And me and Lenny will be in there for the most part, so you'll have to ring if you need either of us. Or we can get some walkie-talkies, or something? Whichever you prefer.'

'How's about I just let you get on with it and I get on with this side?' Jenna suggested, thinking it was all too much hassle. 'I'm not walking all the way around the outside of the club in the dark. If I've got a problem, I'll ring and you can come round here.'

'However you want it,' Tony agreed. 'Before I forget,' he said then. 'I've stocked up the bar, but I'm gonna need to sort out an independent supply tomorrow, 'cos we can't be running round here every time we need a refill. Oh, and I need a couple of the waitresses for tonight.'

'My waitresses?'

'*Our* waitresses. Yeah, I want two for my side. We can spare them, can't we?'

'It's a bit short notice,' Jenna murmured. 'But I suppose we could juggle things for one night. Anyone in mind?'

'Yeah, them two blondes – JoJo and Vanessa.'

'Really?' Jenna was surprised. She'd have expected him to go for some of the older, more respectful girls, given the type of clientele he was catering to.

'Yeah, they'll go down a bomb,' Tony said. 'They're young and attractive enough to please the eye, but sassy enough to fend off any nonsense if the grandads get out of line. And they're friends, so there won't be none of that bitching we get with some of the other girls.'

'Well, it's your choice.' Jenna shrugged. 'I'll have a word with them when they come in, see what they think.'

'If they're all right with it, send 'em straight in to me,' Tony said, glancing at his watch now. 'I want to talk them through my rules before we kick off.'

'Rules?' Laughing softly, Jenna shook her head. 'I don't envy them.'

Tony drew his head back. 'Hey, I'm just a big old softy, you know that.'

'Er, remind me again how you got the builders to finish so fast?' Jenna said, giving him an incredulous look.

★

Summoned to Jenna's office when they arrived a short time later, JoJo and Vanessa could barely keep a straight face between them when she asked if they wanted to try out working for Tony in the new room. They had known about it for ages, way before *she* had even known that he was planning it. Tony had approached them as soon as he got the idea, letting them know exactly what would be expected of them, and what they could expect to get out of it.

And exactly what would happen to them if they breathed so much as one word about it to anyone – ever.

'I don't mind giving it a go,' JoJo said now, shrugging, as if she really couldn't be fussed either way. 'As long as I can come back in here if I don't like it.'

'That shouldn't be a problem,' Jenna assured her. 'How about you, Vanessa?'

'I'm easy,' Vanessa said, coughing to cover a giggle as JoJo gave her a dig with her elbow.

'Right, well, Mr Allen would like you to go and see him now,' Jenna said, standing up and waving them to the door. 'Just make sure you're on your best behaviour,' she went on, following them out into the corridor. 'Mr Allen's catering to a much older crowd than you're used to, so you need to be respectful at all times – which means no swearing, arguing, or flirting. Okay?'

They both nodded, their expressions suitably chaste, even though they were both thinking the same thing: that Jenna didn't know Tony at all if she thought he was expecting respectful behaviour from them.

'Good.' Jenna smiled. 'Give it a week and see how you get on. If you don't like it after that, come and see me and I'll see what I can do. Oh, and you'd best take your things in with you,' she said, walking into the clubroom and glancing at her watch. 'It's not long to opening, and you won't be able to come back through this side once the club's open.'

'What, so we're gonna be, like, locked in?' Vanessa asked. '*We* can't get out, and no one can get in?'

'That's the general idea.'

'Not even you?'

'Not even me,' Jenna confirmed, not noticing the sly glance that passed between the two of them.

'Girls,' Tony drawled when Eddie brought JoJo and Vanessa in. 'Welcome to a whole new world.' Beaming, he put an arm around the shoulders of each of them and walked them to the bar. 'This is my new barman, Juan,' he said, introducing them to the good-looking young man on the other side of the counter. Juan had glossy jet-black hair, and huge brown eyes framed by lashes that were longer than both of theirs put together.

'Hello, Juan,' they both said, eyeing him with immediate interest.

Nodding, Juan got on with polishing his glasses. He knew they both fancied him, and that he could have taken his pick of either of them, right here and now. But they had the wrong parts to get his engine running. Anyway, just like them – he suspected – when he put out he expected a damn good return for his efforts, 'cos nobody got this hot bod and gorgeous face for free.

'Right, girls, tell him what you want, then I'll show you to your dressing room.'

'Anything we want?' JoJo asked.

'Anything at all,' Tony told her magnanimously.

'Great, well, we'll have champagne, then – won't we, Van?'

Clicking his fingers at Juan when Vanessa nodded, Tony said, 'You heard the ladies.'

'It's really nice in here, Mr Allen,' Vanessa said, gazing around wide-eyed.

'Glad you like it,' he said. 'Because you'll be spending a

lot of time in here from now on – depending how you get on. So, what did Jenna say?' he asked then.

'That we should be on our best behaviour,' JoJo told him, smiling slyly. 'She's got no idea what we're going to be doing, has she?'

'None whatsoever,' Tony replied, his voice low as he added, 'and if she ever finds out, I'll know exactly who to blame, won't I?'

'She won't hear anything from us,' JoJo assured him quickly. 'We're not that stupid.'

'Let's hope not,' Tony said, still smiling. Picking the two girls' glasses up when Juan placed them on the bar, he handed them to them, saying, 'Right, follow me. The customers will start coming in at about eleven, so you've got plenty of time to get into your costumes and get your faces on. Oh, and in case you need a boost I've left you a little something in the dressing room.'

'We can't afford to lose two waitresses,' Fabian complained when Jenna brought him up to date. 'The rota is worked out to give us exactly the number we need each night.' Not that he should even have to be telling her this, he grumbled to himself.

'I know. But I imagine Tony forgot in the rush to get finished,' Jenna said, defending him because she'd already okayed him taking JoJo and Vanessa. 'It shouldn't be too much of a problem if we shuffle everyone around.'

'I don't think Maurice would agree with you,' Fabian replied tersely. 'He relies on JoJo when it gets full later on. Patsy's useless when there's a rush on, and this is by far the busiest bar.'

'Right, I'll send Kalli down to help Maurice,' Jenna said, knowing that he was right. 'And tomorrow I'll arrange proper cover. Okay?'

'Not really.' Fabian folded his arms now. 'Kalli's needed upstairs. We can't let that stupid boy run the VIP bar on his own.'

'Austin's a good barman,' Jenna told him, trying to stay calm – Fabian was annoying her now. 'And he'll have Diane to help him, so I'm sure they'll manage.'

'Neither one of them is good enough to run the VIP bar,' Fabian pointed out, a note of exasperation creeping into his voice. 'Kalli's got to stay up there. If anything, we should send the boy down here to help Maurice and Patsy. But I'm still not happy about it,' he added peevishly. 'You should never have agreed to let him take those girls at such short notice. Anyone would think his stupid room was more important than the club.'

'Okay, Fabian, I get the point,' Jenna retorted irritably. 'But it's too late to do anything about it now, so we'll just have to get on with it. I'll sort it out tomorrow.'

'I sincerely hope so,' Fabian said, glancing at his watch. 'Right, I'd best go and have a word with Maurice – make sure he doesn't start sulking, or we'll be buggered.'

'I'll send Austin down,' Jenna said, heading for the VIP stairs.

'Aw, do I have to?' Austin moaned when Jenna told him he was working downstairs tonight. 'I can't stand Maurice. And that Patsy's a right wimp. Please, Jenna, I'll do anything you ask, but not this. I need to be with my Kalli.'

'It's not a bloody crèche,' Jenna snapped, seriously pissed off that everybody seemed to be arguing with her these days. No matter what she said or did, somebody always had an objection. Or, like Tony, just disregarded her opinion.

'*I* don't mind going downstairs,' Diane chipped in help-fully.

'No,' Jenna said firmly. 'I want Austin down there. No

offence, but he can handle a rush much better than you, Diane, and it's the busiest night tonight, so I don't want to take any chances.'

Nodding, Diane stepped back and left them to it.

'Please,' Austin implored, looking up at Jenna through his lashes. 'I really, really hate Maurice. He's a horrible old man.'

Jenna had to fight the urge to laugh. She knew exactly how Austin felt, but she wasn't about to say that, because it was hardly professional. Instead, she gave him a mock-stern look and said, 'Yes, well, just try and stay away from him as much as possible and you'll be fine. If we're still short-staffed tomorrow, I'll think about letting Diane go down. But I need *you* down there tonight.'

Pulling a sulky face, Austin folded his arms. 'Why isn't JoJo doing it? I bet she's skiving.'

'She and Vanessa are working for Mr Allen now,' Jenna told him. 'So get used to it, and stop moaning. I'll get onto hiring some new girls first thing tomorrow.'

'Can't you get boys?' Austin suggested, perking up a little. 'We could do with some fresh blood around here.'

'Don't you mean fresh meat?' Jenna gazed at him knowingly.

'Miss *Lorde*!' he gasped, his eyes sparkling with delight. 'I never thought you'd come out with something like *that*!'

'Yes, well, maybe I'm not quite as stupid as I look, eh?' she replied amusedly. 'There are quite enough boys already, and I'm replacing *girls*, so there we go.'

'Fine,' Austin said, rolling his eyes resignedly. 'Will JoJo and Vanessa be doing whatever they're doing for long?' he asked then. 'Only I thought we were all working for Mr Allen now, anyway.'

'He's got a new project of his own,' Jenna said evasively. 'So they'll be helping him out for as long as he wants them to.'

'New project?' Austin persisted.

'An offshoot club,' Jenna said, refusing to say more, because it was really none of his business.

'In the storeroom?' Austin said, his eyes burning with curiosity. 'I *knew* there was something going on in there. So, what is it? Can I go and see it?'

'Absolutely not,' Jenna told him quietly but firmly. 'If Mr Allen wants you to see it, I'm sure he'll let you know. But don't be making a nuisance of yourself,' she warned then, her eyes clearly telling Austin that he wasn't to approach Tony about it. 'This is his and Mr Drake's project, and they don't want it to be general knowledge, so keep it to yourself. Understood?'

'Loud and clear,' Austin said, his mind already ticking over, figuring how he could get to know more without The Sopranos – as most of the staff now referred to Tony and Eddie behind their backs – finding out.

Leonard Drake! *He*'d tell him. The man had been following him around for weeks, and Austin was starting to believe that Kalli had been right all along. No, in fact, rephrase that – he *knew* Kalli was right. Leonard had the hots for him, but he was obviously too shy to come out and say it. Whether that was because he'd been in the closet so long that he'd forgotten where the handle was, or because he hadn't even admitted it to himself yet, Austin didn't know. But Leonard definitely liked him, and would probably tell him what was going on if he asked nicely enough.

A little bit of flirting couldn't hurt. And why not? Now that he was finally losing weight Leonard was actually quite good-looking. And he was so nice, too – which was more than could be said for Xavier. That two-timing little prick – *little* being the operative word! – had bitched and whined and complained and scrounged his way through seven whole months of Austin's precious life. It might be kind of nice to be with an older man for a change.

All depended how forthcoming Leonard was about this secret project. 'Cos you didn't get nothing for nothing in this life.

'Time you got moving, isn't it?' Jenna said, clicking her fingers in front of his face to snap him out of his trance. 'You'll have Fabian to answer to if you don't get your back-side downstairs in two minutes flat.'

'Great,' Austin muttered, dragging his feet as he made his way around the bar. 'Maurice *and* Fabian. Can life *get* any better!'

'Ignore him,' Kalli said when Austin had gone. 'He'll be fine once he gets down there.'

'I know.' Jenna chuckled softly. 'That boy should be on stage, he really should. Anyway, will you be all right without him?'

'We'll manage,' Kalli assured her. 'That thing you were just talking about,' she said then, lowering her voice. 'What did you mean by offshoot?'

'I can't really tell you too much,' Jenna said, glancing quickly around to make sure that nobody was listening. 'But Mr Allen and Mr Drake have opened a private members' club, catering to old politicians and reclusive stars. But don't tell a soul, because Mr Allen wants it to be strictly private. And I know I can trust you, but some of the others, I'm not too sure.'

'I won't say a word,' Kalli assured her quickly. 'And I'll make sure Austin keeps quiet, too. And don't worry about this bar. Me and Diane can run it with our eyes shut.'

'I know you can,' Jenna said gratefully. 'And thanks, Kalli. It's good to know I've got a friend in here, because I feel like I'm banging my head against a brick wall sometimes.'

Sensing that Jenna was troubled about something, Kalli

reached out and squeezed her hand. 'You sure it's just the club that's bothering you?' she asked, her eyes dark with caring.

'Yeah, course,' Jenna told her, smiling softly. 'It just gets to me sometimes, that's all. Don't worry about me. I'm fine.' Seeing Melody coming up the stairs alone just then, she said, 'If anyone needs worrying about, it's that girl. She's not been herself for ages.'

'I know what you mean,' Kalli said, gazing at Melody. 'I feel really sorry for her sometimes. Mr Allen's not very nice to her these days, is he?'

'Can't say I've noticed,' Jenna lied, thinking it best not to go down the road of gossiping about Tony. 'But I think I'll go and say hello, anyway. See you later.'

'See you,' Kalli said, watching as she went.

Melody wasn't the only one who hadn't been themselves lately. Jenna was getting more and more irritable, and looked tired all the time, too. Come to think of it, she hadn't been herself since Vibes had left. And she hadn't mentioned him for a while, so he obviously hadn't been in touch, which was probably something to do with her irritability. But there was nothing Kalli could do but be here for her if she wanted to talk. In the meantime, she would do her best to keep the other waiters and waitresses in line while they were under-staffed, so that Jenna didn't have to worry about that as well.

Melody was feeling a lot better than she had in a while. And tonight she was particularly upbeat, because Tony wasn't going to be around to keep an eye on her – for a change. He was going to be far too busy with his secret little club – the one that Melody wasn't allowed to go into, because it was a 'man-only zone', according to Tony. She knew he was lying about that, but she didn't give a flying fuck. As long as Fabian wasn't locked in there with him, she didn't care *what* Tony was doing.

Fabian was her favourite-ever man again. He'd been so good to her since that night a few weeks back, keeping her well supplied with coke to ease the pain of smack withdrawal. She didn't know what she'd have done without him, and she was dying to get something going with him again. He'd been keeping her at arm's length so far, but she understood that. It wasn't just the threat of having Tony on his back that put him off, he'd been genuinely disappointed in her for taking smack. But now he could see that she really meant it when she said she would never do it again, Melody was hoping that he would relax and they could start being honest with each other again. And tonight was the perfect time to talk to him about it, while Tony and Eddie were going to be locked away. It shouldn't be too hard, because she was sure that Fabian felt the same way. And now she wasn't looking so ill any more, and was dressed to kill, how could he resist?

But she'd have to wait before she went chasing him down. Zenith had only just opened, and Tony had another hour before his first night kicked off. Better to give it a bit of time and let him get really rolling before she made a move.

Smiling when Jenna came over to her table now, Melody said, 'Hi, how are you?'

'Knackered,' Jenna said, flopping down onto a chair.

'Already?' Melody laughed. 'You've not been open two minutes. How are you going to last the night?'

'With difficulty,' Jenna admitted. 'But never mind me,' she said then, flapping her hand. 'I'm just moaning for the sake of it. How are *you*?'

'Feeling pretty good, actually,' Melody told her truthfully. 'I was a bit sick for a while, but it's dying down now.'

'I did wonder,' Jenna said, smiling again. 'We didn't see you for ages, and you didn't look at all well when you did come in. Tony just said you had a bug.'

'Yeah, that's right.' Melody raised a hand to her throat.

'Think it might have been a touch of Mono, or something. Totally wipes you out, that shit. Feels like the worst flu ever.'

'Ah, the kissing disease,' Jenna said, rolling her eyes. 'I caught it when I first went to college. Nasty stuff. Lasted about three months, from what I remember.'

'That's the one,' Melody nodded. 'Still, it seems to be shifting now – fingers crossed. Fancy a drink?' she asked then. 'Or are you too busy?'

Pursing her lips, Jenna said, 'It is going to be a bit busier than usual – thanks to your boyfriend stealing my waitresses. But go on. Why not?'

'I have no ice,' Juan said, walking into the dressing room where Tony was sitting with the girls. They were in costume now, their sequinned bras and panties sparkling beneath the sheer negligee-like gowns, but Juan didn't even look at them.

'You gotta be kidding me?' Tony frowned up at him. 'I put a bag in there myself this morning.'

'There's an enormous bag of water leaking all over the *fridge*,' Juan said, folding his arms. 'I don't suppose that's it?'

'Fridge?' Tony repeated, slapping himself on the forehead. 'Fuck! I thought that was the freezer. So, where's the freezer?'

'In the kitchen,' Juan told him, his tone ever so slightly condescending. 'Next to the sink.'

'Fuck!' Tony said again, glancing at his watch and seeing that they only had half an hour to go before people started arriving. Zenith was already open, so he couldn't send anyone through the adjoining door to get another bag, and the girls definitely couldn't go outside dressed like this. Leaning back, he stuck his head out of the door and yelled, '*LENNY!*'

Rushing out of the toilet, still fastening his belt, Leonard said, 'Did you want me?'

'Yeah, I need you to go round to the big kitchen and get

a bag of ice,' Tony said. 'Seems someone forgot to put the last bag in the freezer like I asked, and it's melted.'

'Oh, right,' Leonard murmured, not too thrilled at the prospect of walking all the way around the outside of the club and down the dark alley to get in through the back-yard. But he could hardly refuse if *he* were the one Tony was referring to. He genuinely didn't remember being asked to move anything into the freezer, but his head had been so full of arrangements, he must have forgotten.

'Tonight would be good,' Tony was saying now, a sarcastic edge to his voice that didn't escape the girls, who smirked into their wineglasses.

Blushing, Leonard turned on his heel and walked away. That old nonsense had better not start up again. He'd had more than enough of people smirking at him before he and Tony hooked up, and he wouldn't sit quietly by and watch as people started being disrespectful again. Especially not those sluts in there.

Letting himself into Zenith's kitchen a few minutes later he found himself confronted by the sight of Austin, wearing nothing but his shorts as he stood at the sink, rinsing out his T-shirt.

With his back to the door, Austin didn't see who had come in but he felt the icy draught.

'Fucking hell! Hurry up and shut that,' he complained, turning around, giving Leonard a full frontal of his hairless chest and pudgy little breasts decorated with gold nipple rings. 'Oh, sorry, Mr D.' Raising a hand to his mouth, he giggled. 'Didn't know it was you, or I wouldn't have said that.'

'It's okay,' Leonard said, averting his gaze. 'I know you youngsters have your own way of talking.'

'Hey, you're not so old yourself,' Austin teased, leaning back against the sink. 'How come you came in the back way, anyway? You've not been out there the whole time watching me, have you?'

'God, no!' Leonard yelped, afraid that the boy might think him a peeping Tom. 'I've, er, just come round for some ice.'

'It's in there.' Austin pointed out the chest freezer in the corner. 'Is that for your secret club?' he whispered then, letting Leonard know that he knew. 'Don't worry,' he added, tapping his nose. 'I won't tell. I'll carry the ice round for you, if you like?' he offered then.

'Oh, thank you, but no. Best not,' Leonard said, knowing that Tony would not be pleased, even though Leonard would have liked nothing better than to take a leisurely stroll around the block and have a friendly chat right now.

Austin had been nice to him when he'd been a customer, and a positive delight since he became part of the team. In fact, he was one of the few members of staff who didn't treat Leonard like an interfering intruder when he went into the areas that had previously been off-limits to him. Like Fabian, some of the others had been rather cool towards him, if not downright offhand. But Austin was never anything less than friendly, and Leonard found himself seeking the lad out more often than was probably decent. But what was the harm, as long as nobody commented upon it – which, so far, they hadn't. And now that Avril seemed to have lost interest in following him around and was content to get on with her own thing, he was free to indulge himself with these friend-ships that would previously have incurred her scorn, if not her wrath.

'You all right, Mr D?' Austin asked, tilting his head to one side and peering up at him. 'You look miles away.'

'I've, er, got a bit of a headache,' Leonard murmured. 'Best get some . . . Ah.' Spotting the first-aid cabinet, he pointed at it.

Darting in front of him as he headed for it, Austin took

out a bottle of paracetamol. 'There you go,' he said, pressing
it into his hand. 'That'll shift it. If not, just give me a shout
and I'll give you a neck massage. Kalli says I've got healing
hands.'

'Kalli?'

'My flatmate. Gorgeous, bossy little thing. Works the VIP
bar.'

'Oh, yes, I think I know who you mean,' Leonard said,
remembering the pretty little Chinese girl with the highly
suspicious eyes. Or maybe that was just the look that came
into them when she stared at Leonard, because she certainly
seemed to suspect him of something. Though goodness only
knew what. 'I didn't realise you shared a flat.'

'Can't afford *not* to on my wages,' Austin snorted.

'Oh?' Leonard raised an eyebrow. 'Are they low?'

'Try limboing under the door, and you'll get an idea,'
Austin told him. Then, seeing the concern on Leonard's
face, he said, 'Hey, I'm only joking. They're not great, but
they're better than at a lot of places. Anyway, I like sharing.
Better than going home to an empty place every night, eh?'

'I expect so,' Leonard agreed.

'Don't know why I'm asking *you* that,' Austin said,
laughing softly now. 'You've got Mrs D waiting for you,
haven't you? She in tonight, by the way?'

'No, she's busy with one of her charity projects,' Leonard
replied. 'At least, she was earlier. But I imagine she'll be
tucked up in her bed with a book by now.'

'So you're living it up while you can, eh?' Giving him a
conspiratorial grin, Austin turned back to the sink to wring
out his T-shirt.

Trying not to stare at the tighter-than-tight shorts, Leonard
said, 'Erm, something like that, yes. Busy tonight?'

'*I* am, but I can't say the same for that lazy lot out there.
If I had to count the times I've been asked to do someone

else's dirty work tonight, I'd run out of fingers, toes, *and* eyelashes.'

'They're not taking advantage, are they? I'll get Mr Allen to have a word, if you like.'

'Hey, *nobody* takes advantage of me,' Austin said indignantly. 'I might look like a pushover, but this boy's got balls – pardon the expression.' Giggling again, he turned to face Leonard. 'So, how about you, Mr D? Reckon anyone could take advantage of *you* – apart from the wife, of course, 'cos that's a woman's prerogative, isn't it? To make our lives as miserable as possible.' Biting his lip playfully now, he said, 'Oops! Me and my big mouth. I shouldn't be saying stuff like that to a happily married man, should I?'

'You're entitled to your opinion,' Leonard said, feeling a little uncomfortable with the subject matter, yet thrilled that the boy felt able to speak so openly to him. 'So, do you have a . . . *partner?*'

'Not now,' Austin said, shaking the damp T-shirt out and pulling it over his head with a grimace. 'I did, but he cheated on me with one of my friends. And one of his. *And* some lad he met on holiday.'

'Oh, dear, I'm terribly sorry.'

'Don't *you* be sorry,' Austin said, reaching for a tea towel to wipe his hands. 'You didn't do anything wrong. In fact, you're such a decent bloke, I can't imagine you ever doing the dirty on anyone. I just wish there were more fellas like you out there. But oh well . . . we can't get everything we want, can we?'

'No, I don't suppose we can,' Leonard said quietly.

'Right,' Austin said, clapping his hands. 'Best get back to work before Fabulous comes looking for blood.'

'Fabulous?' Leonard repeated.

'That's what I call Fabian,' Austin whispered. 'But for *gawd*'s sake don't tell him, or I'll be out on my arse.'

'Wouldn't dream of it,' Leonard assured him, smiling conspiratorially. 'Mum's the word.'

'Jeezus, you wouldn't say that if you'd met *my* mum,' Austin said, shuddering as he headed for the door. 'She scares the absolute *crap* out of me. Bit like your man in there – the big fella.'

'Eddie?'

'Yeah, *him*. He gives me the *right* willies. Doesn't he bother you?'

'I haven't really thought about it,' Leonard said, realising that it was actually true. He'd been so busy focusing his attention on Tony that he hadn't really noticed Eddie. 'I suppose he can be a little intimidating, now you mention it.'

'A *little*?' Austin gasped. 'Wow, Mr D, you're a bigger man than me. Tell you what, you should come out with me some time, only I could use someone fearless like you to put that useless ex of mine back in line.'

'I really don't think I'd be much use to you,' Leonard chuckled.

'Worth a try.' Austin said, rolling his eyes good-naturedly. 'But, seriously, if you ever fancy coming down to one of my clubs, give me a shout, 'cos I reckon you'd get a kick out of it.'

'I don't really think I'd fit in,' Leonard said, folding his arms as his heart picked up speed.

'Rubbish,' Austin scoffed. 'Everyone's welcome down there. Gay, straight, bi. *Curious*.' Smiling when Leonard dropped his gaze, he said, 'No pressure, but I reckon we'd have a laugh.'

'That's very kind of you,' Leonard said. 'I'll keep it in mind.'

'You do that,' Austin said, adding in a whisper, 'only do us a favour, and don't tell anyone, 'cos I don't want them lot out there gossiping. They're too thick to understand that gays and straights can actually be *friends*. And while we're on the subject of keeping things quiet,' he said then, 'any chance of me getting a sneaky peek at this new club of yours?'

'Oh, I don't know,' Leonard murmured. 'Tony – Mr Allen – well, he kind of wants to keep it exclusive.'

'Oh, right,' Austin said, obviously disappointed. 'Never mind.'

'I would if I could,' Leonard assured him, feeling guilty now because Austin had been kind enough to offer to take him out – as a friend. 'Maybe . . .' Hesitating, he shrugged. 'Well, maybe one day, when no one's around.'

'For real?' Austin grinned. 'Cool!'

'But you won't tell anybody I said that?'

'God, no!' Austin promised. 'Right, well, give me a shout when you're ready – for my club, *or* yours. See you later, Mr D.'

'Yes, bye.'

Waving as Austin danced out, letting a loud blast of Kanye West in before the door swung shut behind him, Leonard put the paracetamol bottle back in the cabinet and went to get the bag of ice that he'd come for. Alone now, paranoia reared its mocking head, and he wondered if Austin's invitation had been innocent or if he were playing some sort of game. But surely not, because he'd never been anything but polite, so why would he suddenly turn on Leonard now? And Austin had asked Leonard to keep it quiet, so it was unlikely that *he* would run around starting sordid rumours. But you never could tell, so maybe it was best not to think about it for the time being. Not until he was sure that there was no ulterior motive behind it, because the last thing he needed was for anybody to get the wrong idea.

'What on earth have you been doing?' Maurice demanded when Austin got back behind the bar. 'And what on earth do you think you *look* like?' he said then, looking him up and down with a sneer of disgust. 'This is *my* bar, not some sleazy little dive running a wet T-shirt competition!'

'Keep your hair on,' Austin snapped back. 'I was talking to Mr Drake, if you don't mind. And as for this –' he plucked at the T-shirt. 'Some dickhead spilled red wine all over me, so what did you want me to do? Carry on serving in it?'

'Don't swear,' Maurice hissed, stomping away. 'You sound and *look* like a little guttersnipe!'

'Let's not *mince* our words, eh, Maurice?' Austin called after him, grinning knowingly.

Turning on his heel, Maurice marched back to him and thrust his face into his, spitting, 'Fuck off! I don't want you on my bar.'

'Tough tits!' Austin spat back. 'Jenna *told* me to come down, because *you*'re not capable of running the bar without JoJo, and I'm the next best thing – so there!'

'If you do not get out from behind my bar right this instant, I will not be held responsible for my actions,' Maurice warned, his eyes bulging from their sockets.

'Oh?' Austin folded his arms, his head wobbling like a *Jerry Springer Show* guest. 'And since when was it *your* bar? Did *you* pay for it? No, I didn't *think* so. It's *Jenna*'s bar, and *she* sent me down.' Holding his hand up palm out when Maurice opened his mouth to reply, he said, 'Say it, don't spray it. And, anyway, I'm not interested. I didn't want to work on this poxy bar to start with, so I'm going back to *my* bar, and you can explain to Jenna why *your* lousy bar fell apart without me!'

Flouncing out from behind the bar then, Austin walked away with his head held high until he was sure that Maurice could no longer see him. Then, giggling, he ran the rest of the way up the stairs.

★

Frowning when Austin came bounding over to the bar, Kalli swiped her hair back from her face with the back of her hand. 'I hope you haven't come to bother me. You might not be busy downstairs, but I'm run off my feet up here.'

'Well, Cinders, you're in luck, 'cos Buttons is home from the ball,' Austin said, leaping over the bar.

'Pack that in,' Kalli scolded, glancing around in case anyone had seen.

'Oh, don't you start,' Austin moaned. 'I had enough of that off Maurice. I was made up when he kicked me off his bar, but I might as well go back if you're just gonna be miserable.'

Tutting, Kalli pushed him out of the way so she could get at the spirit bottles behind him. 'What happened?'

'I got red wine knocked all over me,' Austin explained indignantly. 'So I had to go and rinse it out, yeah? Anyway, the minute I get back, the ugly cunt starts having a go at me, saying it's not a sleazy club doing wet T-shirt competitions, and calling me a guttersnipe – whatever the fuck one of *them* is. And then he tells me to fuck off out of his bar, or he won't be responsible for his actions. So, *I* said, "Oh, right, so it's *your* bar now, is it? I don't *think* so, matey!"'

'Great,' Kalli murmured, rolling her eyes. 'Just what Jenna needs right now. She sent you down there because she knew they'd struggle, so who'll suffer if it gets out of hand now?'

'Maurice,' Austin declared self-righteously.

'No, *Jenna*,' Kalli corrected him. 'Her bar, her club, *her* profits dropping because her staff are unreliable. And if her profits drop, so will your wages. Remember how bad it was getting before she took Mr Allen on as a partner?'

'Oh, per-*lease*!' Austin groaned. 'Let's not *exaggerate*, or anything.'

'Are you going back down?' Kalli asked, pushing him aside again.

'No, I am *not*,' Austin stated adamantly. 'Even if I wanted to, I couldn't, 'cos Maurice is out for my blood now – the big fat poof!'

'Right, fine,' Kalli said. 'I'll send Diane down. But if you're staying, you'd better make yourself useful, and no messing about.'

'*Moi*?' Austin gasped. 'You know you wouldn't have me any other way.'

'I know I'll be glad when you grow up,' she retorted softly. '*And* when you start taking some responsibility,' she added, giving him a pointed look. 'That electric bill hasn't gone away just because you turned it upside down and shoved it under the bread bin, you know.'

'Nag, nag, nag,' Austin droned, covering a mock-yawn with his hand. '*Bor*-ing!'

'Oi!' Kalli slapped him hard on his bare arm. 'I'm serious.'

'You always are these days,' Austin moaned sulkily. 'Where's my fun little gal pal gone?'

'She'll be in the flaming bin with all our stuff if you don't get your act together and start paying your share of the bills,' Kalli snapped. 'The landlord came round when you were chasing Xavier around the other day. He said—'

'Yes, I know what he said,' Austin cut in. 'You have told me a million times already.'

'So, what are you going to do about it?'

'Fucking hell, man! I might as well be straight, putting up with shit from me bird, the way *you* go on!' Austin grumbled. 'But if you'd quit nagging for long enough, I *was* about to tell you to stop worrying, 'cos I'm going to sort it all out.'

'How?'

'Never you mind.'

'What are you talking about?' Kalli demanded, peering at him. 'You'd best not be planning to do anything stupid, because you know they've been checking the till rolls every night since Mr Allen came in. If there's a discrepancy, he'll be all over it till he finds out who did it.'

'When you've quite finished, you suspicious little bitch,' Austin said, giving her a mock-offended look. 'I have *not* had my fingers in the till, and if you ever accuse me of it again I'll slap you so hard your eyes will be round in the morning!'

'All right, if it's not that, what is it?'

'Nothing yet,' Austin gave her a mysterious smile. 'But watch this space, 'cos I'm looking to get me a sugar daddy.'

'Oh, Austin.'

'Never mind *Oh, Austin*. I deserve someone nice after that little prick messed me about. I'm sick of always giving, giving, giving.'

'Stop being such a drama queen,' Kalli scolded. 'And don't you dare go after a rich man from this club, or Mr Allen will skin you alive.'

'Who mentioned *this* club?' Austin said, his face a picture of wounded innocence. 'If you must know, I'm going out after work. And when I find someone, I'm gonna rub him right in Xavier's ugly little mush. You can stand here worrying about bills and landlords if you want, but I've had it with struggling. It's time someone took care of *me* for a change.'

Shaking her head when he flounced away, Kalli sighed. She hoped he was only sounding off after being dumped by Xavier. But if he wasn't, she had a feeling that he would end up with a whole heap of trouble on his hands. Because Austin never did anything by halves; he always had to take every-thing to the extreme.

'Showtime!' Grinning, Tony popped his head back into the dressing room. 'Are we ready?'

'I am,' JoJo said, jerking her head in Vanessa's direction. 'Don't know about her, though. She's well sick.'

'Nerves?' Tony asked, his grin slipping.

'Probably,' Vanessa muttered, clutching her stomach. 'I've never done anything like this before.'

'Aw, you'll fly through it,' Tony assured her, coming in and clapping a reassuring hand down on her shoulder. 'Would I have picked you if I didn't think you could do it?'

'No, but—'

'But nothing,' Tony said firmly. 'You're the girls I wanted, because you're the best. Now get yourself up and give yourself a good jiggle about, 'cos I've got twenty-five horny old men waiting to be shown the time of their lives. So get out there, and blow the false teeth right out of their heads!'

'If they give us money, can we keep it?' JoJo asked, giving him a flash of tit when she put her hand into her costume to adjust herself.

'You earn it, you keep it,' Tony told her, thinking that he might just give this one a bit of what she was looking for one of these days. She had something about her. Kind of reminded him of Melody before she turned all Hollywood on him. And her breasts were decent enough. Bit of surgery, they'd be spectacular.

'Hear that?' JoJo gave Vanessa a nudge. 'We earn it, we keep it. And there's some serious money out there, Van. How hard is it gonna be to get them to get their wallets out? They'll probably have a heart attack with a flash of boob, never mind the rest. It'll be a doddle.'

'Attagirl.' Tony gave her an approving wink. 'Leave you to sort her out, shall I?'

'No, I'm all right now,' Vanessa said, taking a deep breath and standing up. 'I'm nervous, but I'm always the same when I get on stage. I'll be fine when I get started.'

'What's that about stage?' Tony asked, only half listening as he cracked the door to look out at the 'crowd'.

'She's a singer,' JoJo told him. 'Lovely voice. Does all that Motown, and old soul stuff.'

'Really?' Tony turned back. 'That's interesting. I reckon we could do something with that. Get you a little rig-up; give the old guys a bit of a cabaret. What do you think?'

'What, instead of the other stuff?' Vanessa asked.

'Maybe.' Tony shrugged.

'Hey, that's not fair,' JoJo complained. 'I'm not doing it by myself.'

'You'll do whatever I tell you to,' Tony told her sharply. 'But we'll stick to the plan for tonight. Talk about the singing tomorrow. And you,' he said directly to JoJo now. 'Come see me later, 'cos we got some things to sort out.'

'I didn't mean anything,' JoJo said quickly, scared by the intensity in his dark eyes. 'I was only sounding off.'

'Yeah, well, we'll talk later,' he said. 'For now, you can get your asses out there and give your audience something to dream about.'

After closing, Austin told Kalli that he was going on to a club and would be home in a few hours. Waving her off in her cab, he waited until she was out of sight and then nipped around to the yard. Standing in the dark alley outside the gate, he hopped from foot to foot, waiting for Leonard to come out and get into his Jag, which was still parked up.

Cursing when somebody walked out of the back door into the path of the security lights, flooding the yard and alley with brightness, he pressed himself back against the wall and waited to see who it was. Luckily, it was Leonard.

Unlocking the gate, Leonard pulled it open and went to his car. Switching his headlights on, he reversed out into the alley and got out again to close the gate. Jumping when Austin stepped out of the shadows, he cried, 'Oh, my good Lord! What on earth are you doing there? I thought I was being attacked.'

'I'm sorry,' Austin said, his fearful eyes swivelling every

which way. 'I was being chased, so I ran down here to hide, but the gate was locked so I couldn't get into the yard. I've just been hiding in the shadows.'

'Are you all right?' Leonard asked, full of concern. 'Who was chasing you?'

'Some men,' Austin told him, shivering visibly. 'But don't worry about it. You get yourself off home to Mrs D. I'll just stay here until I know they've gone.'

'I'm not leaving you in this state,' Leonard said, nervous himself now. 'Get into the car. I'll take you home.'

Folding his arms now, Austin shook his head. 'No, I couldn't ask you to do that. I'll be fine.'

'I insist,' Leonard said, getting back into the car and pushing the passenger door open.

Taking a last look around, Austin got in, saying, 'I'm really sorry about this, Mr D. I wasn't expecting you to do anything.'

'It's not a problem,' Leonard assured him, activating the central locking and easing out of the alleyway onto the road. 'Where to?'

'You can drop me on Kingsway, at the roundabout at the Levenshulme end – if you don't mind?' Austin said, settling back into the leather seat and gazing around. 'Wow, nice car. Is that a DVD player?'

'Yes, but I've never actually used it.'

'How about the CD player? You must have CDs.'

'Probably nothing to your taste,' Leonard said, overly conscious of his size in the confined space. 'I tend to listen to boring old stuff when I'm in the car, I'm afraid.'

'Like what?'

'Oh, you won't have heard of any of them.'

'Try me.'

Shrugging, Leonard said, 'Etta James. Ray Charles. Barbra Streisand.'

'You're kidding me,' Austin yelped delightedly. 'Streisand's an absolute diva; gays *love* her. And didn't you see that film called *Ray* with Jamie Foxx? The man was the *bomb!*'

'You really like it?' Leonard asked, his eyebrows raising with surprise. 'I was sure I was the last person alive who appreciated good music. Avril detests it, says it's too old-fashioned. And people at the club seem to prefer much more modern stuff.'

'Yeah, well, course,' Austin said, opening the glove compartment in search of CDs. 'They go there to dance, don't they? But you'd be surprised what they listen to when they go home. Loads of my friends like trance and techno when they're out zinging off their boxes, but they shove Will Young and Kylie on when they get in and want to come down.'

'I see,' Leonard murmured, not understanding a word of it.

'Oh, wow,' Austin yelped, finding a Streisand CD and reading down the titles. 'God, I love this album. Can you put it on?'

'Yes, of course,' Leonard said, taking the CD and slotting it into the machine.

'Man, listen to *that*,' Austin groaned, leaning his head back as the first haunting strains of 'The Way We Were' seeped in through the speakers like liquid gold. 'That's some expensive system you've got there.'

'Bang and Olufsen,' Leonard told him proudly. 'I had it fitted when I bought the car. No point settling for inferior quality on those long journeys.'

'You must have some dosh,' Austin said, quickly adding, 'Not that I'm being nosy, or anything. But, well, you can tell you're minted. You've only got to look at your clothes; and you've got a dead posh voice, too. I bet you went to university, and everything, didn't you?'

'Well, yes, I did my time,' Leonard admitted modestly. 'Three years at Oxford.'

'Check the brainbox,' Austin said, laughing softly. 'So, what did you do before you came to Zenith?'

'I was a politician,' Leonard told him, resting his arm on the door now and driving one-handed as he reached into his pocket for his cigarettes. 'I used to be on TV quite a lot.'

'So you're famous?'

'Moderately so.' Leonard smiled. 'Before your time, though.'

'See, that's what I mean about you,' Austin said, gazing at him admiringly. 'If you look at you, you're just any old posh man – well, not old, but you know what I mean. Then you get talking to you, and find out all this stuff you're into, and it's like, *wow*! I mean, I'd never have guessed you had such cool taste in music. I'd have expected you to be into really boring old white-man stuff.'

Leonard was flushed with pleasure. Nobody had ever described him as *cool* before, and he would never have expected it from a trendy young boy like Austin. Opening the cigarette packet, he offered one to him.

'Nah, I don't do straights,' Austin said, sliding one out of the pack anyway. 'I'll light yours for you, though – seeing as you're driving.'

Taking the lighter, he let his fingers graze Leonard's thumb, smiling to himself when the older man didn't immediately jerk his hand away. Good. Leonard was starting to relax. Handing the cigarette to him, Austin rested his head back again and sang along to 'You Don't Bring Me Flowers'.

'You have a very nice voice,' Leonard commented, admiring the way that Austin did both the male and female parts. 'Have you ever considered taking it up professionally?'

'God, no. Karaoke's enough for me,' Austin said. 'There's

a pub in the Village where we all go on a Thursday. It's run by a trannie called Marilyn, and everyone gets up and does a bit. You should come some time, you'd love it. They do all this kind of stuff.'

'Sounds nice.'

'It's *fab*. And everybody's dead laid-back. None of that nudging and winking, and "Ooh, what's he doing in a place like this?" Everyone just goes to have a good time, and your business is *your* business, know what I mean?'

'I think so,' Leonard murmured.

'Well, any time you fancy it,' Austin said. Humming along to the music for a while, he said, 'So, Mrs D does charity work, does she?'

'Yes. Spring and summer are her busiest seasons,' Leonard told him. 'As soon as the sun comes out, you can guarantee that I won't see her for weeks on end. She's invariably already left the house when I wake up in the mornings and, now that I'm involved with the club, she's usually tucked up in her bed by the time I get home, so our paths rarely cross.'

'Ahh,' Austin said sympathetically. 'I bet you really miss her, don't you?'

'Mmm,' Leonard murmured beside him. 'Well, here we are,' he said then, turning onto Kingsway. 'Where would you like me to stop?'

'Anywhere here,' Austin said, sounding disappointed that the ride was at an end.

Pulling up, Leonard glanced out through the window at the deserted street. 'Are you sure you'll be all right? I can take you to your house, if you like?'

'Best not,' Austin said, smiling sheepishly. 'I don't want anybody thinking anything if they see us in the car together. It'd be all over the club by tomorrow that we were having an affair, or something. And I'm sure you don't need that, do you? And I'd hate for you to stop talking to me just because other people can't keep their opinions to themselves.'

Leonard's heart was hammering in his chest. The boy genuinely liked him, and was trying to protect him. There were no games being played; no danger of turning up at the club to find his reputation in tatters. No danger of Avril finding out.

'I, er, have to pass this way on my way home, you know,' he said quietly. 'So, why don't I, um . . . well, I could give you a lift after work, couldn't I? Save you having to waste your money on cabs.'

'Really?' Austin peered at him as if it was the kindest thing anybody had ever said to him. 'Oh, wow, that'd be great. But what about your wife? Wouldn't she mind having me in the car?'

'Well, actually, now you mention it, she probably would,' Leonard said, tapping his fingers on the steering wheel. 'Probably best if we restrict it to when I'm alone, then. Like you said, we wouldn't want people to gossip, would we?'

Gazing at him, Austin sniffed softly. 'You know what, Mr D, you're one of the nicest men I've ever met. I'd give you a hug, but I don't want to scare you off.'

Swallowing hard, glad of the masking darkness, Leonard said, 'I'm not easily scared.'

'Oh, well, go on, then,' Austin giggled, lurching across to Leonard's side of the car and throwing an arm around his neck, his other hand accidentally-on-purpose landing on Leonard's thigh, high up. Near the groin.

17

JoJo and Vanessa couldn't resist nipping into Zenith to show off before going round to The Diamond on Sunday night. Going in through the kitchen door, knowing that all the other waiting staff would be in there getting changed, JoJo coughed loudly and struck a pose in the doorway before strutting into the centre of the room, calling out, 'All hail Queen JoJo and Princess Vanessa!'

Smiling smugly when everyone surrounded them to admire their new shoes and clothes, all wanting to know how they'd managed to afford them, they would say nothing, except that Tony Allen was the best boss – ever!

They had earned themselves a nice little wedge the night before, and all they'd had to do was lap-dance for a load of horny old men. Vanessa had hated the dancing, but she'd got on with it, knowing that she wouldn't have to do it for long if Tony went ahead with the idea of the cabaret. And she'd been more than happy when they'd hit the shops today and she'd realised that she didn't have to buy the cheapest of everything, because they would probably earn as much again tonight. Plus, Tony had lined up a private session for them with an old judge at a hotel later in the week – a session which, he had promised, would be very profitable.

JoJo had been nervous when Tony had called her into the dressing room after hours. But she'd soon cheered up when she'd realised that he wasn't going to bollock her – even more so when he'd slipped her an extra fifty for one little blow job. If things went on like that, her days of scrimping and scraping on her poxy waitress wages would be long gone.

They were still showing off when Austin came in a few minutes later. Giving their shoes a cursory glance, he sniffed dismissively and plonked his foot on a chair, casually examining his nails as everyone turned their attention to his new trainers.

'Wow, man, they're *bum!*' one of the waiters said enviously. 'I saw them in Foot Locker the other day. They cost, like, one-sixty, don't they?'

'Uh huh,' Austin drawled, as if the money meant nothing. 'But you've got to pay if you want the best in this life.'

Hanging back on the edge of the circle, Kalli narrowed her eyes suspiciously. Where had he got the money to be buying expensive trainers? And if he was that well off, why hadn't he paid the bills instead of treating himself? There was something funny about this. Last night he'd said that he was going to get himself a sugar daddy, but she knew he hadn't been to a club to find one, because he'd got back to the flat just one hour after she had. So he wouldn't have had time.

Pushing the door open just then, Fabian came in and glared at the staff. 'Oh, so this is where you're all hiding, is it? You *do* know we open in fifteen minutes?' Standing back as they trooped out, he raised an eyebrow at JoJo and Vanessa. 'Are you supposed to be here?'

'We're fine, thanks for asking,' JoJo replied cockily. 'Our club doesn't open till eleven, so we can do what we want.'

'Not in here, you can't,' Fabian retorted, looking them up and down, taking in all the new gear they were wearing. And what had they done to get the money for *that*? he wondered. There was no way that Tony Allen was stupid enough to pay them up front – or that much – for waitressing. So what else was going on behind that closed door?

Staring insolently back at him, JoJo said, 'Something taking your fancy, Fabian?'

'It's Mr King to you,' he snapped. 'And no, it bloody well isn't taking my fancy. Quite the contrary, in fact.'

'You can't talk to me like that,' JoJo retorted, facing up to him in the knowledge that she had powerful friends now. 'I don't work for *you* any more, I work for *Tony*.'

'You work for *me*,' Jenna corrected her, having come in just in time to hear what JoJo was saying. 'Which, in turn,' she added frostily, 'means that Mr King is still your manager – in here, *or* in there. Understood?'

'Yes,' JoJo murmured, dropping her gaze.

'Good,' Jenna said, nodding towards the back door now. 'Off you go, then.'

'Out the back?' JoJo gasped. 'But it's raining. Can't we just go through the club?'

'No, you can't,' Jenna said firmly. 'The adjoining door stays shut during club hours – as I'm sure you've already been told. If that's a problem for you, I suggest you go straight there in future, instead of coming in here bothering people.'

Gritting her teeth, JoJo turned on her new heels and marched out with her nose in the air. Just *wait* till she was Tony's proper girlfriend. See if that pair of dipsticks ever dared talk down to her like that again!

Smiling nervously at Jenna, Vanessa said, 'Sorry,' then followed her friend out.

'Cheeky bitch,' Fabian muttered when the door slammed shut. 'She's lucky you came in when you did.'

'Don't let it get to you,' Jenna told him, guessing that he must be even more annoyed to hear the insolence in JoJo's voice just now than she had been. The girl obviously thought she was onto a good thing working for Tony, but Jenna wasn't having her coming in here rubbing it in everyone's face. And she certainly wasn't going to let her get away with being disrespectful to management.

'Any idea what's going on over there?' Fabian asked now. 'Only I couldn't help noticing what those two were wearing just now. Obviously new, as well, which they certainly couldn't afford on their wages. Doesn't that strike you as odd?'

'I've got no idea what they're doing,' Jenna admitted guardedly, not really wanting to get into any sort of speculation with him – although she was wondering much the same herself. 'I'm just going to grab a quick coffee while we've still got time,' she said then, changing the subject. 'Would you like one?'

'No, thanks.' Fabian glanced at his watch. 'I'd best go out front and make sure everyone's where they're supposed to be.'

'All right. Well, I'll be out as soon as I've had this,' Jenna said, switching on the kettle.

Following Austin when he rushed into the foyer to show his new trainers off to the girl on the pay-desk, Kalli grabbed him. 'I want a word with you.'

'Not now,' he said, wrenching his arm out of her grip. 'I've only got a minute.'

'I don't care,' she hissed, jabbing a finger at his feet. 'I want to know where you got the money from.'

'I told you last night,' Austin whispered, wishing she'd pack in glaring at him in front of everyone like a tiny little monster. 'I found a nice old man to take care of me.'

'Where?' Kalli demanded disbelievingly. 'You weren't out long enough to go to a club. So, unless you picked one up on the street, you're lying.'

'For your nosy information,' Austin told her, 'I *did* meet him on the street, after you took off in the cab last night. I already knew him, but we just haven't *talked* before.'

'And you *talked* last night, did you?'

'We sure did.' Austin grinned. 'And then some.'

'And he gave you money?'

'Enough to buy these *and* pay the bills. Which is exactly what I'm planning to do first thing Monday, so you can stop nagging now, can't you?'

'You are disgusting,' Kalli snapped, her lips as tight as a drawstring purse. 'That's prostitution.'

Widening his eyes, Austin drew his head back. '*Whoa* there, Miss Dynamite! Isn't that a bit kettle-potty?'

'Don't you *dare* compare what you've done to what happened to me,' Kalli warned him, her eyes sparking with hurt and anger. 'You had a choice, *I* didn't!'

Bringing both hands up to his mouth, Austin said, 'Oh, God, Babe, I'm sorry. I should never have said that. I didn't mean it.'

'Didn't you?' Kalli said, still peering at him with pain-filled eyes. 'I wonder sometimes. But, no, you're right. It's got nothing to do with me. You can do whatever you want.'

Reaching out as she turned to walk away, Austin took one of her hands in his. 'Let's not fall out, sugarplum. I'm doing this for you as much as for me. Honest, I'm really gonna pay the bills on Monday. You don't even have to pay me back.'

'I've already got my share, thank you,' Kalli told him curtly.

'Well, keep it. Buy yourself something nice.'

'No, thanks. If I want anything, I'm quite happy waiting until I can afford it.'

'Okay, fine,' Austin said, losing patience. 'You play the martyr if you want, but I've done nothing wrong, so don't think I'm going to grovel. And it's not dirty, because I really like him – so there!'

Watching as he stomped away, Kalli exhaled loudly. She didn't agree with what he was doing, but she sincerely hoped that he did like this new man of his, because it would just be too nasty for words to have taken money off him otherwise.

Opening the door just then, Bobby stuck his head inside and looked around. Seeing Kalli, he waved her over.

'Do us a favour, and go tell Jenna there's a bloke out here asking to see her.'

'Sure,' Kalli said wearily. 'Who is it?'

'Dunno.' Bobby shrugged. 'Some black guy. He reckons he's been told to come and see her about picking up some stuff an old DJ called Victor Brown left here. Can you go now, though? Only we'll be opening in a minute, and them at the front of the queue are gonna get funny about him walking in ahead of them.'

'Won't be a minute,' Kalli said, already setting off.

Jenna had just sat down with her coffee when Kalli popped her head round the door.

'Sorry to disturb you, but there's somebody out front asking to see you.'

'They'll have to wait,' Jenna said, taking a sip of the coffee. 'This is the first cup I've had all day.'

'I think you should come,' Kalli urged. 'I think it might have something to do with Vibes.'

'Oh?' Jenna immediately put the cup down and stood up. 'Why, what did he say?'

'I haven't actually spoken to him, but he told Bobby he's been asked to come and see you about something you're storing for an old DJ called Victor Brown. Bobby wouldn't let him in because we're not open yet, but he told me to let you know he's out there.'

Thanking her, Jenna rushed to the foyer and told Bobby to let the man in. She felt ridiculously nervous all of a sudden, because Vibes hadn't been in touch for months, and their last conversation had been so stilted and short that she hadn't dared ring him in case he'd decided to cut ties with her.

The man was tall and pleasant-looking, and when he spoke Jenna heard that he had the same soft American accent as Vibes. She wondered if Vibes had actually sent him over to get his stuff. Or, worse, had he come, too, and was waiting around the corner somewhere so that he didn't have to see her? Oh, God! He must really hate her. And, what about this man – did *he* know her shameful secret too?

'Hi,' the man said, his eyes smiling as he held out his hand. 'It's Jenna, isn't it? I have seen you before, but we didn't actually meet.'

'Oh?' Jenna gazed up at him questioningly.

'New Year's morning. You gave Vibes a lift home.'

Remembering, Jenna said, 'Ah . . . you must be one of the men in the garden?'

'Running around with the Super-Soaker,' he admitted, grinning sheepishly. 'Yeah, that was me.'

Just then Bobby opened the door and tapped his watch.

Nodding, Jenna turned back to the man and said, 'I think we'd best get out of the way. It'll get rather crowded in here in a minute.'

'And I'll probably get lynched for jumping the queue,' he said, looking around as the first people came through the door.

'We'll go to my office,' Jenna said, waving him through the clubroom door. 'Sorry,' she said then. 'I didn't ask your name.'

'It's Kenneth,' he told her, gazing around. 'Hey, this looks great. I came in once, when Victor first started here, but it looks way different now.'

'Thanks,' Jenna said, a confused frown on her brow. 'Sorry, did you just say your name was Kenneth?'

'Yeah, that's right.' He looked down at her with a half-smile. 'Don't tell me Vic's been bad-mouthing me?'

'No, nothing like that,' she assured him, opening the door to the offices. 'I just thought Kenneth was his son's name, that's all.'

'He doesn't have a son,' Kenneth told her quietly as he followed her up the stairs.

'Oh, I see,' Jenna murmured. 'I must have misunderstood. When he was talking about the baby, he mentioned Kenneth, and I assumed it was another child. Sorry.' Unlocking her office door, she went in, switched the light on and waved him towards the couch. 'Can I get you a drink?'

'A light beer would be good,' he said. 'But I'm cool with whatever if you haven't got any. Neat shot,' he said then, looking at the picture of the tramp on the wall. 'Sure looks happy.'

'Simple pleasures,' Jenna said, pouring him a brandy and handing it to him. 'No beer, I'm afraid.'

Thanking her, Kenneth went and sat down. 'Sorry for dropping in at such an awkward time,' he said when she joined him. 'I came earlier, but I couldn't get an answer, so I thought I'd best try again when I knew someone would be here. I just wanted to set up a time to come get Vic's stuff out of your way. He was concerned that he'd left it too long already.'

'It's not been any trouble,' Jenna replied, her mind whirring with questions. 'I, er, haven't actually spoken to him for a while. I assume he's been busy with his family?'

Looking at her, a flicker of sadness came into Kenneth's eyes. 'He hasn't told you, has he?'

'Told me what?' Jenna asked, aware that she was gripping her glass a little too tightly. Could it be that Vibes's wife had found out about the kiss and was giving him a hard time? She didn't want to be responsible for causing them trouble.

'His family are dead,' Kenneth explained quietly.

'Oh, my God,' Jenna gasped, instinctively putting a hand

to the necklace that she hadn't taken off since Vibes had
fastened the catch. 'That's terrible. How? *When?* He sounded
fine last time I spoke to him. Did something happen after
that?'

'It was three years ago,' Kenneth told her, sighing heavily.
'A gang broke into their house while Vic was out playing a
gig. They were actually looking for the house next door but
got into theirs by mistake. Vic's kid brother must've
confronted them, and they shot him. Then they went on to
kill his mom, his wife, and his daughter, before going after
the guy they really wanted and taking off.'

'So they got away with it?' Jenna asked, her face completely
drained of colour.

'For a while.' Kenneth nodded slowly, his eyes dark with
painful memories. 'But they got caught a few months ago.
That's why Vic went back so fast – for the case.'

'I didn't know,' Jenna murmured, shaking her head. 'I
can't believe he's been walking around with this for so long
without telling us. It must have been killing him.'

'It damn near did,' Kenneth confirmed softly. 'That's why
he came to England in the first place. Me and Gina made
him come, because we knew he'd never get over it if he
didn't get a break from that place.'

'So Gina's *your* wife,' Jenna said, putting the pieces
together. 'And the teething baby?'

'Mine.' Kenneth smiled. 'Not teething any more, though,
I'm glad to report. Sleep's never felt so good.'

'I bet,' Jenna said, still reeling from what she'd heard. 'So,
how is Vibes?' she asked, thinking that it probably sounded
strange to Kenneth because he called his friend by his given
name. But she couldn't bring herself to do the same. 'Have
you heard from him recently?'

'Yeah, he called this morning. The case has been dragging on because of conflicting witness statements, or

whatever, but the prosecution think they've got it nailed now. The jury have been out for the weekend, but they should be ready to give their verdict tomorrow.'

'I hope it turns out the way he wants it to,' Jenna said quietly. 'What will he do after it's finished?'

'I don't think he's really thought about it yet,' Kenneth said. 'But he'll have all the time in the world once this is out of the way. It's always been there in the back of his head, stopping him from moving on. But once it's done, he can start over.'

'So he's not made any plans to come and stay with you again?'

Sighing, Kenneth shrugged. 'He's more than welcome, but it'd have to be *his* decision. No pressure.'

Sensing that he was warning her not to expect too much, Jenna said, 'Do you think it would be all right if I called him? Just to say hello – let him know that we're all still thinking about him. He was very popular here – everyone would be devastated to know that he was going through something like this on his own.'

'I'm sure he'd love to hear from you, but I'd leave it for now,' Kenneth advised, his voice soft. 'Just till they get the verdict.'

'Of course.' Jenna nodded. 'But do you think *you* could let me know what happens?' Getting up, she went to her desk and jotted her numbers down. 'These are my mobile, office and home numbers. I'll always be near one or other of them. I just want to know he's all right.'

'Sure.' Taking the numbers, Kenneth smiled. 'Soon as *I* hear, you'll hear.'

Thanking him, Jenna sat back down. Then she said, 'About his stuff, by the way. When he left it, he said he didn't want to leave it at the house because there wasn't enough room. Is that still an issue?'

'Well, there's no room inside,' Kenneth admitted. 'Especially now Gina's pregnant again.'

'Really?' Jenna smiled. 'Congratulations.'

'Thanks.' Kenneth gave a proud grin. 'Wasn't planned, but, hey . . . God and his mysterious ways, huh? Anyway, I'm gonna make some space in the garage for it. Vic was stressing, 'cos he promised he'd send over for it. But he's been stuck in the courthouse almost every day, and catching up on his sleep when he's not, so he hasn't managed to sort anything out yet.'

'It's not a problem, it being here,' Jenna told him. 'I honestly don't mind. It's quite safe, and definitely not in my way.'

Shrugging, Kenneth said, 'Okay, well, I'm sure he won't mind if you don't.' Finishing his drink, he put the glass down on the table. 'I guess I'd best let you get on, then. I'll give you a call as soon as I hear anything, and I'll tell him you were asking about him.'

'Send him my love,' Jenna said, standing up to show him out. '*Everyone*'s love,' she added quickly, not wanting him to think that she was planning to make a move on Vibes now that she knew his situation.

'I'll do that.' Kenneth smiled. She obviously had feelings for Vic and, if he was any judge, it was mutual. She seemed like a real nice woman, and was probably exactly what Vic needed to put his life back together. But it was too early to tell how Vibes would feel when all of this was over.

Coming back into the club when she'd shown Kenneth out, Jenna went up to the VIP bar to tell Kalli what she'd heard.

Kalli was as shocked and upset as Jenna to think that Vibes had been carrying that burden alone for so long. Her eyes immediately brimmed with tears. 'Please let me know when you hear anything,' she said. 'And give him my love when you speak to him. Tell him he *must* come back, so we can take care of him.'

'I'll give him your love,' Jenna assured her. 'But his friend doesn't want to pressure him into making any decisions, so I won't say the rest. Maybe when he's back on his feet and contacts *us*, we can hint that we'd love to see him again.'

'Good idea,' Kalli said, sighing heavily.

'Everything else all right?' Jenna asked perceptively. 'You seem upset about something.'

Pursing her lips, Kalli shook her head. 'Just Austin doing my head in. Nothing new.'

'Oh?' Jenna gave her a sympathetic smile. 'Want to talk about it?'

'No point.' Kalli shrugged. 'He's an idiot, but he's going to have to learn by his own mistakes – because I'm sick to death of trying to protect him.'

Just then, a group of Manchester City players arrived. In high spirits because they'd won an important match earlier that day, they came up the stairs arm in arm, singing loudly.

'Looks like you're going to have your hands full,' Jenna said, glancing around as the footballers neared the bar. 'I'll leave you to it. Give me a shout if you want to sound off.'

'Thanks,' Kalli murmured, smiling gratefully. Then, switching on the professional smile for the players, she said, 'Evening, boys. What can I get you?'

Leaving her, Jenna strolled around chatting to people for a while. But she wasn't really in the mood for socialising, so she went to her office to get away from it all.

She seemed to have lost all enthusiasm for the club lately, and she wasn't sure why. They were doing fine financially now, and the customer numbers were better than ever. But the place just didn't feel like hers any more, and she resented constantly having to assert her authority with people like Maurice and JoJo.

Maurice was a perpetual pain in the arse with his super-
cilious sneers and thinly veiled disrespect, but something was
really bugging Jenna about JoJo and Vanessa. Like Fabian,
she was wondering where they'd got the money for those
new clothes. The Diamond was Tony's project, sure, but
the staff wages were still going through Zenith's books, so
they shouldn't be getting any more than usual. And if they
were, it was totally unfair to the rest of the staff – and totally
out of order on Tony's part because Jenna had not agreed
to that. She'd have to ask him about it, but she wasn't looking
forward to it because he was bound to make her feel like
she was making a silly fuss about nothing. She couldn't just
say nothing, though, because he'd think he had free rein to
do whatever he liked. And they were partners – Jenna more
so than Tony, albeit by only two per cent – so every decision should be jointly made.

That said, she didn't want to jump in and start shouting
the odds when there was so much other stuff going on in
her head that might cause her to overreact. Not least the
matter of Vibes.

It had been bad enough walking around with the guilt of
thinking that he had cut ties with her because of that kiss.
But now that Jenna knew about his family, she felt not just
sad, and angry that something so terrible had happened to
such a good man, but even *more* guilty that she hadn't seen
the pain that must surely have been there beneath his smile
the whole time she had known him.

Just as Jenna left the room, Leonard came in from the kitchen.
Keeping his head down, he made his way up to the VIP bar
in search of Austin. They had arranged to meet on the corner
by the train station after work, but he needed to see him
now, to gauge where his head was at after last night's little
'incident'.

Not a lot had actually happened, but it had been enough for Leonard's heart still to be singing when he'd awoken this morning. Thankfully, Avril had been out already, so he hadn't had to suffer her sarcasm or suspicion, and he had spent the day just waiting for night to roll around so he could see Austin again. He couldn't stop thinking about him, but it wasn't just the joy of what had happened between them that was on his mind. It was the worry of what Leonard had learned about Austin's financial state, too.

They had spoken for some time, and Leonard had been dismayed to hear how much of a struggle it was for Austin just to get through each day. Austin had explained that he wouldn't get better wages anywhere else, given his poor upbringing and education, but his acceptance of his situation didn't make Leonard feel any better. Blessed with a wealthy family, a fabulous education, a well-paid career and a substantial inheritance, Leonard had never really believed that people actually lived like Austin did. In fact, during his time in politics Leonard and his colleagues had heard the same sob stories many times and had never paid them any mind. They believed that the people who complained of poverty were simply greedy layabouts who were unwilling to get off their backsides and support themselves and the multitude of brats they insisted on burdening the system with.

But the boy had quite opened Leonard's eyes to the inequalities that undoubtedly existed. Austin worked harder than most of the politicians Leonard had ever met, for a fraction of the pay, and all because he had never been given the opportunity to better himself. And Leonard felt that the responsibility for this lay partly on his shoulders, for having been a part of the system which kept Austin down. Not the rest of the spongers, just Austin. And now that Leonard had shown the boy a glimpse of how the other half lived by allowing him into his plush car, he couldn't, in all conscience, refuse to help him out.

Which was why he had driven the lad to the cashpoint last night and given him three hundred pounds from his private account. Small change to Leonard, but the look in Austin's eyes had made it feel as though he had given him a million pounds – and Leonard had never felt so good about anything in his life before.

The buzz had lasted right up until he'd arrived at the club tonight. But it had soon been dampened when he saw the looks passing between the blonde slut JoJo and Tony.

It was obvious that something was going on between them, just as it was obvious from her new attire that JoJo had been well paid for whatever it was. And the thought that she had wheedled her way into Tony's wallet sickened Leonard – almost as much as the so-called 'high-class entertainment' that his friends had been subjected to the previous night.

Tony had assured Leonard that the dancing would be completely tasteful and decent. But it had turned out to be little short of porn as the sluts paraded their naked bodies around the small stage. Leonard had been mortified that his friends – some of whom had been his *father*'s friends – had been tricked into paying for such a disgusting spectacle. He could only assume that the tarts had put their clothes back on soon after he had left the room in protest – given that nobody had actually complained. But he thanked God that Tony had decided to make it a men-only club, because if Avril had witnessed the shenanigans there would have been hell to pay.

Spotting Austin behind the bar now, Leonard approached him cautiously. The small Chinese girl was busy at the other end of the bar, and Leonard hoped that she wouldn't turn around and see him. He knew that his face would betray him if she looked at him with those penetrating eyes of hers.

Austin was equally nervous. Casting a quick glance at Kalli to make sure that she wasn't watching, he whispered, 'What are you doing here? I thought we were supposed to be meeting later.'

'Yes, we are,' Leonard whispered back, glad that Austin didn't seem to have changed his mind. 'I just wanted to make sure you were all right, after . . . well – you know.'

Smiling, Austin said, 'Never better. But you'd best go before someone sees us talking and puts two and two together and makes a porn film.'

'Yes, of course,' Leonard said, reluctant to leave now that he had seen the boy but knowing that he must for safety's sake.

'Oh, before I forget,' Austin said as Leonard was about to turn away. 'When you see JoJo, can you tell her I need to see her for a minute after work? I saw her earlier, but Fabulous chased us out before I got a chance to speak to her.'

'Well, I'm not sure *I'll* be speaking to her,' Leonard said, his tone clearly conveying his disapproval of the slut. 'Is it something I can help with?'

'No, it's just something she owes me that I need to get back before she forgets,' Austin said evasively. 'What's she doing in there, anyway?' he asked then, changing the subject before Leonard could ask what it was that she owed. 'Only she came swanning in here like the cat with the cream earlier, showing off her new shoes and stuff, and I was thinking there's no way she got them on our wages.'

'She's doing the same as she was doing in here,' Leonard lied, aware that he was blushing. Not the best of traits for a politician when lying played such a major part in the game, but he hadn't suffered from it so much in those days. Only now, speaking to people he liked on a personal level, had it become a problem.

'Mmm,' Austin murmured disbelievingly. 'Well, I'd have a word with Mr A if I was you,' he cautioned Leonard now. 'Only I know how secretive he's being about his business, and if she's doing nothing different that ain't the impression she's giving everyone in here.'

'Why, what are people saying?' Leonard frowned.

'That it's a whorehouse,' Austin told him quietly, casting another glance at Kalli and seeing that she only had one customer left to serve. 'Look, you'd best go. Kalli'll be over any minute, and she's too nosy.'

'Right you are,' Leonard said, still frowning deeply. 'I'll meet you as arranged.'

'Yeah, see you.'

Kalli reached Austin just as Leonard went down the stairs. 'What did Mr Drake want?'

'Dunno.' Austin shrugged. 'He was looking for Jenna, but I said I haven't seen her.'

Kalli narrowed her eyes. He was lying, she could tell.

'Are you going to stand there staring into space all night?' Austin asked, nudging her. 'Only there's still two hours to go, and a shit-load of glasses to collect.'

'Start collecting, then,' Kalli snapped, marching away. Whatever he was hiding, she would find out sooner or later.

Outside just then, Phil Dixon had his head down and his collar up against the pouring rain as he approached Zenith's front door. Tony had told him not to come to the club, but after several unsuccessful attempts to reach him on the phone over the last few weeks Phil was so pissed off that he'd thrown caution to the winds and had turned up to see him in person.

Bobby was standing in the doorway, his head barely covered by the arch. Looking Phil over when he reached the door, he shook his head. 'Sorry, our kid, you can't come in here wearing trainers.'

'I'm not a punter, I'm here to see Tony,' Phil told him, taking a last deep drag on his cigarette and flicking it into a puddle.

'Is he expecting you?' Bobby asked, guessing that he wasn't or he'd have told the man to go to the door of The Diamond, which was around the corner, down the dark, narrow alley between Zenith and the café next door.

'He knows me,' Phil said, pulling his sleeve back and glancing at his watch. 'No offence, mate, but I don't wanna be standing around in this all night. Just give him a shout for us, will you? Tell him it's Dix.'

Telling him to wait there, Bobby went inside. Seeing Fabian passing the clubroom door, he called, 'Yo, Fabian. There's a bloke out here asking for Mr Allen. D'you wanna deal with it?'

Already annoyed because Melody had been sitting with Jay Kay and his mates all night, making it impossible to get near her, Fabian tutted loudly. 'Who is it?'

'He said to say it was Dix,' Bobby told him. 'I'm not letting him in, though, 'cos he ain't dressed right.'

Opening the door, Fabian jerked his chin at the man. 'What can I do for you?'

'Nowt,' Phil said, blowing at the raindrops dripping off his nose. 'I want to see Tony, so be a good lad and go tell him Dix is here, will you? And don't take the piss and forget I'm here, or I'll have to start making noise – know what I mean?'

Frowning, Fabian folded his arms, safe in the knowledge that Bobby was right behind him. 'We don't take kindly to being threatened in here, so why don't you go away and come back when you've found your manners? Oh, and change the gear,' he said then, looking Phil up and down. 'We've got a dress code.'

'Bit of a joker, eh?' Phil sneered.

'Oh, yeah, I'm a regular comedian,' Fabian said, his face dead straight. 'But as the manager, it's my decision who does and doesn't get in, so I'd suggest you drop the attitude.'

'Are you for fucking real?' Phil snorted. 'Just get your arse inside and get Tony before I knock you the fuck out, you cunt.'

Peering at him, Fabian was about to tell him to piss off when he caught sight of his gold earring, which had a tiny boxing glove hanging from it – just like the one Jenna had described when she'd been threatened in the yard. Letting his gaze slide surreptitiously down to the man's throat, he saw the thick gold chain, but he couldn't see if there was a dog at the other end of it because the man had the collar of his jacket turned up. It had to be the same man, but why was he here asking for Tony when Tony had supposedly warned him off?

Suspicions seriously roused, Fabian stepped back and opened the door to let the man in.

'Sorry for being irritable,' he said, forcing himself to smile. 'I've been rushed off my feet tonight. But if you'd like to wait here, I'll have somebody find Mr Allen for you.'

''Bout time,' Phil grunted, brushing past him. Inside in the warm, he shook the rain from his hair and flapped his jacket.

Seeing the gold bulldog clear as day now, Fabian told him he wouldn't be a minute. Going to Bobby, who was back outside now, he whispered to him to make sure that the man stayed in the foyer and didn't go wandering. Then he went into the clubroom and tried to reach Tony on his mobile. Getting no answer, he snapped his phone shut and gazed around. There was no point trying the adjoining door because they wouldn't answer it, but there was no way he was walking around to The Diamond in the rain, and the doormen would laugh in his face if he tried sending one of them.

Austin passed just then. Grabbing him, Fabian said, 'I

need you to go round to the side door and tell Mr Allen that someone called Dix is here to see him.'

'Like this?' Austin gasped, holding his arms out to indicate that he was wearing shorts and a T-shirt. 'I'll get soaked.'

'Just do it,' Fabian snapped.

Sighing loudly, Austin said, 'Right, fine. But don't blame me if I get pneumonia and can't work for a month!'

'Don't worry, I'll have your cards sent on if we don't see you,' Fabian told him, pushing him out through the foyer.

'He won't be a moment,' Fabian said, giving Phil a tight smile. 'If you'll excuse me, I've got a couple of things to do.'

Letting himself into the pay-booth then, so that he would be able to hear what was going on when Tony came back with Austin, he told the cashier that she could go. Sitting on her chair, he sank down as low as he could in the hope that Tony wouldn't notice him, and started bagging up.

Austin was dripping wet when he came back a couple of minutes later. Shaking himself all over the polished floor, he looked around for Fabian. 'Where's he gone?' he asked Phil in a loud whisper.

'No idea,' Phil said, lighting another cigarette. 'Did you find Tony?'

'Oh, are you Dix?' Austin asked, giving him the once-over. 'Yeah, he'll be round in a minute. Couldn't give us a quick drag on your ciggy, could you?' he asked then. 'Only we're not allowed when we're working, and I'm fucking gagging.'

'Knock yourself out,' Phil said, handing him the cigarette.

Turning away from the clubroom door, Austin took several quick drags and fanned the smoke away with his hand before handing it back to Phil. 'Ta for that; I owe you one. Best get back,' he said then. 'If you see the funny fella, tell him to go fuck himself from me, will you?' Giggling then, he said, 'No, don't! I'll only get the sack.'

Smiling slyly, Phil said, 'Don't worry about it, mate.'

In the pay-booth, Fabian pursed his lips furiously. Just wait till he got hold of Austin. The little poof wouldn't know what had hit him!

Tony came in just then. Seeing Phil, he jerked his head and took him off into a corner.

'What the fuck are you playing at? I told you not to show your face in here.'

'So try answering your phone,' Phil retorted gruffly. 'Look, I ain't come for an argument,' he said then. 'I just want what you owe us, 'cos my lads are bugging me for it.'

'I don't appreciate being hassled,' Tony told him darkly. 'I said you'd get it, and you will.'

'Don't take the piss,' Phil hissed. 'It's been fucking ages, and you ain't been in touch once. Anyone'd think you was trying to avoid us, and that ain't on, 'cos we did our bit.'

Sighing, Tony ran a hand through his hair. 'I've had a lot on, it slipped my mind. Anyway, here, I guess you earned it.' Reaching into his pocket, he took out a thick wad of money. Peeling off several notes, he thrust them into Phil's hand, saying, 'There's a bit extra for waiting.'

Glancing down at the money and seeing how much extra there was, Phil grinned widely. 'Anyone else you want heavying, you know where I am.' Holding out his hand then, he said, 'Nice doing business with you.'

Shaking Phil Dixon's hand, Tony showed him out. Turning to Bobby with a furious scowl on his face when Phil had gone, he said, 'Who sent that waiter round to my club?'

'Fabian,' Bobby told him.

'And did he let that other dickhead in here?'

'Er, yeah.'

'Cunt!' Tony growled. 'I'll break his fucking legs when I get my hands on him.'

Marching inside, he stormed through to the clubroom in search of Fabian. Not finding him on the lower floor, he went up to the VIP lounge and stood at the head of the stairs, peering around narrow-eyed.

'Tony!' Brenda Thompson cried, coming over to him and pulling him into a hug. 'You've been neglecting us. Come and have a drink and let's catch up.' Linking her arm through his, she tried to pull him towards her table.

'Sorry, doll, I've got no time,' Tony said, gently peeling her hand off his arm. 'I'm looking for someone.'

'Who?' she asked, not giving up so easily. 'Maybe I've seen them.'

'Fabian,' he said, his teeth gritted.

'The cutie?' Brenda said, sighing lustfully. 'He was here a few minutes ago. I can never see enough of those toned buns of his. They're so delectable, it makes you want to bite them.'

'Huh!' Tony snorted. 'Probably 'cos they see so much action.'

'Excuse me?'

'He's an ass raider,' Tony elaborated scathingly.

'*Fabian?*' Brenda gave a deep husky laugh. 'Don't be ridiculous, darling. The boy's as straight as a die.'

'Believe me, he ain't,' Tony told her. 'Melody's in showbiz back home, and she's got a nose for that kind of thing. Anyway, you've only got to look at him to know he's got more woman in him than man.'

'My darling, I too am in the business,' Brenda reminded him. 'With a good few years on *your* little chickie, I might add. And I assure you that Fabian is no more gay than you or I. He may take care of his appearance,' she went on, with a theatrical shrug. 'But that, my love, is because these young ones have at long last realised that we girlies like a good-looking, sweet-smelling man in our beds, whose hair is clean enough not to stick to our inner thighs like glue and leave us with a nasty mess to clean up afterwards. Anyway,' she said then, flapping her hand, 'he's had several of my girlfriends, so I know he's straight. And they all gave such *glowing* recommendations that I'd be tempted to go for him myself if my little gigolo wasn't already wearing me out. Worth it, though,' she added with a satisfied sigh. 'So very liberating to pay for what you want and not to have to bother with the tedious endearments. Don't you think?'

Tony wasn't listening; he was too busy mulling over what Brenda had just said. If she was telling the truth – and there was no reason for her not to be – then Melody had either been mistaken or had lied outright when she'd told him that Fabian was gay. And he suspected the latter, because she'd have known full well that he wouldn't have let her dance with the cunt if he'd known that Fabian was straight. He didn't know what kind of idiot they took him for, but they would both be sorry if they'd been fucking around behind his back.

Filled with white-hot fury now when he spotted Melody flirting with a scruffy pop star whom he vaguely recognised, Tony shook Brenda off and made his way over to her table.

'Yo!' he barked, snapping his fingers at her. 'A word.'

'What's the matter, Tony?' Melody said, her eyes huge with fear when he dragged her over into a quiet corner. 'I wasn't doing nothing. He was just telling me about his tour. They've been in LA, and we were—'

'Shut the fuck up,' Tony yelled, gripping her arm tightly. 'I'm not interested in him. I want to know about the other fella – your fucking dancing partner.'

'Fabian?' Melody gasped. 'What do you mean?'

'What's going on with you and him?'

'Nothing!' she yelped when he tightened his grip. 'You're hurting me, Tony!'

'I'll do a damn sight more than hurt you if you fuck me about,' he snarled. 'You told me he was queer.'

'He is,' she whimpered, petrified now. 'Please, Tony, you're hurting me. And people are looking.'

'I don't give a fuck,' he said, bringing his face down close to hers. 'I've just had it on good authority that your friend is no more queer than *me*. So what's the game, Mel? You been fucking around with him?'

'Don't be stupid!' Melody protested, wincing when he raised his fist. 'Sorry! I didn't mean that. I just meant don't say stupid things. Of course I'm not messing around. Would I risk doing something like that when I know what I'll get? I swear on my mother's life I thought he was gay. If he's not, I didn't know, hon, I honestly didn't. I'll never speak to him again.'

Sidling past them, Austin ran down the stairs. He didn't think he should interfere, but Kalli was concerned that Mr Allen might start beating his girlfriend up and so she'd sent him to get one of the security guards just in case. Legging it down to the foyer now, he pulled the door open and told Bobby what was happening.

Back upstairs, Tony had decided to give Melody the benefit of the doubt – for now. Shoving her away roughly, he said, 'All right, I'll take your word. But if I find out you're lying, you know what's gonna happen.' Giving her a last warning glare, he turned on his heel and marched back down the stairs.

Shoving past Austin who was on his way back in with Bobby, Tony made his way out and walked quickly back round to The Diamond, deep in thought.

Still hiding in the pay-booth, Fabian was shaking. He shouldn't have sent Austin round there, and now that Tony was gunning for him he'd have to stay out of his way until he forgot about it. Which would be kind of difficult, seeing as they both worked here, but would still be better than having his legs broken.

'You been in there the whole time?' Bobby asked when Fabian came out with the money bag in his hands.

'No, I've been out back,' Fabian lied. 'Why?'

'Good job,' Bobby chuckled. 'Mr Allen's in a right strop with you. Apparently he's just had a go at his bird, 'cos she told him you was gay and he's just found out you ain't. Accused her of fucking around with you.' Laughing now, he shook his head. 'You're a right one, you.'

'Aren't you supposed to be outside?' Fabian snapped, fronting it out even though his knees had turned to water.

Waiting until Bobby had gone out, Fabian walked through the club and out through the kitchen door. He didn't know what had just happened with Tony and Melody but he wasn't sticking around to find out. Jenna could lock up. And she could open up tomorrow as well, because there was no way he was coming back until he knew it was safe. Melody wouldn't dare admit it, so hopefully she would convince Tony that it was all in his head. But until Fabian knew for sure that he was out of the firing line, he was on indefinite sick leave.

And there was no way he was risking telling Jenna about the man with the boxing-glove earring. Not yet, anyway. Much as she probably needed to know, that would be all the excuse that Tony would need to kill him.

Austin was already changed and on his way out of the door when Kalli caught up with him at the end of the night. Pulling him to one side, she said, 'Wait for me.'

'I can't,' he told her, leaning down to kiss her cheek. 'I'm meeting someone, and we're going to a club.'

'We need to talk,' she persisted, trying to hold him there. 'I'm worried about you.'

'Well, don't be,' Austin said irritably. 'It's getting on my nerves. I don't tell *you* who to go out with, so stop trying to tell *me*.'

'I don't want you to get hurt,' Kalli said, looking him straight in the eyes as she added, 'or anyone else.'

'No one's going to get hurt,' he assured her. 'It's nobody's business but mine and his.'

'And what about his wife?' Kalli asked quietly. Shaking her head when she saw the flicker of surprise in his eyes, she said, 'So I'm right. It *is* Mr Drake.'

'Sshhh!' Austin hissed, glancing quickly around.

'Why?' Kalli asked, pain and anger in her eyes. 'If it's all as nice as you were trying to make out earlier, why wouldn't you want the world to know?'

'Don't be stupid,' Austin snapped. 'It *is* nice, and I really like him. But you know exactly why I can't tell anyone, so keep your nose out.'

'You're making a mistake,' Kalli said softly. 'And I'm your friend, so I'm not going to ignore it.'

'Well, you'll have to, if you want to carry on being my friend,' Austin told her bluntly. 'Don't try and make me choose, 'cos you won't like the outcome.'

'You'd really do that?' Kalli gazed defiantly up into his eyes. 'For money?'

'It's not just the money.' Austin sighed heavily. 'I really like him, Kal. But if you can't understand that, there's nothing I can say.'

'You don't even *know* him.'

'Yes, I do. Don't think last night was the first time we've ever talked. You lot have been treating him like shit since he first started coming here, but I've always talked to him, and he's a really nice man.'

'He's an old *married* man,' Kalli reminded him. 'And he's not your type at all. You like dark and handsome. He's blond and fat.'

'You don't have to tell me what he looks like,' Austin retorted. 'I've seen more of him than you have.'

'Don't be disgusting.'

'If you don't like it, mind your own business.' Shrugging, Austin gave her a take-it-or-leave-it look. 'I like him, and I'm not going to stop seeing him. Not for you, or anyone.'

'Well, I hope it's worth it,' Kalli said sadly. 'When his wife finds out, and you're left with nothing but your fancy trainers to remind you of the job you used to have and the *friends* you lost for him.'

'Whatever,' Austin said glibly. 'See you later.'

Using all her self-control to keep herself from crying, Kalli got changed and made her lonely way home, knowing that things would never be the same between her and Austin again. She'd tried her best, but there was nothing more she could do. When this fell apart, as it undoubtedly would, she just hoped that Austin would learn something from it.

'Anybody seen Fabian?' Jenna asked the security guys as they made their way out.

'Yeah, about an hour ago,' Bobby said, sharing a conspiratorial smirk with Flex. 'He wasn't looking too well. Maybe he's in the loos?'

'His car's not out back,' one of the other doormen said, coming through from the kitchen just then. 'I've just been out there checking that the gate got shut behind the staff, and it's deffo gone.'

Tutting softly, Jenna went back up to her office to get her keys. She'd be having words with Fabian in the morning. He might have let her know if he was leaving early. She could have been waiting all night to lock up.

18

Vibes couldn't settle. Sitting in the bar around the corner from the courthouse, he repeatedly checked his mobile to make sure that he hadn't missed the call telling him that the jury were in.

Sipping his beer, he stared at the screen of the TV above the spirit bottles on the other side of the bar. It was on a news channel, but the volume was down. Vibes was trying to lip-read the female newsreader but was finding it impossible because, like most of the women he'd come across since he got home, she talked way too fast. He'd forgotten that about American women. They got so animated about the stupidest things. Aliya had been no better. Much as he'd loved her, the girl could run her mouth off with the best of them when she got to bitching.

Smiling at the memory, Vibes took a sip of his beer – and almost choked when a still photograph came up on the screen. It looked to have been taken in some kind of night-club, and showed several men sitting around a table, all grinning at something that was resting on the table between them. The image had been blurred, but it didn't take a lot of imagination to guess what it was, nonetheless.

'Yo! Turn the volume up,' Vibes yelled at the bartender. 'The volume, man! Come on!'

'. . . *Trial of Mafia boss Stelios Zagorakis a.k.a. "Zorba",*' the newsreader was saying, '*who is charged with a variety of offences from kidnap to extortion to murder.*

'*This photograph is one of a set recovered by police from a safe found buried beneath Zagorakis's home on the exclusive Palmira Estate complex, and is believed to show the severed head of a rival Mafia boss, Paolo Vitto.*

'*Police are now trying to locate the other men pictured with Mr Zagorakis, and have today named them as Raoul Perusa, Anthony Cerrullo, Peter Gossam and Edward Derby. They are wanted in connection with what police are estimating could amount to dozens of murders, dating back as far as 1960 when Mr Zagorakis first arrived in the United States. They are also suspected of involvement in the murders of brothers Martin and Deke Johnson, who were in the custody of the US Army at the time of their deaths, being transported to high-security witness-protection units.*

'*Anybody who knows the men's whereabouts is asked to contact their local police force immediately, but under no circumstances should the men be approached directly, as they may be armed.*

'*Well, those are today's headlines,*' the woman said now, smiling widely. '*We'll keep you updated on these, and all the other stories as they come in throughout the day. But now we go to Frank Highfield for the weather . . .*'

Vibes stared at the screen long after the picture had been replaced by a grinning weatherman who was promising a long-awaited break to the heatwave being suffered across the country. He wasn't certain by any means, because the photo had been a grainy black and white shot, and was obviously a good few years old, but two of the men around that table had looked just like Tony Allen and Eddie. And could it be a coincidence that two of the names given had been Anthony and Edward?

His mobile rang just then, snapping him back to the present.

'They're in,' Molly, the DA's assistant, told him when he answered. 'You okay?'

'Yeah, I'm fine,' Vibes assured her, gathering his things together. 'I'll be two minutes.'

Judge Mackay looked at the written verdict, his expression giving nothing away to Vibes who was staring intently at him. Nodding, he asked for the jury spokesperson to stand.

Vibes could barely breathe as the spokesman began to give the verdicts, and he could hardly hear above the sound of roaring wind in his ears as his heart raced and pounded. But, somehow, above the storm he caught the word *guilty*.

He sat in stunned silence as the judge picked up the gavel and passed sentence: life without parole for each of the five gang members.

Despite Molly's kind assurances, the forensic evidence and the witness statements, from the very start of this trial Vibes had thought that the jury, with its majority of young white males, would swing in the accused's favour, given that two of the gang were also white. But race hadn't reared its ugly head at all, and Vibes was truly humbled by that. *And* truly grateful.

'Man, it's over!' Tyler exclaimed jubilantly, throwing his arms around Vibes. 'It's *over!*'

Shaking his head in disbelief, Vibes stood up. It really was over. Justice had been done, and he was free to start his life again.

'We're all going to the bar around the corner for a celebratory drink,' Molly told him quietly. 'Are you up to it?'

Looking down into her kind eyes, Vibes shook his head. 'I can't face people just now. I've got to . . .' Trailing off, he bit his lip and raised his chin. 'Sorry, I just need to go.'

'I understand,' she said, reaching up to kiss him on the cheek. 'Congratulations – if that's the right thing to say?'

'Thanks,' he murmured, managing to hold it together as he added, 'for everything. I wouldn't have got through it without you.'

'My pleasure,' Molly said, blushing prettily. Dipping her gaze then, she reached into her pocket and took out a card. 'I, er, don't mean to be presumptuous,' she said, handing it to him. 'But if you ever – you know – want to meet up for a drink, or something . . . ?'

Taking it only because he didn't want to offend her, Vibes slipped it into his pocket and thanked her again. Going to Tyler then, who was busy shaking hands with everybody on the prosecution team, he said, 'I got to get out of here, man.'

'No problem,' Tyler said, seeing from his face that he was close to the edge.

Back at Tyler's house a short while later, where Tyler's mom Delores and sister Talisha had laid on a fantastic spread of soul food, Vibes sat quietly in a corner, accepting all the handshakes and kisses and good wishes from his old friends and neighbours. This was home, and these were his people, but he'd never felt so alone in his entire life.

Coming over to sit with him after a while, Talisha said, 'So it's over, huh?'

'I guess.' Vibes nodded, sipping his beer straight from the bottle.

'What you gonna do now?' she asked, stretching her long legs out. 'Planning to stay around – I hope?'

Smiling, Vibes reached for her hand. She'd been a pretty, slightly gawky sixteen-year-old kid when he'd left, with a serious crush on him. Nineteen now, she was a beautiful woman, with a low mellow voice, and dreamy nut-brown eyes. Any man would be proud to call her his own, but Vibes's love for her was the brotherly kind – even though it was plain to see that her crush had developed into some-thing more fiery and adult.

'I wasn't sure until this afternoon,' he said, gazing around the room at the people he had known all his life. 'Part of me wanted to stay and put all the bad stuff behind me, but another part wanted to get up and run and never look back.'

'And which part won?' Talisha asked, her fingers entwined in his as though they belonged there.

Looking at her, Vibes smiled fondly. 'You're a beautiful girl. Why haven't you got yourself a decent boy yet?'

Biting her lip, she smiled shyly. ''Cos I been waiting on you, Victor. You know that.'

'Don't,' he said softly. 'It's a waste of life to wait around on a dream. You got to get yourself out there and live while you got the chance. You know I love you, right?'

Biting her lip now, her eyes moist with tears, she nodded. 'Uh huh.'

'Then do it for me,' he said. 'Stop kicking it with these idiots, and do what your brother did. Move somewhere nice. Start college and get yourself a future. Do anything, but don't wait on me, 'cos I've moved on and I can't turn back.'

'It's the woman who gave you this, isn't it?' Talisha asked, surprising him with her perception as she stroked her fingertip over the face of his watch. 'You think about her most of the time, don't you?'

Sighing, Vibes nodded. 'Yeah, I guess I do.'

'Do you love her?'

'Mmm-hmm.'

'Then go back to her and be happy,' Talisha said quietly, resting her head on his shoulder. 'She must be some kind of special if you feel that way about her. And I'm damn sure she must love you, too, 'cos she'd be crazy not to.'

'I don't think so,' Vibes murmured softly. 'I left it kind of bad with her.'

'How?' Talisha gazed up at him.

'I kissed her,' Vibes admitted, sighing heavily. 'And I shouldn't have, because she's already got a man.'

'Did she slap you?' Talisha asked. 'Scream? Push you away? Tell you you're disgusting?'

'No. But—'

'She loves you,' Talisha stated with certainty.

Smiling, Vibes put his arm around her and hugged her. 'You're one special sister, Tal.'

'I guess,' she murmured, rolling her eyes. 'And I suppose that'll have to do if it's all I'm gonna get. You'd best invite me to the wedding, though, 'cos I ain't letting go of you for nothing.'

'If it ever happens,' Vibes said, sincerely doubting it, 'you'll be the first to know.'

Putting her arm across his stomach now, Talisha cuddled up closer. 'So, when you going?'

'Soon,' Vibes said, feeling a sudden lift in his heart. 'But I'll have to call first, make sure she ain't mad at me. And I need to let Kenneth know what's happened. But first, I need to get me some sleep, or I won't know if I'm coming or going.'

'You can go to my room,' Talisha told him, smiling up at him mischievously. 'Don't worry, I won't follow you. But Mom's used your room as a coatroom so you won't get near the bed.'

Thanking her, Vibes said, 'I don't suppose you've got a TV in there, have you? 'Cos there's something I really need to check out on the news.'

19

Fabian rang Jenna first thing in the morning, waking her up.

'Sorry for taking off like that last night,' he said. 'I wasn't feeling too good.'

'Yeah, Bobby told me you looked ill,' she said, stretching. 'Anyway, it's all right. I was a bit pissed off, but I figured you must have been feeling pretty bad for it to make you leave like that.'

'I, um, had a bit of an embarrassment,' Fabian told her. 'Dodgy stomach.'

'Nasty,' Jenna said sympathetically. 'I don't blame you for going home. Are you feeling any better?'

'Not really,' he lied, rubbing his stomach as he said it. 'Think I might take a couple of days off, if you don't mind.'

'I'm sure I'll manage,' she told him. 'You just stay in bed and sleep it off. And drink lots of water to flush it out.'

'Thanks, I will. And don't worry about the takings. I'll keep them safe until I can get in.'

'I'd forgotten all about them,' Jenna admitted. 'But don't worry about it. If it stretches on, I'll pop over and pick them up. Hope you're feeling better soon.'

Hanging up when they'd said their goodbyes, she pushed her quilt aside and got up. It would probably do her as much good as him if he had some time off. The way she'd been feeling lately, she'd all but given up on the day-to-day running of the club. Without Fabian to do everything for her, she'd be forced out of the rut she'd dug herself into.

Getting dressed, she had a quick coffee, then went to the club to let the cleaners in. Seeing Tony's car already parked up, she tutted softly. If she'd known he was coming in early she'd have had an extra half-hour in bed.

Making her way up to the office, Jenna was just looking through her bag for her keys when Tony came marching up the corridor towards her with a face like thunder.

'Morning,' she said, glancing around at him. 'I didn't know you were—'

'Where's the cunt?' He cut her off, the ferocity in his voice and eyes making her jump.

'Who?' she asked, frowning up at him.

'That prick, Fabian!' he snarled, his breath coming hard and fast as he stood over her. 'Where is he?'

'He's not well, so he won't be coming in for a few days,' she told him, glancing down the corridor to where Eddie was leaning against Fabian's open door. 'What have you been doing in there? That's Fabian's private office.'

'He ain't entitled to privacy,' Tony spat, barely controlled rage flashing from his eyes. 'Not when he's been fucking my girlfriend!'

'Are you sure?' Jenna was frowning now. 'I've never seen anything going on between them.'

'That right?' Tony growled, peering down at her.

Thoroughly innocent, Jenna looked right back at him. '*Yes*, that's right. I've never seen or heard the slightest thing to indicate it. Wherever you've got this from, I'm sure you're wrong. Fabian's a very professional—'

'Oh, don't give me that shit,' Tony interrupted, running a hand through his hair. 'And if you didn't know, you obviously ain't got a clue what's going on under your own fucking nose.'

'I resent you speaking to me like this, Tony,' Jenna said quietly. 'I haven't done anything to warrant it, and I'd appreciate it if you'd stop it – now.'

Tony inhaled deeply. Then he jerked his head. 'Come with me.'

Following him to Fabian's office, Jenna's mouth dropped when she saw the mess. Everything was turned upside down; every drawer opened and emptied; the safe door stood wide.

'What on earth have you *done*?' she gasped. 'This is a complete invasion of privacy.'

'Sit down,' Tony told her, righting the chair that he had minutes ago thrown across the room. 'I'm gonna show you something. But first, take a look at this.' He held up a small plastic bag half full of white powder.

'What is it?'

'Coke. From his safe.' Letting that sink in, Tony held up a pair of panties with a diamante thong. 'Know whose these are?'

'Should I?'

'They're Mel's.' Sneering, Tony crumpled them in his hand and threw them hard at the wall.

Wincing, Jenna raised a hand.

Groaning, Tony squatted down in front of her. 'Hey, don't be scared of me, Jenna. I'm not mad at you.'

Snatching her hands away when he reached for them, Jenna shrank back in her chair.

'Don't,' Tony said, softening his tone. 'I would never hurt you, I swear it. But you've got to understand that I can't let this go.'

'I just don't understand where this is coming from,' Jenna said. 'I mean, okay, so you've got a pair of panties. But you don't know they're Melody's for sure. They sell stuff like that everywhere.'

'They're hers,' Tony said flatly. 'I bought them myself, back in the States. You don't got that label over here. And they were in his safe.'

'That doesn't mean anything,' Jenna said, knowing it

sounded stupid but still convinced that he was wrong, that there had to be a simple explanation for this. 'Melody loves you. She'd never do that to you.'

'You sure about that?' Tony asked, his eyes still too dark for Jenna's comfort. 'Show her,' he said then, clicking his fingers at Eddie.

Slotting the DVD into the machine in the cupboard, Eddie pressed *play* and stood back, his arms folded.

A frown creased Jenna's brow as she looked at the screen and saw a shot of this office. 'It's a CCTV tape.'

'Keep watching,' Tony said quietly, his own eyes riveted to the screen.

Fabian came into the shot, quickly followed by Melody, and Jenna gasped when she saw Fabian lay out two lines of coke on a mirror and snort one. Handing the straw to Melody then, he came up behind her as she leaned down to snort hers and ran his hands over her body. Rocking back against him when he slipped his hand between her thighs, Melody moaned, 'Oh, that's good. Oh, yeah . . . keep doing that.'

'Seen enough?' Tony asked.

Nodding, Jenna lowered her gaze. 'Yes.'

'See,' Tony said when Eddie had switched the DVD off. 'The bastard's been fucking my girl *and* giving her coke, right here in this room!'

Shaking her head, Jenna looked at him. 'I'm so sorry. I had no idea.'

Tony nodded. 'I know. But now can you see why I've got to find him?'

'What are you going to do?' Jenna asked, fearing that she already knew the answer.

'Rough him up,' Tony lied, shrugging. 'Nothing else I can do, is there? He can think himself lucky we ain't in the States, or I'd do a whole lot worse.'

'And Melody?'

'Don't worry about her, I ain't gonna touch her,' Tony said, semi-truthfully. She was going to get the beating of her miserable life when he got back to the hotel, but he needed her alive to finish what he'd started and get his ticket to stay in the country.

'I don't know where Fabian is,' Jenna said now, flapping her hands. 'All I can do is give you his address from the staff files.'

'Good girl,' Tony said, patting her knee. Standing up, he reached for her hand and pulled her to her feet.

As she went into her office, Jenna's mind was reeling. How could Fabian do something like that? Having an affair with somebody was one thing – but with his boss's girlfriend? And giving her drugs. *Having* drugs on the premises, full stop, knowing that Jenna could have lost her licence at any time because of it – that was unforgivable.

But he didn't deserve to die for it. And, whatever Tony said, she knew exactly what would happen if he got his hands on Fabian while he was in this kind of mood.

Giving him the address, Jenna said, 'Please don't be too hard on him. I know he's done wrong, and I'm going to sack him as soon as I see him, but please don't do anything to get yourself into trouble.'

Kissing her on the cheek, Tony gave her a reassuring pat on the shoulder. 'Quit worrying. All I'm gonna do is warn him off.' Then, turning to Eddie with murder in his eyes, he jerked his head. 'Let's go.'

Jenna waited a couple of minutes, then reached for her mobile. Hands shaking wildly, she called Fabian.

'Come on,' she muttered as his phone rang and rang. 'Pick it up, damn you.'

'Hello?' Fabian said sleepily, answering at last.

'Where are you?' Jenna asked him.

'Still in bed. I'm off sick, remember?'

'Are you at home?'

'Yes, why?'

'You've got to get out of there,' Jenna told him, the urgency in her voice getting through to him at last.

'What's the matter?' Fabian said, fully alert now.

'Tony and Eddie are on their way round,' she told him. 'They've found a DVD of you and Melody in your safe, and some panties that he bought her in the States. They'd ransacked your office by the time I got here, and got your address.'

'Oh, my God,' Fabian muttered. 'What are they going to do?'

'What do you think?' Jenna said sharply. 'Just get out of there, Fabian. And if you've got Melody's number I think you should warn her, too. But get yourself out of there first.'

'Right,' Fabian said, sounding scared and confused. 'Thanks, Jenna.'

'I'm only telling you because I don't want them to do anything stupid,' Jenna told him. 'I know what you've been doing, Fabian, and you had no right to keep stuff like that in my club.'

'Jenna, I—'

'Don't,' she cut him off, not wanting to hear it. 'It's too late.'

'No, you don't understand,' he persisted. 'There's something you should know, about that man who threatened you in the yard.'

'What about him?' Jenna asked, frowning deeply now.

'He was at the club last night,' Fabian told her, breathing hard as he pulled his jeans on. 'He came in asking for Tony.'

'Don't be ridiculous.'

'It's true, Jenna. Ask Bobby and Austin. That's why I went home, because Tony got mad about me sending Austin round to The Diamond to get him. I heard him telling Bobby he was going to break my legs.'

'So, what did the man want with him?' Jenna asked, not sure that she wanted to hear this.

'He said he'd come for the money that Tony owed him. Tony was annoyed with him at first, said he'd told him never to show his face at the club, but the man said he'd waited long enough, that his boys were hassling him for their money.'

'Did Tony pay him?'

'Yeah, and gave him extra for waiting. Then the man said if he ever wanted anyone else heavying, he knew where to find him.'

'How can you be sure it's the one who threatened me?'

'Because he had a boxing-glove earring, and a gold chain with a bulldog on it.' Pausing, Fabian inhaled deeply. 'I'm really sorry, Jenna, I should have told you last night, but I was worried what Tony would do to me, 'cos he was already mad at me.'

'It's all right,' Jenna murmured, feeling sick to her stomach. 'Thanks for letting me know.'

Hanging up then, she exhaled shakily. If it was true, and it obviously was or Fabian wouldn't have told her to ask Bobby and Austin, it could only mean one thing: that Tony was behind those men jumping her in the yard that day. And if he was behind that, he'd probably organised the other trouble, too. The fights that had kicked off for no good reason; the raids – during which, she realised now, Tony had been conveniently out of town; the taxi firms blacklisting them – everything. Wearing her down, eroding her profits and damaging the club's reputation, then, finally, sending those men to put the fear of God into her, all designed to leave her with nowhere to turn but to him – the one person she'd believed could help her. And all so he could get a stake in her club.

And now that he had it, there wasn't a single thing that

Jenna could do about it, because if he was willing to do all
that just to get it, he would surely be willing to do whatever
it took to keep it. And the police couldn't help her, because
Tony's name wasn't even on the contracts. Hiding behind
Leonard Drake's respectable name, he would say that she
was crazy if she complained that he had conned her.

How could she have been so stupid?

Jenna's mobile began to ring. She switched it off without
looking at it, fearing that it would be Tony checking up on
her – making sure that she hadn't warned Fabian.

Well, tough: he was too late. Because she *had* warned
Fabian – and Fabian had warned *her*. And now she knew
where she stood, she had to find a way of getting Tony out
of her life and out of her business before he took everything
from her.

Getting up, Jenna grabbed her bag and headed out.

Dressed, Fabian grabbed his wallet, cards and car keys and
ran down the stairs. Fearing for his life, because Tony and
Eddie would surely kill him if they got hold of him, he jumped
into his car and took off in a squeal of burning rubber. He
didn't know what he was going to do now. Jenna knew about
the coke, so he might as well kiss his job goodbye – not that
he could go back there anyway, because Tony owned half
the business. But at least he had some savings to tide him
over while he found a new job. In a new town. Somewhere
far away from Tony Allen.

Driving to the old part of Hulme now, Fabian parked up
under one of the covered open-ended garages and ran up
to Bubba's flat on the third floor of the scruffy block. Bubba
would let him hang out there for a while, until he'd figured
out where to go.

Hammering on the door, he took out his mobile and rang
Melody to warn her while he waited for Bubba to answer.

'Wha's up?' Melody said groggily. 'You woke me up.'

'Tony knows,' Fabian told her quickly. 'Him and Eddie are on their way to my place now.'

'How?' Melody demanded, sitting bolt upright in her bed. 'Don't tell me you *told* him?'

'No, I didn't fucking tell him,' Fabian snapped. 'Do you think I'm an idiot? He must have got it from you.'

'It wasn't *me!*' Melody retorted, her voice panicked. 'He was asking me last night, but I totally denied it. I'd be dead by now if he didn't believe me.'

'Well, he obviously didn't,' Fabian snapped. 'Sure you don't talk in your sleep?'

'Fuck off!' Melody snarled, throwing the quilt back and leaping out of bed. 'Who told you he knew, anyway?'

'Jenna just called from the club. Him and Eddie have ransacked my office, and they found your knickers in my safe.'

'Which knickers? I haven't left any knickers there.'

'Diamante thongs,' Fabian reminded her.

'Oh, my God,' Melody muttered. Then, 'Okay, that's cool. If that's all he's got, we just say I took them off in the toilets one time, and the cleaners handed them in to you as lost property.'

'That's not all,' Fabian admitted. 'There's CCTV footage of us together in the office. My, er, security camera was still running the first time, but I didn't notice till we were leaving. I meant to delete it, but I forgot.'

'*Forgot?*' Melody yelled. 'How could you forget something like that? What's on it, anyway? If it's just us doing coke, I can—'

'Everything,' Fabian interrupted quietly. 'You can see everything.'

'So you've watched it?' Melody said, stunned that he could be so stupid. 'If you only realised when we were leaving the office, you must have watched it after you went back or you wouldn't know what was on it. So why the fuck didn't you delete it then?'

'I don't know,' Fabian muttered.

'You shit!' she snarled. 'You kept it on purpose, didn't you?'

'It was insurance,' he admitted, getting irritated now. 'In case you did something stupid.'

'Oh, well, congratulations,' Melody shot back sarcastically. 'You've just won first prize in the knob-head of the fucking *century* awards! I never said a goddamn word, but you've dropped us *right* in it, haven't you?'

'I'm sorry,' Fabian murmured, reaching behind him and rapping on Bubba's door again.

'Where are you?' Melody demanded, holding the phone between her cheek and her shoulder as she struggled into her jeans.

'At a friend's,' he told her evasively. 'Where will you go?'

'Tell me where you are – I'll catch a cab over to you,' Melody said.

'No!' Fabian yelped. 'Sorry, Melody, but you said you couldn't get away from Tony because he'd find you and kill you. And I can't risk being with you if he does.'

Melody opened her mouth to call him a bastard, but stopped when she heard another voice in the background say, 'Yo, dude, what's with the rat-a-tat-tatting?'

Staring at the phone when it went dead in her hand, she tried to remember where she'd heard the voice before. But she couldn't quite put her finger on it.

But she'd worry about that later. She had to get out before Tony got back. And as soon as he found out that Fabian had done a runner, he *would* be back for her.

Throwing a jumper and jacket on, she grabbed her handbag, then ran to the closet and pulled the pack of sanitary towels out of her toiletries bag. She had no idea where she would go, but at least, with the money, she'd be able to hide out for a while.

Melody had just reached the door when Tony walked in and knocked her clean off her feet with the hardest punch she'd ever felt in her life. Dazed, she opened her eyes in time to see him running at her. Screaming when he kicked her in the back, she rolled into a ball and prayed that he would kill her before the beating came to an end.

20

Vibes's instincts were prickling. Something was wrong, he was sure. He'd tried calling Jenna, but she had switched her phone off. And that was odd, because Kenneth had said she was looking forward to hearing from him. She would have seen his name on the screen, so why would she turn her phone off if that were the case?

Taking a chance on her being at work, he tried her on the club phone instead.

'Hello, Zenith. Anna speaking. How can I help you?'

'Hi, Anna,' Vibes said, remembering her as the girl who worked on reception. 'It's Vibes.'

'No way!' she cried, her voice ringing with surprise and delight. 'How are you? Wow! Wait till the others hear that you've called – they'll be so jealous that they weren't here to speak to you!'

'Say hi to everyone for me,' he said. Then, 'Sorry I can't chat, but do you think you could put me through to Jenna's office?'

'Oh, you've just missed her,' Anna told him. 'I can try Mr Allen for you instead, if you like? He went out earlier, but he's always in one door and out another, so he could still be around somewhere.'

'Mr Allen?' Vibes repeated. '*Tony* Allen? Why would he be there?'

'Oh, didn't Jenna tell you? He's her partner now.'

'Her *partner*?'

Chuckling softly, Anna said, 'I forgot how long you've been away. A lot's happened here since you left. We had a load of trouble – fights, and police raids, and all sorts. Then Jenna and Mr Allen went into partnership, and everything got sorted out. It's been great for ages now. He's even opened an offshoot club in the old storeroom, but we're not allowed in there so I can't tell you what it's like.'

'I gotta speak to Jenna,' Vibes said, feeling sick. 'Do me a favour and tell her to call me if you see her before I reach her, will you? It's urgent.'

Cutting the call then, he found Kalli's number and called her.

'Oh, my God!' Kalli said when he told her what he'd found out. 'Jenna's got no idea. She can't have, or she'd never have agreed to let him buy into the business.'

'Any idea where she might have gone?' Vibes asked. 'I know I'm probably overreacting because of what I know about him, but I've got a feeling something's wrong. My friend told me she'd be happy if I called, so I can't understand why she'd turn her phone off if she saw my name. She wouldn't do that, would she?'

'Definitely not,' Kalli replied softly, hoping that he'd get what she meant when she added, 'she really, *really* likes you.'

Completely missing it because he was so concerned, Vibes said, 'I don't suppose you've got Fabian's number, have you? I could call him, see if he's seen her.'

'I haven't got it, but I can get Anna to look it up for you, if you like?'

'Would you?' Vibes said gratefully. 'I'd appreciate it. I'll call you back in ten.'

Disconnecting, he sat down on the bed and looked at the newspaper he'd picked up the previous morning, which had the same photograph on its front page as the one he'd seen on the TV news bulletin. And, having scrutinised it with a magnifying glass, he was positive that the men were Tony and Eddie.

He had considered calling the police, but he wanted to speak to Jenna first, to find out if they were still hanging around at the club. But now that he knew she'd gone into business with the man, he was thinking that maybe he should call them anyway – just to be on the safe side. If Tony Allen – or Cerrullo, or whatever his goddamn name was – could sit and laugh over a severed head, he was capable of anything. And there was nothing Vibes could do to protect Jenna if he set his sights on her, not from all the way over here.

Startled out of his thoughts when his mobile rang, Vibes frowned when he saw Kalli's name on the screen.

'You shouldn't have called me,' he said, answering it. 'It'll cost you a fortune.'

'It doesn't matter,' she assured him. 'I got Fabian's number, but I rang him to save you doing it, and it's switched off.'

'His, too?' Vibes frowned.

'Yeah, and I thought I'd best tell you what happened last night,' Kalli said, her tone grim now. 'Some man called in to the club to see Mr Allen, and Fabian sent Austin round to his *new* club to get him. Mr Allen was really annoyed about it, and came looking for Fabian. Then, apparently, somebody told him something he didn't like about Fabian and his girlfriend, and he started threatening Melody, so I sent Austin down to get security, because he looked like he was going to hit her. Anyway,' she said, taking a sharp, much-needed breath, 'when Anna just went to get the staff file to get Fabian's number for me, she said that his office door was wide open, and the office itself has been turned upside down. And she said Mr Allen and Big Eddie went storming out just as she got to the club today, so she thinks they probably did it. And then Jenna just left without saying a word a few minutes later.'

'I've got to go,' Vibes said suddenly. 'Thanks for that, sweetheart.'

'Do you want me to go to Jenna's flat and see if she's there?' Kalli asked.

'No, stay out of it,' Vibes told her quickly. 'I'll call you later.'

Hanging up, he mulled everything over for a few minutes. There might be nothing going on, but could he really sit here and do nothing if there was even a chance that Tony was posing a threat to Jenna? He didn't think so.

Reaching for the phone, he dialled the contact number listed at the foot of the newspaper article.

Putting the phone down, Detective Bill Martinez stood up and, tucking his shirt in, strolled across the office to his colleague, Matt Knight. 'Just had a call from some guy,' he said, handing him the sheet of paper he'd written the info down on. 'Claims Anthony Cerrullo and Edward Derby are in Manchester, England, staying at some hotel called the Waterford.'

'Sound genuine?' Knight asked, looking at it.

'Yeah. Says he's been working over there, came back just a few months ago. Seems Cerrullo's going under the name of Allen now. Hanging out with an actress called Melody Fisher.'

'Oh, yeah?' Knight said, peering up at him now. 'I wondered where she'd gone.'

'You know her?'

'Nah, the wife was raving about her. Saw her in some movie with Sandra Bullock and rated her. Mentioned that she hadn't heard anything about her for a while.'

'Could be worth looking into, then?'

Grinning, Knight reached for his desk-phone. 'Best let the big guy know. You never know, there could be a trip in it for us. Passport up to date?'

Getting up quietly, Susan DeLornio wandered across the office and put a couple of letters she'd just finished typing in the out-tray. Looking at her watch then, she said, 'I'm going out for coffee, guys. Can I get you anything?'

'Depends what you're offering,' Martinez said, giving her a leering smile.

Tutting loudly, she walked out.

'You've got a hope in hell,' Knight chuckled. 'She's one of the untouchables.'

'Leper?'

'Catholic.'

'What a waste,' Martinez grumbled. 'Why can't they ever get any horny temps in this goddamn place?'

Taking the elevator down to the ground, Susan walked out into the open. Smiling at the security guard who held the door for her, she crossed the square and walked casually around the corner. Then she went into a phone booth and dropped her quarter into the slot.

'Cerrullo and Derby are in Manchester, England,' she said quietly when the call was answered. 'Waterford Hotel, under the name of Allen. They've got Melody Fisher with them.' Smiling when she got her reply, she said, 'My pleasure. But you'd better hurry. The Feds are gonna be all over the place soon as my boss gets the green light.'

21

Leonard's car wasn't in the drive. Pulling up outside the locked gates, Jenna peered at the house, but there wasn't so much as a whisper of movement behind the elegantly curtained windows.

Annoyed with herself for driving all the way over here without calling first, she banged a hand down on the steering wheel. She didn't know what she'd hoped to achieve by coming here, anyway. She supposed she'd just wanted to hear Leonard say that he hadn't known about Tony when he'd agreed to put his name to the contracts. Some reassurance that she hadn't been the only one he'd taken for a ride. If Leonard was in the dark, as she truly hoped, then maybe, between them, they could come up with a plan to get Tony out.

Reaching into her bag, she took out her mobile and switched it back on, intending to call Kalli and see if she was available for a coffee. She didn't want to go back to the club just yet, and she didn't want to go home, either, in case Tony decided to visit her there. Jumping when the phone immediately started to ring, she saw Vibes's name on the screen.

'Jenna, are you all right?' he asked, his voice sounding so concerned that Jenna thought something bad must have happened to him.

'Yes, I'm fine,' she told him. 'Are *you*? Kenneth told me all about the case, and he said the verdicts were coming in soon. Have you—'

'Never mind that now,' Vibes said quickly. 'I don't know what's going on over there, but I think you're in danger.'

'Why?' Jenna asked, shocked that he was saying this when he couldn't possibly know anything.

Explaining everything to her that he'd found out at his end, Vibes said, 'I had no idea you'd gone into partnership with him. I can't believe you did that.'

'Neither can I,' Jenna admitted shamefacedly. 'I was in such a mess, I couldn't see any other way out of it. But I've just found out that he probably set everything up from the start.'

'I'm coming over,' Vibes told her. 'It'll probably take a few days, but I want to be with you.'

'Oh, God, that would be fantastic,' Jenna gasped, aware that she was crying. 'We've all been missing you so much.'

'Have *you* been missing me?' he asked, his voice quiet and low now. He was dreading a negative reaction.

'More than you'll ever know,' she admitted. 'But I didn't want to call you, because I – well, it doesn't matter now. Kenneth told me everything. Just come back, Vibes. I really need you here.'

'What about Jason?' Vibes asked. 'Is he gonna be a problem?'

'Jason?' Jenna repeated. 'Why on earth would he be a problem? I haven't seen him in almost two years.'

'For real?' Vibes sounded confused. 'But I thought . . .'

'Ah,' Jenna said, remembering when she'd made that slip of the tongue during one of their conversations. 'I said his name in the present tense, and you thought I was still with him. Well, no, I'm not. He lied to me, because he was married the whole time we were together, and I got as far away from him as possible when I found out. I never want to see him again. Okay?'

'I see,' Vibes said, trying to remember that he'd called for far more serious reasons, even though his heart felt like it was busting right out of his chest with joy. 'Okay, well, I'll be with you soon, so we'll talk more then. But right now, you need to be careful.'

'What should I do?' Jenna asked, feeling a little safer now.

'Nothing,' Vibes said. 'If you're not in any immediate danger, don't say or do anything out of the ordinary. Just do what you usually do so you don't raise his suspicions. Let him think everything's fine, so he can't blame you when the Feds move in on him.'

Exhaling shakily, Jenna said, 'Okay, I'll try. But I hope they don't take too long.'

'I don't know what they'll have to put in place to do it,' Vibes said. 'They might have to liaise with your cops, or your government, or something, to get permission to come after him. But if they want him bad enough, they'll get to him. It's just a matter of holding out till they make their move.'

'Right, well, I'll pretend I don't know anything,' Jenna promised. 'But please hurry up and get here.'

'Soon as I can, I'll be there,' he assured her. 'Do me a favour,' he said then. 'Go see Kalli – make sure she doesn't do anything stupid. Not that she'll mean to, but she's seriously worried about you and she might give something away.'

'I was about to call her when you rang,' Jenna told him. 'I was going to take her out for coffee.'

'Do it,' Vibes said. 'I'll call you later, to make sure everything's all right.'

Hanging up, Jenna leaned her head back and hugged the phone to her breast. Swiping the tears away after a moment, she called Kalli and arranged to meet her. Then she turned the car around and set off back to Manchester.

She'd have to act as if nothing were out of the ordinary for the next few days, and it would be hard now that she knew exactly what Tony Allen was really about. But, with luck, then it would be over.

22

The men came out of the airport and paused to light cigarettes. They had one small suitcase each, containing just the essentials for a week-long stay, although they had no intention of staying that long if they didn't have to. Hailing one of the waiting cabs when they had finished their smokes, they climbed into the back with their cases on their laps.

'Waterford Hotel,' one of them told the driver.

'Americans?' he asked, setting off. 'I got a sister lives up that way. You might know her? She lives up in Richmond. Name's Pat Hillman.'

'Maybe,' the man replied, his eyes hidden by dark shades.

They stayed silent for the rest of the journey. Paying the driver when he pulled up around the corner from the Waterford, they got out and walked around to take a look at the hotel. Watching the front doors for a while, they gave each other a nod and entered the foyer.

'Two singles,' one of them said to the receptionist.

'Certainly, sir.' She smiled. 'If I could just take your details?'

Handing their room passes to them when they had been processed, she said, 'Would you like one of our porters to carry your cases up for you?'

'No, thanks, we can manage,' he told her, smiling. 'Have a nice day, ma'am.'

'Oh, I love it when you people say that,' she giggled. 'It sounds just like The Blues Brothers. We've another

American gentleman on the third floor who sounds just like you, and it makes me go all weak when he says it.'

'That right?' the man said, still smiling as he walked away.

Melody was asleep on the couch when she heard the knock on the door. Groaning, she picked herself up and hobbled to answer it. It had been two days since Tony had beaten her half to death, and she hadn't set foot out of the room since. Even if Tony had let her – which he definitely wouldn't – she wouldn't have wanted to, because she was too ashamed of the bruises.

Thinking that this would be the room-service boy delivering the painkillers she'd sent down for earlier, she opened the door a crack and stuck her hand out.

Knocked back by the force of the man's shoulder barging the door, she landed in a heap of agony halfway across the room.

'Who are you?' she screamed when the man and his friend came in, closing the door behind them. 'Don't you fucking touch me!' Opening her mouth, she screamed at the top of her voice.

Pulling a gun out of his pocket, the man slammed it butt-down on her nose. Then, waiting to see if anybody had heard the scream and was coming to investigate, the two men relaxed after a few minutes and set about searching the room.

23

Tony and Eddie found the duty manager waiting for them when they got back to the hotel at four that morning.

'Excuse me, sir, but could I have a quick word?' he said, approaching them nervously.

'Yeah, what?' Tony grunted, hoping this wasn't some stupid shit that could have waited till morning.

'It just that, well, some of the other guests have been complaining about the noises coming from your room while you've been staying with us,' the manager told him, feeling more awkward than he'd ever felt in his life before. 'Now, I realise that people do argue,' he went on, trying to be diplomatic. 'But I'm afraid that this cannot be allowed to continue.'

'What you getting at?' Tony interrupted snappily. 'I ain't uttered a sound in days.'

'With respect,' the manager said, 'the, um, screams were loud enough to reach the guests on the floor below your suite this evening.'

'Screams?' Tony narrowed his eyes.

'Yes, and as it isn't the first time your, um, wife has been heard to scream in that manner, I'm afraid it's fallen to me to ask that you refrain from whatever activity you're involved in that may be causing it.'

'You couldn't just say that in plain fucking English, could you?' Tony snarled. 'I haven't got a fucking clue what you're talking about. I've been out all night. I've just this second got back.'

'Well, then maybe you could speak to your wife?' The manager raised an eyebrow. 'I did try knocking earlier, after the other guests complained of the noise of furniture being moved about up there. I didn't get an answer. But I would have been within my rights to use my pass key to gain entry. It was only the fact that you've been with us for so long that prevented me from doing so. But I would appreciate it if you could resolve the matter so that we don't have to have any more complaints.'

'The furniture being moved about?' Tony said, looking at him with dark eyes. 'Was that before or after the screams?'

'After,' the manager said. 'Which was why I eventually went up there. But I don't really think—'

Trailing off as Tony and Eddie abruptly walked away, he turned to the receptionist and flapped his hands.

Taking the stairs at a run, Tony and Eddie came out at the third floor and walked cautiously up to the door of Tony's suite. Pressing his ear to the wood, Tony listened for a minute. Hearing nothing, he took his phone out and called Melody on her mobile. They could hear it ringing inside, but Melody didn't answer. Cutting his phone off, Tony eased the door handle down. Just as he'd expected, the door was unlocked. Cracking it open, he stayed to the side and peered in. Melody was lying on the floor a few feet in, her face a bloody mess, her nightdress pulled up over her bruised thighs, her legs spread wide and displaying her nakedness.

Muttering 'Fuck!' Tony waved Eddie in and told him to watch the door. Then, creeping quietly around the room he checked every corner and cupboard. Then he went into the bedroom and did the same in there and in the bathroom. Satisfied that no one was hiding, he switched the lamp on.

Illuminated, Melody looked even worse. Her tongue was hanging out of the corner of her mouth and her bulging eyes were already clouded. She'd been strangled, raped and, for good measure, shot through the middle of her forehead.

Gazing down at her, Tony shook his head, then reached for the quilt off the couch and threw it over her. Sticking his hand down the back of the couch then, he dragged all his money out.

Stuffing everything he had into one of his cases, he and Eddie left the room, locking the door behind them, and made their escape through the fire exit.

24

'Have you seen the news?' Kalli gasped when Jenna answered the phone.

'No, I'm on my way to the airport,' Jenna told her. 'Why, what's up?'

'Melody Fisher's been murdered. They found her at her hotel, and the police are looking for Tony and Eddie.'

Swerving onto the hard shoulder, Jenna pulled up and grabbed the phone from its hands-free holder. 'You're joking?'

'No, it's all over the news. Big pictures of her, and everything. They reckon she was shot through the head. It's so awful. She looks so beautiful in the pictures, but to think of her shot dead like that, it just makes you feel weird.'

'Right, I'll pick up some papers when I've met Vibes,' Jenna said, restarting the engine. 'Stay at home. I'll come there as soon as I get back.'

'With Vibes?' Kalli asked.

'Of course. He's dying to see you.'

Vibes saw Jenna as soon as she walked through the automatic doors. Swallowing hard, because she looked just as beautiful as ever, he got up and called out to her.

Turning, Jenna saw him and threw a hand over her mouth.

Seconds later she was in his arms, kissing him and telling him that she loved him too.

25

'No, Mr Allen was not my partner,' Jenna told DI Seddon, who was questioning her along with two American detectives. 'He was a customer. Mr Drake here is my partner.'

'Yes, that's right,' Leonard affirmed, aware that Avril was glaring at him, making sure that he didn't get the story wrong. 'As Miss Lorde has already told you, Mr Allen was a customer. Unfortunately, however, I allowed him into my life when I agreed to sell some of my paintings to him. He – Tony, that is – paid for them with a banker's draft, which I deposited in my account. But not long after, he began to call on me for favours, and before I knew it he was demanding money, and threatening to hurt my wife if I didn't pay.'

'And you never thought to report this to the police?' Seddon asked, frowning.

'I'm not the bravest of men,' Leonard admitted, blushing deeply. 'And I'm afraid I took his threats at face value.'

'So, none of this business belonged to Anthony Cerrullo?' Detective Martinez chipped in, looking Leonard over with a scornful sneer.

'None whatsoever,' Jenna told him, drawing his attention to herself to give Leonard a break. He was having a hard enough time keeping it together as it was without these men looking down on him. Getting up, she took the contracts out of her safe and showed them. 'See, just me and Mr Drake.'

'Fair enough,' Knight said, looking them over and handing them back.

'Has anybody come over to identify them?' Jenna asked, afraid that she might be faced with a whole new problem if Tony's relatives tried to stake a claim on his shares. If he'd told them the arrangement, and they were anything like him, they'd be bound to try and muscle in.

'We don't know of any family, as yet,' Martinez replied, giving her a whole different look than the one he'd been giving Leonard. 'But it's highly unlikely that their own mothers could ID them, the state they're in. The ID we found scattered about the canal bank in back of the hotel indicates that they were the bodies of Cerrullo and Derby – or Tony Allen and Eddie, as *you* knew them. We'll go on that for now, see what the DNA turns up when we get them back to the States. Maybe we'll trace family that way.' Pausing, he shrugged. 'Someone's got to bury them, and it sure as hell ain't gonna be at our expense.'

Shaking her head, Jenna exhaled loudly. 'I can't say I particularly liked them, but it's horrible to think of them being shot in the face like that.'

'Typical Mafia execution,' Martinez informed her knowledgeably. 'We deal with this kind of shi— *stuff* every day back home.'

'So, have you any idea who did it?'

'Oh, yeah, and our guys are already onto it,' Martinez told her, puffing his chest out proudly. These English cops were so disorganised, they hadn't even thought to check the hotel register after they found the bodies. If they had, they'd have found out about the two American-Italians who had booked in earlier that day, then disappeared without so much as touching their minibars or beds. And they might then have followed it up, as Martinez and Knight had, and learned that the men had caught an early-morning flight back to New York.

'Right, well, we'd best get moving,' Knight said now.

There was nothing worth sticking around for, and Bill looked to be getting a little too friendly with the lady boss. 'Nice meeting you folks. Sorry to put you out with this.'

'It's no problem,' Jenna assured him, standing up to show them out. 'I'm just sorry we couldn't be more help.'

Walking them down to the front door, Jenna shook Knight's and Martinez's hands and wished them a safe journey home. Thanking DI Seddon then, she said, 'You will let us know if you find Melody's family, won't you? I'd hate to think of her being buried with no one to pay their respects.'

'I'll keep in touch,' Seddon promised. Lowering his voice then so that Knight and Martinez wouldn't hear, he said, 'Think yourself lucky you weren't involved with Cerrullo, 'cos I've got a feeling these guys would have been all over your club and your accounts.'

'Well, there's nothing here for them,' Jenna told him, folding her arms. 'And there never will be, because I've got no intention of ever letting anyone worm their way into my club.'

'Good for you,' Seddon said approvingly.

'Do you think they were convinced?' Avril asked when the detectives had left and Jenna had come back.

'I think so,' Vibes said, reaching for Jenna's hand. 'You did good, Princess.'

Gazing into his beautiful eyes, she smiled. 'Thanks.'

Winking at her, Vibes turned back to Leonard and Avril. 'Bet you're glad it's all over.'

'Oh, yes,' Leonard said, sighing softly. 'It's been quite an ordeal, I must admit. I was, um, thinking,' he said then. 'Maybe we should think about having the ownership reverted back to Jenna, now that Tony is no longer around.'

'I don't think so,' Avril chipped in firmly. 'With respect,

Jenna, my husband's name is on the contract as a legitimate partner.'

'Yes, and I'm quite happy for it to stay that way,' Jenna assured her. Turning to Leonard then, she smiled. 'I've thought it through, and it seems a waste to let everything slip now. So, if you're willing, I'd be quite happy for you to pick up where Tony left off and continue running your private members' club.'

'Really?' Leonard gasped, hardly able to believe his good fortune. 'Well, of course, I'd be delighted. Oh, but there are a few changes I'd wish to make,' he said then, casting a quick glance at Avril. 'I wasn't too happy with the waitresses, you see.'

Chuckling softly, Jenna said, 'I'm not really surprised. I never thought they'd suit your more *upmarket* clientele, but Tony wanted them, so what could I do? Just send them back in here. I'll put them back on their regular posts.'

'I'm not sure you'd want to do that if you knew what they'd been doing in there,' Leonard told her quietly. 'I'm afraid they weren't very . . . *nice*.'

'Oh?' Vibes peered at him with a smile in his eyes. 'How so?'

'They were lap-dancing and prostituting,' Avril told him bluntly. 'If I'd known, I would have put a stop to it there and then. But Leonard isn't the most forceful of characters, as you've probably surmised, and he went along with Tony Allen's orders not to tell me. Didn't you, dear?' She gave Leonard a spiky smile.

'I'm afraid so,' he muttered, folding his arms.

'Well, I can't keep them on if they were doing that,' Jenna said. 'I'll let them go when they come in tonight. Better still, I'll find their numbers and call them, so I don't even have to look at them.' Sighing, she shook her head. 'Never mind. There's plenty more will be glad of the work. But in the meantime, you'll have to choose some of the others, I suppose.'

'Oh, right,' Leonard said, licking his lips nervously. 'Well, um, if you're in agreement, I wouldn't mind taking that polite girl from the VIP bar.'

'Not Kalli,' Jenna said quickly. 'Sorry, but I can't lose her. In fact, I'm planning to promote her to bar manager. She's been practically running the place anyway, and now that Maurice has decided to retire I think she's the perfect replacement.'

'No, no, not her,' Leonard said. 'The other one – the quiet one. Diane. That's it.'

'Oh, right, well, fine.' Jenna shrugged. 'I'm sure she'd be an asset. Anyone else in mind?'

'Um, yes, maybe the boy who works with her – Austin, I think his name is.'

'I don't think so,' Avril snorted.

'He's very good,' Jenna told her. 'And he and Diane do work well together.'

'No, dear, I don't think he's at all suitable,' Avril said firmly. 'Leonard will take another of the young ladies, won't you, Leonard?'

'Yes, of course,' he murmured, looking down at his hands. She obviously knew. And if she knew, it was over.

Tapping on the door just then, Kalli popped her head in. 'Anybody want anything? Only I'm about to go.'

'Wait a minute,' Vibes said, smiling up at her. 'We'll walk you out.' Standing up, still holding Jenna's hand, he said, 'If everybody's ready?'

'Yes, absolutely,' Leonard said, jumping lightly to his feet, already over Austin because the future looked quite bright without him. 'We shall see you tonight, then.' Turning to Jenna, he bowed. '*Partner.*'

Smiling, Jenna looped her arm through Vibes's and held on tight as they all walked out together. Now that she'd got him back, she was never letting go again.

EPILOGUE

Avril was roused by the sound of rustling in the corridor outside her bedroom door. Opening her eyes, she glanced at the clock. It was only just past two, and The Diamond didn't close until three, so what on earth was Leonard doing home already? And why was he at her door? He surely didn't think that she was going to welcome him into her bed? Oh, no, no, no! It hadn't even been a month yet. He had *far* more grovelling to do before she forgave him his latest indiscretion.

Sitting up when the door handle turned, she was about to call out to him to bloody well forget it when she heard a voice that she recognised all too well.

'It's locked. She's gotta be in there.'

She inhaled sharply. No, it couldn't be. They were dead.

Getting out of bed, she tiptoed to the balcony door.

The wind was high tonight, and a forceful gust tore the door from her hand when she eased it open. Licking at the curtains, it knocked a jar of cream over on the dressing table, sending it rolling noisily into her perfumes and deodorants.

'Kick it in!' the voice in the corridor hissed.

Bursting in seconds later, Tony saw the hastily vacated bed and the open door and turned back to the stairs. 'She's climbed out. You go look if you can see her, I'll go after her.'

Walking quickly to the balcony, Eddie stepped out and peered over the rail into the dark gardens below.

Holding her breath, petrified that he would hear her, Avril crept out of her walk-in closet with the heavy steel poker held firmly between her hands. Raising it above her head, she came up behind Eddie and slammed it down as hard as she could on the back of his neck.

Letting out a tiny gasp of fear when his knees buckled, Avril hit him again and again on the top of his head, not even aware of the sounds of splintering bone and squelching tissue, just conscious that she needed to make sure he was properly unconscious so that he couldn't retaliate.

'You seen her?' Tony's voice hissed up a moment later. 'Ed?'

Ducking so that she was almost sitting on Eddie's battered head now, Avril squinted out through the ornate balcony rails. She couldn't see Tony, but she could hear him mooching about in the pitch-dark gardens below. The security lights should have come on by now, but they had obviously disabled them along with the alarms.

Letting out another tiny gasp when Eddie made a sighing sound, she reached down to steady herself, and almost fell over when her hand landed on the gun he was still holding.

Bringing her hands up to her mouth in shock, Avril recoiled when she felt and tasted the blood on her lips.

'Yo!' Tony hissed. 'What you doing up there, man? I can't see her. I'm coming in.'

Heart hammering in her chest, Avril wrenched the gun out of Eddie's hand and stumbled back into the bedroom. Running back to the closet, she crouched on the floor inside the slightly open door so that she could see Tony when he came in. She felt sick, and every nerve in her body seemed to be sparking, every muscle taut with terror.

Running into the doorway a minute later, Tony made his way to the balcony door in search of Eddie. Pointing the gun at his back through the crack, trying desperately to still her wildly shaking hands, Avril closed her eyes and squeezed the trigger.

There was a slight popping sound, followed by a grunt and the sound of something falling heavily to the floor.

Hardly breathing now, Avril opened her eyes and looked out.

Tony was lying in a heap a few feet away. Standing up, Avril ventured out warily. Screaming when he moved, she shot him again, not even sure if anything had happened because she couldn't hear anything at all this time – she just saw the flash of light that illuminated Tony's darker than dark eyes.

Turning, she ran for her life.